PENGUIN BOOKS

Darling Daffodils Farm

Brittanée Nicole lives in New England with her husband and their two children. Known for writing swoony men who always fall first, Brittanée loves stories centered around strong friendships that form the basis of a found family and messy, beautiful love. When she's not writing, she enjoys spending time outdoors by the water with her children, reading at the beach or by the pool (or really anywhere), dancing with her friends, singing karaoke, spinning, taking long walks by the water, and boating.

Darling Daffodils Farm

BRITTANÉE NICOLE

PENGUIN BOOKS

PENGUIN BOOKS

UK | USA | Canada | Ireland | Australia
India | New Zealand | South Africa

Penguin Books is part of the Penguin Random House group of companies
whose addresses can be found at global.penguinrandomhouse.com

Penguin Random House UK,
One Embassy Gardens, 8 Viaduct Gardens, London SW11 7BW

penguin.co.uk

First published in the US by Putnam, an imprint of
Penguin Random House LLC, New York 2026
Published in Penguin Books 2026
001

Book design by Lorie Pagnozzi

Printed and bound in Great Britain by Clays Ltd, Elcograf S.p.A.

The authorised representative in the EEA is Penguin Random House Ireland,
Morrison Chambers, 32 Nassau Street, Dublin D02 YH68

A CIP catalogue record for this book is available from the British Library

ISBN: 978–1–911–74607–2

Penguin Random House is committed to a sustainable future
for our business, our readers and our planet. This book is made
from Forest Stewardship Council® certified paper.

For the dreamers. It's never selfish to go after your dreams.
And to the readers who have been with me since the beginning.
This one's for us.

Darling Daffodils Farm

Chapter 1
TALLY

March

I can't believe you talked me into this." I pass the welcome sign for Hope Harbor and shake my head, baffled as to how my older sister got me to return home to our small New England town before ski season even ended.

Penny's laugh comes out raspy over the car's Bluetooth. "Please. I've been dealing with Mom for the last few months. You're lucky my failed engagement gave her something to focus on, but I'm tagging you in now, Tally. You're it."

"What if I just stay until we find someone who actually knows how to plan a wedding? Or better yet, I'm sure the ladies' auxiliary has someone who would want to help out."

The ladies' auxiliary is a group of women a bit older than our mom who call themselves the Liberty Ladies. Their charter dates back to the 1600s and says something about supporting the soldiers' families during wartime. Nowadays, they plan town celebrations, including the Daffodil Festival that will take place on our farm in just over three weeks.

The festival is the perfect event to ensure the farm is ready for wedding season. Maybe the Liberty Ladies would want to help. That, or they'd drive Mom just crazy enough that she'd kick them off the farm and finish the job herself. Either would be better than having me, the vagabond who rarely comes home and never stays in one place longer than three months, do it. That's what everyone believes, anyway. It's easier to let them think that than to explain the truth: that I never wanted to leave but had to. That I've been counting down the days until I can come back. That I'm on the precipice of being able to do just that. One more season, that's all I need.

Tears prick my eyes, and I swipe them away quickly. Those truths won't change a damn thing, and telling anyone now will only make things harder for everyone else.

"Mom doesn't need *help*." I can practically hear my sister's air quotes. "She needs you. Her daughter. The one most similar to Dad. The one who was *supposed* to take over the farm."

I slow to a stop at an intersection, feeling like I've gone back in time. Nothing ever changes in Hope Harbor. Old colonial buildings line the quaint streets with eclectic shops like Twisted Tea and Wicked Wine and Cheese occupying their first floors. The properties beyond Main Street have mostly been converted into condos, since nowadays people don't have the need for six-thousand-square-foot homes with multiple dining rooms and kitchens. American flags fly proudly from every home, and flowers—likely from our farm—decorate many of the stone steps leading up to their front doors.

My eyes trail down the cobblestone sidewalk in search of Mabel's , the bakery I worked at during high school when I wasn't helping Dad on the flower farm. It's where I discovered my love of baking. As I drive past it now, I notice it's more run-down than the last time I saw it. Someone must be looking after it, however, because the wisteria that snakes up all the buildings doesn't cover the windows, which have clouded with age.

Now that's a business I would happily take over. The farm? Not so much.

The farm was never my passion. It's always been Mom's baby. And my father's one true love was my mother, which meant he spent his whole life nurturing the various fields of flowers that she adored. Every season brought a different blossom facilitated by my father's hard work; a sonnet written just for his wife. Their love bloomed vivid pinks, purples, and yellows in the spring. There was even a garden dedicated to her favorite flower, the iris, that burst with different shades of blue. He'd grown it as a surprise one spring, planting it right in view of their bedroom window. I understand why my mother isn't ready to do this without him yet. I'm not sure I am either.

The only reason I know what needs to be done with the land is because I was a daddy's girl who spent all of her free time helping him after school and on the weekends. It was our special time together. Meanwhile, my sister always had her nose in a book. It became a running joke in our family that I'd take care of the farm and Penny would become a librarian. They were mostly right about Penny. She's now the proud owner of Bonfire and Bliss Books, the most adorable romance bookstore right in downtown Hope Harbor. I, on the other hand, let everyone down when I left after high school graduation for my first adventure. I haven't been back home for more than a long weekend since. That was eight years ago.

I thought I'd have more time to make my father's dreams come true. I'd get my culinary degree, return home to Hope Harbor, and open a small bakery. Maybe bake cakes for the weddings the farm hosted. I'd have a simple life and a purpose in this town. And I would be here to help Daddy with the farm. That was the plan. He was the only one that knew it, though. He was my confidant and my biggest cheerleader. He understood me in a way no one else ever did. He always said, "You can't keep a wildflower in one place. They sprout up wherever they choose."

I never expected to lose him so soon.

"You're right. I'll do what I can for Mom," I say, turning my attention back to my sister. "But I need to be on the first ferry out to Nantucket the weekend before Memorial Day or I'll lose my spot at The Chamber House."

"I know the drill," my sister agrees, her tone dismissive. "New season, new job. But this spring, you belong to the farm."

I pass by my sister's bookshop and grin as I sound the horn. "That's me! Sure you don't want me to stop at the store first? Bet you could use some help picking out your next thriller."

"Ha ha," she deadpans. "You know the only books I carry have *happily ever afters*."

"And spice. We can't forget the spice!"

"Sex is a part of romance," Penny says defensively. "Not having it on the page would be ignoring an entire portion of a relationship. A very important one at that!"

I've heard this argument more times than I can count. My sister can get quite heated when people call the books in her shop porn. Ironically, it's not the older women in town who complain. Nope, the Liberty Ladies are all about their Spicy Saturday reads. It's strangers on the internet who have my sister up in arms. Maybe if she just stayed off TikTok, she'd be less stressed.

"And no, I don't want you to stop here," she continues now. "I want you to stop procrastinating and get settled at the . . . farm so you can help get things ready for wedding season."

"Fine." I let out a heavy sigh as I press on the gas and continue down Maple Lane. "It's just going to be so strange being in that big house without Daddy."

"About that," my sister starts. But before she says anything else, a woman walks right into the street.

I slam my foot down on the brake, and my car screeches to a stop. "I've got to go," I tell Penny as I slide the car into park and end our call. After looking both ways, I open my door and rush to check on the pedestrian.

March in New England is still cold, but I barely feel the bite of the wind; it's at least thirty degrees warmer here than it is up on the ski mountain where I spent the last few months.

"Are you okay?" I ask the woman, who continues to slowly stroll across the street. She's got chin-length silver hair that's perfectly coifed and is clutching a brown purse to her shoulder.

She whips her head in my direction, and her eyes blink wide in surprise before her lips tip up in a smile. *Oh no*, I think as realization sets in, *it's Rayna McGovern*. I can't backtrack fast enough. Now that the town gossip has set her beady blue eyes on me, I know it's only a matter of time until the entire town hears I'm home.

"Well, I never," Rayna says, her voice aghast. "I heard a rumor that Tallulah Darling was coming home for the season. But I never believe rumors."

Strange, because normally she's the one spreading them.

In her sixties, Rayna is about a decade older than my mother. When I was in high school, she was always the head of the PTA. I vaguely remember Penny mentioning that she's now *the* Liberty Lady, the prestigious title awarded yearly to the leader of the group.

"Here I am," I say with a wide smile. "And it's Tally now. Always has been, actually."

When she reaches out for a hug, I allow her to circle her arms around me and pull me against her chest. Like almost every woman in this town, she's got the familiar floral scent that my best friend Rosie accidentally created years ago and now sells exclusively in the boutique at her brewery. Mrs. McGovern is wearing lavender and lime. I've got on the wild honeysuckle that Rosie made just for me. It's the only perfume I've ever worn.

"Well, if you're okay," I pull back, thumbing toward my car, "I'll get going. My mom is waiting at the house, and I don't want her to worry if I'm late."

Rayna frowns. "Why wouldn't I be okay?"

"Because you walked out into the street without looking both ways?"

"Oh, nonsense. Cars stop." She waves her hand as if I'm crazy.

"Yes, a car stops if the driver sees you in time to slam on their brakes."

Rayna shakes her head again. "You've been gone too long, Tallulah. In this town, cars *stop*. They don't want to hit you."

Rayna is right about one thing at least: I have been gone for a long time.

"Got it. I'll make sure to keep an eye out for jaywalkers," I tell her as I head back toward my car. In any other town, there'd have been a backup of traffic behind my stopped vehicle. But in Hope Harbor, not a single car has passed.

"Say hi to Walker for me!" the woman calls as I'm shutting my door.

Walker? Who the hell is Walker?

Rayna might be getting a bit batty. Walking into streets without looking, mentioning random people I've never heard of.

I shake my head and press the button to start my rented Kia, and I head off, driving extra slow. Apparently a little too slow, as a few minutes later a truck behind me lets out a quick beep.

I glance in the rearview mirror to glare at the out-of-towner—people in Hope Harbor never beep their horns—only to find the road empty again.

"Well, if it isn't Tally Darling!" a familiar voice calls.

I'm beginning to feel like a celebrity with everyone using my first and last name. It's drastically different from my culinary life, where I wince whenever someone calls me "Darling." The guys find my last name hysterical. Male chefs are extremely egotistical, and because I don't have a degree, I'm never called "Chef," even if I take on that role many a night.

Not that I even want that title. No, the title I want is simple. "Baker."

And finally, it's within reach. Just one more summer of dealing with egomaniacs and then it'll be my turn.

Well, after I help my family get through this spring.

Turning, I realize the vehicle that was behind me is now pulled up beside me—in the opposite lane of traffic—and the driver is none other than Eli Davis.

I smile at the man beside me; honey-brown hair with a wave most women would kill for, chiseled cheekbones covered in more-than-day-old scruff, and blue eyes that still have the same charm they did back when he was in high school with Penny.

"Still driving too fast all these years later," he says in the flirty way he says everything. Eli doesn't know how not to flirt with you. It's in his nature. I'm sure plenty of women have been crushed by his demeanor, not realizing that he means nothing by it. Eli doesn't date—long-term, that is—nor does he lead anyone on. But I'm surprised to see him here because last I knew he was still living in New York City and playing in the NHL.

"I almost ran over Rayna McGovern, so I'm just being extra careful. Don't want to take any chances."

Eli gives me one of his slow smiles; it spreads across his face and reaches his eyes, making the blue in them twinkle. It's impossible not to smile when Eli smiles. "Heard you were helping out your mama on the farm. Make sure you stop by The Ice Cream Barn one day this week. Your mom loves the cherry cobbler. I'll put a tub aside for you to bring home for her."

At the mention of cherry cobbler, my brain starts to think up recipes for desserts that I could pair with that flavor. Maybe a cherries jubilee? I'd need the sweetest cherries to simmer with some sugar, lemon juice, and vanilla. Oh, and the zest of an orange. My mouth waters as I can practically taste the tart, sugary sauce dancing on my tongue.

"Wait, The Ice Cream Barn? What's that?" And more importantly, where?

"A barn where I sell ice cream. It's part of my groveling."

"Groveling?"

"Yeah. Since I played for New York, I have to pay my penance in hopes of forgiveness."

I laugh because few things are more sacred to New Englanders than their sports teams, and when Eli was drafted to New York—New England's sworn enemy in almost every sport—a few people took up weekly prayers for him to be traded to their beloved Boston Bolts. Though that never happened.

"Got it. Will do. It was good seeing you, Eli!"

He tips his chin at me, and as I begin to drive forward, he hollers, "Say hi to Walker for me."

Who is *this Walker?*

Taking a left, I head toward the farm, which is set back from town on the other side of the harbor. As I cruise along, I eye the smattering of sailboats bobbing in the deep navy waters, waiting to be taken out for the next boating season. The view of the farm from here has always been one of my favorites. The harbor in front of it, the small bridge that connects the town to our land, and, in the distance, the outline of New England's craggy mountains.

One of my other favorite views? Rosie's Brewery. It sits adjacent to our farm in an old barn that she's worked hard to transform into a thriving business. It's angled perfectly so the back faces our fields of flowers and the mountains, giving her customers a show that is constantly changing depending on the season: daffodils and tulips in the spring, sunflowers and dahlias in the summer, and roses and mums in the fall, not to mention the apples for picking and the pumpkin patch. In the winter, when the farm is mostly blanketed in snow and the flower beds rest in preparation for the next season, the trees are lit up with Christmas lights. Or they were, before Daddy died.

Blinking back the memories, I turn into Rosie's driveway. I'm not ready to see my mom just yet.

The weathered wooden brewery sign with the red rose welcomes me to my best friend's business. Shaking my head as I get out of my car, I smile up at the place. She really did it; she created a place for herself in this town, just like she always said she would.

The brewery boasts a walk-up window where you can grab coffee, and I offer a wave to the person manning the counter before pulling on the copper handle on the barn door, which swings open to reveal the whitewashed boards of the main room.

A long black bar lines the back of the space, and oversized chalkboards hang on the wall just above it, decorated with bright writing that details the day's specials.

I scan the mostly empty room for Rosie. It's barely lunch time, but in twenty minutes, this room will be full.

"Well, if it isn't Tally Mae Darling," a familiar voice sings.

I turn, searching her out, my lips lifting into a smile as soon as I spot the red locks my best friend is known for. Today they are piled high in a messy ponytail that somehow looks like it was intentionally styled that way, wisps hanging down around her ears, next to her signature gold hoops. The same rose from the welcome sign is stitched above her breast on a black long-sleeve shirt, and tight jeans hug her slim hips. A pair of black worn-in cowboy boots—also decorated with the brewery's rose—completes the look. She gifted them to herself three years ago, after she got the business off the ground.

"Rosie!" I squeal as I rush toward her, pulling her in for a long hug.

As I step back, her familiar scent—rose and citrus—dances between us. Somehow Rosie always smells just a little bit better than everyone else.

"You don't even look surprised to see me."

"Penny texted. She figured you'd stop here rather than going to your mom's."

I roll my eyes as I let out a heavy sigh and point toward the bar. "Are you going to offer me a drink?"

She shakes her head. "Nope."

My eyes narrow in surprise. "What do you mean, 'nope'?"

"Your sister said I need to send you along to the farm." Her head lifts at the jangle of the bell announcing another customer. Her eyes bounce in recognition, and her gaze stays on the door as she keeps talking. "You've delayed enough."

"Since when do you take Penny's side?" I counter.

She hasn't taken her eyes off the door, so I turn to see who's stolen her attention.

A man wearing a pair of jeans and a heavy, dark sweater and holding the leash of his chocolate Labrador is headed toward the bar.

"Mut," my friend growls beside me.

"I thought you loved dogs," I murmur, watching the man as he stops at a table in the corner to say hello to an older woman who reaches down to pet his dog.

"I love dogs," Rosie responds with a pasted-on smile, her lips barely moving. "I just don't like Fletcher."

"And Fletcher is the dog?"

I must ask the question too loudly because the man answers it as he reaches us.

"No, the dog's name is Brewer. I'm Fletcher." He holds out his hand to me, and his warm brown eyes stare into mine. "Fletcher Matthews, Hope Harbor's mayor. And you are?"

"Tally Darling," my best friend answers for me. "And she was just leaving."

My head whips in her direction. "I was not."

Her green eyes cut to me. "You were."

"Oh, the other Darling girl. I've heard a lot about you. Your farm is treasured by our whole town. We're all really looking forward to the Daffodil Festival."

"Thanks," I say uncomfortably, because I most certainly am not.

Fletcher barely acknowledges my words, however, as he focuses in on Rosie. "I'm having the pale ale today."

"Good for you," she says in a bored tone, waving him away.

"Odd way to treat a customer," I mutter as he walks off, chuckling.

Before he settles at the bar, he turns back to me. "Oh, Tally. Say hi to Walker for me, okay?"

"Who the hell is Walker?" The words are a hiss between my teeth.

With a gleam in her eye, Rosie smiles. "Nope. I'm not telling you."

"What?"

"It'll be more fun this way."

"No." I pull on her arm, keeping her close. "It will not. And as my best friend, it's your job to tell me what's going on."

She shrugs. "Nah."

"Are you being serious right now?"

She shakes my hand off her arm and starts walking toward the bar. "Go home, Tally. You'll know him when you see him."

"*Where* will I see him, though?"

The only response I get is another arch of her brows.

Determined to get to the bottom of this, I make the trek to the farm in my rental. My mother will tell me what's going on. She's never been good at keeping a secret.

"Mom!" I yell as I open the unlocked door. No one locks their doors in Hope Harbor. My eyes scan the familiar living room, comforted that nothing has changed. "Mom?" I call again, peering into the kitchen.

I hear a noise upstairs and turn around to head to the second floor.

A rush of excitement fills me at the thought of seeing my mom again. She and Penny came to me for Christmas in Vermont this season. With it being so soon after Dad's funeral, my sister thought it would be a good idea to stay off the farm during the holiday. There were too many memories in the house.

The floorboards creak in my bedroom and, keen to surprise her, I don't call her name again as I run up the stairs. I swing open the door to my room and squeal. "I'm home!"

But it's not my mother standing in my bedroom.

No, it's a six-foot-something wall of a man, gripping a towel so tiny with hands so big my eyes bulge. The towel barely makes it around his waist, dipping dangerously low and exposing hard lines and an indecent dusting of dark hair.

I'm not supposed to be seeing this. He's not supposed to be here. Even though those facts blink brightly in some part of my brain, I can't look away from all that tanned skin. My gaze slides higher, over a muscular chest slick with water; up to a corded neck, the muscles of which flex; and farther still, to a strong chin covered in day-old scruff.

He's holding a cell phone up to his ear, but his mouth isn't moving.

When I meet his hard eyes that are narrowed into black slits, my brain finally catches up. Yup. There's a naked man in my childhood bedroom.

Shit. There's a naked man in my bedroom.

With nothing useful to protect myself, I do the next best thing and scream bloody murder.

Chapter 2
WALKER

Ah, what the fuck? "Billie, I gotta go."

"Who is that?" my sister asks, although it's hard to hear her through the phone with the woman in front of me screaming her head off. Even with her face red and contorted in anger, it's easy to see she's pretty. I've seen pictures of her around the house, so I know who she is. I just don't know why the fuck she's here.

"It's the other Darling girl. I'll call you back in a second." I toss the phone toward the bed, not waiting for my sister to acknowledge me. She's used to few words. She'd be more concerned if I actually tried to have a conversation with her.

I tighten my towel and hold out my free hand to the banshee in front of me. I'm not sure she's all there right now. She's screaming like the noise itself is all she knows to do. Like her brain has stopped working.

Approaching her carefully, I take a step forward. "Ma'am."

She flails her arms at me. "Don't you come near me. I'm trained in Krav Maga."

I straighten. "What?"

The woman nods aggressively, the chestnut hair that frame her face bouncing with the movement. Then she puts her hands up in a fighting stance. Or at least what *she* might call a fighting stance.

"Yup. So go on, get out of here. We've got nothing but

flowers on this farm. No money, no liquor. You got your warm shower, now get out of here."

It hits me that this woman has no idea who I am. Interesting. Figured her sister would have warned her about me, considering how distrustful she's been. Or maybe her mom.

The nosy people in this town can't help but run their mouths, so she must not have stopped anywhere before arriving at the farm.

For what seems like the thousandth time today, I ask myself why I'm still here. Why I stayed after Peter Darling died. It's certainly not for the money. The only reason I said yes to Peter in the first place was because of my sister, Billie, and my nephew, Quinn. They deserve a place like this, a safe place to land. Which is exactly what the farm was—until this woman walked in.

I really didn't think she'd come back. The way everyone talked about Peter Darling's youngest daughter, it seemed like she was addicted to the road.

"Stop casing the joint. There's nothing here you want." The woman's words draw me back to the present. When I focus on her, I find her amber eyes trailing around the room. With her attention not on me, I take the opportunity to study her. Wearing a pair of jeans that mold to her curvy hips and small waist and a green ribbed sweater that dips down low, exposing perky breasts that would more than fill my hands, she makes it hard to focus on anything else. Wild caramel waves almost hit her elbows as she continues the slow perusal of my space.

"Not much I want here, either," she whispers to herself.

"Exactly. So why don't you go on and get back to where you came from?" The words slip out gruff. My voice is gravel—

staring at this woman has my throat dry and my heart beating rapidly. Every second I spend in her presence I find another thing attractive about her. Long black lashes that flutter in surprise, a golden ring hanging from her neck, dipping between her breasts. Pouty lips that pop open in rage.

I don't normally censor myself, but from the look on her face, I know I've fucked up. I was supposed to be easing her into the truth, letting her come to terms with the fact that this was no longer her room, before kicking her out.

Except a few seconds in the presence of a pretty girl already has me forgetting the plan.

Her eyes widen and then she's back to screaming again.

Ah, hell.

"Tally!" A voice hollers from downstairs. Thank fuck someone is here to talk some sense into her. Footsteps thunder up the stairs and then Penny appears in the doorway, out of breath and holding her chest. "Tally—" Her head falls forward as she tries to catch her breath. "There's a man staying in your room."

Tally glares from me to her sister. My hand grips the towel tighter, and I realize just how naked I am in front of both of Peter Darling's girls right now. Something I promised him would never happen.

"Why?" is all Tally grits out.

Penny shakes her hand, her head still hanging forward. Unlike Tally, she's got much darker hair that's thick with blunt bangs across her forehead and braided to the side. She's much curvier than her sister, too; more in line with their mother's shape. True to her name, Penny's eyes are copper and she's got a spattering of freckles that cover her cheeks.

"Give me a minute. I thought Mom would be here to

handle this, but when she walked into the bookstore just now, I knew this was going to end badly. Which is why I ran here straightaway."

"You ran here from the bookstore?" Tally's voice is filled with shock.

Penny raises her head, "No. From the driveway. But that's as much running as I've done lately, so just—" She pauses and breathes deep. "This is Jesse Walker. Walker, this is Tallulah Darling, my sister."

I nod. Already figured that out.

"You're Walker?" She's heard about me already. I can't imagine any of it would have been good: talks in grunts, never smiles, refuses to make small talk, doesn't date. That's a quick list that I came up with on the fly; I'm sure people in town would find plenty more to add.

I grunt in agreement.

"Why is he here, and why did everyone in town tell me to say hello to him?" she asks Penny.

My scowl deepens. This fucking town.

"He's helping Mom with the farm." *That's one way to put it.* "And he's living here."

Warily, Tally's gaze falls back to me again.

"With Mom? Are you, like, dating her?" Her palms cover her flushed cheeks and then she peeks between them. "Oh God, Mom is having an affair with a hot farmhand. This is what happens, isn't it? Younger guys find out about poor widows and hit on them and then suddenly we're having to call this guy 'Daddy' and he brings his brothers around and they're groping us under the Thanksgiving table while telling us we're not really related."

"What the fuck?" Penny growls, taking the words right

from my mouth. "No. What sort of afterschool specials have you been watching on the ski slopes? Dad hired him last year to help with the soil. He was living in one of the cottages, but after Dad died—" Penny's voice goes soft, and suddenly I feel like I'm interrupting a family moment. I shouldn't be here. Though I can't exactly leave considering I'm still naked.

"After Dad died what?" Irritation coats Tally's tone.

"I moved in here." There, I said it. Kept it simple, and now they can go. "Now if you don't mind—" I nod toward the door.

Tally doesn't head that way, though. Instead, she steps closer to me, and the smell of something sweet has me almost leaning in. Fuck, she smells good. "Moved in here? As in into my bedroom or with my mother?"

"As in into this house. Gail—" The damn scent of her is fucking with my head. I can't put together a proper sentence. And those eyes. Fuck, I could get lost in them. I shake my head and blow out a breath. "*Your mother* moved into the cottage I was staying in."

"Why?" she practically yells. "Can one of you just tell me what's going on?!"

Penny presses closer to Tally, placing a hand on her back. "Why don't you sit down and I'll fill you in."

Tally nods, and they both look toward the bed.

No. Fuck no. I'll be stuck in here all day.

"Could you have this conversation downstairs?" I ask.

Both women whip their heads in my direction, and finally it dawns on them that I'm naked. And still dripping wet.

My sister, Billie, had called just as I was getting out of the shower, and I never let her go to voicemail. Tally had barged in while I was on the phone with her and my nephew, Quinn, who was telling me about the hockey league in Hope Harbor run by the former NHL player Eli Davis. It's the first time Quinn's shown any excitement about moving here.

But now, with Tally back, there probably won't be a job for Billie. Which means there's no chance she'll move to the farm. Before, I was able to pitch it as her getting me out of a jam. My sister is incapable of saying no when someone needs help. Now, however, she'll see my plan as charity. I'm proud of how she's raising my nephew on her own, but I want to help. It's what family does. She won't accept that, though. Instead, she works herself to exhaustion providing for her and Quinn. And they both suffer.

Anger courses through me. *No.* Tally needs to go. The Darlings and I had an agreement, and I, for one, intend to hold their family to that promise. Whether they like it or not.

Chapter 3
TALLY

O h, you're naked." My sister blinks at Walker as if seeing him for the first time. Then her gaze sweeps to me. "Why is he naked?"

I hold up my hands. "Don't look at me! You guys are the ones who've been hiding everything. Maybe you're the one having a secret relationship with the hot cowboy."

"Not a cowboy," he grumbles. "And that's the second time you've called me hot."

My sister and I look in his direction simultaneously, shocked that he said so many words in one go. If he'd started talking earlier, I wouldn't have screamed for so long.

Walker's got this look on his face that tells me he's slightly amused, even with a scowl fully in place. His eyes are no longer as narrowed.

"Now, can you both get out?" This time his words are gritty and filled with warning.

It's irritatingly hot. Much like Walker.

"Why does the man have to be so good-looking?" I ask my sister. Her body sags with a nod, like she's agreeing with me. "Maybe it's because he's naked. Although, I can think of quite a few people I've accidentally seen naked who I didn't find hot." I look back at him to explain. "Working in seasonal tourism, and mostly in hotels, means this happens more often than I'd like. It's not like I'm a Peeping Tom."

"Why are you still talking?" He grits out the words.

Oh. Right. "We'll just—" I point toward the door. "Leave you to it."

A bull-like huff escapes his lips as we leave, and I make sure not to turn around, even though I still have a thousand questions and zero answers.

"Start talking," I say to my sister as I drag her down the steps and into the kitchen.

As soon as I spot the L-shaped counter, specifically the woven stools my dad always pulled out for us to sit on and have our chats, the memory of my father's voice grounds me. *"Breathe, Tally. Just breathe."*

This is where I'd go when someone made fun of my clothes at school, or when I got my heart broken by a boy. A few fights were fixed between me and Rosie, too, with diet cokes in glass bottles—one of my dad's special treats—right in this very spot.

"God, I miss him," I whisper, my hand going to my chest and rubbing as if I could ease this pain. I don't dare walk into the living room, where my father used to sit in the worn blue chair that matched the couches we had when I was a kid. We got new couches when I was in high school, but his chair remains. There's probably still a LEGO block or two lost in the cushions. He was always putting together a new model.

Penny leans her head against my shoulder. "Me, too."

"What's going on, Penny? Why is there a man living in our parents' house? Why did Mom move out? Why did you really ask me to come home?"

My sister rolls her lips before nodding toward the counter. "Let's sit."

Wearing a pair of jean overalls that hang haphazardly on

one side, Penny leads us over to the counter. With a roll of her shoulders, she straightens. "I'm not exactly sure what is going on with Mom. She refuses my help on the farm. Not that I'd even know what to do. Like Walker said, she moved into the cottage and gave him free reign over this house." She pauses, looking around the kitchen. "I haven't been in here in months because of that. Looks about the same, though."

I nod in agreement. If Walker has been staying here, he can't have touched much. Why, though? Why is he here? Why would he want to live among my parents' things? It's such an odd choice for a bachelor.

"Wait, is Walker single?"

Penny's mouth falls open. "Wow, you're interested in the farmer?"

"No. Obviously not." My cheeks heat. "I am just wondering if anyone else is going to jump out of the rafters and claim they have the right to be here."

Penny lets out a breathy laugh. "Not that I'm aware of. Dad hired Walker last year to help with the soil. He was trying to extend the wedding season."

My stomach clenches. "Extend it?"

"Yeah. The daffodils only last a few weeks and then the tulips are gone by end of May. Dad figured if he could find a way to extend those time periods, more brides would want to have their weddings here."

This is news to me. "But that wasn't possible, right? You promised you only needed me through mid-May."

Penny nods. "don't think any magical soil has been produced. You're safe to return to your exciting life as soon as the season ends."

My exciting life. Right. Everyone thinks I left because I

wanted to. The truth is that I *couldn't* stay. Or at least that's the lie I've always told myself. Now, Iee how I let everyone down. How I let my father down.

He had to hire some stranger to run our farm. Dammit, I should have been here. I should have known about this . . . Jesse Walker's presence wouldn't have been a surprise if I'd paid even a little attention.

The guilt is enough to eat me alive. But I can't change the past. I may have failed my father once, but I won't do it again. Which means I need to figure out what Walker is up to.

"Why is he still here? If he didn't do what he said he would, why did Mom have him move into our house?"

"Because she needs help, Tally. She can't oversee the farm. The flowers need a lot of attention. Attention Dad always gave them. I don't know the first thing about how to maintain them, and Mom *can't* do it. But if you're so concerned, you could stay and do it yourself?"

I bite my lip. She knows I don't want to do that. She also knows I never back down from a challenge. "I don't like it. How much digging have you done into this guy? Are we sure he's not trying to take advantage of Mom?"

Penny rolls her eyes. "Have you seen him? Do you really think he needs to con our middle-aged mother into sleeping with him?"

"Ew."

Penny laughs. "Exactly."

"I don't trust him. There's just something about him."

"Dad trusted him."

"Dad liked everyone. He was a terrible judge of character."

"Tally!" My sister's mouth falls open.

"What? Daddy was my favorite person in the world, but

I'm not about to rewrite history so you can get me to agree that this guy is good."

Penny sighs, but there's something about her expression that makes me feel like she's not convinced, either. "Everybody in town loves him."

"This town loves everyone."

She shrugs but doesn't disagree. The people of Hope Harbor are good, hard-working people. They may be gossips, but ours is a town filled with warm hearts, with people who will give you the shirt off their back and, *apparently*, never hit a pedestrian.

"Where will I stay?" I ask, realizing my next dilemma.

"Mom's cottage has a double bed."

"Penny!"

"Or you could stay here?"

"You want me to stay in a house with a man I don't know?"

"You've stayed in many houses with men you don't know. Don't try to tell me that your accommodations over the years haven't been way worse than this."

I blow out another long breath. She's not wrong. Seasonal employment leaves few options when it comes to housing. Often I'm sharing a small hotel room with another employee or a house with a group of strangers.

"I'm going to be completely useless, Penny. I don't know a thing about the wedding business—"

"I've got someone." The gruff voice startles both of us. I turn to see the grump from upstairs, now dressed in a pair of worn-in Wranglers and a dark green Henley. Dammit, he's still attractive with clothes on. His brown hair curls a bit at the sides, and I can't help but think that it's the perfect length to tug on.

Yep, if I'm ever going to survive this season, this guy needs to go.

"Got someone for what?" Penny asks.

"My sister has worked in the wedding business for the last few years. She's got a degree in hospitality and event management. She knows how to handle brides and everything they need, and she's available to move in and help."

"That's why I'm here," I say, possessive over a job I don't really want.

"For how long, though? My sister knows what she's doing." My eyes narrow at his words. "And she doesn't have another job to rush off to." My scowl deepens. "And whoever is in this position will have to deal with me daily because I'm the one running the farm." Folding his arms across his chest like he's proud of himself, he squares his shoulders and waits for my reaction.

I don't like the way he's looking at me. Don't like his insinuation that I'm going to run. And although I might have left eight years ago, he has no idea why. I don't want this job, but I never back down from a challenge.

"I'll be the one dealing with the weddings."

He frowns. "So you keep saying."

"It's *our* family's farm."

His jaw ticks. "I'm aware."

Hmm. He's aware it's ours, but that doesn't make him happy. What the hell does that mean?

Chapter 4
TALLY

"So I hear you finally met Walker?" Rosie says as she slides a shot glass over to me.

"How'd you—" I glance at my sister sitting next to me and scowl. "Oh, for fucks sake, can the two of you stop sharing secrets? She's supposed to be *my* best friend."

Penny laughs. "Rosie's my friend, too."

Rosie pushes a shot toward her. "Yeah, and you're the one who's been gone for years. The two of us had to commiserate over missing you so much. Right, Pen?"

Penny doesn't answer and instead grabs the shot and downs it quickly. There's a band set up in the corner of the brewery, and a decent crowd has gathered to listen to them play. My mother was supposed to meet us for dinner, but she texted that some meeting had run late. I know she's avoiding me because she's going to have to explain how she gave not only our house but also my room to a stranger.

Without dinner plans, Penny and I decided to come down to the brewery.

"I don't know why you all wanted me to say hello to Walker for you. He doesn't seem very friendly."

The man barely talks. After our little showdown in the kitchen, he grumbled that he had work to do, and I haven't seen him since.

Rosie's lips slide into a wide smile. "The town loves to

tease him *because* he doesn't talk. So everyone's always saying hi to him, being friendly, trying to strike up some meaningless conversation. It drives him nuts."

I swirl the liquid around in my shot glass. "You talk like the town is in cahoots."

Penny and Rosie share a look and then Rosie lets out a raspy laugh. "Oh, honey, you've been gone too long. *Of course* we're in cahoots. We had an entire town meeting about it."

I groan in aggravation. "And he's still here? I don't get it. Something isn't adding up. Do you know *anything* about him?"

Rosie shakes her head. "Only that he and your dad used to come in here often for lunch. Your father really liked him."

"So Penny says," I grumble. "But I'm telling you, there's something suspicious about him. You know he told us his sister could do my job?"

Rosie raises her eyebrows in surprise.

"Exactly. Said I could go to my next job because his sister knew how to plan weddings and was happy to come and stay."

"But you're not leaving, right?" Penny almost sounds panicked.

"No," I say quickly. "Walker told me that whoever was working the weddings would have to answer to him because he's running the farm."

Rosie settles her forearms on the edge of the bar and smirks. "So let me guess. Because he offered to bring his sister to do the job you don't even want—and insinuated that she'd do it better than you—you're now committed to stay?"

I stare at the Fireball she's poured for me and then meet her gaze. She arches her brows again, and I brace myself for what she's about to say. "Remember the rule: If you don't tell the truth while drinking, you'll be cursed with bad sex for ten years."

I practically choke on my laughter. Rosie came up with this stupid rule when we were drinking peach schnapps in high school and I refused to admit that I had a crush on the guy who had asked her to prom. We both threw up for hours the next day, but she didn't go to prom with Kyle and we've never told a lie while drinking since.

I lift my glass and grin. "Yup."

Rosie grabs the bottle of Fireball and pours herself a shot before filling Penny's empty glass. Then she lifts hers in the air in my direction. "Girl, you're just as crazy asthe day you left Hope Harbor."

As the Fireball hits my throat, I relish the burn. I haven't felt this wild in a long time.

When Penny disappears to the bathroom, Rosie eyes me. "For what it's worth, I'm glad you're back. Your family needs you. But a word of advice."

I nod, knowing that if anyone is going to give it to me straight, it'll be my best friend.

"Walker's not going anywhere. You're going to have to figure out a way to get along with him."

I shake my head at her words. I'm going to find out the story behind Jesse Walker's scowl. And I'm not leaving Hope Harbor until I prove to everyone that he is up to no good.

—

HOPE HARBOR TOWN CHAT

UNKNOWN NUMBER: Did you know Tally Darling's back in town?

UNKNOWN NUMBER: Oh yes! Ran into her downtown today. Or more like she almost ran into me. Good thing cars stop.

UNKNOWN NUMBER: Of course they do. What else would they do?

"What the heck is this?" I ask my sister as I hold up my phone and point the screen in her direction. We're sitting in her car outside our house after sunset, and I'm trying to work up the courage to go inside. Messages continue to pop up by the second, all from numbers I don't recognize.

My sister smiles. "Oh, it's the town group chat."

"The what?"

She giggles. "The group chat. You know, so everyone can get up-to-the-minute updates."

Confused, I stare down at the screen that's filling with more messages. "How did I end up in it?"

Penny shrugs. "If I had to guess? Rosie. She *loves* the group chat."

I frown. Everything feels so different from when I lived here last.

"You sure you don't want me to walk you up to the house?" Penny's eyes cast longingly in the direction of what used to be our family home.

"I'll be fine. Hopefully the man of the house is already sleeping."

Penny giggles. "Come by the store tomorrow," she says

before turning to me with a more serious look. "I'm glad you're home, Tal."

My chest aches as I throw my arms around her before grabbing my stuff from the back seat.

When I get out of the car, I stare up at the white Victorian with the farmer's porch my father never got around to fixing. My mother always wanted a few rocking chairs and cushions so she could sit and drink her tea and look out at her meadows. But the porch is bare. Like so much of this house, Dad only finished half of it before he got pulled into something else.

My father was the type of man who was always offering to help—he was at every town meeting, and if he wasn't at home, he was probably helping out a neighbor. A familiar pang of sadness grows as I climb the steps and lean against the banister, which just barely holds my weight because one of the stakes is missing. Laughing, I look up at the sky, knowing my dad is saying he'll get to that soon enough.

Silence greets me when I enter the house, and I sigh in relief, knowing I can sneak up to my sister's room without having to talk to Walker. But as the floorboards creak under my weight, a throat clears and I find the man in question sitting in my daddy's chair with a slew of papers laid out on the table in front of him.

The last time I visited, my dad was in that same position, reviewing taxes. I cough out a laugh at how ridiculous it is that he was worried about business expenses and write-offs that he didn't even live to deal with.

"Are you okay?" Walker pushes back in his chair, studying me. I'm sure I'm quite the sight, with the delirious smile on my face from laughing so I don't start sobbing.

I give a quick nod and shift toward the stairs. "I'm going to stay in Penny's room if that's all right."

Walker shrugs. "It's your house."

I rush out of the room without a response. Because it sure doesn't feel like it.

Chapter 5
WALKER

D o you think he keeps the rink open in the spring?" my nephew, Quinn, asks as he takes a bite of the pancakes Gail made this morning. It's a new tradition she started a few weeks ago when she found out my sister was interested in helping with the weddings. Billie and Quinn come over to the farm for breakfast and then Gail and my sister chat while Quinn joins me out in the meadows. The fresh air is good for him, and I like to think that Gail and Billie's new friendship is good for them, too. We normally do it on Saturday mornings, but Quinn had an odd day off from school today so my sister is joining us for brunch and then heading to work while Quinn hangs with me for the day.

Billie and I never had a home like this or a mother as warm as Gail. Giving Billie a taste of what life would be like here is the best way to get my sister to move in.

I shrug noncommittally. "I'm not sure." To find out, I'd have to actually make conversation with Eli Davis, and I try to avoid the overly talkative former NHL player as much as I can.

"I bet he does." Quinn smiles, causing the dimple in his cheek to pop just like my sister's does when she's genuinely happy. I've got one, too, although no one's seen it in a long damn time. "I can't wait to start playing hockey. Mom even said I could get new skates."

Billie pauses her conversation with Gail to look at Quinn. My sister and her son are twins, with matching dirty blond hair and almond-shaped chestnut-brown eyes.

"I told you I'd consider it," she says to him. "Don't go putting words in my mouth."

I'd get the kid new skates. Hell, I'd even talk to Eli if it means my sister and nephew would move here. The house has three bedrooms, and Gail swears it has more life when Quinn is here. She's happy to have us stay on the farm.

"But if we move here—"

Quinn's words are cut off by my sister's stern glare. "Quinn."

My nephew sighs, looking down at his pancakes, and I glance at my sister. I know better than to overstep in front of her son.

"Did I tell you that we got another two wedding bookings for June? At this point, we may need you to come on full-time," says Gail.

Quinn sits at the head of the table like a proud king, with Billie and I flanking either side of him and Gail at the other head. It's clear to me that Gail's trying to fill the void Peter left, but since Billie and I never had much of a home life, neither of us mind .

Growing up, I worked hard to keep Billie and me out of my father's way. By the time I was sixteen, he'd stopped coming home most nights, anyway. By eighteen, he was dead. Food wasn't an easy commodity to come by, but I did my best to raise Billie after our mother left, just before my sister's sixth birthday.

Now I survey the scene in front of me—a family and home like I've only ever dreamed of having. Strawberries, bananas, whipped cream, and syrup, along with stacks of pancakes in all different flavors, are spread in front of us on the table.

"Really?" Billie almost sounds excited.

Gail breaks out into a big smile. "Yup, and Penny thinks we could get even more weddings if we'd advertise more."

Billie laughs warmly. "Yes, I'm sure that would help drum up business."

"Your brother is doing a good job with the socials," Gail says proudly, eyeing me across the table.

I offer a grunt in response as Billie's eyes lift, amused. "I've never seen him use any form of social media. What's your handle, Jesse?"

Even though I hate social media with a passion, I do enjoy the lilt in my sister's voice. "I don't have one. We use the farm's."

Billie immediately pulls out her phone, and I know when she's found the page because she snorts. I try to not roll my eyes, but when Quinn sits up on his knees and begins to reach across the table, a growl escapes from the back of my throat.

"I wanna see," he begs.

"Don't," I start, right as the front door swings open, dragging in the cool March air.

From my place in the dining room, I watch as Tally, in a pair of sleep shorts that barely cover her toned thighs and an oversized sweatshirt, cautiously steps inside. "Mom?"

"In here, dear," Gail replies.

Tally's amber eyes go wide when she realizes there's a crowd.

"I was just looking for you in the cottage. You've done a great job avoiding me," she says pointedly.

Gail gets up and greets her daughter, pulling her in for a

hug. "Give me a hug, then you can hit me with more attitude. Missed you, baby girl."

Tally's stance relaxes as she melts into her mother's arms, and I look away.

"Missed you, too, Mom," I hear her whisper, not so quietly. "But could you please tell me why there's a man living in our home and you've moved into a tiny cottage?"

My head snaps back in their direction, and I can't help but scowl. My sister gives me a swift kick to the shin. "Stop staring."

"We'll talk later," Gail replies as she guides her daughter toward us. "This is Billie, Walker's sister, and his nephew, Quinn."

When Tally blinks but still says nothing, Gail sighs. "Manners, Tally. Introduce yourself."

Tally shakes her head, and the long, thick caramel waves of her hair shift with her. She's gorgeous. "Sorry, I didn't expect anyone to be here. I'm Tally. Nice to meet you."

"Nice to meet you, too," Billie says.

"Billie is going to be helping me with the weddings," Gail continues. "And her son will be starting first grade at Gardener in the fall."

Tally's eyes widen again. "I'm helping you with the weddings."

Gail frowns. "I thought you were only here for a few days. Don't you have to get back to Vermont?"

Tally steps farther into the dining room. "I left my job, Mom. This is my job now. Penny asked me to come back for wedding season." She glares in my direction as she says it.

My sister shakes her head nervously. "Oh, I didn't realize. I don't want to step on any toes."

"You're not," I grind out. "Like Gail was saying, Tally *isn't* staying."

"I am," she retorts.

"Does that mean we can't play in the fields today?" Quinn questions.

My fists clench as Tally stares him down silently.

"Of course you can," Gail tells him. "Tally, we'll talk logistics later. But for now, are you joining us for breakfast or not?"

The woman's eyes flutter shut as she tries to regain some composure. "I need to shower."

"About that," Gail starts as I push back my chair. "Your father and I had started renovations on the bathroom before—" She doesn't finish the sentence as she stares out the window. The only other full bath in the house is attached to my bedroom.. "You'll have to use the one in the cottage. But there's no hot water."

"You didn't say anything." I cut in. "I can take a look at it later."

"It's fine," Gail replies, brushing me off. "The cold water is good for your skin."

Tally sighs. "Well, I guess I need a shower more than hot water." She points to the door and then does a little wave. "It was nice meeting you," she tells my sister and then makes a point to look at Quinn. "Enjoy the fields today. The one in the back where the wildflowers grow was always my favorite."

I follow her to the door, reaching for her arm and snagging it before she can escape. "You can use the shower in my room—it's working just fine—and I'll go look at the heater in the cottage." I know it's a mistake before she even turns, because with her this close, the sugar-like scent of her invades my senses and my whole body tenses..

"My room," she spits out, her head whipping around to me. "It's *my* shower in *my* room."

This damn woman. Try to give her an inch, and she takes back the whole house.

I've still got her elbow in my grip, and this close, the tiny specs of gold are visible in her amber eyes. She shakes me off, and I can see her pulse thrumming as we go toe to toe. Fuck, why does that thrill me?

"Just use the shower," I clip, annoyed that everything is a fight with her. But even more annoyed that I can't stop staring into those damn eyes.

"I'd rather take a cold one." She storms back toward the cottage, and I stare after her, my own pulse racing.

"I like her." My sister's voice startles me from stewing. I snap back to reality as I catch Quinn in the background, laughing at something on Gail's phone. She must be showing him the pictures of me on the farm's social media.

I glare at Billie. "There's nothing to like."

"She doesn't take your shit. *Of course* there's something to like. And it looks like you don't need my help, after all."

My sister walks toward the kitchen with the dirty plates she picked up from the table, and I follow. "She's not staying."

"That's not what she says." Billie's soft voice calms my pounding heart. I haven't felt this way in a long damn time, and I'm not sure I like it. "Does she know?"

I turn on the faucet and hold out a hand, waiting for my sister to give me the dirty dishes. When I don't reply, Billie raises a brow, holding the plates hostage.

I grab the dishes from her and dunk them in the water, ignoring her wary expression.

"You didn't tell her?"

I remain silent as I pour soap into the basin. No, I didn't tell her. And yeah, she's going to be pissed when she finds out. But that's not my problem. Tally isn't my responsibility; Billie and Quinn are. And eventually Tally will learn that they have just as much right to be here as she does.

Chapter 6
TALLY

HOPE HARBOR TOWN CHAT

UNKNOWN NUMBER: Can someone confirm that the Daffodil Festival is still going forward?

RAYNA: Oh, I think that's why Tally's home. She's here to help.

UNKNOWN NUMBER: Tally? Can you confirm? She's in here, right?

ROSIE: She is! And it is. Rumor has it she was at the brewery last night and chances are if you stop by for lunch this week you'll get a Tally sighting.

I snort. Rumor has it? Rosie knows it's not a rumor because she saw me with her own eyes. My best friend is a little marketing genius when it comes to this small town stuff, but I wish she didn't use me as collateral.

Another five texts roll in, and I silence my phone. I can't leave the chat because I want to know what they're saying about me, although I'm annoyed they're talking about me at all. Especially since I don't know who most of them are. Although, I did figure out Rayna's number based upon her last few texts.

I sigh. This so isn't my day. I'd woken up feeling awkward in my own house—in Penny's old bed, which oddly still smelled like her—and before I could think too long on it, I decided to sneak out the back to avoid running into Walker. I headed to my mom's cottage to finally confront her on all of this insanity, but of course I couldn't find her. After a quick walk into the fields to calm my nerves, I found my mother playing house with Walker and his family.

And then there was the little boy sitting in my father's chair. It's silly, I know. My father is gone. And it's just a chair, but jeez, did that one hurt. Everything that once existed on the farm has changed.

I never appreciated it before. Never knew how I'd miss it all. But God, do I wish I could have it back.

Rather than spending the rest of the morning dwelling on things I can't change, I throw on some running gear and prepare to jog into town.

The first mile offers views of our farm, the brewery, and the beautiful mountains that lie just beyond. The spring air is cool against my skin, but it's got nothing on the frigid Vermont temperatures.

Running is a way to clear my head. I often use the time to think up recipes or work through a possible menu change. Not that I had a ton of say in the restaurants I worked in.

Today, though, my mind can't possibly fathom a recipe because all I can think about is how my mother has given away our house.

It's impossible that Penny is fine with this. I just have to get her to admit it.

Everyone seems cagey. It's not like I expected the red carpet to be rolled out upon my homecoming, but I thought my mother would be a little bit more excited that I'm here. Even Rosie has been weird.

I'm used to not having many people in my life. When you travel as much as I do, spending seasons in different kitchens, there's no time for long-term relationships. For the most part, I've always been okay with that. I've had one goal with every kitchen I've worked in: to work under the pastry chef.

We didn't have a lot of money growing up—my father always said the earth was our wealth. We got by because he was creative in using the daffodil and tulip season to host weddings on the farm as a source of income, but it wasn't enough to put both my sister and me through college. Everyone thinks I ran away, but I did what I had to do so I could chase my dreams and my family could chase their own.

My father would have mortgaged the land—or sold some of it—so I could go to culinary school, but I couldn't allow that. He was already putting Penny through college, and I saw how it wore on him.

So I made a decision to do it myself. And I've had a great time learning, even though it's nearly impossible to work as a pastry chef without a culinary degree.

Nantucket is my chance, though. A pastry chef I worked with two years ago has been hired as head baker at a prestigious restaurant, and she reached out to me to join her this summer.

It isn't a long-term position because Nantucket is a seasonal destination that slows down considerably in the fall, but after this season, I'll finally have enough money saved up to attend culinary school. Then maybe one day I can open up my own little bakery.

I turn onto the road circling the harbor and revel in the

beauty before me until I hit Maple Lane, Hope Harbor's main street, and my quiet peace is interrupted. Traffic rolls in both directions, and I wave at the men drinking coffee on the corner as I run by.

The cobblestone sidewalk tests my balance, but I manage to stay upright and watch workers hang wicker baskets filled with flowers at every street light, the yellows, pinks, and purples waterfalling off the ornate Victorian arches. There are signs everywhere detailing that Hope Harbor was founded in 1682 and is home of the Daffodil Festival. They'll be changed in the fall to remind us that it's home of the Maple Festival as well.

This town loves its festivals. And fortunately for my family, it loves its flowers, too. That's the one thing that's kept my family's business running for as long as it has.

I slow my pace as I pass Pretty Things and Paper Rings, a boutique for cards and jewelry, and glance at the window display that boasts an entire section dedicated to St. Patrick's Day.

Continuing on, I pass more windows, each one a glimpse into a different local shop. My mom's favorite hair salon sits on one corner, its pink-and-white awning reflecting the sun although the lights inside are still off.

I stop at another intersection and turn to look at Mabel's Bakery. A twinge of longing hits my chest as I glance at the wisteria-covered building, something wild and uncontrolled that calls to me. I shake my head—no time for dreaming today—and force myself to cross toward my sister's bookstore.

A bell announces my arrival when I open the door. Despite the fact that it's spring, the store smells of cinnamon and pumpkin spice. Even as a child, my sister's favorite season was fall, and she was pumpkin obsessed far before the latte craze.

Her gold-and-burgundy bookstore is eclectic with hand-drawn designs dancing across the walls and oversized navy velvet chairs dotted strategically throughout. Noah Kahan's smooth voice drifts over the speakers at a low enough volume that I can barely make out his words, but I find myself swaying anyway. It's been a long time since I properly danced.

My brain immediately summons Walker, and I can't help but wonder if he's the type of man to spin a girl around the dance floor. He doesn't seem like a romantic. Or like he has much of a personality at all.

Which is a pity because that chest and those strong arms would feel incredible to lean on.

"Welcome to Bonfire and Bliss Books," my sister says as she peers around a bookshelf, not realizing her new customer is me.

"Why thank you," I say with a dramatic curtsy. "I'm in the market for a book with sex. The good kind."

Penny rolls her copper eyes as they land on me and swipes at her bangs.

"What kind of sex do you consider *good*?"

My eyes stray to the corner where books featuring hot men on the covers line the shelves. "I'm guessing *that* kind."

Penny nibbles on her lip and pulls a book with an adorable pink cover off the shelf. "You'd be surprised. This one is very kinky."

I take the book she hands me and study the illustrated cover. "Go figure. A cartoon character is having better sex than me."

Penny snorts. "Maybe you'll have good sex with the hot cowboy."

I place the book on the counter and glare at her. "There

will be no sex with the cowboy. He's probably bad in bed, anyway. Too selfish and grunts all the time." I mimic two quick pumps of my hips and a grunt.

Penny shoots me a sly grin. "Bad sex is definitely worse than no sex."

"Spoken like someone who knows."

Penny flops down on one of the cozy couches. "I'm sure you didn't come over here to hear about my horrible sex life with douchebag Dick."

I plop down beside her and wrap my arm around her. "Oh, we're going with my nickname for him now? I thought he preferred to be called *Richard*." I say the name the way his mother always did, as if he was famous.

"Yeah, well, douchebag Dick doesn't get to dictate what we call him after ending our engagement, now does he?"

I lean my head against hers. "You okay?" Dick was offered a job in LA and told my sister to sell her little store because his job was real and hers was just a hobby. When my sister refused, he called off the engagement.

"Ha," she says with a loud breath. "He did me a favor. I'm done with men."

"Me, too," I say softly.

"Book boyfriends are better."

"They sure are."

"I'm really glad you're home."

Her soft admission makes me smile. "Me, too."

"But?" she says, staring at me. "Come on, tell me what you really think and how you're dying to get out of here."

My shoulders fall. Despite the rumor mill, I don't hate it here. I just don't fit in like everyone else. Penny and Rosie made a place for themselves in Hope Harbor. They're so ingrained in the fabric of this town they can't see it, but I've always been like the ball of yarn that never got woven in.

I also might have watched too many YouTube knitting videos due to my lack of a sex life.

"There's no hot water, Mom gave our house away to a stranger, and it seems like she'd prefer Walker's sister as a daughter over me." The words rush out, and I groan loudly. "Why am I like this?"

Penny lets out a breathy laugh. "Mom loves you. She just knows you don't want to be here. You need to make it clear that you *want* to be."

"I *do* want to be here," I say aggressively. "But she doesn't seem to need me. She's got someone to help, and honestly—" I take a deep breath because it sounds so judgmental to even say. "Mom seems fine. Like—" I glance around the store, searching for words as if the books will offer them up. "Like she's not devastated that he's gone. Like she's just *moving on*."

Penny gnaws on her lip, and I know my sister agrees with me.

"Wait a second," I hiss.

Penny looks away from me.

"Penelope Iris Darling, look at me." My sister's big round eyes give away all her secrets. "You agree with me. You don't trust Jesse Walker any more than I do. You're just as bothered by the way Mom basically gave away our home to play house with his family!"

Finally, she breaks. "*Fine*. Yes. Okay. I got distracted with my engagement falling apart, and Mom seemed—well, like you said, she seemed fine. It's weird, right? Like everything is the same but it's completely different. And Walker's running the farm, and Mom is basically acting like Dad never existed, and I don't know what to do about it because you're the one who always went toe to toe with her. You and Dad had this special bond, and I was always close with Mom, but I don't know how to talk to her anymore. Tally, she gave away our house!"

I laugh. It's loud and obscene, and the situation is not in the least bit funny. But this is the first time in twenty-four hours that I don't feel like I've entered the twilight zone. Finally, someone is acknowledging that what's going on isn't normal.

Penny grabs my shoulder and shakes me. "You're freaking me out."

I let out an exaggerated sigh. "I'm just relieved you're not on the Walker train."

"Honestly, I don't know what I am. Maybe he really is just trying to help, but it doesn't make sense, right? If I told you ahead of time what I thought, I'd never be sure I wasn't putting my insecurities on you. I wanted your blind reaction, but I'm sorry I didn't warn you."

As much as I hate the way she tricked me, I get why she did it. "You were right to call me. Nothing adds up. How can Mom afford him full-time? Plus, I don't trust him. It feels like he's trying to steal Dad's business. But Mom thinks he's genuine, which means she's not being reasonable. She's avoiding me and pushing me out of the wedding business. How the hell am I going to get to the bottom of all of this if she refuses to talk to me?"

Penny huffs out an exasperated breath as she gets to her feet. "I don't know." She begins moving books around on the shelf and I follow her, studying the titles as she touches them.

"Jake Montgomery. That's a name from the past," I mutter.

My sister shrugs.

"I thought you only had books with happy endings here." I turn over the thriller in my hands. Monty and my sister were best friends in high school, which means he's one of few authors I've followed through the years.

She grabs the book and puts it back where it was, beside the corner counter with the rest of his books. There's a little chalkboard sign that reads LOCAL AUTHORS. Only Monty's books are on display.

"If you're so worried about Walker taking over the business, you should be over there, not here," she says pointedly. I know she's changing the subject, but I allow it since my sister has been through enough these last few months. She doesn't need me poking at old wounds, too.

The bell above the door jangles again, and both Penny and I spin around to see the Liberty Ladies enter the store, led by Rayna.

"See, I told you she was here," she says, her silver coif barely moving as she bobs her head up and down and points in my direction.

Penny snorts but covers her laugh with a book.

"Oh my goodness, you've gotten so big," Ruby Simmons says as she pats me on the head. My eyebrows shoot up in surprise; Ruby's always had an issue with personal space.

Before I can say anything, she steps back as Angelina Rhinehart, the owner of Twisted Tea, steps forward like she's about to do the same thing. I'd rather avoid a hug, so I wrap my arm around my sister. "Hi, ladies. Yes, I'm really here."

The trio is joined by Babs Wilcox and Mindy Robins, who co-own the local hair and nail salon, A Breath of FresHair.

Babs has always been the beauty of the bunch, with her blond hair, voluptuous figure, and flirtatious attitude. Even at sixty-five she turns heads. However, it's often because of the things that come out of her mouth. As she begins to speak, I brace myself. "Well, now you'll have to join us for our Spicy Saturday Book Club meeting! Do you have a Kindle?"

"Can't. The farm has weddings on Saturdays," I say, an exaggerated *oh shucks* expression on my face.

Mindy shakes her head. "Oh, that's no good. Maybe we can move the day we meet?" She's always been the most agreeable of the women. She's also still stuck in the eighties with her brown hair teased high and feathered at the edges.

"Impossible." Rayna barely looks at us as she picks at her red sweater set. "Besides, it's how we keep Penny company on what would be a date night now that she no longer has a fiancé."

My sister is unable to hide her wince. She might say she doesn't care about douchebag Dick, but it's obvious that she's not taking the breakup as well as I thought. I loop my elbow in hers and tug her closer. "Well, now she'll have busy Saturdays as well. The farm is a family affair, after all."

"Hmm, I thought your mother hired Walker's sister to help with the weddings," Rayna says. "She's such a sweet girl, raising that boy all by herself."

I glance at my sister, who shrugs.

"Oh!" When Rayna's hawk eyes dance between Penny and me, I know I'm going to hate what she says next. "If we switch to Monday nights, then your mother can come, too. What do we think, ladies? Monday nights for the season?"

"Works for us," Babs says, her red lips lifting excitedly. "The salon is closed Mondays."

"Great," I say through gritted teeth as the women bid us goodbye and remind Penny to give me the name of this week's book.

"It's *The Alien Baby Daddy*," Penny says, not even trying to hide her amusement.

Though it's at my expense, I'm glad Penny's smiling. "Alien?"

"Don't knock it 'til you try it. Two alien penises might just be better than none."

I chuckle. Well, she's got a point there.

Chapter 7
WALKER

"M orning, Walker." A chorus of voices greets me as I walk through the meadow Wednesday morning.

I've spent two nights with Tally Darling one room over from me, which means I've barely slept and I certainly can't say it's a good morning, but I nod toward the Liberty Ladies, who are out for their early morning walk. They never miss a day to gossip and circle the farm; they're heartier than our winter daffodils, and the cold weather has yet to stop them from showing up.

I check on the bulbs, where our first tulips are set to bloom, hopefully any day now. The first wedding is in three weeks, and the bride expects a refined yet organically colorful display—her words, not mine.

We could use a few more days of rain. Then, if I had my way, a slew of sunny days so these girls could strut their pretty petals and sun themselves until they're the perfect shade of magenta.

Digging my hands into my jean pockets to keep them warm, I march toward the west field where the floating row covers still blanket our late bloomers. I put blankets over the tulip bulbs in early January and won't take them off until mid-April. Not only will it bring up the tulips faster, but protecting them from the frost should hopefully extend their life, too.

I drop to the cool ground and army-crawl under the covering to check on the bulbs' progress. It was one hell of a project filling all these sandbags to weigh down the blankets through winter, but it was worth the work.

This was only one suggestion I made to Peter for how to extend the season. Another has been protecting the meadows from deer. They love eating the early bulbs, but with the new protection, they can't destroy them. It's a tactic used in Holland that I'd read about in a study two years ago. I'm excited to see how it turns out.

I crawl back and kneel in the dirt, looking up as the sun peeks through the clouds. An osprey, native to the area, soars overhead. She was here last spring when I started working with Peter. I close my eyes. It's crazy how only one year ago Peter was teaching me all about his farm, and now he's not here to see the fruits of our labor.

I miss him more than seems reasonable, but in the short time we knew each other, he gave me more attention than my father ever did, and more opportunities, too. He took an interest in me as a person. And fuck do I miss his loud laugh and optimistic attitude. The man saw the best in everyone and was never faced with a problem he couldn't solve.

Earlier this week, I'd spread out all of his papers on the dining table, hoping to make sense of the farm's bank accounts. It's clear we need more money, which means we need to refinance the loan Peter took out against the house. Soil, flowers, chemicals—I can make sense of those. My degree in agriculture prepared me for that. But the bills and loan paperwork aren't so easy.

Unfortunately, the loan has a balloon payment due on June first. If we don't make enough to pay that, all of my hard work this year will be for nothing. We'll have to sell the farm before I ever have a chance to own it.

I never imagined I'd have my own farm. Dreamed of it, sure, but thought of it as an actual possibility? No.

My whole life my father grumbled about how this land should've been ours, but I never thought it would be. The most I hoped for was a warm bed and a soft woman beside me. Maybe a few kids one day.

I blow out a long breath. Dreams change. I might have lost the woman, and it's likely the only kid I'll ever have is my nephew, but God, does the earth beneath my fingers feel good.

My thoughts are interrupted as Tally Darling rounds the path that the Liberty Ladies just passed by on. In a pair of yellow leggings that mold to her curves and a matching yellow sports bra, I bet I could see the swell of her breasts if I was closer. Maybe even the peaks of her nipples, too, and the drips of sweat meandering their way down between those beautiful tits. What is she thinking wearing something like that in this weather?

Or better question—what is she thinking wearing something like that in front of me?

I watch as she folds her lithe frame and stretches out her legs. Fortunately, I can't see her ass right now because if I did, I'd probably be hard.

Fuck, this woman needs to go.

I don't have time to be staring at her. Don't have time to be fighting with her, either.

My focus needs to be on these flower beds, this soil, and how to make this farm successful so my sister and her son have a place to stay.

That's how Peter enticed me into considering his proposition. He saw my love for my family and knew I'd do anything for them.

Thinking of those early days, and the way Peter walked me around this farm with such pride as he told me all about his family, his girls—*Tally*—has me swallowing thickly.

"She's my wildflower," he had told me. "Vibrant, with big dreams and a big personality. Easy to love but impossible to keep."

When I moved into the cottage, he warned me that she might visit now and again. He also warned me to stay away from her. Well, both of them, although Penny had been engaged at the time. I promised him it wouldn't be an issue. What interest would I have in his young daughter?

Problem is, I'd never seen Tally. I had no idea she'd have the ability to tie me up in this damn knot with only a few words. That she was too gorgeous to look away from.

I roll back my shoulders and stand, walking in the opposite direction of the wicked woman who won't leave my thoughts. I don't watch as she continues to stretch.

And I absolutely don't hum the very same melody of Alex Warren's "Burning Down" as I march toward the south fields to check on the daffodils.

I made a promise to Peter Darling. And it's one I intend to keep.

Chapter 8
TALLY

The ground crackles beneath my feet as I walk across the meadow in search of Walker. We avoided one another yesterday after our run-in during breakfast, but I can't avoid him forever. After a decent night's sleep and a warm shower, thanks to Walker's absence when I returned from my run this morning, I feel renewed. I even liberally applied the white cypress moisturizer I've been saving since I splurged on it in Nantucket last year. The sweet smell has me feeling brighter; determined and refreshed.

This is my town. My farm. My house. And I've got a job to do.

I will figure out what's going on, but the only way I can do that is to talk to Walker since my mother won't answer any of my questions.

Now I just have to find the guy. Though the white farm-house has always been a focal part of the sprawling ten acres of land, there's a lot of ground to cover as I search for Walker. I start in the barn near where the weddings are normally held. It's also where we host the Daffodil Festival, and since that's just a few weeks away, there's a decent possibility Walker is over there.

At the entrance to the farm, there's a long dirt road that cuts two ways. If you go right, you end up at the main house. Take a left, and the path winds through the farm, toward the barn and the meadows where people pick tulips after the last of our weddings.

Basically, anything my father could think of to create another source of income, he leveraged. This time of year was critical to get us through the summer season, when our farm was already picked over, until we reached fall, when we had revenue from the pumpkin patch and maze. Though if memory serves, the pumpkin patch had gotten smaller since my sister and I graduated from high school. Maintaining the farm is a hell of a lot of work. And since my father did most of it on his own, or with seasonal help from high school kids, things had fallen to the wayside as he'd gotten older.

Another burst of guilt hits me as I pass the old cottages next to the wildflower fields. My father had a dream to fix all these up. As children, Penny and I used to sneak into them and pretend they were our own houses. When I got older, I snuck boys in there, and I'm pretty sure Penny used them to hide away with her books.

I take a few tentative steps onto the wooden porch of the first one and wince as I hear the wood strain under my weight.

"What the hell're you doing?"

Walker's bark takes me by surprise and I nearly stumble sideways but catch myself on the door to the cottage. Grasping my chest, I turn around and glare at the man I'd been looking for. "What the hell am *I* doing? What about you? Do you routinely go around scaring the hell out of people?"

Walkerwears a baseball cap so it's hard to see his eyes, but it's clear he's glaring at me. And by the way his chest is rising and falling, it's clear he isn't thrilled to see me.. His chin is covered in far more scruff than when I first got here, making him appear meaner, maybe even dangerous. And his jeans are dirty, like he's been rolling around in the fields, although his shirt is still clean. The deep green henley compliments his olive complexion, and a shiver runs through my body at the sight of him.

Perhaps I hit my head when I tripped, because I'm blinking like an idiot, fawning over a man I don't even I like.

"The cottages aren't safe. Why the hell are you snooping around over here, anyway?"

Oh, this ass. "Snooping? First of all, I was looking for you. Second, I can snoop wherever the hell I want because this is *my* property."

He grunts and kicks his Timberland-booted foot into the dirt.

"Well, you found me. What do you want?"

I straighten my back because I will not be railroaded by his attitude. "I'm here to help, and it's clear there's a lot of work to be done, so"—I hold up my hands, affecting the most sarcastic offering—"what can I do?"

Walker's head bows down, and he grips his waist, , like he's trying to summon some patience. I guess the disdain is mutual. "What you can do is go back to the house and spend time with your mom. Or go into town and hang out with your sister. I've got the farm covered."

"There's ten acres, Walker. The festival is in mere weeks, and the farm is a complete mess." I swipe my hand against the glass windowpane on the door, creating a circle in the dirt. I hold out my palm, showing him the years-old grime.

Walker shakes his head but turns and starts walking away.

"I was trying to be nice," he calls over his shoulder. "But

if you want to clean all the windows on the cottages, be my guest. Feel free to tackle the chairs in the barn when you're done. They'll need to be spruced up for the weddings!" He's hollering now because he has put a good distance between us.

I chase after him. "What about the flowers, Walker? The two hundred and fifty thousand tulip bulbs. The hundred thousand daffodils. Who's taking care of *those*?"

Finally, the man spins around and stalks back toward me. With each step he eats up three times what mine could cover, which means he's standing right in front of me in barely a breath's time. He grabs his hat and flips it backward so I'm victim to those eyes again. They're as angry as a thundercloud, yet I can't look away. The thrill of the potential electric bolt that charges through the air whenever he holds my gaze has me stuck stupidly in place.

"Do not *touch* the flowers, Tally." His voice is a low growl, a warning. I don't like the way it heats my cheeks.

Annoyed, I step forward so we're practically chest to chest. We both breathe heavily, and I grit my teeth.

"Why won't you let me help?"

His nostrils flare as he shakes his head. "Why can't you just do what I ask?"

I poke his chest, ignoring the way my finger barely budges as it's met by a wall of hard muscle. "Why are you so bossy?"

He stares down at my finger like he wants to remove it but refuses to touch me. Without looking up, he growls out, "Because I'm the boss."

I push off him with a loud sigh and stomp away. Fine, I'll do his stupid chores. I'll do them so well he will be amazed. And then maybe he'll lower his defenses and slip up to reveal what exactly is happening here.

—

Hours later, I'm convinced today was a bust. Walker disappeared sometime around lunch, and I haven't seen him since. I'm tired, my arms hurt from rubbing the windows so hard they sparkle, and I'm starving.

I go to text Penny and Rosie to ask what they're doing tonight when I see the town group chat blowing up.

HOPE HARBOR TOWN CHAT

BABS: What time is skinny dipping?

RAYNA: I'm not coming.

BABS: I didn't ask if you were going. I asked what time it was.

STEW: Mayor Fletcher! I don't think this should be in the town chat.

RAYNA: Well, it is an event that takes place in town so I would disagree.

BABS: Oh, go fly a kite Stew. The mayor doesn't monitor this chat. We can talk about what we want.

I'm glad I forced Penny to go through my phone to update the contacts of everyone in the town group chat, because now at least I know who's making these absurd comments, but I still have no idea what they're talking about. I open up a text thread with the girls to find out.

ME: What the heck are they talking about?

PENNY: don't ask.

ROSIE: Some of the elders in town like to get freaky when they play pool so they call it skinny dipping.

ME: Oh god, why did I ask?

PENNY: told you.

PENNY: How was today? Did you learn anything?

ROSIE: Oh, what's she learning? What's happening? Can I bug someone's phone?

ME: excuse me, what?

PENNY: Rosie's just being dramatic.

ME: Oh, well nothing happened really. My arms hurt. Walker is nowhere to be found, but the cottage windows are cleaner than ever.

PENNY: I don't think that's going to lead to answers about what's going on with Mom or the farm.

ROSIE: Your mother is currently sitting at my bar having dinner with the Liberty Ladies. Then they're probably going to play pool at Wicked Wine and Cheese.

ME: What?

PENNY: I told you she's been weird.

ME: Yeah, for real. Okay, well, I need food.

PENNY: Want me to pick something up when I close the shop? Or you could come here?

ME: I'm too tired to move. I'm just sitting on the porch of one of the cottages out in the fields. Do you think there's some peanut butter leftover from when we were kids?

PENNY: Maybe a snickers bar.

ROSIE: ew. Just come here. I'll feed you.

ME: can't move.

ROSIE: I forgot how dramatic you are.

ME: It's fine, I'll scrounge something up from the kitchen. I want to get a shower in before Walker returns so I can get to bed early. Maybe if I wake up before he does tomorrow I can get some real snooping done.

ROSIE: Oh yes, check the fireplace.

ME: the fireplace?

PENNY: Pretty sure that thing hasn't worked in at least a decade.

ROSIE: Exactly. It's a great hiding spot.

I stare at that last sentence and wonder how I got here. How is my dad gone, my mom acting diabolically different, and a man we don't know controlling our family business?

PENNY: they don't really get naked while they play pool. They just think it sounds more scandalous. Mom's acting weird but not that weird.

I slowly blink at the phone and then decide I'm not going to touch that. I don't want to think about my mom and the word *naked* in the same sentence. It's bad enough that I've already had visions of her with Walker.

ME: I'll talk to you guys tomorrow.

I shove my phone in my pocket and push up to stand, letting out the loudest of sighs, and then head down the path leading back to the house. The sun is setting over the meadow, and I'm reminded just how vast this land is. At the bottom of the wildflower-covered hills, the bay sparkles as though it's covered in a pink sequined blanket. Across the harbor, downtown Hope Harbor sits proudly.

Of all the places I've traveled, none has held a candle to Hope Harbor. As much as I fought coming back, and as much of a pain in the ass as Jesse Walker is, it sure is nice to be home.

Chapter 9
WALKER

Question."

I grip the kitchen counter to find some damn strength before turning around to deal with the current bane of my existence. Even her voice has me on edge. Soft and melodic, with a hint of sass. How she's able to do all of those things with only one word must be some fucking talent.

I know the moment I turn around I'll likely find her in one of her damn bright, colorful outfits. It's all she seems to wear. Spandex that clings to her curves.

She's too young. She's Peter Darling's daughter. And most pertinent, she drives me fucking insane.

With my head on straight, I finally turn around to answer Tally's question.

All the goddamn mantras in the world couldn't prepare me for the sight before me.

"What are you wearing?" I ball my fists, trying not to reach for her. Trying not to touch the soft fabric of *my* T-shirt that barely covers her thighs or the expanse of her bare legs, which glisten below it. They're probably so goddamn smooth. The spandex was bad; this is torture.

Tally blinks those golden eyes of hers like she's unaware of the problem and pushes back the damp chestnut waves surrounding her face. "Oh, this?" She tugs on the shirt. "I forgot clothes when I went to shower, and when I heard the front door shut, I grabbed the first thing I saw rather than running down here naked. I didn't want to miss you."

So many words and yet none of them mean a goddamn thing because my brain isn't working right now.

Digging my fists into my eyes, I try to blur her out. But she's fucking perfect, and I'll never forget the image of her standing in this kitchen, looking the way she does right now.

"So can I ask my question now?"

I still don't know what the fuck she's talking about so I just nod. It's better this way. The less I say, the quicker this conversation will be over.

"I was out in the tulip fields yesterday and noticed there are tarps over like dozens of the flower beds."

Tongue in my cheek, I nod.

Tally takes a deep breath like she's summoning some damn courage, which amazes me because the woman seems to have boundless amounts of it. "We've never had covers on the tulips. I know my mother trusts you for some reason—"

I don't hear the rest of her words as anger starts to flood through me. My whole damn life I've had to prove myself. Prove to my mother I was worth sticking around for, even though she still walked out on us. Prove to my father that I would amount to something. It was fruitless, he was too wrapped up in drinking himself to death to even care, but still, I tried to raise my sister and bring in money to help with the bills. And then when I met my ex, Gina, I thought I'd finally found someone who believed I was worth something. But the moment Billie got pregnant and I asked Gina to wait a little longer to start our own life together, she decided I wasn't worth it.

Now I don't make the effort for anyone but Billie and

Quinn. Still, it stings to hear Tally questioning me. I've been running this farm for the better part of a year with her father, and doing it on my own almost six months. Where has she been? And what right does she have to question my choices?

I steel my back and hold up a hand. "Both of your parents knew my plans for the farm. The tarps are there for a reason."

"But why?" she presses on.

"Because I said so, and I'm the boss. Remember?"

Flames dance in Tally's eyes as she narrows her gaze. She steps forward, and suddenly that sweet goddamn scent of hers infiltrates my space. I don't know what it is, but it drives me fucking insane.

"I'm here, so I might as well be useful." She takes another step toward me until she's close enough to touch. Close enough that if I reached out, I'd be able to skim my knuckles against her bare thigh. "*Use me.*" The words are a whispered rasp that turns me on and wakes me the fuck up at the same time.

Heels digging into the floor, I push back from her and fold my arms across my chest so there's no chance I'll accidentally run my hands against her flesh. "You want to be useful? Handle inventory."

Her lips tip up like she's won some fucking prize, and I almost smile because she's going to hate this.

Or maybe it's her proximity. Or her in my shirt. Or those goddamn bare legs.

Fuck. Me.

I force my gaze to the incredible view of the fields out the window, toward the rolling green hills that are beginning to sprout pinks and yellows, and to the sparkling ocean beyond.

"I need an inventory of the daffodils. Count every one in the west field, and let me know how many we have."

"I'm sorry, what?"

I finally glance back at her, and this time I don't hide my smirk.

"What, is that too hard for you? I thought you wanted to be useful."

With a lift of her chin, she quells her anger and shrugs. "Fine. If that's what you want."

"That's all I want," I grit out, reminding us both that I don't have time for these games. Don't have time for these thoughts, either. Though, unfortunately, I can control only one of those things.

Chapter 10
TALLY

It's day five, and I've learned absolutely nothing since moving in with the grumpiest man alive. I've rarely seen Walker, which is fortunate for him, because I think I'd kill him if I did.

I spent the last two days counting flowers. Each freaking daffodil. Well, maybe not each individual one. After counting three flower beds and finding they all had almost the same number of stems—give or take ten—I decided to count the flower beds instead. Much quicker work than counting one hundred thousand bulbs separately. Though it still took me two days to verify.

The only thing that kept me half sane was trying out that cherries jubilee recipe. As predicted, with the ice cream that Eli dropped off, it was utter perfection. Of course, once I got on a baking kick, one thing led to another and I ended up making pineapple upside-down cake, cherry cheesecake brownies, and cherry winks, a cookie made with cornflakes that is surprisingly delicious because of the maraschino cherry baked inside it.

Walker was undeserving of my treats so I took them over to the brewery and the bookstore to share. I hope his stomach was growling, though, when he smelled all the sugary perfection that he never got to taste.

Clearly, the ridiculous chores he's given me are his way of

trying to keep me out of his hair, which I don't mind, because who would want to spend time with someone so completely miserable? So what if he's stupidly good-looking? Or if there's something in the way he looks at me that makes my pulse thrum. Makes me seek out his attention even though I tell myself I don't want it.

Shit, I've got some issues to work out. But today is not the day. No, today I'm sneaking around "his" bedroom—can it be considered breaking and entering if it's your own room?—in hopes of finding something that will tell me why he's so invested in the farm.

I heard him get out of bed at 5:30 a.m. On a Saturday. The minute I heard the front door shut behind him, I ran into his room and have spent the last few hours scouring every inch of it—under the bed, in the closets, in his bedside drawer. That was risky. I was almost positive he isn't the kind of man with toys, but you never know.

Of course, boring grumpy Walker just had a picture of his nephew on the end table and a lighter, some spare change, and ChapStick in the drawer.

Defeated, I stomp downstairs and step out onto the porch, my eyes searching for the man in question.

It's infuriating that I've learned basically nothing since I got here. From what I can see—outside of him laying blankets over the flowers despite their requirement for sunlight to freaking bloom—he knows what he's doing. He's hard at work every day, and my mother seems happy and settled, too. She spends her mornings walking with the Liberty Ladies, then she checks in with me and we share a cup of coffee before I start my chores.

Maybe she's just handling grief differently than I imagined she would, and this is her way of moving forward. The farm is too much to handle on her own, and considering all the work I've done this week, it's clear she needs Walker. I just wish I knew what Walker was getting out of it. Although, I guess he has a place to stay and she must be paying him a wage. With what money, I have no idea. We won't turn a profit for a few more weeks based on past years. And my parents were never great at saving.

I stretch my legs on the porch and finally catch sight of him coming out of one of the cottages near where my mom is staying by the wildflower fields. I haven't cleaned any of those properties yet. What is he doing over there?

A fog has settled over the farm this morning, like a cozy blanket hanging heavy in the air. Walker seems almost mystical as he emerges from the mist. He's wearing his trademark Wranglers, work boots, and a long-sleeve Henley. He hasn't noticed me yet, and I take this opportunity to study him: the scruff that covers his hard jaw, how the lines of his face deepen as he looks into the distance, and the way his lips part and his eyes flare the moment he catches me spying on him.

His steps don't falter because the man is good at going toe to toe with me, so I straighten my hips and prepare for battle. "You checking my numbers?"

Walker grunts as he climbs the stairs to the big house until he's standing right in front of me.

I push on despite his silence. "Have any other pointless tasks you want me to do today?"

Walker lifts his ball cap from his head and flips it backward, then arches a single brow. "Pointless?"

"Yes, Walker. Having me count each individual daffodil is pointless."

"Did you know that daffodils multiply each year and can crowd each other?"

I blink at him. "Um, no."

"If we have too many," he continues, taking a step toward me, "they'll stop blooming and our crop will be destroyed next year. So, Tally, it's not pointless. It's important that the numbers in each flower bed don't tip too high in one direction. And if they do, I can adjust by digging and dividing them more evenly."

Well, fuck me. I nibble my bottom lip, worried now because I didn't actually count them, and consider the mammoth task of starting all over again.

"Anything else you want me to explain to you?" he grits out.

I shake my head.

"Then do you mind moving so I can go inside?"

Shit. Do I tell him the truth? It's probably fine. None of the flower beds look overcrowded, and I can check myself. "Sure. Um, is there anything else I can do? You know, like maybe help take off those tarps."

"Leave the tarps alone." The grizzly warning instantly has my hackles up again. Why is he so damn insistent on keeping the bulbs covered? I might have been wrong about the daffodils, but I know tulips need sunshine. I listen to the sounds of Walker's boots hitting the wooden planks until he stops and turns to me again. "If you want to help with the flowers so much, why don't you mist them?"

"Don't we have an irrigation system for that?"

Walker's brows lift again and I realize he's probably going to mansplain. "Flowers like *little* drops of water."

I sigh as I study Walker's position. With his arms crossed

and the cocksure expression on his face, it's as though he's king of this farm and I'm his lowly servant. "And how does one *mist* a flower?"

"With a mister." He holds up his hand and squeezes his fingers to his palm, as though he's explaining science to a six-year-old.

"That seems ridiculous," I mutter.

"Well, they aren't standing as tall as I'd like, so it would be great if you could mist them. Unless you're ready to quit?" He grins.

I realize this is the first time I've seen him smile. Even though it's a cruel one, my stomach flips as I discover that Walker has a dimple. And now I am unreasonably turned on. Great.

I raise my brow and cross my arms, trying to remain calm and professional.

"No. Of course not. Are you going to tell me why you haven't taken the blankets off the flowers?" I can't stop pushing. Or maybe I don't want to stop pushing. I shouldn't want to spend another second in his dark cloud, but I seem to be chasing the lightning. Chasing the electric current that thrums just below the surface of my skin whenever he's around.

"No," he growls. And without another word, Walker storms into the house, taking all that energy with him.

—

I'd like to say it was hard to find a mister in the tool shed, because why in the fuck would anyone actually mist plants?, but there are several of them.

God, I wish I could talk to my father right now. To have

five minutes to ask him all the questions circling in my head. *Why did you hire Walker? Why did you like him? What the hell am I supposed to do now that I'm here and you're not?*

The wind howls around me as I stomp down the path toward the fields. The frustration inside me swirls and builds until I feel like I'm out of control. Dropping the misters, I fist my hands and look to the sky. "Why, Daddy? Why did you have to leave? Why?"

"*Breathe, Tally.*" I can hear the words he'd utter so often when I'd spin out like this. "*Just breathe. Take a minute, sit down, and breathe.*"

"I don't know how to do it, Daddy," I whisper back as I suck in a lungful of air and try to pull at his memory to ground myself. My heart settles more with each breath I take.

I close my eyes. "I'll probably need to do more than breathe if you want me to survive the next few months with this man." I smile at my own joke, knowing my dad would be smiling, too. He didn't expect people to be perfect and somehow found the good in everyone. God, I wish I was more like him.

Feeling calmer, I take the path to the fields near my mother's cottage.

Her new home—which is the only property on this part of the farm that isn't tattered and run down—is dark at the end of the long lane. I take in the sad state of affairs of her porch. At our house, my mother always had flowers adorning the steps leading up to the porch.

Daddy would pick them for her daily—and in seasons when we didn't have beautiful flowers blooming, he'd use other decorations to make her day brighter: a random garden gnome with a silly face, pinwheel flags that spun with the warm breeze, or whatever he could find in town.

That's what my dad did: He looked for ways to make life brighter. Not just for Mom, but for everyone.

I smile as I think of him and rush toward the wildflower meadow. I won't dare touch Walker's other flowers, but these should be safe. No one else ever seemed to notice the beauty in this field, but I have always loved it. The fresh aroma of earth and damp soil clings to the dewy air as I enter the field, which overlooks the marina. The fog hangs heavily above the water, and the sound of the boats rocking gently back and forth is a soothing balm after such an infuriating morning. Humming, I pluck the prettiest flowers I can find. Pinks, purples, and my favorite golden ones. The grass is a vibrant green because it's left mostly untouched and it almost appears to be preening beside the wildflowers, as if searching for the sun.

The raindrops start slow. It's really nothing more than a mist to begin with, and I start to laugh before throwing my head back and hollering, "Thank you for helping with the chores, Daddy!"

My smile grows bigger as I let the raindrops gently wet my face. It's like a baptism. A rebirth. In this field, under the New England sky, I promise my father I'm going to do better. I'm going to make this daffodil season the best one yet, and help Mom get through this. I'm going to put our family back together.

Finally, I allow myself to let go of the guilt I feel for not returning sooner. All the *what if*s and *maybe I should have*s. From here on out, I'm going to live like my dad did. While I'm on this farm for the next nine weeks, I'm going to find ways to make everyone's life brighter. Ease their burden. Help.

Without judgment and sarcasm.

I snort. That's probably too big of a goal.

Renewed, I grab two metal planters from the shed and arrange wildflower bouquets in both before setting them on my mother's porch. It might only be step one, but it's a step in the right direction.

Chapter 11
TALLY

The rain is quick, but because my chores are now done for the day—*Thank you, Dad*—I'm in a better mood than I've been in since I arrived back in Hope Harbor. It only seems to get brighter when Walker stalks past me, heading to his car and grumbling something about having to go out and that he won't be back 'til late tonight.

I decide now is the perfect time to do some more snooping. While there may not be anything in Walker's room, there's got to be something around here that will tell me what's going on with the farm.

Which is how, twenty minutes later, Penny and I end up army-crawling through the house.

"Are you sure Walker isn't going to be back anytime soon?" my sister hisses at me.

"No, he said he'll be gone for the day."

Penny stops her forward crawl and goes to turn around, shoving her foot into my face as she spins.

"Ow!" I yelp.

Penny sighs in aggravation. "Why were you so close to me?"

"Can you not yell at me? I think you got dirt in my eye."

"I don't have dirty feet."

"You do, too!" I rub at my eye, sure I've got something stuck in it, as Penny harrumphs again.

"I'll go grab a washcloth." She goes to stand up, and

knowing our mother could be just outside the door and then our cover will be blown, I grab her arm and pull her to the ground.

"What are you doing?" she squeals.

"We're undercover, remember?" I dip my head against my shoulder, rubbing my eye until I feel like I can see again. I blink a few times and then point at the fireplace. "You check in there. I'll keep a look out for Walker and Mom."

Penny huffs before dropping down again and scooching her body across the rustic hardwoods. "Lotta good that'll do us when you can't see. I think this is dumb, anyway. Do you really think the man would leave a trail of his nefarious plans if he actually is up to something?"

I throw my hands up in the air. "I don't know! But he's so cagey. He refuses to let me do anything to help with the Daffodil Festival or do any real work around the farm. It's almost like he's trying to put us out of business. He has freaking blankets covering the tulips, Penny. You know as well as I do that Daddy never did that. And all I have managed to find online is that tulip bulbs are hardy and that covering them can actually destroy a crop. It doesn't make sense."

I'm still facing the door, watching for any movement in the fields, when I hear Penny's loud inhale of breath.

I spin around to see her holding up a piece of paper, her eyes moving quickly as she reads.

"Unless, of course, you were right and he is trying to tank the business!" Penny says loudly.

I give up on crawling and lunge toward her, reaching for the letter. "What does it say?"

"Well, it's addressed to a Mr. Jesse Walker." Her eyes cut to mine and she shakes her head. "It's an offer to buy the farm. Basically details how this—" She pauses to annunciate the name. "—*Frank Seymour* looks forward to hearing if Jesse has discussed this with our mother and that he thinks the offer is fair based on the poor profit margins this year." Penny's mouth drops open. "Do you think that was his plan all along? What if he's been working with this Frank guy to get Mom to believe he could turn around the farm only to destroy everything at the last minute and make her sell it to him?"

Something about that feels . . . *far-fetched*. "Kind of sounds like a book, Pen. What would be in it for Walker?"

Penny nibbles on her lips. "Think about it, Tally. If the farm is losing money, Mom would have to sell it, which means Walker could buy the land for so much cheaper. And she trusts him, right?"

I nod. As much as I hate to agree, Penny's not wrong. My mom seems to believe everything Walker says when it comes to the farm.

"And it was addressed to Walker, not Mom."

That part is hard to argue. And the damn blankets on the flowers. He refuses to tell me why they're there. It's concerning. Very concerning.

"I say we take this to Rosie. Get an outsider's perspective." Penny blows her breath up and her bangs fan out, clearing her vision. She holds out a hand to help me stand.

I take it and then dust myself off. "Okay, let's go."

—

An hour later, I'm seated at Rosie's bar, waiting with bated breath for her thoughts on the letter.

"Hmm." Rosie taps her long pink nails against the wooden countertop. There's a little rose design on her ring finger nail.

I feel like I might jump out of this chair and scream. Notonly has the letter got me all antsy, but the lack of work this week is driving me batty. Going from slaving away in tourist-filled hotels, where the kitchen staff is always overworked and never had free time, to this nothingness leaves me itching to move my body. To use my mind. To do *something*.

"Want me to cover the bar while you read that?" I offer, ready to bounce off my chair if she says yes.

Rosie raises a single brow and then dashes my excitement with a shake of her head. "Stay."

"Come on. You are killing me here. Do you think Penny's right? Is Walker up to no good?"

My sister had to go back to her bookstore because she has an actual job, which left me with the task of getting to the bottom of the letter.

Rosie drops the paper and rests her elbows on the bar, leaning in close. "It does seem a bit suspect."

My stomach sinks. Rosie and Penny are always the more reasonable ones. Sure, Rosie is over the top sometimes, and she got me into plenty of trouble growing up, but she doesn't jump to conclusions. I'm an "act first, ask questions later" type of girl. Rosie is fearless, but she always assesses the risk first and somehow manages to make the right choice. The brewery is the perfect example. She saw something she wanted and didn't let anything stop her from opening it, despite the town's initial objections.

Penny, on the other hand, has always had her head in the clouds. A dreamer for which life seems effortless. Though I suppose I'm seeing cracks in both my best friend's and my sister's facades. Penny doesn't have her life nearly as put together as she had me believe while I was away. She's hurt and jaded. More than I expected her to be. Penny believes in happy ever afters. Hell, up until Dick the douche, it was basically her entire personality. I like that she's suspicious of Walker because it makes me feel less crazy. But I'm not sure I like that she's lost that innocent belief that everything will always be okay in the end. Somehow having my big sister believe that so strongly made it all seem possible. Made it feel like one day I could also have that.

The bell above the door announces a new customer. My lips curl the minute I see it's Fletcher Matthews walking in with his dog. "Eleven o'clock on the dot," I tease Rosie, trying to make her smile.

She grabs a cloth and starts vigorously scrubbing the bar.

"I still don't get why you hate him so much. Did you know he's a widower?" I ask out of the side of my mouth as I watch him greet Rosie's customers with an easy smile and friendly conversation. This week, when I had nothing to do, I spent the afternoon with my mother and some of the other Liberty Ladies. They told me that his wife had died suddenly and that Fletcher has been raising his son alone since the boy was only six months old. It's a tragic story. Yet the guy is always smiling. How does one smile through all that heartache?

Rosie lets out a heavy sigh. "Yup."

"Rosie," I chide, sounding an awful lot like my mother.

She rolls her eyes. "Maybe he killed her." She shrugs her shoulders and throws her hands up in the air. "Maybe he was so bad in bed she decided death was the better option."

"Oh my God!" I clamp my hand over her mouth right as Fletcher pulls up a stool next to me.

"Hi, Tally. How's everything on the farm?"

I don't reply for a second, paralyzed with the fear that he just overheard our conversation.

"Muts should sit outside," Rosie grumbles even as she grabs a treat from behind the bar and comes around and kneels in front of the dog so he can eat it straight from her palm. "I'm talking about you," she says, glaring up at Fletcher.

The man flashes her one of his mega-watt smiles. One day I will get the story behind these two.

"Farm is good. Boring. But good," I mumble.

"Everything ready for the Daffodil Festival?"

I shake my head. "I really don't think it is."

Rosie's head pops up from her position on the floor, and I can feel her glare. She doesn't want me involving Fletcher in the farm's business. But he's our mayor, and the farm is an integral part of the community. If someone is threatening our community, he should know about it.

"All the tulips, which would normally be blooming by now, are still covered in tarps. I'm not sure why Walker hasn't taken them off." I shrug my shoulders innocently. "My father never put tarps on his plants."

Fletcher frowns. Like everyone else, he probably thinks Walker knows exactly what he's doing, so I change tactic. "Or maybe Walker didn't want to ask for help. The Daffodil Festival is only a few week away, and there is just so much work still to do. It is his first season doing it all himself." I let those words hang there. Wait for Fletcher to take the bait.

"You think he's too proud to ask for support?" Fletcher

asks. This time, I don't get the feeling he finds the idea preposterous.

"Yes, I do. Maybe I'll just do the work myself," I say brightly. "Surprise him."

"You're going to uncover all the flowers?" Rosie asks suspiciously as she pushes to a stand and leans against the counter.

"Yeah, sure. Why not?"

Rosie's bun flops around on her head as she laughs at me. "Because it's a ton of work."

"I could help," Fletcher offers, walking straight into my plan.

She lets out a derisive sigh. "Of course you can. Don't you have a town to run? A child to raise? *Somewhere else* to be?"

"You'd really help?" I ask hopefully.

"Of course. Hope Harbor is nothing if not helpful," he says proudly. "I bet I can have a group of us over there this afternoon, and we'll have it done by dinner."

"Really?" I ask, hope blossoming inside me. This is how my dad got stuff done. Everyone in town always lent him a hand because he was the guy who helped everyone else. He actually engaged in conversation with his neighbors, unlike my roommate. I can't wait to see my mother's and Walker's faces when they see the farm blooming just like it used to.

And it will be a good test. If Walker's upset that everything is finally ready for the festival, it will only confirm Penny's and my suspicion. Either way it's a win because the farm needs to be ready, and this is step one.

"Really," he says. "I'll call Eli."

Fletcher pulls a phone out of his pocket but just before he

walks away, he flashes Rosie a smirk that could kill a woman. "And, by the way, I'm definitely not bad in bed."

With that, he hits Eli's number and walks toward the porch, leaving my jaw on the floor and Rosie throwing daggers his way.

Chapter 12
WALKER

For the first time in a long damn time, I feel relaxed and content. Hell, I'm even smiling.

I'd like to say it has nothing to do with Tally, but of course it does.

I've successfully avoided the woman for two whole days. And *that* is something to smile about.

We only have two weeks until the start of the Daffodil Festival now. And the following weekend, we have our first wedding of the season. The magenta flowers in the east field were standing tall this morning, ready to dazzle the happy couple and their guests. The tulips in the west field are still warm and covered beneath the tarps, ready to bloom when I release them—which won't be for another three weeks so they're still pretty for the late-May weddings and maybe even the early June ones.

The daffodils need a bit more time, but by next week, they, too, will be showing off, right in time for the festival.

All in all, things are good. Right. Exactly as they should be.

I pull the ball cap off my head, spinning it so I can see Quinn as he takes the plate and prepares for the first pitch.

It's Little League, but this is the first year the kids are pitching rather than the coaches, so the ball has been a bit wild. My sister grips my arm as the ball releases from the pitcher's hand. Quinn shakes his little butt like he's a professional, and when the ball gets close, he swings wide, missing it completely.

"That's okay, Quinn. Eye on the ball," I shout. "You'll get the next one!"

Beside me Billie cheers, "You've got this, Quinny!"

My nephew's head swings back, and he glares at his mom.

"Don't call him 'Quinny,'" I mutter.

"He's seven, not seventeen," she retorts. "I'll call him whatever I want."

I shake my head and clap my hands. "You got this, Quinn!" I holler, annunciating his name clearly.

Billie rolls her eyes and ignores me, cheering louder, though I notice she doesn't use the baby name again. The next pitch is wide, but Quinn doesn't swing.

"Wayne didn't want to come?" I ask, keeping my voice low enough that only my sister can hear me. We're standing by the batting cage, away from the other parents, who are mostly seated in lawn chairs or on the metal stands, chatting away.

My sister is younger than most of the other mothers because she had Quinn when she was only nineteen—something I didn't love at the time—so she's never really fit in with this crowd.

My mind wanders as I try hard not to imagine how well she and Tally would get along. They're about the same age and both enjoy rolling their eyes at me, and in general, my sister smiles a hell of a lot more than I do—so yeah, I have a feeling that they would be friends if given the chance.

Not that they will, because I'm trying my damn hardest to ignore that Tally exists. Plus, she'll be gone in a few weeks, anyway.

Nine weeks to be exact. But who's counting?

Billie doesn't even glance at me as she replies, "Nope. I let him know about it, but I'm sure he had work or something."

"Or something," I grumble, my jaw clicking.

Quinn's father has been very hands off. Eyes off, too. Billie and Wayne were never really together. As much as I don't want to think about her like that, I know my sister didn't have to be in a relationship to make a baby. Still, I wish Quinn's father didn't suck so much.

Then again, he doesn't really give Billie much trouble, either. She has full custody of Quinn, which is all she wants, and Wayne drops in every now and then as if he's a family friend. But Quinn deserves more from his dad. Which means I show up for him as much as I can.

The pitcher releases the ball again, and this time when Quinn wiggles his butt and swings, the bat connects, sending the ball flying . . . five feet in front of him.

"Run!" I yell, right along with his coaches.

Billie covers her eyes. She hates watching him get thrown out. "Tell me what's happening?"

I give her the play-by-play. "He dropped the bat and he's moving. The catcher has the ball. He's throwing it, and *he overthrew the base*!" My voice grows excited. "Keep going, Quinn!" I nudge my sister's arm. "Open your eyes, he's rounding second. The ball is in the outfield, and the other kid just tripped trying to get it." It's like a circus act out on the field. One kid throws it to the next and he misses it, and Quinn rounds third base. "He's coming home!"

My sister finally opens her eyes and grabs my arm, jumping up and down as she screams for her boy. When Quinn lands on home plate, our entire side of the diamond erupts and he turns to flash us the biggest smile. It hits me right in the heart. How his father could miss out on this I'll never understand. But damn, am I happy I didn't.

———

"And did you see when I hit the home run?" Quinn asks again from the back seat. *Home run* is a bit of an exaggeration, considering the ball barely passed in front of the plate, but he's so happy about this win, I'll give it to him this time.

"Yeah, buddy, it was great."

"And did you see how fast I ran? That kid couldn't even keep up with me." The catcher is who he's referring to, and he's right: The poor kid tripped over his own two feet, missing the out completely.

"You are the fastest, Quinny boy," my sister says.

I eye her and then glance at my nephew in the rearview mirror as he whines, "*Mom*, you're so annoying."

"*Quinn*." My voice is hard. Even though I agree with him, I'll never let him talk to his mother that way.

"Sorry, Uncle Jesse."

"It's not me you need to say sorry to."

Billie gives me a small appreciative smile before turning to her son in anticipation.

"Sorry, Mom."

"It's okay. I love you."

"Love you, too," he grumbles before looking out the window toward the cherry and maple trees that line the road leading into downtown Hope Harbor.

My sister settles back in her seat. She looks more relaxed than I have seen her in a while. I'm taking them both out to dinner in Hope Harbor and then to The Ice Cream Barn for dessert. I'm slowly trying to get her to spend more time in this town every week. She might not want to admit that she needs help and that she can't continue working herself to death at the hotel day in and day out, but hopefully after seeing what she *could* have—peace and tranquility and a real home for Quinn—Hope Harbor will grow on her.

Billie and I grew up a few towns over, so we heard about Hope Harbor, and Darling Daffodils Farm, pretty regularly. Our father's favorite topic was how the Darling's land should have been ours. How it was my birthright. His grumbles only became more incessant when I showed interest in farming. Honestly, I almost changed majors just to shut him up, but nothing made me as happy as my agriculture classes. Or to be more accurate, being on the land. Offices and desks have never felt comfortable to me. But being outside among the dirt, the trees, the fresh air, and the birds? That's always been my home.

As soon as we make the turn toward downtown, the drive livens up. Despite the fact it's early spring, Saturday night in Hope Harbor is an experience. Everyone is keyed up from having been stuck indoors all winter, so like typical New Englanders, the townspeople are out without jackets on, braving the cool weather with smiles and pretending they can't feel the chill in the air.

And I've got the windows down because I love it, too.

I turn to Billie, who glances longingly at Penny's bookstore as a few women, who must be only a year or two younger than her, laugh loudly as they walk inside.

Someone on the sidewalk yells "Hi, Walker," and I wince as my sister smiles.

"Aren't you going to wave?"

"And make them think I want to say hello?"

She laughs as she waves at whoever said hello and I keep my focus on the road, though my lips lift slightly. I like seeing her like this. Hell, I'd say hello to everyone in this town if it would make my sister happy.

"Is your roommate home?" I can feel Billie's intense gaze as she tries to read my thoughts.

"Don't know."

"Should you call her and let her know we're coming?" We're stopping by the house to grab one of Quinn's school folders that he left earlier in the week before heading to dinner.

I glance at her. "Why should I let her know that I'm coming home to *my* house?"

"Because you're bringing guests."

"You're not guests," I grumble.

"Why is everything so difficult with you?" she asks playfully. "Just text the woman. Or do you not have her number?"

She reaches for my phone but I'm quicker, pulling it out of the center console and tossing it into my lap. Obviously, I don't have the woman's number, but I don't want my sister going through my phone and seeing how few people I talk to. It's mainly just her and Quinn. Okay, it's only her and Quinn.

"Do I look like I text?"

"I have no idea what you do when I'm not around."

I shake my head and focus on the road. I do nothing when she's not around. I work. And find ways to avoid Tally. And I work some more.

I take the left over the small bridge that leads to the farm.

"She just seems nice is all," Billie says almost wistfully.

"You could text with her," I blurt out. I don't know why I say it, but I hate the tone of my sister's voice. The yearning I saw in her eyes at the girls in town. The loneliness that I understand more than I let on.

"I don't know her," Billie replies, matter-of-factly.

Gnawing on the inside of my mouth, I try to stop myself from my next offer but I could never stand to see my sister sad. "I'll invite her to dinner and you can get to know her."

My sister practically bounces in her seat as she turns to face me. "Really?"

"Really," I mutter with a resolute smile.

Guess I'm done avoiding Tally Darling.

Chapter 13
TALLY

My entire body is sore, and my arms feel like they are on fire. I've never worked so hard in my life. Carrying one-hundred-pound sandbags from the meadows to the storage barn was more effort than I'd bargained for. Dirt coats my hands and stains my fingernails. It'll take at least two showers to feel clean. Maybe three.

But I can't help but smile.

The tarps are off, folded, and put away. The sandbags are organized. It barely looks like we've been here. Even though, for hours, we've worked to get the last of the blankets off the tulips. In two weeks, when they are fully bloomed, all this work will be worth it.

Eli and Fletcher, along with a few guys from the fire department they'd wrangled to help, all sit on the edge of our porch enjoying the iced tea, beers, and homemade sandwiches I'd provided. The sun is just dipping behind a bank of cotton candy clouds, leaving the entire farm in a hazy pink hue.

"So what's the story with you and my best friend?" I ask Fletcher as he tosses a piece of his sandwich to his dog.

Eli perks up. "You and Rosie?" He waggles his brows. "Definitely didn't see that coming."

"There is no me and Rosie," Fletcher replies, and for the first time today, he's not smiling. I know there's more to this story than either of them are willing to share.

"But you want there to be?" Eli asks.

Fletcher rolls his shoulders back and sets his sandwich down beside him. Brewer jumps up, setting his paws on his lap, and Fletcher finally smiles before pushing the dog down. "You've had enough, boy. Go lay down."

He looks up to find us waiting for an answer before shaking his head and letting out a breathy laugh. "I've got my hands full enough with Henry."

"And Rosie would definitely require two hands," Eli says before tipping his beer back and taking a swig.

"Oh yeah, she would," I agree. My best friend is more than a handful for sure, but she's worth the effort, and I have a feeling Fletcher realizes that as well. Though I don't push him. Neither of them seem ready to deal with whatever is brewing beneath the surface, and Lord knows I have enough on my own plate to not try to play matchmaker.

We all laugh right as my mother's car appears in the driveway. Excited to show her our handiwork, I hop off the porch and pat down my dirty clothes, waiting for her to park. Right as she's getting out of her car, Walker's Ford F-150 swings into the lane. It's an older model, obviously well loved, and it suits him.

The truck pulls up next to my mom's car and Walker hops out, his movements slow, his body tense. Something about the way he peruses the entire area has nervous energy buzzing through me.

Shit.

His nephew leans out the window and waves. "Hi!"

His boyish charm settles my nerves. I smile and wave back.

"What's going on?" Walker mumbles to my mother.

She shrugs. "I was just about to ask the same thing."

Eli's hand lands on my shoulder, and he squeezes me against his side. "Tally here had a great idea today. And she roped us all into helping."

Nervously, I give him a closed-mouth smile. But before I can say anything, Walker speaks. "Roped you in to help with what?"

"We uncovered the rest of the tulip bulbs!" I say brightly. "Tada." I do a little jig. I have no idea why—probably because I feel nervous about the way my mother and Walker are looking at me.

Walker's brows pull together. "You what?" He takes a step closer, and even though he's still ten feet away, I feel the itch to back up.

Instead, I straighten my back. "With the Daffodil Festival around the corner, the flowers need time to bloom." I sound more sure of myself than I feel. But this is how we always did it. The end of March meant the start of tulip season. By mid-April, we'd be in full bloom. Despite knowing all of this, however, something doesn't feel right. It might be the panicked expression on my mother's face. Or the simple shift in Walker's stance; the way his jaw ticks as he looks off to the fields.

He's angry. As is my mother. Whatever his plan was, they're clearly in this together.

Walker's emotions pass quickly across his face, and soon, he's his usual stoic self. Unreadable. He glances at the men surrounding me. "Thanks for the help. If you guys ever need anything—"

Fletcher holds up a hand. "It's what neighbors do. I've actually got to go pick up Henry at my mother's. You all good?"

He directs the question at me. I think he can sense that something is off.

I give a quick nod and fake a smile. "Yes. Thank you again. If you ever need a sitter for Henry, I'm your girl."

He smiles and then the rest of the guys begin to pack up, heading for their trucks. Eli pauses next to me before leaving. "Walker doesn't look happy. I'm not making that up, right?" He mumbles it out of the side of his mouth, his focus on my mother and Walker, who are talking together in quiet tones.

I shake my head as Eli gives my arm a gentle squeeze. "Want me to stick around?"

"No, I'll be fine."

His blue eyes study me for a beat longer before he nods and carries on his way. As he passes Walker and my mother, he stops to gives her a gentle squeeze and does some fist-bump thing in Walker's direction, which Walker just stares at before Eli shrugs and gives up. Then he seems to notice Billie's son hanging out the back of the truck and walks up to say hello. The way the little boy lights up, it's clear he's a big fan of the hockey player.

I stay where I am as everyone leaves, wondering what bombshell is about to be dropped. As soon as the last car pulls away, my mother spins on me. "*Why* would you uncover the flower beds?"

Confused, I look between her and Walker, searching for an answer to their concern.

"Why wouldn't I? The festival is coming up. The flowers won't have time to bloom if they're covered."

The sound of a car door slamming echoes as Walker's sister comes around the truck. She gives me a nod of her head and an uneasy smile. "Hi, Tally."

"Hi." I suck in a lungful of air. "Will someone please tell me why you're acting like I killed someone?"

Billie glances at her brother, but his gaze is focused on the uncovered tulip bulbs.

"Because," my mother says slowly, pain evident in her every syllable, "Walker was trying to extend the season. By keeping them covered, they'd still be in bloom by the end of May, maybe even into June. We have two weddings booked right up 'til June sixth."

"But we never have weddings that late," I protest, even as the sick feeling grows in my stomach.

Walker clenches his teeth and finally looks at me. "Because we never have flowers for brides to take pictures with."

"Well, why didn't you tell me that? I asked you repeatedly why you weren't uncovering them." I'm angry now. I tried to talk to him. Tried to get him to open up. It all would have been so simple if the man had just used his damn words. "*And* Penny and I found the letter from Frank Seymour in the fireplace."

My mother sucks in a surprised breath. Ha! See! I knew Walker was up to no good.

Vindication has me stepping forward, my back straightening. "It was addressed to him," I tell my mother.

Walker sighs, his demeanor not indicating that he's the least bit concerned that I know about this.

My mother shakes her head. "Frank's been after your father to sell for years, and Walker was here the last time he stopped by. He offered to take care of it so I didn't have to deal with the guy. He's pushy."

"And I threw the letter in the fireplace because I'd already told him weeks ago your mother wasn't interested." Walker says before glancing at my mom. "I was annoyed that he did again. I thought I'd made it clear where you stand."

Shit. "But the fireplace doesn't even work," I say weakly. I'm losing my fight. It seems Walker has an answer for everything and, more importantly, my mother knows every one of them.

"I fixed that a few weeks ago, too," Walker grumbles.

"Oh." My eyes fly to his, and where I expect to find anger, I find exhaustion.

"What will we do?" my mother addresses Walker. My heart pinches at the worry in her voice.

The way she looks at Walker makes me think things are even worse than I imagined. Is it possible that my daddy hired Walker because we are at real risk of losing the farm? Our home?

"I was just trying to help," I say softly, though my words are lost in the wind.

A gust kicks up right as Walker's nephew whines from the window. "Are we getting dinner? I'm hungry."

Billie reaches for my mother's hand and squeezes. "Why don't you join us for dinner? We were just heading out. We can figure out a plan for those late weddings. Don't you worry."

Walker stares out at the uncovered flower beds, his breathing heavy. His head drops and he nods. "Yeah, Gail, come with us. We'll figure it out."

Loss settles deep in my bones as I feel the familiar clang of not only screwing up, but also of not belonging. It's not me my mother needs; it's Billie. I don't know why I even came home. I just keep making everything worse.

"Want to join us, Tally?" Billie asks.

"I'm sure she's got plans." Walker's tone is harsh enough. The way he won't look at me, though? That stings. Creates this empty ache in my chest that I want to rub away.

Somehow I find my voice despite the utter devastation that sweeps through me. I hold up my dirty hands to Billie. "Yeah. I've got to shower. Enjoy your dinner."

As I watch the four of them leave, I will my mother to turn back and look at me. To see how sorry I am. To tell me she forgives me.

But the truck disappears in the same direction it came from, and no one inside even looks my way.

Chapter 14
WALKER

She meant well."

My sister's words play on repeat in my head as I drive back to the big house. After dinner, I dropped Gail at the farm and then took my sister and Quinn home. The extra alone time in the car was needed. Even now I'm not sure I'm ready to have a rational conversation with Tally. Hopefully, she'll be hiding out in her room and we can avoid talking for a few days—or ideally for the rest of the spring.

Banging my fist against the steering wheel, I groan. That's not what I really want at all. If I had my way, Tally would not be someone I'd be avoiding. Then again, if I had my way, Tally would have never taken the tarps off the damn tulips.

"Fuck." I smack the wheel again. This is so fucking bad. My sister had all sorts of ideas that will help us for next summer—seeds we can plant and other attractions we can tout to brides—but none of them fix our immediate problem. We have a bunch of weddings scheduled for the end of May, and I highly doubt any of the tulips will make it that long. Even if they do, they won't be the beautiful blooms that the brides expect. They'll be wilted. Maybe even grazed over by the deer.

I'll need to invest in a better system to keep the flowers we do have safe.

Plus, for the next two weeks, I'll have to devote my attention to the tulips, which weren't in my planned rotation.

Basically, I just have a lot more fucking work to handle and no idea what we'll do about the potential loss of income.

"*She meant well.*" Billie's words taunt me again as I pull down the long driveway and the big white Victorian comes into view. I still can't forget them as I park and hop out of my old truck, my boots kicking up dirt as I stomp up to the house.

"*She meant well.*" I pause at the door, staring toward the meadows. I love this land, I love this farm, and I know she meant well, but fuck, she's making it really hard for us to keep it.

Things are worse than Gail and Peter let on when they brought me onboard. Every bill I uncover makes that clear. Frank is right. They would have only a season left if they kept going the way they were. We've got a season left if I don't figure this shit out.

I'm about to head inside when I hear a whimpering cry.

"*No.*" It's a moan. A *female* moan.

"Hello?" I call into the wind, walking across the porch and peering out into the dark night. The evening sky is filled with stars, but there's no light coming from the farm in any direction. The closest source is Gail's cottage, which has a faint glow behind her curtain, and then the brewery in the distance.

"Shit, shit, shit. Why did I do this?" The voice gets louder as I rush off the porch and head toward the fields.

This freaking girl. Can she not listen to a word I say? What could she possibly be doing now? I half expect to find her pulling the tulips from their bed since I told her to stay away from the flowers and she tends to always do the exact opposite of what I ask.

"Tally!" I call louder as I continue my search.

"Go away!" she yells back, and as my eyes adjust to the light, I can just make out her slow limp.

"Dammit, what did I tell you?" I growl as I start to run.

As if she can sense my speed and urgency, Tally starts to rush forward. Though she only takes two faster steps before she drops to the ground with a loud thud.

"Gah!" she yells. It's hard to tell if she's hurt or just angry.

"What the hell are you doing?" I hiss as I reach her. She's on her back with a sandbag flopped on top of her.

A hundred-pound sandbag.

What. The. Fuck?

Tally lets out a heavy sigh before pushing it off. I watch as she drops her head to the ground and stares up at the sky. "Go away."

Hands on my waist, I glare up at the glowing moon, which taunts me as it lights up the field. I know when I look down I'll be able to make out every one of Tally's features. Tally sounding broken and angry in the dark is hard enough to resist, but seeing her desperate sadness when I'm trying to focus on my anger instead of her whimpers? Not so easy. But of course, I'm a glutton for punishment, so I barely brace myself before glancing down at her. When I see the wet marks trailing down her cheeks, I know I've lost the battle.

"Are you okay?" I rasp.

Tally closes her eyes. "Just pretend you didn't see me. I'll get everything put back where it was by morning. Promise."

Obviously, that's not going to happen. I rough a hand over my face and blow out another breath. "Come on Tal, let's go inside."

"No."

This woman.

"Tally."

"I'm serious, Walker, this isn't your problem. *I'm* not your problem. Let me fix this."

She's right. She's not my problem. But dammit if that makes a bit of a difference. Not sure what else to do, I drop to my ass beside her. "You can't fix it. It's a day's worth of work at least when there's a full crew to help. It would take you a week to do on your own."

She huffs. "You don't know me. I'm a very hard worker, and I'm stubborn."

I cough out a laugh. "That sounds about right."

She nudges me with her knee, and I smile as I drop my head back beside hers. The ground is cold, but something about it also feels good. I relax for a second and stare up at the moon again, giving her a second to breathe and get used to my presence.

Yes, I'm angry that Tally didn't listen to me. But she was right earlier, I never told her my plan.

"Can I be honest?" Tally's soft voice breaks through the quiet night.

I turn my head toward hers and smirk. "Since when have you not been?"

She laughs, but I can tell she's still sad. From this position, I can see the glittering swirls of gold in her eyes from her tears. My smile dies as I stare into them. A man could get lost in those eyes. Hell, I probably will if I look at her any longer.

"I didn't want it to be true," she whispers as she rolls her teeth over her bottom lip and my mouth goes dry. "I didn't want you to be trying to steal my farm. To destroy my family's business. I'm glad Penny and I were wrong. I'm sorry I screwed everything up. I just don't know how to be here now that he's not. I think Penny and I are struggling with how everything keeps moving forward when we're still stuck. And you're doing things so differently . . ." Her voice shakes and her head lolls to the sky again. "I miss him so much, and I don't know how to do this. I'm sorry."

Without thinking, I reach for her and pull her body against my chest, hugging her to me. I shiver at how right she feels in my arms. "I was probably an ass and haven't made any of it easier."

She laughs against my chest, though it's mixed with a sob. "Yeah, you are definitely an ass."

I chuckle and run my hands through her soft hair.

"Did you guys figure out what to do about the weddings at the end of the season?"

I continue stroking her head. I can't stop touching her. "No. But we'll figure it out. We may just have to contact the brides and let them know the situation."

"I can do it." She looks up at me, those golden eyes pleading with me. "I'll follow whatever script you want. I know I screwed up. Like I said, I thought you were messing with my daddy's farm. Thought you were keeping a secret, trying to steal our business." My chest clangs because she's not wrong. I am keeping secrets, and one of those is that Darling Daffodils Farm is not her daddy's anymore. "But I was wrong," she says earnestly. She licks her lips, and my gaze follows the track of her tongue. "I'm sorry. I know you're only trying to help my mother. She trusts you. I should have, too."

Guilt claws at me. My sister's warning to just tell her the truth beats a steady rhythm, but it's not my secret to tell.

"Do you forgive me?" she asks softly.

I look down at her, and my eyes roam over her lips, which taunt me with false promises. That she'll ease this ache. That touching her isn't wrong. That all of this would be so much damn easier if we worked together.

"You were just trying to help." I repeat my sister's words and trace a finger down Tally's jawline.

Her eyes light up. "I swear I was."

Her skin is so smooth beneath my fingers. Just one breath closer and I'd be able to taste it. To feel the warmth of it on my lips. I'd devour her, and maybe it'd all feel better—just for a little bit.

A car door slams in the distance, probably at the brewery, and I pull my hand away. I have no business touching this woman. "Come on, it's getting late."

Tally blinks like maybe she was in the same daze as I was and sits up quickly. The second she tries to stand, however, a pained sound flies from her throat.

"You hurt?"

She bites her bottom lip. "I think I might have twisted my ankle when I went down."

Of course she did. I stand up and scoop her into my arms.

Tally squeals. "What are you doing?!"

"Carrying you."

"Okay, Captain Obvious. I mean you don't have to carry me. Just give me a hand."

I grunt, ignoring her. Like I'm going to allow her to limp back to the house. Besides, for the moment I have an excuse to hold her, even though I'm not going to think too long on why I like having her in my arms so much. Instead, I quietly lumber back toward the house and enjoy the feeling of her against my chest. Her heart pounding an unsteady rhythm as mine gallops.

As soon as we reach the porch and the lighting is better, I can see the dirt that coats both of our clothes from lying on the ground. "You should probably shower before bed," I say as I pull open the door and then kick it shut behind us.

"Is that your lame excuse to get me naked?" she taunts.

Her words don't annoy me, though. Tally sounds more like herself now, and I'd rather be the butt of her jokes than hear her sad or lost again.

Ignoring her, I carry her up the stairs and don't let go until we've reached the bathroom. "Okay, I was just joking. You don't really have to bring me in the shower," she huffs.

I roll my eyes as I head toward the door. "I'm not. Just don't fall. Wouldn't want to have to come save you again."

"God. I was just about to say thank you. But then you had to go and be an ass again."

I smile as I head down the steps, happy she's back to her stubborn self. This I can handle.

Even though I know that, after she opened up to me tonight, things have changed. I can't keep lying to Tally. As soon as I reach the kitchen, I grab a beer from the fridge before pulling out my phone and shooting off a text to Gail.

ME: You need to tell your daughters about Frank.

Chapter 15
TALLY

Sunday morning, I wake up determined to fix things. With my mother. With Walker. With the farm. Unfortunately, however, when I make it downstairs, I can't find Walker anywhere. And after traipsing across the farm, I realize that my mother isn't in her cottage, either. So I settle for coffee at Rosie's. I could use a pick-me-up after yesterday and, to be honest, I need my best friend.

The first thing I notice when I make the right toward Rosie's property is the number of cars that fill her parking lot. It's only nine a.m. What are all these people doing here?

The second thing I see is my sister's old Toyota Camry. I remember the day Daddy handed her the keys. I was fifteen and thought my sister was the coolest person in the world. That fact grew exponentially when she told me I could sit shotgun and we took off from the farm. Before then, the farthest I'd ever gone was Mabel's Bakery. But on that October day, Penny and I drove for hours through New England in search of the perfect fall foliage. Listening to Incubus and Coldplay while I looked out the window at the passing trees and the coastline, I realized there was an entire world outside of Hope Harbor. A world I wanted to explore.

My feet quicken as I head inside in search of answers. I bypass the to-go coffee window to scour the bar for my sister or best friend. They're definitely here, though there's not one person in the open room.

A melodic laugh that I'd recognize anywhere pulls me to the left, where I spot Rosie's signature red hair. She's standing outside, on the back porch, next to Penny, a coffee cup in hand and laughing at something my sister just said.

What are the two of them doing together? And why didn't they invite me?

Penny spots me first and smiles in surprise. "Hey! You came to the farmers market! I wasn't sure if you got my text since you never replied."

I reach for my phone, only to realize I don't have it on me. Shit. I hope I didn't leave it in the fields last night. "Yeah, I don't actually know where it is. What are you guys doing?"

Rosie takes a sip from her cup, a coy smile curling her lips. "Drinking."

Penny rolls her eyes before taking a sip out of her pastel pink mug that says THIS IS DEFINITELY COFFEE.

"Why are you guys being weird? And where can I get some coffee?"

"Oh, this isn't coffee," Rosie says.

"Huh?"

Penny giggles as she tips her cup forward and I spot the green juice.

"It's green mimosas," Rosie mumbles, "because it's St. Patrick's Day!"

Aha.

"Besides," she continues, "we always have mimosas on Sundays. They help us get through the farmers market. Well, that and *that*." Her chin lifts in the direction they'd been gazing before. I follow her eyes to a row of tables. Behind each one is a different man wearing a flannel shirt and Wranglers. One table has jams on it while another boasts leather goods next to a stand of pottery.

"It's like a meat market for hungry women," I mumble, my mouth watering. Apparently, I'm starving.

"Yup." Rosie pops the *p* and then licks her lips. "The market was Penny's idea. A way to drum up business for the brewery." She grins at my sister in appreciation, and a sense of pride swells within me at everything they've accomplished since I've been gone. "I'd say your farm has the best setup, though."

My eyes cut down the line in search of my mother. When I spot her talking to a man in a cowboy hat, his body facing away from me so I can only make out the way his jeans mold to his ass, I smile. That is one fine cowboy.

"Oh, did she hire a cowboy to bring attention to her table?" I glance at my sister. "That's a pretty good idea, Pen."

Rosie's head falls back as she lets out a loud laugh. "That's not a cowboy! That's Walker."

My body heats as I realize I was just checking out the bane of my existence. Dammit, why does the man have to be everywhere? And why does he have such a nice ass?

"Okay. I'm going to need one of those mimosas now," I grumble, looking away from the display for our farm. Rosie wasn't wrong; ours is the best table. It's covered in magenta and baby blue peonies, my favorite dahlias that dazzle anyone who sees them because of the pink and peach hues that sprout from one petal to the next, and of course a few bundles of freshly cut daffodils. The stunning array of flowers brightens up the entire market and attracts a large crowd.

"I got you covered," Rosie says with a wink before disappearing inside.

I turn back to the stand, and my gaze is immediately drawn to the man I'm trying to ignore.

"Are we going to talk about it?" Penny eyes me over her cup.

"Oh, you mean the great deflowering?" I say with a roll of my eyes.

Penny snorts. Okay, maybe I need to come up with a better name than that for the untarping of the tulips. But I haven't had any caffeine yet, and I feel like complete shit.

"It was so bad," I mutter as I watch my mother and Walker. They are both smiling, though I'm sure it's all a ruse. There's no way they aren't still pissed off at me and stressed about what is going to happen next. "I'm going to go to the grocery store later so I can load up on every ingredient I can find to make an apology cupcake or fifty for Walker. And I'm going to bake Mom her favorite cake, too."

Basically, my goal in life is to sweet-talk my way out of trouble.

"Oh, can you bring some by the bookstore after? I miss your cupcakes."

"You don't deserve them. You made me do bad things yesterday."

Penny's jaw drops open and her mouth flaps like a dead fish. "At no time did I tell you to uncover the damn tulips. You were supposed to talk to Rosie! Did she tell you to uncover the tulips?"

No. In fact, she pretty much told me it was a bad idea from the start. But I'm not letting Penny off the hook so easily. "You should have seen Mom's face, Pen. This is so, so bad."

Penny sighs. "She should have been honest with us. What was she thinking?"

I roll my teeth over my bottom lip. I have no idea why my mother is being so secretive, but I wish she'd stop. I wish she'd let Penny and me help. "What are we going to do?"

Penny shakes her head. "I'll do some research on other ways to attract brides. And we'll bring back the pumpkin patch and the maze this fall. Maybe talk to Walker about stuff for Christmas?"

All things I didn't plan on being here for. Shit. I can't leave now, knowing how much trouble our farm is in. But how the hell do I stay? What would I even do? I've been nothing but a nuisance since I arrived. I'm sure the last thing Walker wants me to do is stay.

I stare at the man in question for a beat longer, attempting to ignore the pull I feel whenever he's in my immediate vicinity.

"So what's with the hat?" I ask Penny.

"Cowboys are all the rage nowadays on BookTok," she says, like I have a clue what she's talking about. My face must say exactly that because she sighs. "Well, and aliens. Women find the cowboy hat hot."

"But we don't have animals on the farm." Even as I say it, I can't help but smile. The grumpy asshole who hates being called a cowboy is wearing a cowboy hat.

My smile gets bigger when Rosie returns with a matching pastel purple mug with THIS IS DEFINITELY COFFEE scrawled across it. Before I can take a sip, she tips her mug in my direction. "Admit that you find the cowboy hot, or suffer bad sex for ten years."

I clink my glass against hers. "The cowboy *hat* is hot."

Rosie's loud laugh rings out across the market, and Walker's head snaps in our direction.

The second our eyes meet, I'm reminded of the way he looked at me last night. Of how my body vibrated with want as he pulled me against his chest. How those eyes of his warmed as he stared at my mouth. How the words *Fuck it* were on the tip of my tongue right before a car door slammed and he jolted like he'd been shot.

I've got a lot of things to fix, but the way Walker is staring at me isn't one of them.

I wiggle my fingers in greeting, and as I take my first sip of what is definitely not coffee, my mood, for the first time since I arrived in Hope Harbor, is positively giddy.

Chapter 16
WALKER

Y ou like the daffodils?" Gail asks Fletcher's little boy, Henry, who's hiding behind his chocolate Lab. Henry doesn't say much, which only makes me like him more. He's like my kindred spirit.

Fletcher signs the words that Gail just asked, and I remember that Henry is deaf, though the piece from his cochlear implant is barely visible under his trademark ball cap. I'd guess he's around four years old; he looks younger than Quinn but older than a toddler.

We're working the farmers market that Rosie hosts at the brewery every weekend, and thank God we've had a great showing. If the crowd keeps up, I may even need to go back to the farm and grab a few more bouquets, which is good because we'll need to sell a shit ton to make up for the disaster that was last night.

"You must be happy to have your daughter back home," Fletcher says to Gail in the same way he says everything: with a big smile and his attention duly focused on whomever he's speaking with in that moment. Fletcher is the quintessential mayor, and everyone in town loves him.

"It's always good to see her, but I doubt she'll stick around too long. Like my husband always said, you can't keep a wildflower in one place." Gail laughs lightly, though I can sense pain behind her words. I think they both missed Tally terribly when she was gone, and I'm not sure Gail knows how to handle that feeling now that her youngest daughter is here but Peter's not. As much as I want Tally to go back to work so my sister can have the job, I do feel for Gail.

The first thing I did this morning was go out to Gail's cottage to talk to her about having an honest conversation with her daughters. They need to know the truth. If she'd told them to begin with, Tally never would have uncovered the damn tulips. Then again, I'm guilty of the same damn thing. Though, to be fair, Gail is keeping me from telling the girls what is really going on. Her and the ironclad NDA I signed when I first got myself involved in this whole mess.

She said she'd think about it. I guess that's the best I can do.

I'm surprised the girls haven't made more of an effort to come over and say hello yet. Maybe offer to help. Instead, they've stayed on the porch with Rosie all morning, catching up and drinking coffee like it's water. I've seen Rosie go inside to refill their cups at least three times. Not that I'm watching them.

I let out a sigh. At least Tally isn't wearing another one of her spandex outfits that makes my dick hard. Today, she's wearing a long lavender floral dress with buttons all the way down her body. It has a little bow tied between her breasts that, if I was closer, I'm sure I'd be studying way too intently.

My gaze tracks over in the girls' direction again, but now the porch is empty. Though my stomach pinches in disappointment, I don't want to think too hard on why. Instead, I focus on the mayor's conversation.

"Have you considered vegetables?" Fletcher is asking Gail.

"We're not set up for it," I respond quickly, before Gail

gets another thought in her head. Peter told me she used to do that all the time. She'd hear about something like composting and go out and buy everything to set it up. It just made another project for Peter. And when he was already running a farm with hundreds of thousands of flower bulbs, it meant he was always in over his head.

I don't know how he did it on his own for as long as he did. Especially without the right equipment. Fortunately, after working on several different farms, I know a group of guys who all help each other out in season. Planting that many bulbs is far easier with a tractor and ten guys than by hand, by yourself.

"Well, if there is anything the town can do to get you set up for that, you just call," Fletcher says.

"Maybe in the fall I'll reach out. Thank you."

Gail beams like I've just made her the greatest promise. Fletcher's face lights up, too.

"He really does have good bone structure," Tally's voice breaks through our conversation.

"Yup. And he wears the hell out of that hat," Rosie croons.

"Give me that camera, I'll get it," Penny says.

My brows pull together as I whip my head toward the three women now camped out in front of our table. Their heads are tilted to the side as they study . . . *me*. God knows why.

Penny is the first to break as she reaches into her pocket and pulls out her phone. "Could you just turn back that way? The sun is hitting perfectly, and I think you might have even smiled."

"No. Definitely wasn't a smile. More of a lip curl," Tally says. "But we don't want him smiling. Don't want to give false impressions. Right, cowboy?"

I growl and almost reach for my hat to toss it to the dirt. "*Not* a cowboy."

She snorts. "You sure about that?"

"I'm trying to do what's best for the farm," I say slowly and with a hint of threat in my tone. Tally's eyes flare. Her long hair blows in the wind, and while my nose twitches to try to inhale the scent I'm sure is floating through the air, I realize I've overplayed my hand again.

"Well, by all means, since you want to do what's best for the farm, *Cowboy*, smile for the camera."

And *that's* how I end up spending the next two hours posing for the farm's damn social media with a cowboy hat and a shovel.

———

"My personal favorite is the one where you're lying in the mud." I pull the phone away from my ear because my sister's cackle is so loud it hurts.

"You see what I'm dealing with. Can you come work here now?"

I pause on the steps outside the house, not wanting Tally to overhear my conversation. I have no idea where she disappeared to after the photoshoot from hell, but I've stayed out of the house for as long as I can. I'm starving and my body is tired. I need a shower, an ice-cold beer, and silence. But I have a feeling that when I go inside, I'll get none of those things.

"Not a chance. You've got Tally there, and from the looks of it, she's got everything covered."

"'From the looks of it'?" I pull my baseball cap off my

head and swipe at the sweat that's forming just from thinking about the damn woman. "What have you seen that gives you any indication that she knows shit about weddings? Were you and I not part of the same conversation last night when we came upon her destroying the tulips?"

My sister's laughter drifts through the phone and grabs me by the chest. Shit. I haven't heard her sound this free in a long time. She's normally too busy rushing around between jobs and Quinn's activities to focus on anything else. "I don't think I've ever heard you so tied up about a woman," she says.

"I'm not." I suck in a deep breath in a bid to calm myself. I don't like being short with Billie. Plus, I don't want to give her any reason not to move here.

"I'm not tied up. I'm—" I grapple for words.

"You're tripping over yourself, you like her so much."

"The last thing I feel for that woman is *like*." My mouth sours on the word.

"Oh, more like *want*?" she singsongs.

"*Billie.*"

My sister pauses, then her voice softens. "It's been five years, Jesse. It's okay to put down those walls a bit and open yourself to falling for someone again."

I let out a long sigh. I don't like thinking of Gina or what she did to me all those years ago. "I've got a farm to run. Wedding season to get through—"

"And don't forget that modeling career," she teases.

I smile. I can't help it. I like hearing my sister like this. "Even if I didn't have any of those things, I assure you, Tally Darling is the last person I'd date." I pause, trying to ignore the way the lie feels on my lips. "Please, Billie, this would be so much better with you here."

"Quinn has to get through the school year, anyway," she says under her breath. I hear footsteps and then the sound of a door shutting. "Have you talked to her about what Gail did yet? Does she know about our grandfather and the land?"

Instinct has me looking around, as if somehow, someone can hear my sister's soft voice through the phone. It's quiet except for the birds singing to one another in the cherry tree. Soon enough, that tree will be sprouting beautiful pink-and-white petals and then it'll make a mess that I have to clean up. Because I'm the one who's handling the farm. I'm the one who's responsible for it all. "I told Gail she needs to talk to her."

"She needs to know, Jesse." My sister's tone is soft but chiding. She's never been the type to raise her voice.

"It's not my place," I grumble. "Besides, I signed an NDA, remember?" Before my sister can respond, I change the subject and ask for an update on Quinn's week ahead and then we make plans to have her come by for dinner this week. After a few more minutes, we say our goodbyes and I slip the phone in my pocket to head inside.

As I do, the first thing I notice is the music playing loudly in the kitchen. Taylor Swift, I think, with the hint of a pretty voice singing alongside. The second thing I detect is the scent of dinner—something barbecued. My stomach growls, and as if my body has no choice but to go to the singing siren, I find myself leaning against the kitchen wall, arms crossed, watching the wicked woman sway her hips as she dances between the stove and the counter, placing platters of food between two place settings in front of two stools. Clearly she's having someone over for dinner so I start to leave, ready to get back in my truck and head into town to grab a burger. Though my stomach seems determined to find barbecue now.

"You're home!" The happy lilt of her voice makes me pause, and my head whips in her direction, confused.

I look behind me to see if someone snuck into the house after I came in. Wouldn't have been hard since my entire focus has been on her.

She laughs. "Talking to you, Cowboy."

My eyes narrow.

She holds up her hand. "I come in peace. I made us dinner because I think we got off on the wrong foot." She squints her eyes. "Well, a bare foot maybe? Because you were naked," she whispers loudly.

"Are you drunk?"

Her lips fold in on themselves and her eyes grow wide. "Don't tell."

I sigh and look around her. "So that food's for me?" I can deal with her drunken giggles if I'm fed.

She waves her hand at the counter island like she's Vanna White.

"Yup. I found some stuff in the fridge and put this together. Figured I shouldn't drive into town to go shopping."

"Must have been all the coffee," I mutter as I head to the sink to wash my hands.

"I've got a secret," she says, coming right up next me, her hip bumping mine as she sticks her hands under the water, too. Instantly the smell of barbecue is replaced by her sweet, intoxicating, floral scent, and I have to hold my breath to keep from inhaling her. Otherwise, I'm afraid that if I do, I'll be searching out that smell for the rest of my life.

Fuck, this girl needs to go. I step back to let her finish washing her hands.

"Don't you want to know my secret?" She settles on one of the stools at the counter.

I close my eyes because those words coming from her mouth make me want a lot of things. Though none of them are her secrets.

"Not really," I grunt.

"It wasn't coffee."

"No shit."

She barely bats an eye at my bad attitude. "It was mimosas because my sister and Rosie drink mimosas on Sunday mornings."

I take a stack of ribs from the platter and a scoop of the mashed potatoes. Tally reaches over and spoons some broccoli onto my plate. "You're a growing boy, Cowboy. You need your greens."

"Not a cowboy."

"Whatever you say."

I take a bite of rib and practically moan from the delicious flavor of the meat as it falls off the bone.

"Good, right? Sorry, I stole your ribs. If we're going to be living together, we should probably figure out how to split the expenses."

"You cook like this every night, and we can call it even," I reply without thinking.

She blinks up at me like I told her she was the prettiest woman I've ever seen, and the most gorgeous shade of red fans across her cheeks. "I'm glad you like it," she murmurs softly before taking a bite of her food.

I slide off my stool and head to the fridge for a beer, holding one up for her. She raises her glass bottle of diet coke in response and shakes her head, so I grab just one beer and pop the top. Before digging in and forgetting my own name, I add, "I've got a business credit card. We can use that."

She shakes her head, but I hold up a hand for her to let me finish. "If you're determined to work here, you're an employee. It's only right."

Her lips twist and she nods. "About that—I'm really sorry about the tulips."

"It wasn't all your fault. You were right. I should have told you my plan." Her eyes light up. "You still should have listened when I told you not to touch them. But I could have done a better job of explaining why."

She nods and then her tongue goes to her cheek. "Well, while we're being honest, I have something else to confess."

Oh Christ, what did the woman do now? I lift my brows, waiting for her to continue.

"Remember how you told me to count the daffodils?"

I almost snort because fuck, just picturing her doing that has me ready to laugh. Somehow I manage to maintain a serious face. "Yes?"

Her eyes focus on the ceiling before she mumbles, "Well, I kinda sorta fibbed when I said I did it."

"Oh yeah?" I work to keep my tone devoid of humor.

"I thought it was you being bossy and mean and all grumpy, but then you explained why it's important, so I promise I'll go out there and count every stalk this week."

I dip my chin. "All right."

"And I can do the grocery shopping if you tell me what you like to eat," she adds. A warm feeling spreads through me as I realize she wants me to like her. Though I don't think there's a damn thing she could make that I wouldn't like if this barbecue is even a hint at her talent. I haven't had a home-cooked meal this good in—well, fuck, I don't think I've ever had a meal this good.

"Where's your mother?" I ask, reminding myself that it's not just the two of us living on this farm.

"She said something about dinner plans and disappeared." Tally slides her fork around her plate. "And I think she's avoiding me. I really screwed up yesterday. I keep screwing up when it comes to her."

Getting to know anything else about Tally is dangerous. Yet somehow I find myself asking, "Why do you think that?"

When she looks back at me, her amber eyes so wide and sad, it's like a punch to the gut. "I think I remind her of my dad."

I shake my head. She looks nothing like her dad. And she certainly doesn't act like him. This girl is all bright and shiny and loud. Her father was kind but quiet.. A hard worker. Maybe she's got that in common with him. Time will tell. But I don't see the resemblance, even a little bit.

"It's fine," she says with a forced cheer to her voice, making it so I don't have to respond. "I'm going to prove to her that I want to be here. You, too. And I'm going to do whatever I can to save the farm."

She flashes me a smile. It feels genuine, which is awfully bittersweet because I'd like to see it a lot more but know I don't deserve it.

I try to move the conversation in a different direction. "Your mother said you were in Vermont."

Tally's eyes widen. "Is that, like, an actual question?"

She's teasing me. I know she's teasing me, and even though I don't want to play these games with her, I feel my lips twitch into a half smile.

"Yes, Tally. You said you're here because you want to be. But I'm confused as to why. Did you lose your job?"

That might make more sense. If not, why did she choose to come home? Why now?

Tally shakes her head and sets down her fork. "I work seasonally in different places."

"Yes, your father mentioned that."

Her chest rises and falls with that information, and her eyes settle on the glass soda bottle in front of her. She reaches out to play with the straw, swirling it around the top. "I want to help you all get through this first season without him. I know I can be of use." She raises those pretty eyes of hers, and it's like she's pleading with me to let her. To believe that she really does want to help.

And maybe she does. Maybe her heart is in the right place. Maybe she's just gone about it all wrong.

I give her a singular nod. I can do this for Peter. I can help his family heal, help them get the farm up and running for the season, turn around this business, and save the land for all of us.

And I can do it without getting trapped in his daughter's golden eyes.

Tally goes back to humming the song playing on the radio, and that's when I realize it's the same damn song that was on when I entered the house.

I pause, trying to figure out which Taylor Swift melody is playing, but it's not familiar. "What song is that?"

Tally's eyes glitter with delight as she replies, "Cowboy Like Me."

I can't help the laugh that slips out. "Why does it keep playing?"

"Put it on repeat for ya." She nudges my elbow with her own, and I focus on my food to keep from laughing more.

"You're something else."

"That sounds like a compliment."

"You don't get many compliments, huh?"

Tally's brows rise and she shrugs. We eat the rest of the meal in silence, the damn song playing over and over. By the time I'm done with my plate—it took seconds, I'm not ashamed to admit—I know every lyric. I snag her plate, too, and walk toward the sink.

"Oh, chores!" She bounces off her chair and follows me to the sink. "We should discuss that, huh?"

I glance over at her. She's close. Once again standing hip to hip with me in front of the sink. I glare down at our feet, which are practically touching. "How's your ankle?"

When she doesn't reply, I lift my eyes to hers, and dammit, that was a mistake. Because she's looking at me like I just told her I loved her. Like she's not used to people caring. A soft smile plays on her lips. "It's fine. Think the alcohol took away any of the residual pain."

She turns back to the sink, and I'm left staring after her again. She's so damn happy and pretty and perfect and easy to talk to. I can't stand myself for how much I like it. I reach for a plate and grunt. "What're you doing?"

"Helping you clean," she says. "I figure we can rock-paper-scissors for all the chores."

"Rock-paper-what?"

She pantomimes the game.

I shake my head. "I know what you're talking about. Why would we do that?"

"So you can't say I stuck you with all the bad ones."

I sigh. This woman is exhausting me. My entire body is tense because I'm trying not to smell her or let her get too close, but her constant yammering makes it so I'll probably never actually get hard.

Who the fuck am I kidding? She could be covered in cow shit, and I'd probably still be attracted to her.

Taylor sings another line about dancing, and I have an urge to pull Tally closer. An urge I resist by dunking my hands in the water. "Grab the rest of the dishes. You cooked. I'll clean."

"Oh, so we have roles. I'll do the cooking, you do the cleaning?" She knocks her hip against mine before rounding the kitchen to get the rest of the dirty dishes. "Look at us, being such good roommates already."

"You're giving me a headache with all your talking," I mumble.

She rolls her eyes and sways her hips but remains quiet while we finish cleaning up the kitchen. "I'm going to head up to bed," she says after a few minutes, right before reaching past me to put the last dish away.

As if she wants to torture me, that floral scent floats right around me, forcing my body to turn like a damn sunflower in search of the sun.

"Good night." I grunt.

Tally pauses in front of me, nibbling on her lip. "What's your plan for the morning?"

"Got stuff to do on the farm."

"Like what?"

It's like she has some power over me as, once again, I find myself turning back to stare into those eyes of hers. "If I say cowboy stuff will you let it go?"

Her lips hook into another heart-stopping smile. "Glad you're coming around to my way of thinking."

I run a hand over my mouth to hide the beginnings of a grin. "And what are your plans?"

She smacks her palms together in excitement. "Oh my gosh, look at you, having a full conversation!"

My smile turns into a glower. She giggles, and fuck it, my stomach flips. I'm like a teenage girl with all of these emotions. My nostrils flare in irritation.

"I'll go to the grocery store," she tells me. "Get some food for the week."

I reach into my pocket and pull out my wallet, searching for the farm's credit card. When I push it toward her, she steps back, shaking her head. "I've got it."

"It's how things run on the farm. The business pays for it all."

"But—"

I refuse to back down on this. "It's how your father wanted it done."

A somber expression softens her face, and she swallows with a nod. Fuck, I shouldn't have said that.

She takes the card and turns to leave, but I have to make this right before she goes to bed. "You as good at making Italian as barbecue?"

Tally spins back to me, her eyes shining. "You like Italian?"

I hold her stare as I nod.

"I can handle that," she says softly before holding out her hand. "Give me your phone."

"What?"

She rolls her eyes. "I'll give you my cell phone number, and you can text me if you think of anything else you want tomorrow."

Once again my body betrays me and I do as she says. When she hands me back my phone, I stare at the number there with her name and a yellow flower beside it.

"Now is when you give me yours so I can do the same," she goads.

I stare at her. Why did she just give me her number? Why did I take it? She snatches back the phone and works some more magic before handing it back to me with a laugh and then disappearing up the stairs. When I look down at my screen, I see that there's a message, and dammit if I'm not fucking smiling again.

TALLY: Have a good night, Cowboy.

Chapter 17
TALLY

HOPE HARBOR TOWN CHAT

RAYNA: Don't forget book club has been moved to tonight!

BABS: I'll be there with my giant blue alien dildo for the presentation

STEW: Mayor! Mayor! Someone should be monitoring this chat!

PENNY: There will be no dildo demonstrations at the bookstore. We BUY, READ, and DISCUSS books. We don't present them!

FLETCHER: Ladies, could you take this to a private group chat?

BABS: Oh, Fletcher, don't be such a prude!

* * *

Unlike most people, I enjoy the rain. I like the way it sounds when it drums against the roof. I especially loved it when, growing up, I would retreat to one of the cottages that had skylights in it. When we were in high school, Penny and I used to grab sleeping bags and spend the night out there if there was a rainstorm. I felt like I was a flower on those nights, wild and free.

Which means that when I wake up and it's raining, I'm thrilled. It feels like a second chance. Like maybe my dad is washing away all the bad from the last week and giving me a fresh start.

Pulling on my rain jacket, I head outside and pad lightly down the path toward my car, hoping to not get my legs too wet, only to spot one of the metal canisters I'd placed on my mother's porch tipped over sideways with the flowers spilling out. The wind from the rainstorm must have knocked it over. I should clean up the mess before she has a chance to slip on it. I'm just setting it back in its place when the front door swings open.

"Tally!" my mother says in surprise.

I glance up from my crouched position and stand, swiping at my now wet knees. "Hi, Mom."

Her face breaks into a smile, and she leans against the door, holding it open. She's wearing a cozy sweater and a long skirt, and her glasses hang on a beaded chain around her neck. In this moment she looks so much like how she used to when Dad was still here: warm and excited to see me. I almost burst into tears.

"Are you the one who put them there? I would have said thank you, but I thought it was Walker."

I try not to let my face fall, even though her words sting.

"I wanted to brighten up your porch," I tell her.

"Well, I love them."

"Good."

I take a step closer. "I'm really sorry about uncovering the tulips."

My mom shakes her head. "You didn't know. As Walker pointed out, we probably should have talked to both you and Penny."

My eyes widen. I can't believe Walker actually said that. Or that she agrees. Before I can say anything else, though, my mother speaks again. "Where are you off to?"

"Oh, I'm heading into town to go grocery shopping." I nibble on my lip, trying to decide whether I should say the next words. "Can I ask you a question?"

"Of course."

"It feels like you maybe don't want me here. Like you'd rather have Billie and Walker than me and Penny."

My mother's entire expression morphs from one of concern to devastation. "Tally, never."

"Mom, be real with me. What's going on? Why did you hire Walker? Why have you been avoiding me?"

My mom opens her mouth and shuts it more times than I can count in just a few seconds. Then she shakes her head. "It's not an easy answer."

"Try anyway."

She lets out a long sigh. "It's not that I don't want you here. It's that I don't want you or your sister to feel obligated to be here. I *hired* Walker and Billie to help so that the two of you can have your own lives. Your father and I chased our dreams, and it's only fair that we let you do the same."

The pressure that had been sitting on my chest eases slightly. "We don't feel obligated, Mom. This is our farm. Our home."

My mother frowns. "But when we saw you at Christmas, you were so excited about your job in Nantucket this summer. What happened with that?"

"I'm still going," I promise her. "But I want to help you

guys with the Daffodil Festival and wedding season before I go. It's so much work. I somehow forgot how massive this place is."

My mother looks weary as she stares out at the place she once saw as magic. "It's not the same as it was, but yes, it takes a lot to maintain. Thank God we have Walker."

"Yes, thank God we have Walker," I mumble. My mother nudges me in the shoulder, and I giggle. "What? The man barely speaks."

"Yet yesterday you seemed to hang on his every word." She grins. "I was young once, too. He's a good-looking man."

I cough out a laugh. "*Mom.*"

"Oh, stop it. I'm widowed, not blind. And I'm not interested, despite whatever silly ideas you and your sister get in your heads." She eyes me like she knows all about the things I was accusing Walker of doing with my mother.

Red in the cheeks, I defend myself. "We're just looking out for you."

My mother reaches out to hug me, ignoring my wet jacket, and I rest my head against her chest. "Well, don't. I'm your mother. Let me watch out for you. Just know that I love you and want you to go after every dream you have."

I squeeze her tight, holding in the tears that threaten to spill over. I try not to focus on all the dreams I used to have and the man that will never get to see me achieve them. "I'm making dinner tonight at the house. Will you come? I even invited Walker."

My mother arches a brow. "You're not going to poison him, right?"

"*Mom.*" She chuckles, and I relax at this change in attitude from her. "I'm glad we talked."

She smiles. "Me, too. And I'll be there for dinner. Can I make anything?"

"Nope. It's my treat. My apology dinner." I waggle my brows. "Any special requests?"

"No, darling." My mother pulls me in for another hug. "And please know I'm happy you're here for the season, and to help us get the farm through the first spring without your daddy. Just promise me you won't stop chasing your own dreams. That's my only request."

—

Half an hour later, I'm dodging puddles as I make my way to the grocery store with the intention of finding all the ingredients for my mother's favorite, chicken Parmesan.

That ticks off something special for her and still meets Walker's request for Italian. I'm trying hard to keep my promise to her—and the one I made to myself in honor of my father. I will try to make these next two months work with Walker.

Last night—and maybe even this morning—I think we made progress. I know I have my work cut out for me to prove to them both that I want to help, that they can trust me to listen and do what they need, but I'm willing to do just that. I'm determined to make this work.

I grab a black cart from outside Tom's Market and head toward the front of the store. The brick building is on the same busy downtown street as my sister's bookstore and has limited parking.. Most of the food is farm to table from local families in the area, though, so it's worth the hefty price tag and difficulty of getting here.

There's a beautiful daffodil wreath hanging on the front door. I recognize it as one of the ones my family was selling at the farmers market. It's nice to see other businesses supporting the farm. It's also exciting that the town is starting to decorate for spring. It truly is my favorite season.

With that in mind, I think of something else that I enjoy. Teasing my new *friend*, Walker.

> **ME:** When you said 'cowboy stuff,' was that slang for playing with your stallion?

I snort as I imagine Walker's reaction to my text and push open the door. Inside, light music plays. I place my phone in the space on the cart meant for a drink and pull up my shopping list before heading to the vegetable aisle.

"Looks like someone is having a dinner party," a familiar voice says from over my shoulder.

I shift my body to face Eli, who is looking as handsome as ever and wearing his typical grin.

"Every night with me is a party," I tease.

He chuckles as he runs a hand down his chin. "I don't doubt that."

My phone buzzes in the cup, and my eyes drop to read the incoming text.

> **COWBOY:** what the hell are you talking about woman?

A loud laugh bursts out of me. God, I wish I could have seen his face when he wrote that.

"Who's 'Cowboy'?"

I eye Eli. "You reading my texts?"

"Just seeing who my competition is." He folds his arms across his chest. "Cowboy?"

I roll my eyes. As if the hot ex-NHL player is actually interested in me.

"It's Walker," I admit.

Eli's entire demeanor shifts and his shoulders straighten. "Wait, he gave you his number?"

Eyebrows raised, I tilt my head to study him. "You interested in him?"

"The man barely says two words. Been trying to get him to hang out with me and Fletch for months."

I pick up my phone. "Want his number?"

Eli looks like he just hit the lottery. "Hell yeah. Text it to me?"

Teasing, I hold the phone close to my chest. "You trying to get my number, too, Eli Davis?"

"I'm much smoother than that, Tally. You won't question it when I'm asking you out."

"Such a shameless flirt," I chuckle with a shake of my head as I hand him my phone, letting him input his number. Then I text him Walker's contact information.

"Pleasure doing business with you, Tally Darling," he says as he stores the number in his contacts.

—

By the time I get back to the farm, my body is soaked through from all the rain. I quickly put away the groceries and head up to Walker's room to take a long, hot shower before dinner.

I text him to let him know where I'll be when he gets home before I peel off my wet clothes and drop them in the laundry room. Fully undressed, I run up the stairs in only my bra and underwear and head straight into the bathroom.

After turning on the shower to let it heat, I open the bathroom door and peek into Walker's—*my*—room.

The other day when I was in here, I was searching for secrets. Today I look at everything in plain sight. I'm starting to think that's how Walker works. What you see is what you get.

I pick up the picture of his nephew beside his bed. He's wearing a Boston Bolts hat that's too big for his head, and he's staring up at the camera with what appears to be the remnants of an orange Popsicle dripping down his face. He's adorable. I set it back down and then stare at the bed. There are two pillows on it—no shams or decorative pillows at all—and a simple gray comforter that isn't familiar.

For some reason, I have this desperate urge to pick up one of the pillows and smell it. That would be weird, though.

Hell, standing in his bedroom nearly naked is weird enough.

Shaking my head, I stalk toward the shower. Once inside, I lather my body and wash my hair, but after a few minutes, I'm so overheated I have no choice but to open the bedroom door to let in some air. I grab my lotion and drop my towel on the floor. Then, without thinking, I rest my foot on the edge of the bed so I can lather my body.

Which is the precise moment the bedroom door opens and my favorite non-cowboy walks in.

Chapter 18
WALKER

UNKNOWN NUMBER: Hi Walker

UNKNOWN NUMBER: Hi Walker! This is Stew! Hope you're having a great day!

UNKNOWN NUMBER: Hi Walker! We have a town meeting tomorrow at 6. I hope you can make it. Oh, this is Fletcher Matthews. The mayor.

UNKNOWN NUMBER: Hi Walker, don't forget to stop by the brewery this Saturday. It's ladies' night!

UNKNOWN NUMBER: It's Rosie!

UNKNOWN NUMBER: Did you hear it's ladies' night on Saturday? Let's go to the bar.

UNKNOWN NUMBER: This is Eli by the way.

What the fuck? I growl and shove my phone back in my pocket. Why is everyone texting me? And how the fuck did they get my number? My phone buzzes again, but I ignore it. I'll be changing my number before I look at that thing again.

It's like it was sold to a telemarketer or something. Combine that with the absolutely asinine text I received from Tally this morning, and I've had one weird fucking day.

To top it all off, last night I discovered the secret behind that incredible scent that follows Tally everywhere she goes.

Wild Honeysuckle. Her perfume.

Also, white cypress. Her lotion.

Oh, and two blue bottles that smell like heaven and hell but have no words on them. Her shampoo and conditioner.

Sharing a bathroom with the woman is going to be a test of my endurance. Last night I won the battle and didn't touch them. Okay, I touched the shampoo just to see what it smelled like. Though I didn't use it.

My fucking cock was rock-hard, though, and I stared it down in the shower, refusing to jack off to the woman. Once I do that, I'm done for.

The thought of her being only a few feet away in her sister's room and my own body lying in a bed she once occupied—*her bed*—did nothing good for sleeping.

The only good thing to come of all of this is that, because I spent the day avoiding her, I got a ton of work done in the cottage I'm working on for my sister. Billie won't move into the big house—I know her well enough to realize that would be too much. But the small cottage at the back of the farm that overlooks the wildflower meadow would be perfect. Hardly anyone is ever back there—all the weddings take place near the tulips and daffodil beds, and Gail's cottage is farther up the path, at least an acre away, so they wouldn't be on top of each other. The cottage for my sister has two bedrooms, a small kitchen that looks out onto the meadow, and even a space for a swing on the porch—something Billie has always wanted.

In total, the farm has thirteen cottages. Seven by the daffodils, four by the tulips, and two by the wildflowers. Though the ones by the daffodils and tulips are best suited for my business plan, the ones that overlook the wildflower meadow have the best views of both the mountains on one side and the harbor and downtown on the other. I want my sister to have that view. She deserves the solace.

There's still a ton of work left to do before I can focus fully on the cottages, though. The chairs for the weddings need to be dusted, and I should also check on the refrigeration system in the makeshift kitchen Peter set up for caterers to use during weddings.

That reminds me: I need to get stain for the dance floor.

Roughing a hand through my hair, I try to figure out which project I should start on first and what—if any—I can ask Tally to help with.

But what does she even know *how* to do? I know what Billie would say. I can practically hear her chiding tone: "*Ask her what she can do. Find out what she does when she travels. Talk to her.*"

A growl works up my throat. I don't want to talk to Tally. I don't want to know anything else about her. Because the more I learn, the more I like. The more I like, the more obsessed I become. I don't have time to be interested. Don't have time to be drawn into her wicked spell. I've spent five years uninterested in the opposite sex unless it was for a quick lay. A few hours of getting lost in someone. And even those encounters I can count one hand since Gina left me.

My stomach rumbles, reminding me that I haven't eaten anything today. With all the rain, it was easier to stay inside and work through lunch. Now I'm paying for that because I have no idea what time Tally plans on making dinner, and I don't want to have a snack and ruin my appetite if it's anytime soon.

Truth be told, if not for Tally, I'd probably skip half of my meals. Growing up, I got used to not eating, conserving whatever food we did have so my sister wouldn't go hungry. Even after we'd moved out, we didn't have much. I went to bed hungry more often than not.

Giving Tally the credit card to buy food last night had been a strange thing. It's not really mine, since it's linked to the farm's operating account. But seeing as we only have debt, I suppose I'll be the one paying for it all. If it was up to me, I'd subsist on cereal and peanut butter and jelly. Though I can't do that while I'm living with Tally and it feels odd that, after just one meal from her, I'm already starving, when for so long I was used to that hungry feeling.

I could text the woman to ask what time dinner will be since she gave me her number, but I have no intention of looking at that phone again tonight.

I'm too caught up in my own thoughts and don't notice the light beneath the door, or the humming that's coming from behind it, until I've pushed it open. It soon becomes apparent that my room is not empty.

Miles of smooth, silky skin that I'll be dreaming of for the rest of my days stretches before me. As if I have no control over my damn self, my eyes trail up Tally's leg to follow her hand as she rubs lotion up her thigh. But then, unlike her palm, my eyes don't dart back down to her ankles. Instead, my gaze keeps going up, to the curve of her hip, the rounded angle of her ass, past her stomach, and up to the most perfect set of tits I've ever seen. To pink, hard nipples that leave my mouth watering. Completely slack-jawed, I don't make a sound. I just continue to watch until Tally's amber eyes lock with mine and she starts screaming.

"Ah hell, woman, you're giving me a headache," I say as I spin around and cover my eyes. Though I'll never unsee that flawless image. Every inch of Tally's perfection is seared into the wrinkles of my brain. I will be dreaming day and night about that woman for a long fucking time.

Fuck. Me.

"Didn't you get my text?!" she yells.

"Obviously not, since I just walked in here." I glance over my shoulder. "Unless it was an invitation to come in. In which case, I still didn't see it and wouldn't have come in if I had."

"Right. Because it's so awful to see this." Tally snorts as she walks over to me and flourishes a hand up and down her body as I choke on my own tongue. I expected the woman to be in a towel. But no, she's naked as the day she was born. And fuck, does she look good.

I snap my eyes to above her chin, knowing that if I spend even a millisecond looking down, I'll get lost in the space between her thighs. One thing is for certain: I don't need to know what Tally's pussy looks like.

Liquid pools in my cheeks and I swallow. "Could you get a towel or something?"

Tally swings the door open, and her hips sway as she tosses a wink over her shoulder, sashaying out of my room with zero shame. "Or something," she calls out.

I slam the door shut and glare at the space she occupied only seconds ago. When she was so close I could have tasted the sweet scent of her skin. Had I taken one step closer, her tits would have brushed against my chest. Would she have liked that? Is that why she was here?

I groan as I dig my knuckles into my eyes before pulling off my sweatshirt and undoing my belt, pushing my pants down in an angry thrust. I stalk past my bed and picture her toes up on my comforter while she lathered her skin. The lotion is still there, cap up, fucking taunting me. *No*, I growl to myself. Not happening.

Unable to help myself, I reach for the bottle and bring it up to my nose, breathing in her intoxicating scent. "Tally Darling, what kind of game are you playing?"

As I head into the bathroom, I'm not proud of the grunt that slips from my throat when I see her panties right beside the shower.

Yellow. That color fucking haunts me. I know how perfect it looks against her pale skin. How beautiful she must have looked in these. How they rested against her mouthwatering cunt.

I will not pick them up.

I will not jack off to her.

I will—

Fuck.

I glare down at my cock, which stands at attention. I've never wanted a woman the way I want Tally Darling. This is a disaster.

She's too young. Too much of a pain in the ass. Too off-fucking-limits.

She drives me fucking crazy and doesn't listen to a damn thing I say.

And she felt so damn good when I wrapped her in my arms the other night.

My breath comes out tortured as I bend down to grab her damp panties, gripping them in my fist. With my other hand I reach in and turn on the shower. It's damp and warm already from Tally, who was just in here. Naked.

A strangled whimper comes from my throat as I lose all fucking dignity and pull her panties up to my nose and inhale.

My other hand grips my cock and I squeeze. Once. Just fucking once. That's all this will ever be. One time. To get her out of my system. Come all over this damn shower like a dog claiming his favorite tree. And then I'll put her out of my mind.

I step beneath the hot water, panties still in hand, and throw my head back as I start to jack myself.

With every stroke, I picture Tally.

Her tits. Her pussy. Those damn lips that have me half smiling before she even says a word. Her smart mouth that I want to fuck. Lick. Kiss.

Shit. *No.* This is about sex. About getting off. I jam my palm, the one holding her panties, against the wall. They grow wetter, and I focus on that. On the color they'd be if she was still wearing them. Wet with her desire for me.

I roll my finger over my tip and then thrust into my hand, faster still.

Then it's her eyes I see. An amber sun. The color of a spring meadow.

And with the thought of those warm, beautiful eyes of hers staring up at me, I come all over the goddamn wall.

—

I walk into the kitchen to find Tally in front of the stove, flipping breaded chicken in a frying pan. She's in another pair of spandex. Tonight's are a deep green, and the crop top she wears is black, exposing her smooth skin, which I know smells as good as it looks.

"Did you have a good shower?" she coos, a flirty lilt to her tone.

When I don't reply, she looks over her shoulder, catching me staring at her tantalizing curves. "Stop growling with your eyes."

"How does one growl with their eyes?" I ask, even though I know precisely what she's saying. I'm like a hungry bear, desperate for a taste of her.

The shower did nothing to satiate me.

She ignores my question and grabs a spoon to stir the tomato sauce that is simmering beside the frying pan. My stomach rumbles again as I realize she's making me something Italian. Why do I like that she went to the store and thought of me? Why do I like that she's preparing a meal *for* me?

It feels personal. Like a da—

"My mom and sister are coming for dinner." She cuts off my train of thought, dashing my excitement in the process. "I texted to tell you, but apparently you don't read them, so now here I am"—she glances at me over her shoulder again—"*telling you.*"

I grunt as I reach into my pocket, pull out my phone, and ignore the ten new texts from random numbers to pull up our chat.

TALLY: Chicken parm work?

TALLY: Well since you didn't reply that's what we're having.

TALLY: My mom and sister are joining us for dinner. I hope that's okay.

TALLY: K cool. Good talk.

TALLY: If you're done playing with your stallion, go find some other cowboy things to do. I'm doing cowboy things in the bedroom.

"My stallion?" I shake my head. "What the fuck Tally? This is not how you tell someone that you'll be naked in their bedroom."

She smirks. "*My* bedroom."

"That I'm staying in. Listen, if you want your room back—"

She rolls her eyes. "Don't go being all chivalrous now." She stirs the sauce and rests the wooden spoon on top of the pot. "I'm fine in Penny's room. No sense in having you move out for the short time I'll be here."

That is precisely the reminder I need. That she's leaving.

I walk toward the fridge to grab a beer. "Want one?"

She shakes her head. "I'll open a bottle of wine."

"I'll do it." The wine is in the dining room so I grab glasses, the bottle, and an opener and set them all on the table, which Tally has already set. I pour one glass and bring it back to the kitchen, red wine sloshing as I hand it to her. "Thank you for making dinner."

Her eyes warm like honey as she lights up, taking the

glass from me and bringing it to her lips before letting out a low, appreciative moan. The entire scene in front of me—her eyes, the little sounds she makes, her floral scent—has my dick stirring in remembrance of what I saw only a half hour earlier.

"So since you're bad with the phone and I obviously will still need to shower in your room"—those peach lips of hers lift in a mischievous smirk—"should we come up with another system? You know, so you don't get a free peep show daily. Perhaps a sock on the door means I'm naked?"

I desperately suck in air to try to keep myself from reaching for her, grabbing those generous hips, and squeezing her against me.

"A sock means you're hooking up. There will be no hooking up in my room, Tally." I say it as much for her as I do for me. I will not fuck this girl. Peter Darling's little girl.

My eyes fall shut because she doesn't look like a little girl and Peter Darling is nowhere in sight. How old is she? She's got to be at least twenty-one. Ugh, why am I thinking about this? I'm thirty-four, and she's my employee. My boss's daughter. Sort of. Gail isn't really my boss, and Peter is—fuck. Whatever. She's off-limits.

When I open my eyes again, I'm reminded that Tally is all woman. My gaze is instantly drawn to her pert nipples poking against the black fabric of her shirt. Please tell me the woman is wearing a bra. Her family is coming over. She must be.

I blink. She definitely isn't.

Tally smiles. She definitely caught me staring at her tits.

"Obviously, there will be no hooking up in your room." She turns away from me and disappears toward the fridge.

Like a damn puppy, my eyes trail her every move. Opening the fridge, pulling out a head of lettuce. Walking toward the counter. Pulling out a knife. Unwrapping the head of lettuce. Washing the head of lettuce. "Unless I'm with Phil."

"Who the fuck is Phil?" I growl, my focus on her actions all but lost as I glower at her.

Her shoulders shake as she slices into the head of lettuce, then she peeks over at me, a sly grin on her lips. "My shower dildo."

"You have a shower dildo?"

Her eyes widen and she shakes her head, a huge smile on her face before turning back to the lettuce. "No. But you should see your face. Are you picturing me in your shower fucking my shower dildo?"

Yes.

"No," I say aloud. "Why are you like this? And stop saying 'shower dildo.'"

Her melodic laughter fills the kitchen as the front door swings open and her mother calls out a hello. I rush out of the kitchen, knowing I need five minutes alone or else I'm going to be facing Tally's mom with a raging boner.

Chapter 19
TALLY

My eyes cut to the spot at the table where my father used to sit—it's empty tonight because I set the table and couldn't bear to put anyone there. If my family or Walker has noticed, they've said nothing. It's a six-person table so I just put us in the four chairs in the middle. With the bowl of pasta in my hand, I note that my mother and sister have left the spot next to Walker empty. Shoot.

Not that I can't be an adult and sit next to him during dinner. It's just . . . I know my entire body will buzz from his proximity. And I'll be itching to turn and look at him all night—and wondering if he's trying to avoid doing the same.

He's attracted to me. He's terrible at masking it—I caught him staring at my ass or my chest five times in the last twenty minutes alone—which is ironic since I can't read any of his expressions outside of that.

"This looks delicious," my mother says when I drop the dish in the center of the table. "Thank you, Tally."

"Yeah, I haven't had your chicken Parm in so long." Penny hums as her eyes lift to me and then twitch toward Walker. "Special occasion?"

"My roommate requested it," I say. "And I'm nothing if not accommodating. Right, Walker?"

He only grunts in response.

The entire tone of the dinner—which I thought would be focused on my apology, the farm, and how to fix the great deflowering—is different from what I expected. Instead, it feels lighter. Something I think everyone at this table needs.

"Glad the two of you are settling in so well together," my mother comments as she plates her own food before passing the platter to my sister.

"Yeah. How has it been, sharing a house?" Penny chimes in. "Word to the wise Walker, my sister is a shower hog. If you want any hot water, make sure you shower before her."

"Oh, we haven't had any shower incidents yet." I turn my entire body and bat my lashes innocently at Walker, who stays totally focused on his food.

"Yup. No shower issues." The words are staccato. Quick. Like he needs to never say the word *shower* again.

The itch to push him sits at the top of my chest, and I can't help but scratch at it. It's clear this isn't some silly little one-sided crush on the hot older man I'm living with—it's a forbidden thing that I can taunt him with. So with that in mind, I reach my hand across him to where the Parmesan cheese is, lean in, and stretch my body in a way that has my chest brushing right against his shoulder. "I wouldn't say *no* shower issues. I mean you did walk in on me naked."

"Tally!" My mother's mouth falls open, my sister squeaks, and Walker curses under his breath, his head falling downward in defeat.

"It was an accident." I plow on, despite everyone's discomfort. "We've figured out a system, though. We're going to hang a sock on the door if either one of us is *using* the shower."

"We're not using a goddamn sock," Walker growls, finally

looking at me. The pained expression on his face has me ready to burst.

My sister snorts and I bite back a smile as my mother huffs. "Why can't you just tell the man when you're using his shower, Tally?"

I shrug innocently. "I tried, but he doesn't read his texts."

Walker's fork clatters onto his plate as he hangs his head in his hands. "Because there are so many of them."

"Tally sure can text," Penny agrees. I love my sister. She's just as good at this game of teasing Walker as I am. My mother shakes her head at both of us. We used to do this all the time to our poor father, who would get all befuddled at our teasing. It was the fast talking. And the fact that we never did secrets in our family. All of us were open books, and my dad had to deal with three women who never shut up. I glance at his chair and smile. He'd be doing the same thing as Walker right now.

"Can we talk about *anything* else?" Walker begs.

My mother smiles. "Of course we can. Penny dear, will you be able to take pictures of the first few weddings for the social media page?"

"Oh!" I cheer. "Will Walker be wearing his cowboy hat again?"

"Jesus Christ," he groans.

My mom shrugs. "If he wants to. Though he does look so nice with his hair done. Doesn't he, girls?" My mom gazes at Walker with a look of appreciation, and Penny and I grin at one another knowingly.

"I don't know," my sister says, dragging out the last word. "Kind of looks like he's been running his fingers through it."

"Or like he's been thoroughly fu—"

"Tallulah Darling," my mother warns before I can finish.

I smirk. "Definitely should wear the cowboy hat."

He sighs and takes another bite of food, the annoyance flushing from his cheeks as he savors his meal. It's what I love so much about cooking, and even more so with baking. Watching someone find enjoyment in a dessert that I made is a high I'll never be able to replicate with flowers or weddings.

"Is there anything I can do to help with the weddings?" I ask my mother, focusing on the real reason I'm here.

My mom twirls her fork in her pasta, deep in thought. "Billie and I will have the bride and the wedding party handled. If Penny's handling social media, I guess that would leave you with Walker. Whatever he needs for setup and cleanup." She glances across the table at me. "Can you handle that?"

I remind myself that my mother doesn't mean to sound like she's doubting me, or like she doesn't want me here, but I can't help the way it hits. "Won't be a problem. What about before the weddings, though? There's got to be stuff to get ready on the farm. Catering—"

"Has been handled," she says quickly, cutting me off. Her focus shifts to my father's chair. "Just do whatever Walker asks of you. *Please.* Everything that your father handled, Walker took over. He knows what needs to be done." She sighs as she looks away from Daddy's chair. My sister grabs her hand and squeezes.

I have to ball my own hands into fists to keep still. I'm a doer. Words of comfort were never my strong suit.

"You can count on me," I promise.

Four loud buzzes interrupt the moment, and I almost sigh in relief as I turn to face Walker. "You going to get that?"

His eye twitches. I think he wants to say no, but he seems just as uncomfortable with emotions as I am so he digs out his phone from his pocket, welcoming the interruption. Then he sighs heavily, breaking the tension in the room. "I don't even know who it is."

He holds up the phone. There are a bunch of texts from unknown numbers, and they all say the same thing: *Hi Walker.*

I snort.

"Oh, that looks like Rayna's number," my mother offers.

"You gave Rayna McGovern your phone number?" Penny's voice comes out confused. "I don't even have your number."

"Oh, you want me to text it to you?" I offer.

Walker barks. "Is that what you've been doing all day?"

"No. I only gave it to Eli."

Penny coughs out a laugh as Walker's phone buzzes again with another *Hi Walker.* "And it seems he gave it out to everyone in town."

Walker massages his forehead as I try to hide my giggle. "I guess the town really is in cahoots."

Another vibration has Walker squeezing his eyes shut. "Jesus, some woman just sent me a picture of her cleavage."

The smile on my face evaporates as an odd sensation twists in my gut. "Excuse me. Who the hell would—" I grab the phone, but when I see what's on the screen, that weird, uncomfortable emotion that I have no intention of identifying dissolves. "Oh, that's Mrs. Simmons."

My mom reaches across the table as I pass her the phone. She nods as she shows it to my sister. "Yup. Damn Ruby. I don't think Mr. Simmons will be happy you asked her for nudes."

Walker erupts. "I don't even know who that is! I didn't ask for this."

"I expected better of you, Walker. She's a Liberty Lady. She walks on our property every day. How is she going to feel, knowing that you looked at that?"

Walker pushes back his chair. "I didn't ask for it, Gail. Jesus." He shakes his head when Penny tries to hand him back his phone. "How do you even know it's her?"

I pluck it from my sister's hand and smile. "She always had that weird mole in the shape of South Dakota right here." I point at my own chest. "And since that's where my head reaches on her body because she's so dang tall, it's hard to miss."

Walker is looking at us like we're out of our minds. Poor guy. We're torturing him.

"Yeah, we told her to get it checked out," Penny tells him. "It's just a birthmark, though, not cancerous."

My mother nods. "We all went and got our moles checked out after that. Made it an annual thing. We even go to the spa the day before so we can study each other's bodies to make sure we know exactly what to show the doctor. Ruby's South Dakota has nothing on Babs's Texas on the underside of her breast."

"Don't forget Rayna's Mexico on her ass," Penny teases. "That one has hair."

Poor Walker shivers at the image.

"She's harmless." I tell him. "You should tell her she looks great, don't want her to get a complex."

Walker glares at me. "Do not text that woman back. I promise it's not harmless."

Smiling, I stand and reach over Walker's shoulder to grab his plate, whispering in his ear so only he can hear, "Well, at least you won't be thinking about my boobs then, right?" When I walk out of the room, I can feel Walker's intense gaze on my ass again. I pause in the doorway, catching him with a wink. "Anyone want pie?"

Chapter 20
WALKER

UNKNOWN NUMBER: Did you hear that Walker asked Mrs. Simmons to send him pictures?

UNKNOWN NUMBER: That doesn't sound like Walker.

UNKNOWN NUMBER: I don't know. He's a good looking man and he's all alone in that big house.

UNKNOWN NUMBER: That's not true, Tallulah Darling is back. Remember? Bet you by the end of the Daffodil Festival they're a couple!

* * *

My head is pounding from the lashing I just took at dinner. The chicken Parmesan was good, and the pie was incredible, but I don't think anything is worth what I just went through. Okay, that's an exaggeration. I'd probably sit through another round just for the crust on that pie. Tally is fucking incredible in the kitchen.

Still, this day has been a lot and I am in need of some fresh air so I can stop sniffing every corner of this house in my search of her and her intoxicating scent. I'm just heading for the front door when Tally appears at the top of the second-floor steps.

"Hey!" she calls to me before I make it.

I nod in her direction but can't seem to find the words for a reply when I catch a glimpse of her. Her hair is piled up on her head, a few tendrils have escaped to frame her face, and her lips shine with a gloss. She's also changed into a white frilly dress with all sorts of buttons that start at her breasts and run down to her mid-thigh, where it's just *open* despite the fabric continuing down to her ankles.

Is she going on a date? Something heavy settles in my stomach at the thought.

"Heading into town?" she asks before following me through the front the door and out onto the porch. The tree frogs sing through the spring night, and I take a deep breath, tasting the dew in the air right before taking in the deep violet of the night sky.

I shake my head. "Just going for a walk."

"Oh, can I borrow your truck then?" She holds out her hand, signaling that she's waiting for the keys.

My head whips over my shoulder as I search the driveway. "Where's that tiny car you showed up in?"

"It was a rental."

"Okay?"

"So I need to borrow your car."

"No."

She folds her arms across her chest and narrows her eyes. "Fine. I'll walk. Goodbye."

Before she can push past me in her temper tantrum, I grab her elbow. "Where are you going?"

"To my sister's bookstore. It's book club night."

I sigh. "You aren't walking."

She tilts her head. "Well, I don't have a car, and you won't let me borrow yours."

I take the steps two at a time and head toward my truck. "I'll drive you."

I hold open the passenger door, waiting for her to take her sweet time sauntering in my direction. When she finally reaches me, she flashes me a huge smile before setting a pink cowboy boot on the step to climb into my truck. "If you wanted to spend time with me, Cowboy, all you had to do was ask."

"Jesus," I mutter before slamming the door and rounding the truck, reminding myself the entire time that I can handle this. I can be in a truck with her. I can ignore her scent and her commentary and her damn smile that drives me to distraction. But the second I get in, my eyes cut to her bare thigh, which is exposed because of how she's folded one leg over the other, allowing her spring dress to fall open.

Whipping my head forward, I turn on the truck and immediately lower the windows. Less chance of that floral scent suffocating me.

Tally's phone lights up in her lap, and she answers without a hello. "I'm coming."

"What's taking you so long?" A voice cuts through. "The ladies are getting antsy to discuss alien dick."

I practically slam on the brakes before we've even made it ten feet from the house. Tally grabs the handle above her head, and she rolls her eyes. "She's joking. Calm down."

"I'm not." Penny's voice continues before dropping down to a whisper. "You should hear them. Blue alien dick with three heads. They're saying they could all just share one. Help me."

My stomach rolls.

"Sorry, Walker wasn't ready to say goodbye yet so he's driving me. He's very needy," Tally explains.

I glare at her and gas it out of the driveway.

"Aw, I'm glad you're getting along," Penny sings.

"Something like that," Tally says with a smile. "I'll see you in five."

She's barely hung up the phone when she starts giggling.

"What are you laughing at?"

Tally turns her entire body, leaning her back up against the door, and studies me. "Have you checked your phone in a while?"

I watch the way the moon makes her eyes sparkle. "What?"

"Your phone? Here, let me." She reaches across the center console and pats my hip.

"What are you doing?" I grit out even as my dick throbs in my jeans. Her hand is too close, and my body doesn't understand that she's off-limits.

"Looking for your phone," she replies as she continues to stroke my side.

I'm thrilled when I spot her sister's bookstore and find a parking spot right in front. I pull in and park as Tally gives up her search. Then, hands on the steering wheel, I keep my focus forward. "Have a good night."

"Hey, about what my mom said tonight." The way Tally's tone has changed from her normal teasing to something more serious, or maybe even nervous, has me pulling my attention to face her.

She sucks her bottom lip between her teeth before rolling it out of her mouth. My eyes flare. Hers almost seem to droop. "Is that going to be okay? Me helping you? I know you don't trust me, but I'll do whatever you tell me. I want this to work." She reaches across the truck like she's going to put her hand on my thigh, and instinct has me jolting back. She mimics the movement, practically hitting the door, and squeezes her fists.

"Tally, I—" Words fail me. I want to say I'm sorry. That yes, I can make this work. But I don't trust myself right now, for a multitude of reasons. Most importantly, the secrets I'm currently keeping because her mom asked me to and the dire state of the farm. Also because her dad warned me to stay away. After all Gail and Peter have given me, I'm not going to be selfish just to make myself feel good for a night. I need to be stronger than that.

Tally lets out a heavy sigh. "Whatever, it's fine. I'll just stay out of your way. Thanks for the ride." Her phone buzzes again and she lets out a hiss of air when she sees the screen.

My heart rate ticks up. "What?"

She rolls her eyes. "Just Eli being Eli."

"What does that mean?"

She points to my phone, which won't stop buzzing.

"What is this, and how do I make it stop?" I ask.

Tally snorts, and the tension from just moments before eases. She hands me her phone and, unlike mine, hers has names that go along with all the messages.

PENNY: Did you hear that Walker asked Mrs. Simmons to send him pictures?

FLETCHER: That doesn't sound like Walker.

BABS: I don't know. He's a good looking man and he's all alone in that big house.

RAYNA: That's not true, Tallulah Darling is back. Remember? Bet you by the end of the Daffodil Festival they're a couple!

ELI: Walker isn't the only man in this town. Maybe she'll end up with me.

ROSIE: Well, things just got INTERESTING.

STEW: Maybe if you played for Boston you'd have a shot, but a New York team? No way.

ELI: I DIDN'T CHOOSE NEW YORK THEY CHOSE ME!

RAYNA: Don't use all caps in this chat young man. Use your manners!

ELI: Sorry Mrs. McGovern.

BABS: They just pulled up to the bookstore and they're sitting in the car staring at one another.

My head whips up and I spot a group of Hope Harbor residents with their noses pressed against the window, watching us. "Ah hell."

Tally's lips puff out with a laugh. "I'll see you back at the house."

I shake my head right as another message pops up.

ELI: What are you all doing at the bookstore? I want to come.

My head falls back against my seat as I watch Tally disappear inside. Everyone else leaves the window except Penny, who stands to watch me for another moment. Then she shakes her head and turns the shop door sign to CLOSED before disappearing as well.

I drum my fingers against the steering wheel for one, two, three—ah, dammit. I stuff my phone in my pocket and turn off the engine. Then somehow I find myself getting out of my truck and walking toward the door.

Just in case Eli really does show up.

Chapter 21
TALLY

Frazzled from my interaction with Walker, I enter the bookstore in a daze. For once, I wish he was just *real* with me.

Because the way he looked at me when I came down the stairs tonight, like his heart was pounding just as wildly as my own, like he saw me and wanted me for more than just this physical attraction, had a fissure of hope slicing through my chest. But it only lasted the briefest of moments before he shut down and shut me out. Again.

I don't blame him, really. Why would Walker be interested in anything with me? I'm a child compared to him. And I've acted like nothing but a child—screwing up repeatedly, acting out when I didn't get my way, taunting him, teasing him. God, it's like I've lost my damn mind since I came back to this town.

I keep saying I'm going to change, that I'm going to do better, and then I go and do something stupid like try to touch the man.

I sigh as my eyes trail to the table where the Liberty Ladies are all grabbing snacks. It seems that everyone brought something for this little shindig; platters of cheese and fancy meats, sweet treats and desserts. A punch bowl is filled with a suspicious blue liquid. I'm just about to find out precisely what it is when Babs slams down an oversized blue rubber dildo with three heads beside the punch bowl with a loud *thwack*.

"What the hell?" Penny hisses.

Babs grins. "I told you I had one, just like in the book."

"Please tell me that's brand new," Rayna says, covering her mouth.

"Can I touch it?" Mindy asks.

Ruby licks her lips. "Where do I get one of those?"

"Amazon," Babs says proudly. "You can get anything on there."

"This is book club?" I whisper to my sister, my eyes unable to look away from the dildo still shaking wildly. "And does that have a suction cup on the bottom of it?"

"Yes, so you can use it in the shower," Babs explains loudly.

My mind goes to Walker again. Great, I'd made it a whole two minutes without thinking about him. Shaking my head, I nod toward the punch. "Is that safe to drink? Or is it somehow related to that other thing?"

Babs's face scrunches. "If you're making a joke about alien cum, that's disgusting."

My mother—who rode over here early with Penny—covers her mouth in a bid to hide her laughter. The rest of the women look at me and shake their heads like I'm the inappropriate one. "No, I wasn't even thinking that. Though now I am."

Rayna tsks. "This is very inappropriate talk, Tally. You're in the presence of the Ladies of Liberty, remember."

Penny snorts beside me as I start to apologize. I steer clear of the blue drink, though, because I can't get the thought of alien cum out of my head. Every time someone gets near the table to fill their plate with food, the suctioned dildo heads dance and one bobs so low it touches the drink.

The blue liquid drips onto the table cloth. "I'm going to be sick," I mutter to Penny.

She shakes her head. "I'll grab us wine."

I'm not sure that will help, but when she returns from behind the checkout counter with two mugs and a bottle of red wine, I take the one she offers and wait for her to fill it to the brim.

"Oh, Penny, did you hear Stew's getting a divorce?" Rayna says.

"I thought his wife died," Babs interjects.

"Who's Stew again?" I ask.

All the woman grow silent as they stare at me. "The mailman, Tally. Really. You've been gone so long you forgot the man who used to deliver you those dirty magazines when you were a teenager."

"*Cosmopolitan*?"

"They always had sex tips on the covers," Rayna says, like she'snot standing next to a three-headed dildo and about to discuss alien dick.

"Wait, wasn't the mailman like forty back when we were kids?"

My mom nods, and Penny stage-whispers, "*Don't engage with them.*" Then to the group, she replies, "Yes. And his wife didn't die. He just said he wished she would."

"So you have talked to him about dating!" Babs claps her hands in excitement.

"No!" Penny huffs. "He talks to whoever will listen. He's in his fifties, and I'm not dating."

"Okay, fine. I guess he's too old for you," Mindy agrees. "But what about Eli?"

"The same Eli who just hit on my sister in a group chat with half the town? Thanks, but no thanks. There's someone

perfect out there for me, I know that. But he's not out *there*"—
she motions to the window outside—"in Hope Harbor. So
stop trying to set me up. I'm all set with my book boyfriends
for the time being."

I mouth a "Sorry," and she shakes her head before pouring more red wine into her glass.

"I mean the book boyfriends do have three dicks, so . . ."
Babs says with a shrug as she stares longingly at the dildo,
shimmying like a wind chime on the table.

At that moment, Rosie rushes in from the back. "Sorry
I'm late." When she sees me her face breaks into a big grin.
"Yay, you made it!"

Just as she goes to grab a seat, the front door swings open
with a loud jangle and a breeze blows in, followed by a grumpy-
looking Walker and a smiling Eli.

"What are the two of you doing here?" Penny exclaims.

The men eye each other and then Eli shrugs and throws a
thumb in Walker's direction. "*He* was standing outside. I was
just walking by and thought I'd come browse."

"The sign says closed," Rosie teases.

"But you're all here," he points out.

I glance at Walker, who still hasn't said anything.

"Well, you're in luck," Babs cuts across. "I've got an extra
copy of *The Alien Baby Daddy*." She waves a copy of a book
with a blue monster standing over a pregnant woman on the
cover. *Strange.* Babs sees my shudder and points a finger at
me. "You'll be eating it up when you find out how many heads
he has."

"Ah, hell," Walker mutters.

"What kind of heads?" Eli asks, reaching for the book.

Babs drops her gaze down Eli's body. "Ya know."

Eli's hand snaps to the front of his pants as his voice hits the highest note. "Mrs. Wilcox!"

"You asked!"

"Okay, let's be serious ladies. It's time to start," Rayna commands.

I glance at Walker, whose face is scrunched up in a painful scowl.

"You can go, you know," I offer.

He shakes his head and grabs a chair near the door. "I'll just be right here. You don't have a ride home."

"I can take her." Eli winks in my direction as he settles in the seat next to me. "I'm sticking around to learn all about the—" He hesitates. "Alien heads."

"I'm going to the same house because *we live together*," Walker retorts, annunciating the words in a possessive way that has my stomach doing a little flip. Then he sits down, tips his head forward like the conversation is over, and stares at Rayna.

"Alrighty then," she claps. "Now, tell me ladies, how did you feel when he first took out his three penises?"

Chapter 22
WALKER

I've come to the conclusion that, when it comes to Tally Darling, I'm screwed. She is everywhere. In my shower. In my fields. In my goddamn dreams.

It's pointless to fight these feelings, so I have to embrace them.

That's why I walked into Penny's bookstore tonight. That and because I can't let Eli hit on her. Seeing him interested in her bothered me. *Bothers me.* Even now, as he says something that makes her laugh while I wait by the door to take her home.

All night I've watched her, a small smile curling her lips every time the damn alien dildo thing swayed. And then her loud laugh when it toppled over into the damn punch had me fucking grinning from ear to ear. Despite the fact that Babs pulled it out and then licked each head clean while staring down Eli and me. My whole body shudders again at the thought. I need to get out of here.

"Walker, are you ever going to reply to my text?" Rayna says, interrupting my attempt to overhear what the hell Eli is saying to make Tally smile.

I grunt as I turn to her. "No idea what you're talking about."

She pulls out her phone and pulls up the town chat that Tally showed me earlier. "Really, Walker, you're going to pretend you haven't seen any of these?"

"How did anyone even get my number?" The words slip out and she grins, knowing she has me.

Rosie snorts. "That'd be Eli."

The man finally stops talking to give us his full attention. "I only gave it to Rayna while we were having lunch at the brewery. It's not my fault that everyone else was listening when I gave it to her."

"Over the microphone," Rosie interrupts with a grin. "They all could hear because he gave it to her over the microphone," she full explains, turning toward me.

Tally coughs out a laugh as I groan. "Can we go now?"

"Sure," she says, before turning back to the group. "Thanks for tonight, ladies. I had the best time."

As annoyed as I am about the phone number thing, seeing Tally smile has my lip itching to do the same. She seems much more at ease with her mother, and in general, since she arrived last week.. I'm not sure why I care so much, but I like that she's becoming more comfortable in Hope Harbor.

The entire ride home I focus on the road ahead as Tally laughs with her mother over Eli's antics. Thank fuck Gail came back with us. If I'd been alone with Tally in the enclosed space of my truck, there's no telling what I might have done. Probably pulled over near the harbor and kissed her right beneath the crescent moon.

I shake my head and swipe a hand over my face, trying to clear these wistful thoughts from my mind as I pull the truck down the path near Gail's cottage.

I haven't had these types of thoughts in a long-ass time. When you suffer heartbreak after heartbreak, it's easy to close off that part of your life. To stop dreaming. Hoping.

But Tally seems to be awakening a piece of me I thought Gina had buried years ago.

I'm on edge as I park outside the big house. It's just the two of us now and I pause, not moving.

"Going inside?" Tally's voice is raspy from laughing all night.

I swallow as I stare at her across the cab. She's fucking gorgeous right now—her cheeks rosy, her eyes a little glassy from the wine. When the wind blows her golden hair in my direction, I catch another whiff of her sweet scent, and my cock awakens in my jeans.

Still, I don't move and she goes to fill the silence. "Thanks for the ride."

I nod, and the tension within the truck feels as though it becomes a living, breathing thing.

"Cowboy?"

"Hmm?"

"Keep staring at me like that, and a girl's bound to get ideas."

"Well, you shouldn't."

Her smile is rueful as her eyes dip down and she spots what we both know is my erection. It's unmistakable, but still, I ignore it.

"If you say so." Tally reaches for the door, but fuck, I don't want her to go.

"What are you doing tomorrow?"

She glances back at me, her shoulder lifted in a shrug. "What do you need?"

You. I don't say that, though. "I found some old Adirondack chairs that could use some sanding."

She lights up. "Oh, out by the wildflowers would be a great spot for them. People could sit out there during the festival, listen to the music, stare at the water."

"That's a good idea."

She bites down on her lip like she's trying to hide how happy my praise makes her. It makes my chest swell.

"Then that's what we'll do. Night, Walker," she mumbles, finally pushing the door open.

I take my time getting out of the truck and watch as she walks up the steps toward the big house. I know if I don't stay here, my boots digging into the earth, I'll follow her inside, push her against the door, and kiss the life out of her.

So I decide to go for a walk instead. Check on the flowers.

I'm laughing at the absurdity of this situation when Tally's sweet voice breaks through the evening air. "Hey, Walker? Will you be around for dinner tomorrow?"

Tongue in my cheek, I nod. "Yeah. I'm around."

"Okay, good. Make sure you're here at, say, seven?"

I tug the brim of my hat down on my head to hide my smile. "Okay."

The moment I turn toward the cottages, my lips curl completely and I feel an immense excitement that I know is nowhere close to innocent. I walk for what feels like hours through the fields, trying to remind myself why I can't go near her. Why I need to stay outside, far away from the gorgeous woman who lies only a room away from me. But when I finally go inside, I'm drawn up the steps by a sound I'll never forget.

"Yes," Tally's voice hums from inside her room. It's quiet and breathy, and I know why.

I should go inside my bedroom and lock the door. I should take a cold shower and forget what she's doing.

But I don't. Instead, I settle my head against her door and listen to her every whimper.

My cock grows impossibly hard, beating against my zipper, and I picture her every movement. How she's probably got her legs spread wide on the bed, her pussy throbbing, her fingers glistening as she teases herself because she doesn't have what she really needs to get her there: *me*.

I imagine how she'd react if I opened this door. She'd try to stop what's she doing, but I'd tell her to keep her fingers right the fuck there. I'd talk her through it and watch as she teased her clit and fucked herself with her fingers. I'd drop a knee to the bed, inhale her sweet scent, and swallow her moans as she came again and again.

I know I should walk away. I know I can't have her. And yet that doesn't stop me from keeping my ear to the door until I hear her cry out my goddamn name.

Chapter 23
TALLY

Other than the wildflower meadows, there's nowhere I love more than the inside of a kitchen. Whether it's the hustle and bustle of a restaurant or the quiet solitude I find in my own home, when I've got a whisk in my hand and flour on my face, I'm content.

Probably because it's the only place in the world where I truly fit and am driven by pure intuition. The moment my fingers sink into a pound of dough, kneading it with just the right pressure, I know what to do.

And when I don't, I play. I test out every ingredient until I find the right mixture. Pinch the right amount of salt or spice without second-guessing myself.

There isn't much else in life that I understand, but here, in the kitchen, I'm sure of myself. It's the same way I feel when I'm with Walker. It seems like no matter how many times I mess things up, he's still standing there, trying to hide a smile behind the brim of his hat. Understanding me in a way I don't think anyone else has ever really tried to.

For so long I've been gone from this town, from my home. I've run from kitchen to kitchen and felt like an imposter in each because, unlike the pastry chefs I worked with, I didn't have the proper schooling. I was the person they hired to make it through the busy season, never really belonging. Just an extra pair of hands.

Maybe after I go to culinary school—when I finally have the proper education and training—I'll be worthy of more. I'll be able to stop and put down roots somewhere.

My mind wanders to lazy mornings spent in the fields, followed by runs downtown and busy mornings in a bakery. Mabel's old bakery. I imagine how amazing it would be to spend my mornings catching up with my sister before rushing back to my own store to do the one thing I love: *bake*.

"What are you doing?" Walker's gruff voice shakes me from my daydream.

I spin, holding up the spatula to him. "Making apology cupcakes."

Walker's frown turns into a long sigh, and he ruffs one of those big hands across his face. "I told you, you're forgiven." He strolls past me and goes to the sink to scrub off the day's work from his hands.

"Still, I wanted to do something for you and my mom." Because, although they both say everything is fine, I still feel terrible about what happened.

Now I study Walker as he drops his gaze to the ground and slides his hands in the pocket of his Wranglers before stepping up next to me. From this close, I can see speckles of green in his deep brown eyes. God, he's beautiful. I step back. If I don't, I'm liable to wrap my arms around his neck and kiss him.

"So you like to bake?" He glances over my shoulder at the mess I've made.

"I'll clean it up, I promise."

Walker sighs. "That's not what I was saying. I'm—" He pulls at his hair. "Fuck, I'm no good at this."

I take pity on him and his inability to make conversation.

Or maybe on my inability to trust that someone actually wants to make conversation with me. That I have anything worth telling. "Yes, I bake."

"Professionally, or . . . ?"

I smile over my shoulder as I take out the measuring cup and begin sifting through the ingredients on the counter. "Yeah. My first wedding cake was probably five years ago in Vermont."

"So you were, what, twenty . . . ?"

As I dump the eggs I've just beaten into the mix, I smirk at him. "Trying to figure out my age, Cowboy?"

He shakes his head but a smile teases his lips. "Something like that."

"I was twenty-one. It was my third winter away—since you're nosy and need all the facts." He nods in response so I continue. "It was my second year at that particular resort, and since the chef I worked with the year before learned I had an interest in baking, he put me on that line."

"So that's what you prefer? Baking?"

I nod. "When I was in high school, I worked in the local bakery in town. It's not open anymore, but I loved it there. There's something so soothing about being in a kitchen. My mind relaxes when it's just me and ingredients." I reach for the vanilla and add a teaspoon to the cake mixture.

Walker folds his arms across his chest and leans against the wall. "That's how I feel out on the farm."

I grab the mixer and turn it on. "My dad was the same way. So was Mom."

"But not you or Penny?"

I pause the mixer, holding it midair. "Just never felt like it was mine. And Penny had books. I guess I always wanted something that was my own, too." I set the mixer back in the bowl and turn it on.

"So why not open up your own bakery?" he asks, loudly enough that I can hear him over the noise. "Is it because you love to travel? Don't want to stay in one place?"

"So many questions, Cowboy." Satisfied no lumps remain in the batter, I turn off the mixer and get out the first cupcake pan. Then I reach for the cooking spray and grease the pan before pouring some of the batter into each cup. "First one down," I mumble as I place the pan in the oven and set the timer.

"Guessing you don't want to answer."

"I'll answer yours if you answer mine?"

He pauses, then shrugs. "Okay. *Within reason*."

I laugh. "Don't worry, I'm not interested in your darkest secrets."

Something passes over his face, an unease that has me wondering what type of secrets Walker could be hiding.

"I'll go first. Do I want a bakery? Sure, one day. It's not that I love traveling. It's just the only way to get real experience in kitchens without schooling."

"And why not go to school?"

"That's two questions."

He straightens. "Okay, you go."

I begin the same steps to make the next batch of cupcakes. "How old are you?"

Walker groans. "Really?"

I chuckle. "What? You wanted to know how old I was. Why can't I ask you?"

"Just didn't expect it, I guess. I'm thirty-four."

"Is there a Mrs. Walker I should know about?"

He glowers. "Do you think I'd be here if there was a Mrs. Walker?"

That answer makes me far too giddy. He's here because we work together. Because we live together. But the way he answered makes it clear that he's not standing in this room right now because of work.

"Also, that was two questions," he says a little less gruffly.

"Yeah, but then you hit me right back with a question."

He huffs and I giggle. I put down the whisk I used to stir the eggs and step closer to him. His chin dips as I press a finger against his chest, then dance two up as I hold his attention. "But ask me another one. I'm an open book."

It takes me a moment to realize what I've done. We're close. Too close. My chin is tipped up. His is down. We're sharing the same breath. If I moved just an inch, our lips would press together. He'd probably wrap a hand around my neck and tug me closer. It'd be perfect.

"I can't fucking think when you're this close to me." His eyes widen as if he can't believe he said that aloud.

Neither can I.

"So stop thinking," I murmur, leaning in. God, I want to kiss him. But I hold myself right where I am, waiting for him to take that miniscule step to claim my mouth.

"I can't do that, either," he mutters before sighing and stepping back slightly. "Is there a Mr. Tally anywhere?"

I shake my head. "I don't do relationships. I don't stay anywhere more than a few months."

The apple of his throat bobs, and his eyes dip to my lips again.

Then my phone rings loudly and my heart rate skyrockets

as I jump back in surprise. "Jeez," I mutter before grabbing the phone and saying hello to my sister on FaceTime.

"Oh my God!" Penny squeals, her normally alabaster skin bright red.

"What?"

"We've gone viral! We're viral! The farm is famous!"

"What are you talking about?"

She lets out a loose, maniacal laugh. "You're both going to be happy I'm so obsessed with social media after this. I'm going to save the farm!"

I set the phone on the counter as I settle on a stool. "How?"

"Walker's cowboy videos! They've gone viral. Everyone is asking about the farm and the hot cowboy."

"Not a cowboy," Walker grumbles as he sidles up next to me.

I glance at him over my shoulder and tell him to shush.

"Whatever, we'll buy you a pony or something." Penny rolls her eyes and then she puffs air at her bangs, trying to get them out of her face. "This is amazing, Tally. The video you made him do walking around the farmers market with his hat on has gone viral. Everyone's asking where they can find themselves a Walker."

I feel a strange surge in my chest, a tightening that makes me want to claw at anyone who even looks his way. I can call Walker "Cowboy." But everyone else better back off.

"How exactly is that going to *save the farm*?" Walker puts the last few words in quotes with his fingers.

Penny's face falls. "Well, I don't know. But the video has one hundred thousand likes. And I've already started re-sponding to every comment, telling them about the farmers market and the festival. Plus, I said we host weddings. We can do something with this. We've got fans, Tally!"

"Well, Walker has fans." I murmur. "We need to make the farmers market bigger. We need more to sell. And for the festival." I'm thinking out loud, trying to figure out what we can do.

Walker leans against the counter. "We've got wildflowers we can sell. The tulips are a no-go for now, as are the daffodils. We need them for the festival and the weddings."

I nod. "Wildflowers work."

"What about your cupcakes?" Walker asks, turning to me.

"Cupcakes?" my sister parrots.

"Yeah, Tally bakes. She can sell cupcakes," Walker says, his voice stronger now, his stature tall.

"Yes! Oh my God, you know what we need? Walker eating one of your cupcakes!"

My thighs clench. I shouldn't be turned on by this conversation, but my brain clearly isn't working properly. Or maybe it's the way Walker smirks at me like he's thinking the very same thing.

"Yeah, Tally, I'd be happy to eat your cupcakes so we could save the farm."

I kick him in the shin, and he buckles over with a laugh. My eyes widen because I don't think I've ever heard him laugh. It's a beautiful, deep sound that has my heart racing.

"What's happening?" Penny asks, completely oblivious as she gets out a pen to take notes.

"Nothing," I mumble, not willing to share this moment. I want Walker's laughs, his smiles, his damn dimple, all to myself. "Walker and I will handle the wildflowers and cupcakes. And the cowboy videos. Need anything else?"

She glances down at her pad, where she's probably got a whole list of ideas.

"No," she replies, sounding distracted. "I'll talk to Mom and Rosie and call you back." My sister's copper eyes meet mine in the phone. "We're going to save the farm."

A smile blooms across my face as I feel a tinge of hope in my chest. "Yeah, we are."

"Bye, Cowboy!" my sister sings right before the screen goes black.

Walker groans. "Look what you started."

I grin up at him. "You think this could work?"

"Maybe."

The oven dings and I bounce toward it to grab the first batch of cupcakes. "Okay, well, I'll frost these and then we can get some video of you eating them."

Walker's head falls back and he lets out the sexiest chuckle I've ever heard. It's shocking and loud and makes my stomach flip. "This is ridiculous, you know that?"

I smile and bite down on my bottom lip. "What do you think of picking some flowers for decoration? It would really sell the farm if the cupcakes are decorated properly."

He nods as he takes a step closer. "I can do that. Any special requests?"

It's not even a question. "Wildflowers."

Walker's lips tip up in a warm smile and he nods. "All right, wildflowers for my wildflower."

He disappears before I realize what he just said. And I wonder whether it was a slip of the tongue, or did he really mean to call me his?

Chapter 24
WALKER

Thought those were my apology cupcakes?" I remind Tally as I lean against the refrigerator, watching as she frosts one cupcake after another and places them on a platter to take over to the farmers market. The woman has been a machine all week, baking and decorating and plotting with her sister far later than I could stay up.

The plan is to bring the baked goods to the farmers market today and make more content. And I suppose hopefully sell some cupcakes. Who the fuck knows. The girls seem to have a plan, and I'm trying not to get in the way of it. My only plan since Tally arrived two weeks ago has been to stay away from her. Which I'm failing at spectacularly because here I am again, staring at the way she sways her damn hips to some sad song.

It's hypnotic really, the way her lilac-spandex-covered ass rolls from one side to the other, the caramel waves on her head jostling with her movement. She's got on a white crop top that falls off one shoulder, exposing the straps of her lilac bra.

I push off the fridge and step closer to her. "You almost done?"

From this close I can smell the sugar from whatever she's making mixed with her shampoo, and the combination has my cock stirring even though the past few days have been nothing but a shit show and I'm stressed to all hell over the tulips.

Although the longer I stand in this room, right behind her, with her warmth so close it sets my skin on fire, the urge to touch her, to smell her, to *taste* her grows exponentially.

I pull back and put my hands in my pockets as she looks over her shoulder. "Almost."

With a cupcake in her hand, Tally spins toward me. I'm expecting her to offer it to me, but instead she takes a huge bite and then closes her eyes as she hums. Forget her hips being hypnotic. The sight and sound of Tally closing her eyes and eating a damn cupcake is downright erotic.

A whimper slips past my throat, and Tally's eyes fly open. "Want one?"

"Well, they were supposed to be for me," I grumble. "Though I don't even eat cupcakes." The pout that forms on her lips has me adding, "But I guess I can try one of yours."

The way Tally lights up fills me with insane pride. *I did that.*

Like a man who knows he's thoroughly fucked, I watch Tally grab another cupcake and slather it with frosting. She watches me pensively as I bite into it. I'd probably have faked loving the cupcake, but I don't have to.

"Fucking hell, that's—" I take another bite and groan, my eyes falling shut. "What is that?" I stuff the rest of it into my mouth. It's the best thing I've ever eaten. Hands down. I had no idea a cupcake *could* taste like that. Sweet and salty, spongy, decadent. "Holy shit, Tally. What the hell?"

Her shoulders relax, and her surprised laugh rings out. "It's a honey cupcake with salted caramel frosting."

I shake my head as I look around her, wanting more.

She giggles and grabs another one, but I'm staring at the frosting bowl I'd like to stick my head in.

"How the hell did you make this?"

"There was this bakery on the Cape my parents used to take us to every year after Daffodil Festival," she tells me as she swipes the frosting onto the cupcake for me. "They had honey cupcakes, and my dad always loved them. I went back a few years ago, wanting to surprise him with a batch on my way home from Nantucket that summer, but the bakery had closed." The smile that was on her face slips and her lips twist. "I told my dad that I wanted to get the recipe so I could make them for him because we hadn't been able to go on vacation for a long time, and he'd just smiled and said he bet I could make them even better. Then he stayed up all night with me and taste-tested every version until I got the recipe just right." She dips her finger into the bowl of creamy frosting and grins. "The salted caramel frosting was my own addition, though. He loved these cupcakes."

It's clear as day she misses her dad, and that ache to make things easier for her squeezes my chest. "Of course he did."

She licks the frosting from her finger and my dick jumps as she pierces me with those golden eyes. "We're going to fix this, Walker."

I take a slow breath through my nose, trying to calm my raging dick.

I'm pretty sure these cupcakes could broker peace, but I doubt they'll put off Frank's plans. Even still, as stressed as I am about the farm, none of our problems are really her fault. The tarps on the tulips were a Band-Aid. To save the farm, we'll need a lot more than cupcakes and a few more weeks of spring.

—

"Is it always this crowded?" Billie asks as we walk to the farmers market with more bouquets of flowers. We sold out of everything on the table in the first half hour.

"It's normally a decent turnout but nothing like this."

My sister shakes her head. "It's insane. And why does everyone keep trying to take your picture?"

I pull the cowboy hat over my face to hide. "People are weird."

"Tally looks pretty today," Billie continues as we reach our table.

I do anything to avoid looking in her direction. She looks gorgeous, and I've already stolen more glances in her direction today than I should have. After setting up the table with us, she disappeared and returned in a yellow sundress that had every man in the vicinity blinking like cartoon characters. It's got light pink flowers on it anddips low enough for me to see the swell of her pretty breasts. She looks so damn beautiful. I just want to pull her beneath my arm and hold her there.

Which is insane since she's not mine and I'm not making the mistake of being alone with her again. It only ends badly, with me wanting to push her up against the wall and taste her mouth. I can't stop replaying the sounds she made the other night in her bed. Whimpering my fucking name.

"Hi, Walker!" Rayna says, cutting through my thoughts, as soon as we place the bouquets on the table. The rest of the Liberty Ladies are by her side like a row of flowers, each one wearing a brighter color than the last.

"Hi, ladies," I say. The cupcakes are now all gone, but there's still a line of people waiting for the extra flower arrangements.

Tally and her mom have been manning the table with Quinn while Billie and I sorted our stock issues.

"Don't forget about book club tomorrow night," Babs says.

"Book club?" Billie enquires.

Tally lights up at her interest. "Oh, you'll have to come! Your brother really enjoys book club. Don't you, Walker?"

I blow out a breath but don't respond.

Gail smiles at my sister. "Oh, you should definitely come."

"Yeah. And we decided next week's book is going to be a cowboy romance in your honor," Babs nods toward me.

"Not a cowboy," I grumble.

My sister laughs and Tally knocks her hip against mine. I glance down at her and get a whiff of her sweet scent right as our eyes connect. Those damn golden eyes. She licks her lips, and I swear the entire farmers market fades away.

Then she reaches up and snatches the cowboy hat right off my head. "Fine, I'll be the cowboy for the day."

"Oh, you know what they say in those cowboy romances?" Penny says, appearing out of nowhere.

With my hat still held tight on her head, Tally turns to her sister. "What?"

Penny flashes her a wicked grin. "Wear the hat, ride the cowboy."

Tally's head falls back, and her loud, raspy laugh has my dick twitching.

"I wanna wear the hat!" Quinn whines.

Without missing a beat, Tally turns and plops it on his head with a smile. "Looks better on you, anyway."

He grins back at her like she's the best thing he's ever seen. I'm right there with him.

The Liberty Ladies all move on down the line as Gail

rings up their purchases, and I try to focus on anything but these feelings swirling in my chest.

Quinn tugs on my arm. "Can I go play in the fields?"

I grab my hat back and look to Billie, who nods, and I give him strict directions to stay within hollering distance. The farm abuts the brewery so I can see Quinn as he runs up and down the rows of pink and purple tulip beds.

When I turn back, Rosie is walking toward us carrying the damn coffee mugs that say THIS IS DEFINITELY COFFEE in one hand and a bottle of champagne in the other. She hands Tally one and Penny takes the other two while Rosie precariously pops the champagne, the cork flying behind her. She giggles as the liquid fizzes over, and she pours each of them a generous amount.

I grunt in annoyance as my sister laughs beside me.

Rosie taps her glass against the other two. "This is some turnout."

Tally smiles and winks in my direction. "All thanks to our viral cowboy."

I'm about to give her a quick response but fall silent as I catch my sister smiling at the three women. She's so focused on their easy banter and teasing. Those sorts of friendships are what she's missing in her life. And more than anything in the world, I wish I could give it to her.

I'm just about to grab Billie's attention so she doesn't feel left out when Tally reaches right in front of me and yanks on the hem of my sister's shirt. "C'mere."

My sister's surprised "Oh, okay," has my stomach somersaulting.

Tally hands her a mug. "Don't make me drink it all myself. I'm a lightweight."

And then she shares her drink with my sister.

She shares her friends with my sister.

And my stomach is in a free fall. I'm so screwed.

—

Hours later, I'm out in the fields, tending to the tulips and trying to forget how good today was. After we finished up at the farmers market, Rosie invited everyone to the brewery for an early dinner. She said it was the best day the brewery had since opening weekend three years ago so she wanted to celebrate.

Billie spent the whole day chatting with Gail and the Darling girls, and Quinn managed to drag Tally and Rosie onto the dance floor as a live country band performed.

The Darlings—and Rosie—welcomed my family into their fold, and it reminded me all of the things Billie and I missed growing up. It's always just been us. And I've always wanted to be enough for her. Enough of a brother, of a pseudo father, a terrible, makeshift mother. But after today, watching Tally, Penny, and Gail laughing and dancing together, I realize that's the kind of family my sister deserves. I'm just one person. I can't be all the people.

When Billie finally took Quinn home, Tally asked if I wanted to stay for a drink with her. I said no because I had work to do and I needed space from her to think.

Now, I'm heading up the hill after checking on the daffodils, ready for a nice long shower and bed, when I see a flash of light coming from the big house. Then someone steps onto the porch, shrieks, and launches off the front steps. My eyes narrow as I try to make out who it is. When the light of the moon hits her like a spotlight, Tally's angelic features come into view and I see a huge smile on her face. She runs straight toward me until she's launching herself right into my chest. I don't hesitate to grab her by the ass, lifting and squeezing her to me so we both don't fall over.

"Eli shared our viral post online!" she squeals.

"What?" I'm slightly out of breath with her so close.

Tally's golden eyes glow in the moonlight. "Eli! He shared the post, and one of his old hockey buddies, Daniel Hall, commented, asking if we had any wedding openings this spring."

"That's a good thing?" I honestly don't understand half the words she's saying, but she seems happy.

Tally laughs and then she squeezes my cheeks between her palms and stares down at me. "Yeah, Cowboy. That's a good thing. Daniel is like a huge hockey star, and his wife is this big-time author. Penny is freaking out. She's obsessed with Hannah. They want to do a vow renewal here! Can you imagine how big this could be for the farm? This is it, Walker. I feel it. Everything is going to be all right!"

Tally is still in my arms, and once again, our lips are too close. Golden waves of her hair act like a curtain around us as we stand in the middle of the meadow, the budding daffodils and glittering stars our only witnesses. A man could act reckless out here and no one would know.

"I like seeing you smile, Wildflower."

Tally's mouth curves. "I like when you call me 'Wildflower.'"

"Yeah?"

Her teeth dig into her bottom lip.

"Yeah." The word is whispered. "But I liked it better when

you called me *your* wildflower." Her thumb slides across my bottom lip and she tugs on it.

I grunt. With her legs wrapped around my waist I can feel her warmth. Can imagine how easy it would be to head right back to the house, slam the door, and forget about everything else.

"*Tally.*" Her name comes out as a rasp. I'm pleading for her to pull back. To stop us from making this mistake.

She leans just a bit closer and rubs her soft lips against mine. "Shhh, Cowboy, let me play for a minute."

My dick throbs against my zipper as her tongue peeks out, and I practically growl when she slides it against my lips, tasting me.

That's all it takes for me to snap. Gripping her ass with one hand, I slide the other up and wrap it around the back of her neck, needing control. "Okay, Wildflower, let's play."

My lips crash into hers, and it isn't a fire that sets my body aflame. No, it's a tidal wave that pulls me out to sea. An out-of-control disaster that could consume us both and drag us under. I don't care, though. I could drown in this woman without even realizing it because I'd rather keep my lips on hers than ever breathe again.

Just as I imagined, her lips taste like sugar—probably from the incredible cupcakes that got us into this mess to begin with—and something else I can't quite put my finger on. I lick into her mouth, seeking more. She moans, and her legs tighten around my waist. Her fingers grip my hair, and she tugs, giving me just that little bit of pain that I crave. Then she scrapes down my scalp and nips at my lips.

Fuck, this woman is perfect.

"Tally," I mumble.

"Shhh, Cowboy, you'll ruin it." She pecks my lips one more time and then she's sliding down my body and pushing down the skirt of her dress, hiding those gorgeous thighs, which I just had exactly where I wanted them. My fingers ache to reach for her. To pull her back against me and take another taste. But she rushes off in the direction of her mother's cottage, her hair bouncing as she goes, a pretty smile on her face when she glances over her shoulder one more time.

And fuck if that's not the most gorgeous view on this whole damn farm.

Chapter 25
TALLY

You're doing it again," Penny mumbles, kicking me in the shin beneath the table.

"Ow." I reach down and rub at the spot as Rosie snickers beside me. We're having dinner at Wicked Wine and Cheese and have a plateful of a variety of cheeses and meats sitting in front us. Basically, it's my version of heaven. Or it was before I started getting the third degree from these two.

"Eventually you're going to have to tell us what happened between you and the cowboy," Rosie teases.

I roll my eyes, pretending I have no idea what they're talking about. Pretending that Walker didn't kiss the life out of me after the farmers market and then act like it never happened. It's been days and, under the guise of getting ready for the Daffodil Festival and the Hall vow renewal, which will require a hell of a lot more work than either of us had anticipated, Walker's been gone before I wake up and returns after I'm already in my bedroom.

I'd be upset, but I haven't minded the space to think. Truthfully, that kiss threw me more than I'd like to admit. I've kissed boys before, plenty of them, but I've never been kissed like *that*.

Kissing—and sex—and all the acts in between are meant for the singular purpose of getting off. Relieving stress. But

Walker's kiss wasn't that. In fact, it did the opposite; it wound me up and tied my stomach in knots.

All I can think about is doing it again.

"Oh look, it's our mayor," I say loudly, excited to turn the tables on Rosie. "Think he's coming here to meet a lady friend?"

Penny snorts as Rosie scowls and violently stabs the cheese knife into the baked Brie.

I study Fletcher as he chats with the hostess. He's a very good-looking man, always smiling, and the curls on his head giving him a boyish charm. The hostess hands him a to-go bag, and Fletcher thanks her before heading our way. I practically squeal in excitement as Rosie's cheeks flame red. She tugs on her signature gold hoops and looks anywhere but at Fletcher as he steps up to our table to say hello.

"Hi, Fletcher. You having a picnic tonight?" I ask.

I couldn't think of a more romantic date. Cheese and wine with my girlfriends is fun, but having a man provide both of those things in a meadow under the stars would be perfect. A vision of me arriving in the wildflower meadow and seeing Walker sitting there with a hopeful smile plays in my head, and my stomach flips at the thought. Shit.

"No. My mother loves her cheese. I wanted to surprise her with some since she's always watching Henry for me."

"I'm sure she loves spending time with him," Penny says.

Fletcher nods—though there's something sad in his expression—before glancing at Rosie, who still has yet to look away from the Brie, which she's murdered seven times over. "Well, I hope you ladies have a good night."

He's barely reached the door when I turn my focus on my

best friend. "I seriously don't get it. Why do you hate him so much?"

Rosie shrugs. "I just do. He's arrogant and always up in everyone's business."

"He's just friendly," I point out.

Penny's oddly silent.

I glance at her. "What do you know?"

Penny and Rosie share a look that I hate. It highlights the time I've been away. The time when the two of them shared secrets. Growing up, it was me and Rosie. Or me and Penny. Maybe sometimes the three of us, but not often. Penny was older and spent all her time with her high school best friend, Jake Montgomery. They were inseparable. Always caught up in a book, or hanging at his house on the water. Rosie and I, on the other hand, spent most of our teenage years sneaking boys and drinks into the cottages at night. During the day we would drive around for hours, dreaming of the day when we'd leave Hope Harbor. Until I did and Rosie couldn't. And now, well, now I'm the one on the outside and I have no idea how to get them to let me in completely.

Finally, I lift up my glass and glare at Rosie, "Tell me why you hate the mayor or forever suffer bad sex."

Rosie sighs and clinks her glass against mine like I'm the worst friend ever. "You know how hard it was to get the brewery approved with the town?"

I nod, relieved that she's finally talking to me.

"Well, he was the mayor back then, too." She shrugs, like that's enough of an explanation. And maybe it is. But I still feel like there's something more.

"Ladies!" My back goes ramrod straight at the sound of Rayna McGovern's loud voice.

Somehow, while we were distracted, the Liberty Ladies have appeared out of nowhere. My mother isn't with them. Though I'm not surprised, considering she's in just as much of a tizzy as Walker is about getting the farm ready. I'm sure she's sleeping right now from sheer exhaustion, even though it's only six o'clock.

"Hello," Rosie says, and the three of us wave at them. "What are you gals up to tonight?"

"Oh, we thought we'd have a little wine while we discussed this cowboy book we're all reading. We're halfway through. What about you?" Babs asks. She's in a low-cut red top, and I work to keep my eyes on her face.

"We'll be ready on Monday," Penny tells them. It's good she's replied because the last thing I'm doing is reading a book about a swoony cowboy. I don't need any help getting carried away in my own mind.

"That's good," Babs replies. "We do love our spicy Mondays."

I offer a polite smile and hope we're done engaging, but Babs steps closer and somehow her breasts really do seem to lunge toward my face. "You know, we were just talking about you."

"Me?" I push back in my chair to get a little breathing room.

"Did you know that Rayna owns the building that Mabel's Bakery used to be in?" Babs muses.

My stomach flips. "No. I had no idea."

"She's looking for someone to rent it," Babs says.

I glance at Rayna, who smiles smugly.

"Have you ever thought of doing something like that?" Babs continues.

"Oh no, I don't have any formal degree. I just like to bake."

"Hmm," she hums. "Well, what about a stand at the farmers market?" She says this to Rosie, who tilts her head toward me in question.

Penny nods. "That's a really good idea. What do you think, Tally?"

"We've got a lot going on at the farm at the moment. The big wedding for one. Plus, they will need the cottages ready for guests because there's no hotel rooms available in town that weekend."

Towering behind Rayna, Ruby Simmons perks up. "Oh, my husband could probably help with that. He's in need of some extra work."

I blow out a breath. "Walker's in charge, and I'm not sure we have the money to pay people right now."

Her lips twist in disappointment. "Okay, well, let us know if he changes his mind."

"Think about the farmers market, Tally," Babs adds, tapping a hand on the table before stepping back. "You're good at what you do."

I smile awkwardly. "I will."

The four of them disappear, and the girls go back to talking like everything the Liberty Ladies just said didn't throw my heart in a tailspin.

"So," Penny interrupts my thoughts. "What do you think?"

I play dumb. "What do I think about what?"

"The bakery," Rosie answers matter-of-factly.

I frown. "Who's going to buy my stuff?"

Penny shakes her head like she thinks that answer is a cop-out. "Okay, maybe not the bakery just yet. But what about your own stand at the farmers market?"

My head swivels, and I stare at my sister. "Where would I even bake?"

Penny taps her lips. "Oh, if only you had a big kitchen to work in. Oh wait, you do."

"Ha ha," I say sarcastically. "You forget that I currently share that kitchen with Walker. I doubt he'd be happy if I set up a whole business in the kitchen."

"I'm sure you could make it worth his while," She. grins at me, her eyes dancing.

"I have no idea what you're talking about," I mumble, stuffing a cracker and a piece of cheese into my mouth.

Rosie's raspy laugh breaks through the quiet of the restaurant. "Sure you don't."

But just like the two of them have their secrets, I'm keeping Walker and his mind-blowing kisses to myself for the time being.

"Why don't you invite him to meet us at the brewery one night to celebrate the Hall vow renewal? Maybe you could even tell him about Mrs. Simmons's idea."

I bite my thumb as I consider it. *Why don't I?*

Chapter 26
WALKER

April

> **RAYNA:** Don't forget book club is Monday! We loved having you when you came, Eli and Walker. Since it's finally April, we are switching over to our spring reads! If you want to come back, make sure you read Her Secret Garden. Promise there's no aliens this week.

> **BABS:** But there is lots of sex! I've got a new toy to share. Hint: It looks like a rose bud so we're staying on theme.

> **FLETCHER:** Ladies, this is what we talked about at the town meeting. Please. I can't keep getting calls about this.

> **ELI:** I'll be there! Let me know what I can bring.

> **ROSIE:** Brown noser!

> **RAYNA:** Walker?

***

The strong scent of vanilla, sugar, and something else—possibly blueberries—assaults me as soon as I walk through the door. For the last week, the house has smelled more like a bakery than a farm. I wake every morning to find muffins with dark chocolate and bananas in them, rhubarb French toast, and pancakes with a caramel nut glaze laid out in the kitchen. In the afternoons, there is zucchini bread, glazed lemon blueberry scones, and strawberry cupcakes.

I'm going to gain ten pounds if Tally doesn't leave soon. But at least she hasn't tried to talk to me about the kiss.

She still has me on edge most of the time. On Tuesday, she sat me down and asked for a list of things she could do to help on the farm. She didn't even bat an eye when I gave her the worst chores. Not because I was being an ass—okay, I was sort of being an ass because I was trying to create some distance—but because it's stuff I don't think she can fuck up and I have some big jobs to be getting on with.

Then her eyes filled with fire as she watched me eat her treats. God forbid I'd told her what a good girl I think she's been. I'm pretty sure she would have spread her legs for me right there.

Fuck. It's only Friday. How am I going to make it through the Daffodil Festival this weekend with her everywhere? More importantly, it's only the first of April. How the fuck am I going to make it through May without giving in to her?

I run my hand down my face when she calls from somewhere within the house.

"Cowboy?"

Yup, she's still calling me that.

"That's me."

And I'm answering to it. I'm so fucking screwed.

"Wait until you see what I made tonight."

I suck in a lungful of air, trying to temper my excitement.

I won't get myself all worked up like a damn puppy jumping at her feet.

"Just going to shower," I say. "I'll be down in a few."

I head for the stairs, knowing I'm going to need to jerk off before I see her.

"Don't be too long," Tally calls back. Then her voice seems closer. "Dinner's ready."

I've made it up only one step when I make the error of turning around and looking at her. She's leaning against the doorframe, a kitchen towel over one shoulder, her wild hair up in a high ponytail with wisps escaping and framing her pretty face. Her arms are folded across her chest, highlighting the swells of her breasts, which spill out of the low-cut pastel pink spandex she's wearing tonight.

"Where's your mother?" The words come out scratchy, growled with a desperation I feel in the depths of my soul. Her mother needs to be here. I can't sit across from her, or God forbid next to her, and keep my hands to myself.

Since the kiss, I've managed to keep my distance. But a man is only so strong. Especially when she's looking at me with pouty lips that I just want to suck on. Lips that I know taste sweeter than any of the desserts she's fed me.

"Out with the Liberty Ladies. They're celebrating the start of the Daffodil Festival early." Tally raises her brows. "So it's just us tonight."

Fucking fabulous. To avoid giving in to my desires, I double-time it into my bedroom to undress. Within seconds, I've got her sweet floral shampoo soaping up my dick as I work myself, hoping like hell this will hold me over until I get into bed tonight.

When I finally make it back to the kitchen, Tally has dinner set at the kitchen counter and she's got an already open beer in front of my seat.

"This looks good," I say as I pull out my stool and set my eyes on the fried chicken she's got covered in some sauce.

Tally hums. "Thanks, trying a new recipe."

I keep pushing closer to the wall until I'm up against it with nowhere to move, and she keeps shifting closer to talk to me as we eat. If I don't keep shoveling food into my mouth, I'll grab her and do ungodly things to her on this counter.

She fills me in on her day, giving me a list of five more desserts she plans to make this week, which all sound mouth-wateringly delicious. Then she asks about my day; about Quinn's baseball game the night before and whether I think my sister would ever want to leave Quinn with her so she could have some alone time and go out.

"If Billie is leaving Quinn with anyone, it's with me," I say in response, to which she suggests we could babysit him together.

"Maybe after the Hall event," I tell her, reminding her of why she's here. "There's only so much time to get the cottages ready."

The Hall event is going to bring in a good amount of money, but since it's so last-minute, the wedding party couldn't find a hotel close enough that had availability. Tally had the genius idea of telling them we had cottages they could stay in. Although it saved the event, I'll be busting my ass 'til the very last minute to get those cottages fixed up.

I'm having to dip into Frank's loan to pay for the renovations. The furniture could easily be sanded and stained, but all the rooms need new mattresses and bedding, which aren't cheap. Though, for the price the Halls are willing to pay to rent out the farm for the weekend, it will be well worth it in the end. Especially if they tell their very well-off friends. We could use a few more high-end events in the calendar and then we might actually have a shot at making it through this season without having to sell some of the land.

"About that," Tally starts, cutting through my thoughts.

It's clear from her voice that she's nervous and priming me for something I'm not going to like.

"Ruby Simmons says her husband's looking for work. She said he could help get the cottages ready."

"And where exactly do you think we'd get the money to pay him?"

She shrugs. "I don't know. I could try selling some of my desserts at the farmers market. And the Daffodil Festival."

I hate how hopeful she sounds. It's naive as hell to believe that some desserts could cover the cost of a contractor.

"Have you been baking all week just so you could pitch this to me?"

The girl would be terrible at poker. It's written all over her face: the light sheen of sweat and the flush of her cheeks that come with the surprise that I caught on so quickly. "No."

For the first time since I met her, Tally reminds me of my ex-girlfriend Gina, and lead settles in my stomach. Gina was conniving. She'd do things with a purpose. And the purpose was always to get her way.

Offering to take my sister prom dress shopping, only so she could send me pictures of herself in a wedding dress. Cleaning every room in our tiny little apartment—that she didn't live in—just so she could point out that Billie wasn't doing her fair share and it was time my sister got a college dorm.

After Quinn was born and I told Gina I planned to help

take care of the him, and that my sister wouldn't be moving out anytime soon, Gina's true colors shown through and I finally realized that everything she had ever done had been so she could get her way. She didn't really care about me or my sister. She was only interested in setting up her own future.

I don't like the way my body buzzes right now, alerting me to someone else bullshitting me.

"Tally." I grunt and stare down at my damn plate. I take a deep breath and then glare at her.

She sighs and her face scrunches up in annoyance. "I'm trying to help."

"You're trying to con me into getting your way." I throw down my napkin, annoyed.

I don't even know why I'm so irritated. There's this small part of me—an embarrassing part—that felt special because Tally was making all these treats for me. Just like I used to feel special when Gina would do ridiculous things to get my attention.

"It's a good idea, Walker." The use of my name instead of "Cowboy" tells me she's pissed. "This farm means everything to me, and I know everyone thinks that because I left, I didn't care. But it's *because* I cared that I left."

A headache blooms between my eyes. "What do you mean?"

She huffs and pushes to stand. "Forget it. I don't even know why I try. No one expects anything from me, so maybe I should just prove you all right and give up."

The way she speaks, the dejected tone of her voice, has me reaching for her. My fingers snag on her wrist, and I tug. "Tally, wait."

When she turns her head, her eyes cutting to wear I'm

gripping her, it's clear she's not looking at me. But that doesn't stop me from noticing the sheen of tears in her eyes. A wave of regret rolls through me.

"*Tally.*" Desperation attaches to her name as a teardrop rolls down her cheek. Her lashes flutter and lift open as I reach for her chin. With the gentlest touch, I tilt her face so she's looking right at me. I've got to make this right. To apologize. But fuck, the moment I've got her chin in my hand, her attention on me, those gorgeous eyes of hers filling with the same desperation I feel whenever I look at her, I forget my damn words.

Tally trails her tongue across her bottom lip so slowly I don't think she even knows she's doing it. My heart pounds, and I tug on her wrist to pull her closer right as she leans in.

And then I remember why we shouldn't be doing this. She's my employee. She's too young. She's Peter's daughter.

And she'll hate me when she finds out what's really going on with the farm.

When I don't take that infinitesimal step closer and simply stare at her, Tally's lips fall open in an *O*.

"I'm sorry." I blow out a breath as I look at her damn lips again. "I like you, Tally. I like you so fucking much, but I'm no good at any of this."

Her eyes soften and she stares at me, almost defiantly. "I like you, too."

I shake my head because she doesn't get it. "I've been burned pretty badly. So I don't do this. My ex—I thought she loved me, but she turned out to be someone I couldn't trust."

She blows out a breath. "I'm not good with words, either. I don't exactly have a great track record since I got here, so I was just trying to show you my idea could work rather than tell you. I should have just told you what I was thinking. I'm sorry if you thought I was scheming."

I know that. Fuck, I know she's nothing like Gina. Which makes all of this so damn hard because I still can't have her. "This still can't happen."

She rolls her eyes, and though it should remind me of her age, I understand the sentiment. I've been hot and cold with her. But I'm serious. This can't happen. "It's not because I don't want you, and it's not even because I'm your boss."

Her brows raise in question.

"It's because there are things going on with the farm that you won't understand."

She steps back, creating distance between us. "Tell me."

"I can't. I promised your mother and father I wouldn't."

Tally's eyes fall to the counter, zeroing in on her soda bottle. "Okay," she finally says.

Surprise and maybe a bit of disappointment hit me square in the chest. "Okay?"

Tally nods. "Yes. Okay."

"I'm confused."

She sighs but her eyes settle on me and I see something in them that wasn't there before. "Did they have a good reason to ask you to stay quiet?"

I run a hand down my face. Gail and Peter had their reasons. Are they good? Maybe. I can't say it's necessarily wrong, and it certainly isn't selfish, so I nod.

"Okay. I trust my parents, and this is their business." Tally's chin dips. "And I trust you."

"You do? Why?"

"Because my dad trusted you." She says it so softly, so sweetly, I just want to pull her against my chest and hold her.

Fuck.

She places a hand against my chest, and I'm sure she can feel my heart pounding wildly beneath it. "Friends?"

I nod because words fail me.

She drops her hand and motions toward the door. "I'm going to go to the bar."

"Okay. I'll clean up."

"You could come if you want," she offers, her voice raspy with emotion and her face full of hope.

"I don't think that's a good idea." I grab the plates from thecounter and empty them into the garbage.

"It's just the brewery." She shrugs and then takes another step back, holding up her hands like she's promising not to touch me. "We don't have to go together. I could walk like ten feet in front of you the whole way there."

"It's not like that," I say, shaking my head.

"Then what's it like, Cowboy?" She licks at her bottom lip when she catches me staring again. "You want to be my friend or not?"

The heels of my palms dig into my eyes as I try to focus on anything but her lips and the way my dick is thumping against my jeans at the mere sight of her tongue. "Christ, woman."

"Well, as your *friend*, I'm just letting you know that I'm going to the bar tonight." She grins at me. "Don't wait up."

Chapter 27
WALKER

HOPE HARBOR TOWN CHAT

FLETCHER: Don't forget the Daffodil Festival kicks off tomorrow! Can't wait to see everyone there.

ELI: I'm heading to Rosie's. Anyone want to meetme there?

BABS: It's awfully last minute.

STEW: Can't have a beer with a New York traitor.

ELI: I DON'T EVEN PLAY FOR THEM ANYMORE!

STEW: Once a traitor, always a traitor.

TALLY: I'll be right there Eli! I'm happy to drink a beer with you. I'll even buy you one.

FLETCHER: That's the neighborly spirit!

* * *

I can't believe I'm doing this. I didn't even drive here. It's only a few hundred feet past the end of our driveway, but still, I always take my truck. Not tonight, though.

Tonight, I walked here because *she* walked here. And if she's walking, I'm walking.

The air feels heavy, the April dew is thick against my skin, and the frogs cry out in a warning. It feels like rain. Fucking great. It'll probably pour on my walk back home.

With every stomp of my boots against the gravel, I get more annoyed with myself. Why am I following her? She let me off the hook. She said we can be friends. We had an honest conversation, and now I can move on.

Yes, I tell myself, I'm just coming here tonight because I want a beer and to listen to some music.

Doesn't matter that I have an entire case of my favorite beer back at the house and I can't stand the seasonal ales that Rosie serves. Or that the music isn't my style.

The moment I open the door to the oversized-barn-turned-brewery, the sound of some wannabe Dave Matthews guitarist strumming loudly over the quiet din of excited conversation makes me want to turn back around.

I almost do.

But then a hand pushes me forward. "Walker! You got my text."

It's Eli. He continues to walk us toward the bar, right smack in the center of the room. If I was going to stay here, which I'm not, I'd find a shadowed corner.

"Huh?"

I don't know what he's talking about because I blocked almost everyone other than my sister and Gail. And Tally.

Eli sets his elbow against the bar and angles toward me. "Glad you decided to come tonight. The guys and I have been hoping we'd see you here since last year."

My brows fold in on themselves. "Why?" It's a serious

question. Why in God's name would anyone want to hang out with me? Since I moved here, I've done everything in my power to actively avoid becoming part of this town.

"Well, mainly because Fletch has a kid and you don't. And most of the guys on the fire department are married. And Stew smells like cheese."

I'm sure my facial expression says what I'm thinking: *What the fuck?*

Eli remains unbothered. "I'm just kidding." He turns and faces the crowd. "Honestly, most of the guys I played hockey with don't talk to me anymore since I got hurt and retired. And coming home and starting over feels more like a failure than I'd like to admit. For some reason, you seem like someone who gets that." He raises his eyebrows, like he's challenging me to disagree.

I let out a long sigh. "Can we drink and not talk?"

Eli's face lights up. "First round's on you."

I huff a chuckle and nod toward Rosie, who is serving a growing crowd.

The band quiets and it gets a little louder in the bar as people start to chat during the break.

"Hello, guys. What can I get you?" Rosie sets napkins down in front of us, and I order a whiskey for myself and a blueberry beer for Eli. It's one of the brewery's specialties. I imagine Tally loves it.

Suddenly I'm bothered that I don't know what she normally drinks. That I don't really know much about her at all, except that she can bake one hell of a cupcake, she has an endless supply of different floral-smelling shampoos that I'm constantly stealing, her curves look incredible beneath her multicolored spandex, and she enjoys running every morning.

I also know that right before she smiles she bites her lip like she's not sure if she should show anyone that she's momentarily happy. It makes me want to punch something because Tally has the kind of smile that should be permanently on display.

I know the way she tastes. The little sounds she makes when she's surprised. And angry. And turned on.

Fuck, I guess I know a lot about her.

"What does Tally order?" The words stumble out of my mouth as Rosie sets my whiskey in front of me.

She lets out an amused snort, nodding behind me. "Why don't you ask her yourself?"

Shit. My elbows fall against the bar and my shoulders slump.

"Don't go shy on me now, Cowboy," Tally mumbles so quietly only I can hear her. Then she's pushing in between Eli and me. "Gimme a shot," she says louder to Rosie.

"*Please*. The word is *please*," Rosie shoots back.

Tally bats her eyelashes. "Boys, do you want to do a shot with me? My bestie owns the bar, so we can have whatever we want."

"That's not how this works," Rosie grumbles, though she gets out three shot glasses and then reaches for a bottle of Fireball.

That answers one question. Of course she drinks Fireball. She's twenty-six.

"None for me. We've got the festival tomorrow," I remind her.

Tally bites on her lip before glancing up at me with a grin. "Just one. I promise."

She turns away from me as Eli grabs his drink and they

tap glasses before shooting them back while Penny comes up and sits on the other side of Eli.

"Walker, did you hear Tally's great idea?" Penny asks.

"Hush, you," Tally tosses at her in the same way she throws grenades at me. Whatever this idea is, she doesn't want me to know.

Intrigued, I angle myself so my body is flush against Tally's side. Anyone who walked in would assume we were a couple. Especially if I wrapped my free arm around her middle and pulled her between my thighs.

But I don't. I turn to address Penny instead. "I didn't. Care to share?"

"She's going to sell her baked goods at the farmers market to help raise money for the cottages. The Liberty Ladies were even angling for her to open her own bakery."

I can't hide my surprise that Tally would consider staying in Hope Harbor.

"It's a dumb idea," Tally says with a shake of her head. "I'll never raise enough money to pay for help."

Penny's jaw drops. "Really? But we only have, like, a month to get everything done before the Hall event, right?"

Everyone's staring at me now, like I'm the idiot here. "I've got it handled."

Tally rolls her eyes and turns away from me to face Rosie. "Can I have another shot?"

Eli steps closer. "If you need help on the farm, I'd be happy to pitch in."

Tally presses her hand to Eli's chest, staring up at him with stars in her damn eyes. "That's very sweet, Eli." Then she looks back toward me and sighs. "But you'll have to ask Walker. He's in charge."

Fucking A.

Eli looks to me. "Happy to help, man. We could probably knock out a bunch of stuff in a few days if we get the fire department guys, too."

"That's how my bookstore was built," Penny adds.

"And this brewery," Rosie says as she pours Tally another shot. "I'm sure a bakery could even be fixed up that way."

"No," Tally says in what sounds like sincere annoyance. "We're not talking about the bakery. This is about the farm." Her eyes stray my way, and the damn hope in them has my heart racing.

"I'll let you know," I say to Eli with a sigh.

Tally lights up like I've just promised her the damn moon and then the strum of a guitar has a smile blooming on her lips. "Wanna dance?"

I sip my whiskey as the familiar tune begins, trying like hell not to be drawn to her.

"Oh, 'Cowboy Like Me,'" Rosie says from the other side of the bar. "Nice one!"

I shake my head as Tally tugs on my belt loop. I like that she's smiling again, but there's no way in hell I'm dancing. Least of all to this. "I don't dance."

"I do," Eli says.

My grip tightens on my glass, but I try to keep my composure as the man who I momentarily considered befriending grabs Tally's hand and pulls her away.

An unfamiliar feeling grips my chest. Still, I can't look away as Eli's hand wraps around Tally's waist and her arms circle his neck. She laughs at something he says as they dance to *our* song. I can't believe I'm angry about a Taylor Swift tune. I don't understand how I even know one.

But I do.

Every single lyric.

"They look hot together," Rosie says from behind the bar.

My jaw clicks.

"She always had a crush on him when we were in high school," Penny continues, reminding me that Eli is the more appropriate choice for Tally. They're around the same age, and he's a happy guy. Always smiling. A much better match for my wildflower girl than the grumpy old asshole who barely strings two words together despite the woman trying day and night to just have a conversation.

But that's just the thing: She's *my* wildflower girl.

"Who didn't?" Rosie adds.

My fists clench.

"I'm sure he'll keep her smiling tonight," Penny adds.

Her words aren't what set me off. It's all of it. Being in this bar. The talking. And the final straw is watching Tally smile at someone who isn't me. I can't handle watching her in Eli's arms when she should be in mine. As I stalk toward the dance floor, Rosie's voice carries over the crowd. "Atta boy."

Somehow, between the time Tally left me in the kitchen and we came here, she changed into another one of her damn floral sundresses. This one is black with white and yellow flowers on it and wraps across her chest, exposing the swell of those pretty tits. There's a frilly thing going on with the sleeves that makes her seem daintier than she is. Same with the skirt, which falls to the floor, a pair of black cowboy boots peeking out below the hem.

"Tally," I grind out as I reach for her elbow, pulling her back toward my chest and away from Eli's.

The man holds up his hands in surrender. Idiot. Who

gives up that easily? But when I meet his eyes, prepared to give him a death glare, Eli's smiling.

Actually, fuck that, he's not smiling. He's practically exploding with joy.

Like this was his damn plan all along.

Asshole.

Tally wrenches her elbow from my grip and spins on me. "What are you doing?"

The damn cowboy song is coming to an end, thank fuck, but Tally's voice comes out loud now that the strumming has stopped. It feels like all eyes in the brewery are on us.

"The Daffodil Festival," I say pathetically, stepping into her space, keeping my voice down.

Tally's hand falls to her hip as she stares me down. "What about it?"

Reaching for any excuse to get out of here, I grumble, "The chairs. We never cleaned 'em."

Tally's face scrunches reasonably in confusion. Because I'm not making any fucking sense.

"Okay . . . ," she says hesitantly.

"So no more dancing. We have to go," I say, digging my grave even deeper.

She rolls her eyes and lets out a heavy sigh before turning toward Eli. "Thanks for the dance."

"Anytime, Tally."

She breezes past Eli and rushes toward the bar, probably to tell her sister and Rosie what an idiot I am. I grip the back of my neck, trying to figure out what the hell I'm doing.

"Don't go soft now, friend," Eli says, stepping up beside me and turning with me to watch Tally grab her things. "You were just about to rip my head off. *Use that.*"

He grins before pushing me toward the bar, and my chest rumbles in annoyance.

I played right into his stupid plan, and now I have to own it. I was jealous. *Am* jealous. I don't want anyone to touch her. But what the hell am I going to do about that? If I'm not going to touch her, not going to claim her, then I can't stop her from letting someone else.

My fists clench and I know I'm not allowing that to happen. But before I can make it to the bar, Tally is storming through the crowd and disappearing out into the cool spring evening.

When I get outside, she's standing there, arms crossed, waiting for me. "Where's your truck?"

"I walked."

Her eyes narrow. "So you walked here but you just didn't want to walk with me?"

She seems even more annoyed by this revelation. But before I can think of a way to tell her I walked *because* she walked—that I want to walk beside her at all times and I hate myself for it—she spins and huffs in the direction of the farm.

"Tally, wait." I run after her. And then I'm chasing her into the field because of course she doesn't stay on the gravel. She goes for the dirt, where there are divots and uneven ground that could take either of us down.

The sky lights up and then, with a loud crack of thunder, a sheet of rain pours down on us. Tally doesn't even pause—if anything, she almost seems to jump in excitement—and then she's heading away from the house and farther into the acres of land that I love.

"Where are you going?" I holler.

"To dance in the wildflowers!" she yells as she rushes toward that field.

"What?"

She spins around, a smile on her face, and continues walking backward. Her dress is already clinging to her incredible curves, the ruffles at the hem getting caught between her legs. "It's my favorite thing to do when it's raining."

She laughs and then turns on her heel, rushing away from me again. Even over the steady cadence of the rain, I hear her warm laughter calling to me like a siren. I can't leave her out here.

And hell, I'm tired of lying because Lord knows I don't want to. I want to dance with her in the damn meadow. Beneath the angry moon that's peeking out between the clouds.

I pick up my pace and catch up with her quickly. Grabbing her by the waist, I spin her toward me.

"What are you doing?" she asks, panting for air.

Her wild hair falls across her face and clings to her mouth. I keep one hand around her waist and with the other, I untangle the locks from her lips, pushing them back behind her ear. "I was thinking I'd dance with you."

Her eyes light up and I swear they keep me warm even as the cold rain falls on us. With a smile on her lips, she whispers, "But I thought you don't dance?"

I don't answer her question with words. I pull her to my chest and then, while humming "Wildflower" by Tom Petty, I twirl her around as the spring shower soaks us.

With her cheek against my chest, I'm sure she can feel the unsteady pounding of my heart. She tilts her head up to me and murmurs, "You're a secret romantic, huh?"

I'd laugh if it was funny. Of all the things I've been called in my life, a romantic isn't one of them. I'm sure my ex would tell Tally to run far away unless she wants someone who does nothing but grunt and ignore her.

But I can't ignore Tally. It's impossible. I grip her cheek and smooth my thumb against her lips. "Only for you, Wildflower."

She beamsat the nickname, and pride swells within me.

"Will you kiss me again?" she whispers.

I barely shake my head. Not because I don't want to kiss her, but because I need something else. "What if I want you to kiss me?"

"It's not going to stop at a kiss," she warns.

"Better fucking not," I growl.

Her eyes light up again and then she lifts her arms and tugs on my shirt, pulling me down so we're nose to nose. "Better make it good, then."

Chapter 28
TALLY

There are moments in your life that you just know you'll remember forever. That when you're old and gray, lying on your deathbed, God willing, you'll still remember every second.

This kiss—*no, this night*—is that moment for me.

I'm positive that no man will ever look at me the way Walker has tonight. Like he can't get close enough. Like he wants my taste infused in his blood. Like he'll hurt anyone who gets between us.

The ache for him has grown during the last few weeks, from a dull, ever-present throb to an overpowering obsession I can't ignore.

I'm reckless in my need for him, dancing in a field as lightning illuminates the sky. Nothing is as scary as the feeling that consumes me when our lips finally touch. When he licks at my mouth, grips my hips, and lifts me into his arms. When he tilts his head just so and devours me.

The rain continues to fall in sheets, and my dress clings to me. Still, I feel none of it. Only Walker. My cowboy.

"Need these clothes off," Walker rasps before going in for another kiss. He hauls me higher in his arms and begins walking forward, though I have no idea where he's going because I can't see and I don't dare break contact to look.

Fingers dig into my hair as he cradles my head, protecting

me from bouncing too much as he carries me to safety. Some-where warmer.

I jostle slightly in his arms as he steps onto a wooden porch, and for a moment he pulls back and I suck in a breath. Oxygen fills my lungs but I still feel dizzy. With want, with this need that makes my vision hazy.

"You okay?" he asks. We're beneath a porch covering so the rain no longer strains my vision, though the water is still streaming down both of our faces. He wipes the droplets from my eyes and, when I open them, I'm met with the most beautiful smile.

"I'll be better when we're both naked."

He laughs. "Getting there, Wildflower."

But before he has a chance to grab for the door, I'm reach-ing for him again. My hands dig into his hair as I press my mouth to his. He groans and lifts me up, his fingers slipping beneath the fabric of my dress as he squeezes my bare cheeks, which are now damp from my dress. "Fuck, you feel so good."

"Don't stop," I whimper as one of his fingers dips beneath the fabric of my thong.

"We should go inside," he murmurs against my lips, but even as he says it, his fingers explore. "Holy fuck, you're soaked." He groans against my moan, sucking on my tongue as my eyes roll to the back of my head.

"Please," I beg. I don't know what I even want from him. All I know is that I need him to keep touching me. Every-where. White-hot flames burn beneath my skin. He's set-ting my body on fire with every swipe of his finger against my cool skin.

"Need me to take the edge off?" His knuckle grazes my clit, and I sigh in relief. Walker's dimple pops as he presses me against the wall of the house, his smile wolfish. "That feel good?"

I nod and our breaths mingle together as he continues to move his fingers slowly, his eyes never leaving mine as he studies my every reaction.

How my eyes dilate. How the whimpers slip from my lips. How a blush fans across my cheeks. In his deep, raspy voice, he details the expressions on my face as his finger slowly slips inside me and my mouth falls open in shock.

I'm going to come. It's embarrassing how quickly he's getting me there, but I know without a doubt that the way he's thrusting his finger and grinding his palm on my clit, I'm going to explode. His brown eyes never leave mine, and his mouth eats my every moan and whimper until I'm clamping down and pulsing, warmth spreading over my body like the jets from a bubble bath.

I'm hot and unbelievably turned on, my need for him nowhere near fulfilled. "More," I groan.

Walker swallows like he can't get a word out just yet, then he reaches for the door handle and carries me inside. He's just set me on my feet and is reaching for the buttons on my dress when I register where we are. It's one of the cottages. I'd worried he hadn't made much progress, but this one is in better shape than I thought. I glance around. Most of the room is covered in white sheets, and the walls look like they've been freshly painted.

"When did you have time to do all this?"

Walker shakes his head. "Later. We'll talk later."

His lips trail down my neck, and all thoughts fall away.

My hands go to his waist, and I tug on the hem of his shirt. "Off."

His laugh is husky as he steps back and pulls it over his head with one hand. Then he's kicking off his waterlogged boots and stripping off his wet jeans.

Though my rain-soaked clothes are dripping all over the hardwood floors, I can't seem to move as Walker stands before me, completely nude. His cock is hard, standing tall and straining toward me.

"Holy big dick," I whisper, unable to get over just how large he is. I lick my lips. "Are all cowboys that well-endowed?"

He grunts as he steps one foot forward, but I hold up my hand. "Wait." His brows raise. "Touch yourself," I demand.

A smirk kicks up the side of his face, pulling that dimple deeper into his cheek. "You want a show?"

I nod. God, do I.

"Need you out of those dripping clothes first. Can't have you getting sick on me."

I push down one of my boots with my heel and then kick it across the room before doing the same with the other one. "Worried about me not being able to help at the festival?" I tease.

He grips his cock and runs his hand down the smooth expanse. "No, I'm worried about you, Wildflower. I couldn't give a fuck about the festival."

Those words are heady. So is the visual in front of me: Walker working himself slowly as I continue to undress. My bra and panties stick against my skin after the spring thunderstorm. I peel off my panties, keeping my eyes on Walker as I bend down, not wanting to miss a moment of what he likes. Learning how he wants to be touched, how I can please him.

If tonight is what I'll be thinking of on my deathbed, I want him to feel the same. I want to ruin this man so he'll never be able to escape the thoughts of the wild night he had with his wildflower.

Finally both naked, he steps closer. "What do you want first?"

"What are the options?" I tease, my eyes dancing.

Walker wraps one hand around my neck and pulls me to him. My skin heats the moment my breasts hit his chest. He pulls my hair tighter, and my head falls back just so, forcing my mouth up. He runs his nose from right behind my ear to my neck, sending shivers cascading over my body. "You can have my mouth." He presses his warm, open mouth against my neck and sucks. "Or my fingers." He breathes against my skin, and my sex clenches, empty and waiting. "Or my cock," he purrs against my ear.

I keen forward and grasp his length, pulling a whispered "Fuck" from him. He's silky smooth as I glide my hands down and cup his balls. "I'll take one of each, please."

His husky laugh against my shoulder is followed by his hot tongue. Then he reaches down and rolls his thumb across the head of his cock. He pushes his glistening thumb between us, all the way up to the edge of my lips, and then commands, "Open."

I do, and when he slides his thumb against my tongue, I suction my lips around it and suck the salty pleasure from him.

My mouth waters, needing more, and a whimper slips from my throat. "You're a needy little thing, aren't you?"

Pulling his thumb back, he glances around and then pushes us back toward the white cloth–covered furniture. He grabs the sheet, exposing what is clearly a new couch. "Sit."

I almost laugh at how, even during sex, he's a man of few words.

"Please," I chide.

He grunts as he grabs his cock, squeezing like he needs it to hold him over. "You want me to beg, Tally girl?"

If I thought I was on a high before, nothing compares to that idea. I nod. "Yes."

Walker isn't a boy like the guys I've fooled around with in the past. This is a man who knows what he wants. Who is comfortable enough in his own body to submit to whatever I ask. Who revels in pleasing me.

He leans closer, pressing a kiss to my lips. "Please, Wildflower," he mumbles against my lips. "Please sit your pretty ass down on this couch, spread those legs, and let me use this mouth the way I've been thinking about since I first saw you."

Even though he's just begged like I asked, he pushes down, gently, on my shoulders, forcing me to lower to the couch. There's something about that juxtaposition that has me overheating—him forcing me down while also begging for my submission. It has me nervous I'll leak all over this brand-new couch, so at the last minute, I grab the sheet before sitting the rest of the way.

"Such a good girl," he murmurs. His praise makes my stomach flip. "You know you're going to make a mess."

I nod as he grips my chin to hold me in place. Then, with his other hand, he runs his cock against my lips, brushing his essence across them. "Lick," he commands, pulling back, making it clear he means my lips.

I make a show of it, sucking them into my mouth.

"I'll never last," he mumbles. "But please, Tally, please suck my cock."

The powerful elixir of his begging has me canting forward, grasping his hips and tugging him to me. I suck him into my mouth in one swift move, and he grunts as he falls forward. I choke because I've never been with anyone this big. "Breathe, Tally," he murmurs, catching himself and then stroking my cheek. My eyes lift and I find that his are filled with so much warmth. "Thatta girl, look how good you're taking me. Those pretty eyes of yours are watering, they're golden for me."

I swallow and he curses again. "So good, Tally. So *fucking* good."

The ache pulses between my legs as I continue to suck him deep, wanting this to be the best damn blow job of his life.

"Can I come down your throat?" he pleads as he trails a finger up and down the center of my neck before wrapping his hand around it.

His eyes flare, and when I moan in delight, his grip tightens. "My wildflower likes it a bit rough, huh? You're going to let me fuck this throat for a second?"

I nod around him and his lips lift. "Yeah, you will. And then I'm going to eat that desperate pussy. You want that, Tally? Want me to feast on you? Drink your cum? Make you squirt down my throat?"

My body spasms at his words, and desire floods between my legs. Oh my God, I'm going to come the minute he touches me again. I'm unable to even speed up this part to get him there because he's holding me in place as he slowly thrusts in and out of my mouth, stealing his pleasure. Taking and taking, while giving me exactly what I need. Because having Walker like this, experiencing this with him, is the hottest moment of my life.

His jaw tightens as his fingers dig in to the side of my

throat and his thrusts become more wild. He's chasing his high, whimpering and cursing, telling me how good it feels. How nothing has ever been better. How I have the best mouth. The hottest tongue. The perfect throat. And then on a growl, he warns me right before he pulses inside my mouth and comes on a curse.

I don't even have a moment to breathe before he's tugging himself back, hauling my thighs forward and dropping to his knees so he can suck me dry, just as he promised. The second his hot mouth hits me I jolt, but Walker is prepared, already having a steady grip, keeping me in place. "Fuck, Tally." He licks at me like he can't get enough. "I've never tasted something so sweet. Can I do this all night?" He sucks my clit into his mouth, and my back arches as I push my pussy against his tongue.

"Oh God," I pant.

"Not God, Wildflower, your cowboy. The man who is going to worship this pretty cunt for as long as you'll let me."

He leans back and I practically cry out, "What are you doing?" My breath is erratic, and my heart hammers. I'm so close to release.

On his knees he stares at my throbbing sex, a satisfied wolfish grin on his lips. "I'm going to make you squirt. Are you ready, Tally?"

I nod dramatically, my head a bobbing mess as I beg for whatever will result in me coming.

He dips down and presses a kiss to my left thigh, then ghosts his lips across my desperate pussy and presses a kiss to the opposite thigh. "Walker," I growl.

He chuckles, his hot breath hitting my clit. "Yes, Wildflower?" He licks between my slit.

"Make me come."

"Now who's the one begging?" he muses.

I wrap my thighs around his neck and squeeze. "I'm about to make you beg for breath."

He laps at me, nipping and sucking, and then, when I think I will die if he doesn't increase the pressure, he pushes a finger inside me, angling and twisting before, without any warning, I'm coming, my vision blurring as an explosion rips through my body. My thighs squeeze, holding him in place as I thrust up against his mouth, and then he's moaning. "There we go, yes, Tally, so good squirting for me." He licks at me, sucking everything from me, prolonging my orgasm while I see stars.

My thighs fall open, and I should be embarrassed by how his face glistens but I can't seem to care. Walker lifts me onto his lap and smooths a hand up and down my back. "You did so good, Tally girl."

I tip up my chin to look at him and he smiles down at me—a smile so genuine that wrinkles form around his eyes. I pucker my lips, needing to kiss him, and he gives in right away. The peck turns heated quickly and then I'm grinding against his already hardened cock.

"Is this okay?" he asks as he leans me back just slightly. His cock is still pressed against his stomach, but the warmth of me wraps around him and he teases my clit with his head.

"Yes," I reply, mesmerized with watching the way he plays with me like this. At how he toys with my pleasure.

"What about this?" he asks as he swipes a finger across one of my nipples, then pinches it lightly.

"God, yes," I whimper.

He pushes me back a bit more and leans down, sticking out his tongue. Then right before he lightly bites my other nipple he asks, "And this?"

Oh God. The questions, the tone, those damn eyes.

"Yes."

On my assent, his tongue laps at me, sucking my nipple into his mouth as he rolls me over his cock again. I'm so close. So desperate for him to fill me.

"Walker—" He glances up at me as I whine. "Can I fuck you?"

He smiles at my question. "You can do whatever you want to me. This is your show."

I lick my lips and then lean forward. He grips my shoulders, stopping my movement. "Condom?"

"I'm on birth control, and I've been tested. I'm good."

His eyes fall shut, and he groans. "You're going to let me have this perfect cunt bare?"

I smile. "If you're okay with that."

His lashes flutter open, and he leans in for a kiss. Before he presses our lips together, though, he pauses. "I'm good, too."

I knew that without him telling me. Walker would never put me in danger. He's a protector. It's clear in everything he does.

"I trust you," I tell him.

He nods, solemn. "You should." Then the tension grows again as he stares down at where I sit on him. "Lift up and put me inside you."

I do as I'm told, holding him between us before slowly lowering myself on him. "Oh God," I cry as I stretch around him. This probably wasn't a good angle to start with because

I can practically feel him in my throat in this position, but I can't take my eyes off us. Can't help but stare as he slowly disappears inside me.

"Christ, woman, that's—*fuck*—" The palm of his hand goes to his eye, and when his hands fall to my hips, squeezing, he blinks at me. "You have the perfect cunt."

A laugh bursts out of me. "So romantic."

"Fuck me, Tally. I'll give you romance later."

Chapter 29
WALKER

Tally sucks in a ragged breath. Her eyes dilate at my request, and my vision goes hazy when her pussy clamps around me.

"You want me to fuck you? Want to come all over this cock?" I grunt as she bounces down on me again.

I'm no match for this woman. She's been going toe to toe with me for the past few weeks and had she just spread her damn thighs, I'd have folded in one second. Handed her control of the flowers, the farm, my heart.

Hell, I probably already have. No one has ever felt so fucking good, so fucking perfect, so fucking mine.

I'm half off the couch, the sheet a mess beneath me. Tally straddles my hips and settles her palm flat on my chest as she starts up a rhythm, grinding her cunt against my pelvis. I'm so goddamn deep inside her, and still it's not enough. My hand goes to her throat and I pull her down, needing her mouth. "I want whatever you'll give me." I lick at her tongue, and she moans as I suck on it.

Tally melts against me at the action, and I take the moment to lift us both and carry her through the cottage. "Where are we going?" she squeals.

"Need to fuck you against every surface," I mumble as she bounces on my cock with every step.

"You taking me on a tour? Want me to tell you what a

good boy you've been, getting all your work done?" She cocks a bratty brow, and I pause to smack her ass.

"Walker!" she shrieks.

"Next time it will be your cunt."

She clenches around me, and I grin. "Oh, my naughty girl likes that, huh?"

She flashes me a smile so wide, it reaches more than just her eyes and grips my heart.

"I didn't know it could be like this," she says, her smile somehow morphing into something more.

Joy. She's happiness personified. And I think somehow being inside her—hell, maybe just being in the presence of that smile—is treating the poison inside me. Her smile chases away all that darkness.

I settle her atop the counter in the small kitchen, keeping her right at the edge, and my hands skirt up her sides, reveling in the ability to touch her wherever I want. Her skin flushes a beautiful pink as I continue my exploration, and I push her wild hair behind her ears to cradle her face. "Like what?"

"Fun. I didn't know you knew how to have it."

I chuckle and press my mouth to hers. "Brat."

When she bites down on my lip and I groan, she sighs into my mouth. "No, I meant I didn't know this could be so fun. That sex—kissing—that it all could be—" She loses her words as I slide slowly out of her and then her forehead kisses mine as we both watch me take her again.

"It can't be like this," I tell her. "Not with anyone else."

Those golden eyes of hers that I swear hold the key to my heart seem to lighten in acknowledgment. I'm under no illusion that she's mine to keep, but I do know that she's meant for me. That, for some reason, we were both meant to be here on this farm at the same time.

The lightening cracks loudly outside the window behind her and sets her alight. She's angelic, and my heart seems to skip along with the booming thunder when Tally throws her arms around me and pulls me closer. "More," she begs.

"Hold your thighs open," I command.

When she leans back and follows my instruction, I start to pick up the pace, fucking up into her as I strum my fingers against her clit. My tongue goes to her nipple, and I flick, once, twice.

She pants, anxious and on the edge. My thrusts slow as I try to decide what to give her, but I keep rolling my fingers gingerly over her clit, toying with it until her teeth begin to chatter with need.

"Please." Tally's skin is shiny, coated in sweat.

"You're so pretty like this, weeping for me to let this cunt explode. Does it ache, baby?"

"Yes." She begins pulsing her cunt, like little Kegel exercises that try to keep me inside with every thrust.

"Fuck." My vision goes black as she steals the blood from me and my balls tingle with this foreign need. I lose control and suck air through my nose. "Fuck!" This time it's a shout, and I pull my dick back just slightly and lift my fingers off her clit.

"I'm going to spank you," I warn her, my hand hovering right above her pussy. "Then I want you to soak me, Tally darlin'."

Tally's eyes are golden pools of trust, but I can taste her nervous excitement as she sucks in a breath and then nods.

I hit her clit—*hard*—and Tally's head falls back as she convulses around me. Then I roll my fingers over it before doing it again and again, rapid little smacks and then soothing circles, as I speed up my thrusts. My legs grow weak as my orgasm draws near, but I give myself no break, knowing she's close and needs the steady cadence.

"Holy fuck, Walker," she cries as she completely comes apart on my cock. I draw her close as she spasms and swallow her moans, right as I lose the battle and paint her insides, forever marking her as mine.

Chapter 30
TALLY

So tell me why you really stayed away from the farm all these years." Walker strums his fingers through my hair, almost putting me to sleep with his touch. We're lying in a brand-new bed in one of two bedrooms in the cottage. This is one of the bigger cottages that I've always loved. Probably because it's in the wildflower field. After round one—or maybe it was round one and a half?—of sex, he carried me in here, telling me he needed more room to play. I wasn't complaining when I had my third orgasm of the night with my head buried in a pillow as he took me from behind. Now we're both still naked, the sheets tangled around our waists as I relax my head on his chest.

Still, I really don't want to answer his question. My fingers curl around the smattering of hair on his chest, and I absently pulse my grip as we talk. It's a mindless movement, but it eases some of the tension from this topic. "We don't have to talk about it."

Walker's fingers dig into my hair, and he tugs so I'm looking at him. "Please. I want to know."

Warmth rolls through me at his interest. "That's sweet, Walker, but—"

"No buts." His grip tightens. "Let me in, woman."

"That's what he said," I respond with a giggle.

Walker rolls his eyes. "I'm being serious."

"Damn. For a man who doesn't like talking, you are saying an awful lot of words."

"I like talking to you." He says it almost defensively. And though it's a soft admission, it comes out a bit harsh. Like he's mad that he feels this way and even more mad that I haven't realized. I have, but sarcasm is my defense mechanism. If I keep people right on the outskirts of touching the real me, there's less chance I'll get hurt when this temporary fling comes to an end. Because it always does. I'll leave, and he'll forget about me. Because I'm just the temporary girl. The one who comes in and fixes things for a bit, not enough to be the one to keep.

Even so, with the way he's looking at me, I find myself spilling the truth. "I never went to college. I'm sure you've noticed that this farm doesn't make a ton of money."

Walker's brows furrow.

"Don't get me wrong, my parents would have mortgaged the land or sold off part of it if it meant I could go to school. I couldn't let them do that. And Penny was the bookworm. She was good at all that stuff, so I just figured their investment was better funding her." I sigh as his grip loosens on my hair and he goes back to running his fingers through it. My gaze falls to the window in the corner of the room; there are no curtains up yet so the lightning storm outside continues to brighten the space. "I figured that if I traveled to different resorts as a seasonal worker, I could save up money and eventually be able to afford culinary school without being a burden to my family. I've enjoyed it, too, don't get me wrong; I've really enjoyed it. I've gotten to work for some incredible chefs, and the one in Nantucket this summer, she's one of the best pastry chefs in the country. Restaurants hire her to fix their menus. To train their staff. And she asked me to help." I bite my lip. "So that's my story. I wasn't running, and I don't hate being here. I just have a plan that I need to see through before I can think about coming back." I tilt my head to look up at him again. "And I've already been accepted into the New England Culinary Institute in the fall."

"Tally, that's incredible." He leans down and presses a kiss to my forehead. "*You're* incredible."

"Well, I can only go if I make enough this summer to get me through culinary school without working. They offer the entire program online, but I want to do it in person." I bite my lip. "I just want to experience it, ya know?"

He brushes his lips against mine. "You will." I'm swept up in the kiss as he breathes me in, as my nerves ping-pong around in relief from finally having told someone everything.

Sure, Penny knows bits and pieces, but even she believes I left here because I wanted to. I never wanted my sister to feel bad that she went after her dreams. I did, too. It's just taken me on a different path and a bit longer than others my age.

"So tell me about your idea to sell baked goods at the festival and farmers market."

I shake my head. "It was a silly idea. There's no time. I'm supposed to be helping you prepare the cottages and everything else around the farm. Besides, I don't have anywhere to bake."

Walker's fingers dig into my hair and he tugs me so I'm looking at him again. "You'll use the kitchen in the big house. We'll make it work."

"We?"

"Yeah, *we*. You help me with jobs around the farm during the day, and I'll help you at night."

My eyes widen. "You can't be serious."

"It's a good idea. You can charge a pretty penny for those cupcakes. I know I'd empty my bank account for a bowl of that frosting alone."

I smile and Walker leans down and brushes his lips against mine. "Besides, the farm isn't paying you for all your help."

"It's the least I can do."

That's the understatement of the year. The guilt I feel for not having done more while my father was alive will forever haunt me. I bite my lip, though, because I know what my father would have done in our position. Walker may not like it, but that's just because he doesn't realize how this town works. "I do think we should take Eli up on his offer, though."

Walker growls and his hands dig into the flesh of my ass as he pulls me close. "Don't mention another man while you're naked in bed with me."

I chuckle. "Men. You're all the same."

"Yup." His dimple pops as he grins down at me, and I'm so shocked by it I almost forget my words. "But I'll think about it."

"Really?"

Walker pulls me onto his lap, and immediately I feel his erection growing between my legs. "Really. Now, no more talking, woman. I need you."

"Again?" I grip him between my fingers, stroking up and down slowly.

He stares down at where I'm holding him. "I've got weeks

of wanting you to make up for. I've fought this since the day you stepped foot on this farm."

"You were in a towel," I say before rolling my thumb over his crown.

A smile hooks his lips. "I was."

I sit up, my breasts hanging heavy, my want making me grind against him. "You looked so good, Cowboy."

That smile expands.

"So three whole weeks you fought these feelings." I grip my breast as he groans watching me. "So desperate I got ya to break."

He laughs and his hands squeeze my hips. "You say it like it's nothing, but you have no idea what a feat it is. I don't want things. Don't dream of people."

My movements stop. My palms fall to his chest. "What do you dream of?"

The apple of his throat works. "My sister being happy. My nephew's smile. The land beneath my feet. A simple, easy life."

His eyes rove over my naked body. "*You.*"

Me. Elation has me lying flat against his chest, and I press a kiss right above his heart.

His mouth goes to the crown of my head. "You make me think of nothing but you. Damn distracting is what you are." His hands roam up and down my back and then he squeezes my ass.

"Can't have that," I whisper conspiratorially.

We hold one another's gaze, and with the light of the moon cutting through the dark cottage, I don't miss the longing in his brown eyes.

I don't like the way he's suddenly looking at me. Like this

is so much more than either of us signed up for. Because falling for a man and raising babies on this farm isn't part of my plan.

I blink, cutting off our eye contact. Giving up my dreams for a man isn't happening. "Well, I'm glad we scratched the itch," I say, even though the words feel all wrong as they come out.

Walker's hands fall away from my body and he shifts, turning on his side and staring at me.

"Oh, you think you've gotten your fill?" He says it like he knows exactly what I'm thinking. No one has sex like that and doesn't want to go back for seconds. Thirds. *He spanked my freaking clit.* I'll be craving that high for a long, long time.

"I'm not the one who's been fighting this attraction, Cowboy."

A wicked smile finds his mouth, and his fingers trail down my legs, spreading me, his middle finger sliding inside me in one indecent stretch. "So you've had your fill, Tally?"

I can't hold back the moan or the way my body arches for his touch.

His lips find my collarbone, and he presses hot kisses against my already heated skin. He stretches me with a second finger, and I cry out in response.

"That's right, Wildflower, open for me. Your mouth might be telling me one time is enough, but your body gives you away."

"Just don't want to distract you," I rasp.

His mouth finds mine in an instant; his tongue licking at me like he's so damn hungry. Like I'm his favorite dessert. "As long as you're on this farm, you're a distraction."

He presses my clit and rolls it so softly that I pant.

"Which means that, until you leave for Nantucket, you'll be in my bed. Letting me fuck you. Letting me pleasure you. I'm not accepting anything less than that."

I shift us so that I'm straddling him again, this time sucking him inside me in one quick thrust. His eyes squeeze shut on a curse. "*Fuck. Me.*"

"Only because you asked so nicely."

Chapter 31
WALKER

The repeated bleeping startles me awake before I hear Tally mumble "Make it stop."

I chuckle and press a kiss to her forehead. "I have no idea where our phones are."

She whines dramatically, but I don't blame her. I can't imagine it's past eight a.m., and we didn't fall asleep until after five. Pretty sure she closed her eyes and stopped talking mid-sentence. But I'd take the lack of sleep every day of the week if it meant having another one of those nights. And it wasn't just the sex. Though, fuck, thinking about it has me hard again. I've never experienced anything like it. Our sexual chemistry is insane. Her body, her mouth, *her* . . . I'm shattered.

The way she opened up to me is what did me in. And now, until Tally leaves, she owns me. Probably will after that, too.

The phone starts ringing again, and she groans. "Okay, okay," I mumble, rolling her off me as I go in search of the phones.

The living room is a disaster; wet clothes litter the floor, and the sheet covering the couch is half on. Her purse is in the corner, dropped just by the door. The phone screams again, and I finally locate it in Tally's clutch.

Mom.

I head back into the bedroom, holding out the phone to her. "It's your mother."

She throws her head into the pillow and groans.

"I could answer for you," I tease.

She shoots up and glares at me. "Don't you dare." Then she answers, "Hi, Mom."

I settle on the bed beside her and press a kiss to her shoulder. Then her neck. She sucks in a breath, and the sheet that was covering her falls, revealing those perfect tits I'm obsessed with. I lean down and suck one into my mouth, and she pulls the phone away to hide the hiss that slips out. Then her mother's voice booms through the speaker. "Tally, where are you?"

"I'm in bed."

"Not at the house, you aren't. I was just there looking for Walker."

Tally looks down at me, all wide-eyed and panicked. I, on the other hand, feel perfectly calm. Last night changed everything for me. Before my allegiance was to Peter and Gail, but now I know Tally means more than all of that. She may be leaving, but that doesn't make these feelings any less real. Gail and I will have to have a conversation. Soon.

"I'm going to shower and then I'll help you look for him."

My brows dance as I push her back onto the bed and pull the sheets off her completely, revealing my other obsession. "I'm right here," I mouth, before putting my lips between her legs.

"Did you go home with someone last night?" her mom asks suspiciously.

"No, Mom," Tally huffs in annoyance. "I stayed at Penny's after we went out."

"I already talked to Penny. She said you left before her and she hasn't seen you."

"Traitor," Tally mouths, and I chuckle.

Tally leans up and smacks a hand over my lips, her eyes like saucers.

"Oh my God, Tally, are you still in bed with the stranger?"

"Not a stranger," she grinds out.

"Eli, then?" Her mom sounds almost excited, and my entire body goes rigid.

Tally shakes her head and runs her fingers against my lips, like she's smoothing my frown. "*Mom*."

"Well, who is it?"

I realize in that moment that I'm not only hearing her mother through the phone. I shift off Tally, and she grabs the sheets, covering herself. "Mom, where are you?"

"Walking out by the fields, looking for Walker. I can't find him anywhere. Figured I'd check the cottage he's been fixing up for his sister."

"He's what?" Tally grits out, glaring at me.

Oh shit.

"I'll talk to you later," her mother says before the pounding on the front door of the cottage starts.

"Go," Tally says, pushing me out of bed.

"Go where?" I whisper.

Tally wraps the sheet around her and steers me toward the door. "Go talk to my mother. She can't know I'm here."

"Walker! Are you here?"

Annoyed, I stomp to the door and almost swing it open before realizing I'm still naked. But I'm too late because Gail's already seen the knob turning and pushes it open. I snag the first thing I see, a pillow on the couch, and cover myself.

"Oh my God, are you—"

I hold up a hand. "Just getting dressed. I slept out here."

"Why?"

Why did I sleep here? Well, because I was fucking your daughter senseless until five in the morning. "Tally brought someone home."

Gail face drains of color. "Oh, Walker, I'm so sorry. I'll talk to her. *That girl.*"

She tsks and I hold up a hand once again, not wanting to continue this conversation. Not just because I'm naked. But because if she says anything negative about Tally, I might lose it.

I'd never raise my voice to a woman, but if anyone makes Tally feel bad after everything I learned last night, we're going to have a problem.

"It's fine. She's a grown woman. She can do what she wants."

"I'd rather she didn't bring strange men into my house."

"It was a woman."

Gail's eyes bulge.

Fucking A. "I mean, I think it was just a friend. They were loud and giggling. It was probably Rosie."

She sighs. "Oh, those girls can make a lot of noise."

I nod, my jaw hard. "Well, if you don't mind."

I'm not sure how I keep finding myself naked in front of the Darling women, but it needs to stop. Well, except for one.

"Right," Gail replies. "When can we go over everything for the festival?"

Fuck, it's going to be a long day.

I promise Gail I'll come find her when I'm showered and wait for her to leave. Then I grab my jeans, which are mostly dry, pull them on, and head back to the bedroom.

When I enter, Tally is in bed, texting furiously. When she sees me, she sets down the phone to give me her full attention.

We have a lot to do, and obviously Gail's interruption was not how I wanted to start the day, but I refuse to let panic ruin everything about last night. So before Tally can open her mouth and tell me how she wishes we didn't almost get caught, how we need to be more careful, or God forbid, how this can't happen again, I stalk toward her, lift her chin, and press my mouth to hers.

Every ounce of stress, every insecurity, every worry, leaves my body with that simple connection. She hums against my lips in response, wrapping her arms around my neck and pulling me down on top of her, deepening the kiss. Time seems to suspend when her mouth is on mine. When she's in my arms, life isn't so complicated.

Spend my days on the farm; spend my nights with this woman. Smile more.

Hell, I can't think of a better dream if I tried.

She pushes me down and straddles me, but I hold her head, keeping our lips together. Tally sighs against me, and I feel the tilt of her mouth as she smiles.

"Now that's how I wanted to wake up," she says, her eyes still closed.

I kiss her once more before releasing my grip on her.

She blinks her eyes open. "So."

I press a finger to her mouth. "Don't ruin it."

A surprised gasp-like laugh leaves her mouth. "By speaking?"

I stare her down.

"Fine." She twists her lips. "Well, if I can't speak, what do you want me to do?"

I grin. I can't help it. This girl makes me happy. And I haven't had something that was just mine make me happy in a very long time.

"Did you know you have dimples?" She pokes my cheek like she's inspecting it.

My laugh takes me by surprise, and her eyes dance in response.

"You should take a bath."

Her brows rise.

"I'll go up to the house and grab you clothes since you can't go walking around the farm in your dress from last night."

She grins wickedly. "I don't do the walk of shame, Walker. I strut like a peacock." She shimmies her shoulders and throws herself back, exposing that beautiful body to me again.

I pinch her nipple, and she squeals. "You can strut like a peacock in dry clothes. I don't want you getting sick. We've got a festival to host, remember?"

Her mouth falls open. "Oh my God, the festival! Shit, you've got to go."

"That's what I said." I laugh as I pull her down to kiss me once more. "Go take a bath. I'm sure you're sore from last night."

She hums as she rolls her hips against me. "Awfully cocky there, Cowboy."

I smirk. We both know I stretched her in ways she's never been stretched before. Worked her over for hours. There's no way she's not sore. I'm going to love watching her walk around today, knowing why she's wincing.

"Don't think we're not going to talk about what my mom said," she says as she shifts off me. "About this place being for your sister."

"I know." My chest strains because the lies are starting to bleed together and I'm not sure what's the truth anymore. "I promise we'll talk later."

She bites on her lip and nods. I don't like leaving her this way. Don't like that we can't just live in the bubble we created last night for a bit longer. Before I make it past the door, she calls after me. "Hey, Walker?"

I grip the door and turn back to face her. "Yeah, Tal?"

She smiles at me. It's big and gorgeous, just like her personality. "I had a really nice time last night."

My heart takes off at a gallop. "Me, too, Wildflower." I knock my fist against the wall. "Me, too."

Chapter 32
TALLY

The sun kisses my cheeks the moment I step outside the cottage. I'd been nervous that once I left the bubble of happiness I'd found with Walker last night, everything would return to normal. But even the air feels different. There's a gentle breeze that rustles the flowers, awakening them as I walk up the path toward the house. It feels like the daffodils are spilling my secrets to one another, leaning slightly in my direction, gawking at my big smile. I can't wipe it from my face, though. Walker brought sunny days after a very dark winter.

I smile up at the sky and feel the sun smiling back. What an absolutely perfect day for the Daffodil Festival. Spinning on my heel, I inhale deeply, soaking up the scent left over from the midnight rain. An osprey takes flight overhead, and I watch as it soars over the meadows, which are now a tapestry of vibrant hues. Magenta tulips, violet hyacinths, rosy pink azaleas, and rows and rows of daffodils, with their petals spread wide and their mouths open. *Gossips.* Just like the Liberty Ladies. It's a good thing Walker got me clean clothes, or I'd have given them all something else to talk about.

The festival starts at one p.m. today and runs until sunset. Then we'll do it all over again tomorrow. It's already nine a.m., which means people will be arriving any minute now to help set up.

At that thought, I hear a car rumbling in the distance, taking the turn from the marina down the long road past the brewery. I've got five minutes tops to get inside and get my act together before our first visitor. As I approach the house, I slow my steps, not wanting to alert my mother to my presence if she's in the kitchen. I've got to text Rosie and get our stories straight so Mom doesn't figure out who I was actually with last night.

"She's probably at the brewery," I hear my sister's voice saying right as I step inside the living room.

I blow out a breath. I can work with that.

"Then why did Walker think Rosie was here?"

I enter the kitchen to find my sister and mom both sipping coffees and eating the raspberry lemon Danish I made yesterday. "Good morning! Is everyone ready for the festival?" I plant a beaming smile on my face and hope the question distracts appropriately.

"Ah, there's the little hussy," my sister teases.

My jaw falls open right as my mother laughs loudly. Despite not loving that it's at my expense, boy, do I love the sound of it. Penny eyes me, a surprised smile on her face as well. It appears she's just as shocked by the melodious noise coming from our mother.

"I was—" I stammer and shake my head. I don't want to lie. I may not be ready to share who I was with, but with my mom finally smiling, I'd rather be truthful. "Oh, forget it. Clearly you've caught me."

"I won't ask any more questions . . ." My mother's brown eyes dance, and she leans back against the counter. "But Tally, this pastry is delicious. Maybe you can give me the recipe? Or teach me how to make it."

I can't help the smile that spreads across my face. I appreciate her changing the subject. But even more than that, I appreciate the opening to spend more time together.

"I'd love that, Mom. All right, what do we need to do to make this the best Daffodil Festival ever?"

My mom holds open her arms. "Just the two of you. Here. With me."

I rush toward her, and taking one side while my sister takes the other, we all embrace. Mom's scent, a blend of peonies and jasmine that is another Rosie special, smells like home.

"We'll make Daddy proud," I murmur.

"He was already so proud of you both. But yes, let's make it the best festival yet."

My sister swipes a tear from her eye and smiles. "Deal."

I push away from the embrace but continue to hold both of their hands. It's time to get down to business. "Okay, we have to get the pastries out and the coolers filled. What else?"

Penny leans over the sink to glance out the window. "We should probably find Walker and see what he wants us to do. Has anyone seen him?" Her gaze flicks to mine and I narrow my eyes in response, telepathically telling her to shut up.

"Oh, I've seen more of Walker than I ever want to again," my mother says with another laugh.

"Mother!" Penny hisses.

"Wasn't my fault the man opened the door naked!"

I cover my mouth but a squeak makes it out nonetheless, and my sister howls with laughter.

"Anyway." My mother drags out the word. "He's out in the back, setting up the tables with some of his farmer friends."

"Farmer *friends*?" I ask.

My mother nods and takes another sip of her coffee. "Guys

he used to work with. He tried to send them away, but they wouldn't take no for an answer. Your daddy always said Walker wasn't good about accepting help, so I pretended to drop the chair I was holding and batted my lashes innocently."

"Mother!" Penny yells.

With another one of her doe-eyed expressions, my mother shrugs. "Listen, you don't stay married for thirty years without knowing how to get a man to do your bidding."

The three of us laugh, and a warm feeling spreads through my chest. I didn't think we'd get here again. Didn't think my mother would be smiling and joking around like she used to. It's nice. Hell, it's better than nice. It's goddamn wonderful.

—

"Do you think it's a prerequisite that all farmers have to be hot?" Rosie licks her lips and takes a sip out of her mug.

Penny shakes her head, but her eyes don't stray from the scene in front of us. "I didn't know jeans could fit that way."

Walker catches us staring mid-laugh and winks. It's the hottest thing he's ever done. Okay, maybe last night when he had his head between my thighs and was whispering dirty words to me was hotter, but only marginally. Fuck. My thighs clench. I need to stop reminiscing.

Walker's wearing a backward baseball cap, and the ends of his shaggy brown hair peek out beneath it. Flannel-covered arms sit across his chest as he talks to two other guys who are dressed similarly. They're pretty, I'll give the girls that. But they have nothing on Walker. One has darker olive skin, like he spends all of his days in the sun. The other is a bit older but has a broad chest and muscles that look like they have their own muscles.

It's not only because I'm sleeping with him that I think Walker is hotter. It's because I'm finally seeing him relaxed. Smiling. With the goddamn dimple. His stance is less tense, too. At least when he looks at me.

"Okay, I know you said nothing happened last night, but you are *so* lying." Rosie finally takes her eyes off the men with Walker and studies me.

"Nothing happened. We're just friends."

Penny snorts. "Right."

"Yeah, I'm not buying it," Rosie agrees.

"Listen. I'm only here for six more weeks. Why would we start something?" It's a good question. And one I'm trying not to think about.

"And he's too old for you," Penny mumbles.

"He is not!" I say a little too loudly.

Rosie lets out a loud raspy laugh, her entire body vibrating with the sound. "Right, they didn't fuck last night."

"Don't be so crass." Penny bites her lip, and a wicked smile forces her eyes to curl. "She got boned by Farmer Daddy."

"Ew." I push her and her champagne sloshes over the side of her coffee cup.

"Cowboy Daddy?" Rosie muses.

"Not a daddy," I hiss. "He's a-a—" I stutter. They break out into a fit of giggles. "Oh, I hate you both."

Rosie gets this look, and immediately my stomach tumbles because I know what's coming. "Fine. If nothing's going on, then you have no problem looking me in the eye and cheersing to it."

I glance at her glass and then down at my own. *Am I really willing to risk being cursed with bad sex to keep it a secret that I had deliciously dirty sex with Walker?*

Rosie arches a challenging brow, like she can read my mind.

"Fine."

Rosie beams. "Cheers to *not* having sex with the cowboy."

I suck in a breath right as Penny mutters "The only thing worse than no sex is bad sex."

I pull my drink back at her threat and shake my head. "I don't think that cowboy knows how to have bad sex. Now, I'm going inside to grab more pastries."

They're still hooting and hollering as I walk away. My secret is as good as dead. Dammit. I try not to focus on the fact that they know about Walker and instead look around at the festival, making sure everything is running smoothly.

We've set up a few tables just outside the fields, mimicking the layout of the farmers market. There are food and drink vendors, live music, and pastries for sale, including raspberry scones, blueberry lemon tarts, and Walker's favorite honey cupcakes. We've also put together dozens of bouquets that customers can grab to go if they'd rather not pick their own flowers.

Before we started hosting weddings, the festival was held in the flower fields, not farther up the drive, but kids would inevitably end up trampling the flowers, and with the limited crop this year—thanks to me—that is not a risk we can take.

My mother is talking to people who have plucked tulips from our pick-and-go field, which bloomed earlier than the rest and would be dying next week, anyway.

These are the things I never considered—the business

side of the farm—and it's clearly a tremendous amount of work. I have no idea how my father did all this by himself.

At least Penny and I are helping now. I'm ashamed to say I'd missed the last few Daffodil Festivals so I have no idea who supported my mom and dad before.

Guilt and grief war within my chest. I should have been here last year. I had no idea it would be my father's last, and I'll never forgive myself for taking so much of this for granted. For taking him for granted.

Right as I'm about to pass Walker, he grabs my hand and tugs. "Tal, I want to introduce you to my friends."

Despite the sadness in my chest, my eyes light up at Walker's words and I grin. "Who knew you had friends."

"Oh, I like her," the older of the two men says. He's got dark hair and a face covered in scruff, but his bourbon-colored eyes are warm as a melted caramel cupcake.

The other man, who's clean-shaven and wearing a backward Boston Rev's baseball cap, glances down at our hands and I realize they're still joined. Feeling slightly foolish, I flex my fingers, figuring Walker didn't mean to hold my hand. I was probably clinging to him because I was having a moment of sadness. But as I pull away, Walker only strengthens his grip and squeezes. With a flash of warmth in his eyes, he smiles down at me. "I like her, too."

"So you going to tell us her name or—?" Bourbon eyes teases.

"You're grown men, you can say hello." Walker gives it right back.

"I'm Tally." I stick out my hand.

When the older man gives me a firm shake, my other hand falls from Walker's, so he wraps his arm around my back and

I feel his warm palm settle into the back pocket of my jeans. I know both of them tell me their names, but I don't hear a word. I'm too stuck on the way Walker's hand fits in mine. How he so easily claimed me in front of his friends. My stomach does that swooping thing, and when I notice all three of them have gone silent, I realize I must have missed a question.

"I'm sorry, I didn't get much sleep last night. Can you say that again?"

The younger one's eyes trail over to Walker, and I know that if I look at him I'll turn as red as a rose because yeah, he was with me, *not sleeping*.

"Jackson asked what you do," Walker mumbles low against my ear. If I turned right now, our lips would touch. My body heats, and one quick look around makes it evident I'm not the only person realizing how close we are. His friends watch us, and when I spot my sister and Rosie standing just ten feet away, I realize they aren't attending to the customers in line waiting for pastries. Instead, they're staring straight at me. Gawking, really. Penny's mouth is popped so wide flies will probably take up residence. Rosie, of course, is wearing a smirk.

And then there's my mother. A daffodil in hand, a secret smile on her face. Shit. She's happy about this. As if there really is a *this* to be happy about.

I stumble back a little, getting some breathing room, because we can't do this. Even if I was sticking around past spring—*which I'm not*—it was just sex. I can't have my mother believing it's anything more. Can't get her hopes up. *Can't get my hopes up*, my sneaky mind reminds me, because I'm leaving. I need to get out of here. But I also need to answer this question.

"I'm a seasonal worker," I say, letting out a long breath.

"She's a baker," Walker says with pride in his tone.

I shake my head, embarrassed. "Not professionally."

Walker cuts me with his eyes. "She is. She's just not good at taking compliments unless I'm telling her how pretty she is."

My cheeks flush. God, he knows me so well. He could say a million things about me, and none of them would make me hot in the way him calling me a baker does. *Because he sees me.*

I don't think anyone has ever seen me quite like Walker does.

"She baked all the pastries over there. Go try one. You'll be begging her to make more."

"Speaking of—" I take that opportunity to escape because if he keeps sweet-talking me like this, I'm liable to drop to my knees right here. Or worse, kiss him.

Flustered, I point toward the house. "I have to grab more since we're running low."

"It was nice meeting you, Tally," Jackson says, and I'm glad at least I know one of their names.

"You both as well."

Without looking at Walker, I rush away. Though I don't even make it to the kitchen before I hear the door slam shut and his heavy footsteps follow me inside. Trying to appear preoccupied, I do what I came in here to do—not hide from him and all these big, oversized feelings that are swirling in my chest but scrounge up extra pastries to sell.

With every step Walker takes in my direction, my stomach swoops wildly, until I'm a bubbling-over pot of tension.

"Wildflower?"

When I don't reply, his arms land on either side of the counter, surrounding me until he presses his chest against my back and his mouth goes to my ear. "Feel my heart, Tal?"

I do. It's beating hard right against my spine. I nod but don't say nothing.

Walker rolls his nose into my hair and against my neck, and he inhales. "There's no need to run from me. I feel it, too," he murmurs.

"You can't—" I start to say but then I stop and let out a long breath. "We shouldn't—"

Walker spins me to face him. "I can, and we should."

"Only a few days ago *you* were telling *me* we couldn't."

Walker's lips lift, sliding into place, and that smirk appears. "And then I tasted you."

Wouldn't it be amazing if life really was that simple? If we could all just go after what we wanted and enjoy it? No worries about the future. No concerns about what others have to say. No guilt for the price we'll have to pay.

"I want it to be just for us," I whisper.

The smirk morphs into a real smile, and his eyes lighten. "We can do that."

I climb my fingers slowly up his hard chest and bite my lip. "So no winking at me in public." His brows dip. "No claiming me in front of your friends." He rolls his eyes. "And no getting attached." His jaw clenches. Palm flat against his heart, I focus on the rapid beat that matches mine. "The sneaking around will be sexy. We'll have to be careful . . . *and creative.*"

Walker's fingers slide into the pockets of my jeans, and his brow quirks. "Creative?"

I kiss the edge of his jaw. "So we don't get caught. Because technically you're my boss."

He squeezes me tight, tugging me closer and tilting his chin down so his lips are against mine. "Does that mean you'll actually listen to me?"

I snort, a happy giddiness warming me. I'm just about to suck his bottom lip between mine when I hear my mother's voice. "Tally!"

Walker and I both push apart, and I turn back to busying myself with arranging muffins on a platter. "I'm coming!"

"You're not right now, but you will be tonight," Walker husks as I walk past him. He's adjusting himself, and I bite my tongue to keep from whimpering at the sight of how hard I've made him. "You can hide from me in public, Tally, but in this house, when everyone is gone"—he leans into my space before I can disappear—"you're mine."

But because I can't ever let him have the last word, I sway my hips, knowing he's still watching. "Who says we have to wait until tonight?" I wink at him over my shoulder. "Be more creative, Cowboy."

Chapter 33
WALKER

I chuckle darkly as I pull Tally into the shed. It's only been a day since she laid down her rules about sneaking around, and already I've had her behind the house while Rosie and her sister called for her to bring out more pastries.

Just now, though, she stuck out her tongue at me because I winked at her across the festival.

No winking. That's another one of her ridiculous rules. Apparently, when I violate her rules, she turns into a brat, which only makes me want her more.

"On your knees, and don't you dare make a fucking sound," I say, my hand covering her mouth to keep her quiet. Day two of the festival is in full swing, and it's possibly even busier than yesterday. All of our hard work during the last few months has been worth it, considering the footfall we've experienced the past two days, but damn if I can't claw back some quality time with my girl. Tally will be pissed if we're caught this quickly, though. And she's not wrong: The sneaking around is fun, and I haven't had fun in—fuck, I don't think I've ever had this kind of fun.

Last night, Tally, Rosie, Penny, and Gail all stayed up late, baking in the kitchen. They were laughing into the early morning hours, and as damn tired as I was because I'd barely slept the night before, I couldn't fall asleep. I liked hearing Tally's happiness drift up the stairs.

Today she's been walking around in another of her floral dresses, those pink cowboy boots that have become my obsession on her feet, delivering drinks to people sitting on the Adirondack chairs out in the wildflower field. We've got a guitarist strumming The Lumineers's "Flowers in Your Hair," which is only enhanced by the harmonious chorus of chirping birds that keep sweeping in to grab crumbs from Tally's raspberry and lemon scones. Those are one of the new additions from last night's baking festivities. The daffodils seem even brighter today, too—maybe jealous of all the attention the wildflower meadow has been getting. Or maybe it's me. The world is all vibrant hues and melodious tunes since Tally became mine. Hell, even the mountains are abloom with rhododendrons. The crimsons, whites, and pinks are an explosion of color behind the dazzling harbor, where boats sway in a dance that seems choreographed to go with the music.

Tally had quite the idea to set up the Adirondack chairs in that meadow. With that view, no one will ever want to leave.

And if these cottages work out, maybe they'll mean more regular visitors.

"Well, you brought me in here, Cowboy. Do you plan on doing something?" She teases now because I've lost my damn words with the way she just settled on the floor so compliantly.

She's the prettiest thing I've ever seen, with her gauzy green dress fanning around her and the bottoms of her cowboy boots upright as she stares at me from her knees.

I grip her jaw and tilt her face up, stroking the smooth skin beneath her chin. "Undo my belt, Wildflower. Show me what a good girl you can be."

Her head falls back in pleasure as she reaches for my belt. Then, like the obedient thing she's pretending to be, she tilts her eyes to me, waiting for instruction.

"Zipper."

She hums as she pops the button of my jeans and then tugs down the zipper.

"Now take my cock out."

My heart is pounding as I watch her lick her lips and then reach up and pull my hard cock through the opening in my boxers.

"Tongue out, just like you did before when you were being a brat."

Her lips twitch as she tries to fight a smile. Then she slides out her tongue and I step closer, rolling my hard cock across her glistening tongue.

"Now I'm going to fuck this mouth, Tally, and no matter how badly you want to, you aren't going to touch me or yourself. Understood?" Her eyes widen, but she settles her palms flat on her knees and opens her mouth wider, waiting.

Fuck, my dick swells and I know I'm in trouble. I've never been so turned on in my life. I grip her jaw and hold her in place while I slide inside her mouth.

"Pinch my thigh if it's too much," I warn right before I thrust deep into her throat. She gags, and blood rushes to my ears. "Fuck, I love that sound, Tally. Do it again," I tell her right before I hit the back of her throat. She splutters around me and her eyes water, but she doesn't lift her hand to stop me. No, she just hollows her cheeks and stares up at me, taking it all.

The feel of her mouth, the way she's staring at me, it's all so fucking good. I push down her dress and bra to play with her tits. She moans around my cock and pushes her chest up, loving having her nipples tugged.

"You're being such a good girl, and you know what good girls get?" She hums around my cock, not stopping, but her golden eyes raise to mine and she watches me as she sucks harder.

"Good girls get fucked." I hold a hand down to help her up and she sighs out a "Thank God."

I chuckle. "Knees hurt?"

"No, but my pussy is throbbing. I need you."

This girl.

I spin her to face the wall and push her hair over to one shoulder, pressing a kiss right behind her ear. "Can't have that now, can we?"

"Please, Walker, quick," she begs.

"Lift up your dress and lean forward. Let me see how wet you are for me."

Like the wanton thing she is, Tally grabs the bottom of her dress and pulls it all the way up, exposing her ass cheeks, which only have a black string between them. I press my fingers between her thighs and revel in the damp fabric. "You're soaked, Tally darlin'."

She hums as I slide one finger inside and then run it between her dripping pussy lips. "Can I have you right here, baby? Can I fuck this tight cunt and keep you quiet?"

She shudders out a whimpering breath. "Maybe."

"No *maybe*s. Do you need something to help you stay silent?"

She nods so I slide the panties off her hips and then bring them to my nose, inhaling. Already I'm addicted to her smell.

Unable to wait another second, I take her hips in one hand and line myself up at her entrance right before I take my other hand with the panties in them and shove them into her mouth at the exact moment I push inside her. She screams around her panties, but it's muffled so no one but me can hear. Then I wrap a hand around her waist and play with her clit while I fuck her in slow thrusts. "That's a good girl. Taking my cock and not letting anyone know. This is how you like it, though, right Tal, my dirty little secret?"

She nods as she bounces her ass against me.

I may be fucking her, but I'm the one who's thoroughly fucked, and as she comes beneath my fingers and squeezes my cock, dragging my orgasm from me, I don't see a damn thing wrong with any of it.

Fifteen minutes later I return from the bathroom, having snuck Tally to her room so she could clean herself up before coming back for the rest of the festival. We've still got a few more hours to get through before I can hopefully get her in my bed. Fucking her in secret is fun, but I crave the quiet we had in the cottage after sex. The midnight confessions under the moonlight with her warm body against mine, her hands strumming against my chest, her heart beating a steady rhythm with mine.

I step off the porch just in time to see Gail staring out at the driveway, the back of a familiar truck disappearing toward town.

I set my jaw. "What the hell did he want?"

My voice comes out gruff, and Gail's shoulders jump in shock.

She turns around and I eat the distance between us in quick steps. "Sorry, didn't mean to scare you."

Gail shakes her head, but her eyes are tired. "It's fine. He was just stopping by to remind me that we owe him another lump sum payment by the end of the season."

"Well, we knew that." There's no need for Frank to remind us. My fists flex. I don't like this at all.

"This big Hall event will work, right? We'll be able to save the farm?" For the first time since we came up with this plan, Gail looks truly lost.

I reach for her and tug her against my chest. She folds herself against me, and I can feel her arms shaking. These Darling women have gone from being strangers to the closest family I have, outside my sister and Quinn, in less than a year. I can't let them down. Any of them.

I blow out a breath and realize I can't do this alone. Tally was right about that. And because I'll do anything to keep Tally happy, I leave Gail and go in search of a solution.

Despite the fact that I was looking for him, when I spot Eli, he lights up like he was the one searching for me. It's clear this guy is starved of attention, but he's seeking it in all the wrong places if I'm the one he's trying to befriend. "The nominations are starting soon," he says as he wraps an arm around me and walks us toward the fields.

"The nomi-what?"

"The nominations. For grand marshal."

I have no idea what he's talking about, and I'm sure my face says as much.

He laughs. "You really don't know? How could you run this farm and not know?"

"Oh, you found him!" Rayna coos as soon as she spots us. The sun is a gorgeous orange blaze as it begins to set, casting a golden glow over the entire farm. I'm glad the festival has been a huge success, and I'm hearing murmurs in every direction about how it's been the best one yet, but I'm beyond ready for it all to be over. I'm exhausted. Even after everyone leaves, we'll still have hours of cleaning up to do before I can crawl into bed. What I need is sleep. What I want is Tally.

The fact that she's leaving in six short weeks means every second is precious. I can sleep in June.

"Sure did. Guy was fooling around in the shed."

My head whips toward Eli, and I drop my arm from around him. "I was not."

Eli coughs out a laugh.

"Then what *were* you doing?" the town's nosiest resident asks.

"Hiding from everyone because they talk too much," Eli says with a sly smirk.

The glare on my face fades. I'm not sure if he's covering for me or if he really thinks that's what I was doing. Because it is.

"All right, well, now that you're done sulking"—she says with a pointed look in my direction—"can we get to the nomination part?"

I have no idea what this woman is talking about, but I'm tired of the attention being on me so I nod and attempt to skulk to the back of a crowd that's gathered around one of the live music stages. I just need this thing to be over so I can ask Eli about the cottages. The ex-NHL player follows me, and when we make it to the back of the group, he mumbles, "Your zipper's down."

I quickly fix myself. "And you're only telling me now?"

He grins. "Figured you wouldn't want me to point it out

in front of Rayna. Oh look, there's Tally. Wonder where she's come from?"

It's clear from the tone of his voice, and the fucking Cheshire cat smile on his face, that he knows exactly where she's come from. I don't respond and try not to look at her. Which feels like forcing myself not to breathe. Eventually, I can't *not* turn in her direction, and even with my head remaining forward, my gaze wanders. Tally's tied back her hair in a long braid that rests on her shoulder. Her green dress is also back in place, leaving no evidence of the way I'd pushed it down while she was on her knees for me in the shed.

Fuck, how is it possible that I'm hard again? She laughs lightly at something Rosie says to her as she joins her best friend and Penny. I want to know what they're laughing about. I want to be beside her, holding her hand while she talks. I've never felt this way, and I hate how fucking needy she makes me.

"And Jesse Walker—" At the sound of my name, my focus snaps back to the scene before me. Fletcher stands next to Rayna on the stage, addressing the crowd.

"What did he say?" I ask Eli out of the side of my mouth as I give a general nod to Fletcher and everyone else who's now glancing back toward me.

"He was thanking you for hosting the festival along with the Darling girls."

It feels odd to accept this gratitude when people don't understand why I'm involved to begin with. Yes, they know I work here, but surely they see this as the Darling's family farm. And I can't imagine that Fletcher knows about the agreement Peter and I had. If he does, he would have said something to one of the girls. Though what the hell do I know?

"As you're all aware, our tradition is to nominate candidates for the grand marshal of the Summer Solstice Parade, which celebrates the end of spring and the founding of our town, at the Daffodil Festival. This is the greatest honor we can bestow on a resident. Nominees must be present at the Spring Fling—which the lovely Rosie has agreed to host at the brewery this year—and present a speech as to why they should be Hope Harbor's grand marshal. Voting will occur that night, when the winner will be announced. So without further fanfare, Rayna McGovern, last year's grand marshal, will handle the nominations."

My gaze roams to Tally, who is needling Rosie, I'm sure over Fletcher calling her lovely. If there's one piece of town gossip I've been unable to avoid, it's that something weird is going on between Fletcher and Rosie. The two of them do nothing but fight whenever they're in the same vicinity.

"Thank you for your kind words, Mayor," Rayna says, taking over the proverbial mic and drawing my attention back to her. "A reminder that the citizens you nominate should be someone who has shown a dedication to our town, who appreciates the significance of our traditions, and who is willing to tirelessly stand up for them."

I roll my eyes. What is this nonsense? It sounds to me like the grand marshal just walks down the street in a parade.

"Hey, while they're doing this," I mumble = without looking at Eli, "do you think you could maybe help get the cottages ready for the the big Hall event?"

Eli's head whips in my direction, and his eyes light up. "Really?"

Fuck, the guy looks so damn happy. He's probably going to make this whole process exhausting. I'm about to backtrack when I hear Tally's laugh and I'm reminded of how much this farm means to her. How much the wildflower fields mean to her. I can't let her lose any of this. And taking any more money from Frank's loan to finish the cottages will only get us in more trouble. "Yes. Do you think the guys from the fire department can help, too?"

Eli grins. "I'm sure the whole town would be happy to help, Walker. It's how we do things."

The chatter around us stops, and we both look up to see what's happening. "All right, nominations are open!" Rayna says loudly, and the crowd cheers like someone just scored a touchdown.

Then silence takes over again as everyone waits for someone to shout out a name. Rosie's the first to take the bait. "Eli Davis!"

The man straightens beside me. "Thank you," he replies with pride.

"Angelina Rhinehart!" someone else screams, and the Liberty Lady beams.

"Stew Garrison!"

More names are shouted and as Fletcher scribbles on a piece of paper. I tune out the noise as I think about what needs to be done at the cottages when I hear a familiar voice over the chatter.

"Jesse Walker!" Tally hollers.

A round of people shout my name, and I try not to growl

out a *What the fuck?* but when I look toward my girl, she's wearing the biggest smile and all that angry energy leaves me in one easy breath.

Eli nudges me. "Looks like we're going to be spending a lot of time together."

Oh, for fuck's sake. What the hell did the woman get me involved in?

Chapter 34
WALKER

HOPE HARBOR TOWN CHAT

FLETCHER: Reminder, the town meeting is at 7 p.m. tomorrow night. Looking forward to seeing you all there.

STEW: Can I add an item to the agenda?

RAYNA: No Stew, you cannot have the old ice-cream truck.

STEW: You don't even know that's what I was going to ask.

BABS: You try to add it to the agenda every week.

FLETCHER: Unfortunately they're right Stew. Federal law regulates the mail. You have to drive the mail truck.

ELI: Can I buy the old ice-cream truck?

BABS: Oh! Are you going to do ice-cream delivery? Maybe without a shirt on?

RUBY: I second that.

MINDY: Approved!

FLETCHER: Ladies, please!

WALKER: Who keeps adding me back to this chat?

* * *

Lying naked with half a blanket covering her ass, Tally looks beyond irresistible.

I glance at my phone and know we don't have much time. Last night, after the festival was over, we crashed out here in the cottage. We had sex but it was quick, and I'm pretty sure we both fell asleep the moment after we came. I'd let her sleep, but I know Tally will be pissed if I don't warn her before they get here and I like to avoid pissing her off.

My cock is hard as I walk across the room and settle beside her on the bed. She moans as the bed dips under my weight but doesn't open her eyes.

"Tally girl, time to wake up."

She shakes her head and buries it in the pillows.

"Sorry, baby, that's not going to work." I pull the sheet off her and land a smack on her ass. Redness blooms, and her hips lift in shock. She moves just enough that I'm able to snake my hands beneath her thighs and pull her up while simultaneously dropping down between her cheeks and sliding my tongue inside her from behind.

"Holy shit," Tally hisses the moment my tongue hits her pussy.

I eat her from behind, my tongue buried inside her, licking and sucking like I'm a man starved.

"God, I could get used to waking up like this," she moans against the pillow as she rides my face.

She's on the edge, but I pull back and slam inside her in one quick thrust. Fuck, she feels perfect, clamping down around me as I buck into her repeatedly.

"I'll wake you up like this every day, Wildflower. But today, we've got to be quick."

Tally looks over her shoulder and glares. "Why?"

I take that moment to flip her over and then slide right back inside her, fucking into her as deep as I can go. Tally moans, and her fingers go to her tits, plucking at them.

She's gorgeous like this; her eyes still a bit hazy from sleep but filled with lust, her lips open on a pleasurable cry, her cheeks flushed, and her cunt dripping all over my cock.

Needing to be closer, I lean down and kiss her. I love that she doesn't complain about having not brushed her teeth. That she lets me have her just like she is.

Finally, I pick her up and carry her across the room before setting her feet on the cool floor, right in front of the window. "Hands on the glass."

She looks at me over her shoulder, a wicked smile on her face. "Are you going to finally make me come, or are we just playing musical chairs?"

That sass. My palm clamps down on her ass again and her giggles quickly turn into a moan as I thrust inside her. I push her right up against the window, tits on the glass, her entire body exposed, and then I lean really close and whisper in her ear, "Better come quickly, Wildflower. Your friends are almost here."

Her gaze flies forward to see a familiar car crossing in

front of the harbor. They've still got a five-minute drive until they get to the big house, where I told them we'd meet, so I'm not concerned—I'd bludgeon Eli's eyes before I ever let him see her this way—but she doesn't know that. As expected, Tally's moans get louder because I know the thrill of almost getting caught heightens her desire.

"Who is that?" she pants.

I reach around and start playing with her clit, knowing she needs the stimulation to get there. "It's the town brigade. They're here to help."

"Really?" Tally whimpers. I'm not sure if it's the way I'm fucking her or the fact that I asked for help. I'm pretty sure both make her weak in the knees, and my cock swells knowing I've made her happy.

She reaches back and grabs hold of the back of my neck, tugging on my hair. "Thank you," she rasps as I push up into her. Then she kisses me, swallowing any response I could give her. When we both come, we share the same breathy moans and I know nothing has ever felt this fucking good.

Twenty minutes later we're both dressed and back at the big house. Penny and Rosie are seated at the counter chatting quietly, and Eli and Fletcher are lounging at the kitchen table, coffee cups in hand and a beautiful bouquet of wildflowers in front of them. I've noticed random bursts of color around the house during the last week. Little vases filled with flowers that Tally picks on her runs. There's even a burst of blue and purple right beside the coffee pot that I have to move in order to pour the second pot for the crowd of people here to help. As I do, Tally comes down the steps in a bright pink spandex outfit, ready to get to work.

The Daffodil Festival brought in a much-needed influx of

cash, and according to Gail, we had more guests than ever before. Still, I'll breathe a little easier once the cottages are ready for the vow renewal, which actually may tip us from the red into the green.

Rosie's eyes dance as she watches Tally, and it's like the two of them have an entire conversation as they stare at each other. After a minute, Rosie smiles. "Why do you look like you were just thoroughly fucked, Tally Darling?"

Eli coughs out a laugh while Fletcher glances down at his shoes and Penny snorts. I try to avoid looking at Tally, but I can't help it and when I glance up, she's throwing daggers at Rosie. "Get fucked," she mutters as she heads to me and the cup of coffee I'm holding.

She steals it right from my hands, and I smirk as everyone eyes us. I don't even think she realizes she just did that in front of them all. Did I prepare my coffee the same way as Tally just so she'd enjoy it if she stole it? Maybe. Though I'll never admit it.

There's a creak from the front door opening and then Gail appears, a bright smile on her face. "I thought I heard a few cars this morning. What's everyone doing here?"

· "Walker invited us all to help get the farm ready for the Hall event ," Eli explains.

Gail's jaw falls open. "Really?"

She glances at Tally, who shakes her head but holds out an arm to welcome her mother. "Don't look at me. I'm just as surprised as you." She glances at Penny. "Though it would appear Penny was aware, since she's here bright and early to help."

Gail settles beside Tally and wraps an arm around her. "Penny was always better at keeping secrets than you."

Penny lets out a loud laugh. "Coming from the best secret keeper ever, that's a compliment."

"So what's the plan today?" Eli asks.

I pour myself another cup—black, like I like it—and then turn to face our team for the day. "There are seven cottages that still need a lot of work. Let's break into groups of three and get them cleaned up today and then hopefully painted tomorrow. Then we need to sand down the furniture so I can re-stain it. Tally already took care of all the windows, so that's one less thing."

"And to think you thought Walker was being an ass when he made you do that," Rosie muses.

Penny laughs and Tally rolls her eyes, then shrugs. "Sorry, but you kind of were."

I was. But it worked out.

Turning back to the group, I say, "We appreciate all of your help."

Fletcher shakes his head and holds up a hand. "It's what we do."

"Still," I start.

Rosie nods toward her archenemy. "He's right. And thank you for doing this for our girls." She holds up her cup in cheers, and Penny drops her head on Rosie's shoulder in solidarity.

Gail clears her throat. "Yes, thank you, every single one of you." She looks around the room, making sure to meet everyone's eyes. In contrast, Tally holds her coffee cup in front of her face to shield her emotion. But when Gail turns to face her, she smiles at her mother, and the look between them has my heart pinching. I glance away, not wanting to interfere.

After everyone finishes their coffee, the conversation gets

louder as the smaller groups head to their respective areas. I'm heading out the door to follow them when Tally grabs the sleeve of my shirt, stopping me.

"Hey." She nods to the group as they walk the path toward the cottages, laughing and smiling as they go. "You've got people."

"No, Wildflower." I smile down at her. "*We've* got people."

Chapter 35
WALKER

For a week our friends show up in shifts, helping out whenever they're not at their own jobs. The fire department guys manage to get all the furniture sanded in one afternoon, and I spend the next day staining every piece with Eli by my side.

When we're not working, I spend every possible moment with Tally, though none of it feels like enough. We don't have any real conversations because we're too tired after a long day of work and we barely get ten minutes for a quickie before the first of the crew show up in the morning.

Everyone's taken to walking straight in and helping themselves to coffee when they arrive. I can't complain because they're working for free and we'd never get this done without them. Still, it feels cruel that I've finally got Tally all to myself but can barely have her.

The clock is ticking on her time here. She's taken calls all week from her boss in Nantucket. They've been working on different menu ideas, and when she finds the time, she grabs ingredients and tests them out on our friends during breaks to get their blind reactions. I love everything Tally makes, but it's all a reminder that she was never here to stay.

The fact that I can't just grab her hand and hold it when we're walking out to the fields in the mornings—or that she pulls away from a kiss when a door opens—only makes me more needy.

If I can't have her for long, I at least want her completely. Though I can't bring myself to tell her how I truly feel. It wouldn't be fair to her.

It's early Friday morning, and we've got our first wedding tomorrow, when Tally finds me out in the shed, scrubbing down all the chairs.

"Do you ever take a day off?"

I hold open my arms. "That your way of telling me I've been neglecting you?"

She hugs my chest and sighs. "No, that's my way of telling you you're neglecting yourself. Have you even slept for more than a few hours this week?"

"Tuesdays are my day off." I settle my hands on her ass.

"And yet you worked all day Tuesday, and I'm sure you'll do it again next week."

I shrug. "I like working."

She rests her chin on my chest. "I know, but there is more to life than work. You deserve some free time. Go get off the farm for a few hours and relax."

"*I can do that when you're gone*," is what I want to say. I can take a day off and disappear and do nothing when she isn't here anymore, but right now, there isn't a chance in hell I'm leaving this farm without her.

"What if," she walks her fingers up my chest, excitement teasing her words, "we have Tally Tuesdays?"

"What?" Transfixed, my eyes remain locked on the place where she touches me.

"Tally Tuesdays. You'll actually take a break if it's about me."

I smirk. "Oh, will I?" My hands settle on her hips again, and I hold her there. I don't want her to take even a minuscule step away from me.

She smirks back. "Won't you?"

I squeeze her hip. "Probably."

The joy that radiates off her could light an entire stadium. "All right, so Tuesdays are officially Tally Tuesdays—we're going to hole up in the cottage and do absolutely nothing but each other."

"Now that is a way to get me to take a day off."

She presses her lips to mine. "I'm very persuasive when I want something."

"Oh yeah, and what do you want right now?"

Tally's eyes dance with mischief and then she snags the cleaning towel right out of my hand and starts running toward the fields. "Guess you'll have to catch me to find out."

I take off after her, my cock already half hard knowing it's about to get some attention. The early morning sun lights Tally's golden hair, giving her an almost ethereal look as she runs straight toward the wildflower meadow. The harbor glitters in the distance, a pastel pink shimmer coating the still waters, and a gull squawks overhead just as I hear the telltale sign of a car coming round the bend. Dammit.

I hasten my steps, and when I'm finally right behind her, I wrap my arms around her waist, pulling her tight against my chest. My fingers skim the smooth skin of her stomach, and my palm flattens against her side. I move my mouth to her ear as I hold her against my pounding heart. "Caught you."

She's breathless and her head falls back against my chest. "Damn."

I chuckle as I press kisses against her shoulder, then her neck, and when she grinds her hips against my dick, I smile. Maybe Tally is going to give me a little attention this morning after all. I twist her so she's facing me and take her lips in mine. Our tongues tangle as my hands explore her body, kneading her ass before lifting her up into my arms. I drop us to the ground, and she grinds over me, her lips never leaving mine. "You going to fuck me right here, Wildflower?"

Her golden eyes are lust filled, and the space between her thighs is warm. Something comes over me, this need to possess her, to claim her, right here in the field she loves so much. Right out in the open.

And from the look in her eyes, it feels like she's on the same page. Like maybe she hates the sneaking around as much as I do. Like maybe she's ready to say fuck it like I want to.

Just as I'm about to skim my fingers across her tits and pull down that yellow fabric, a car door slams and raucous laughter fills the air. Tally's eyes widen, and she lets out a loud groan. "Sounds like they're here."

"Stay with me," I beg, holding her hips to mine.

Tally's eyes soften as she grins and presses a quick kiss to my lips. "We can't. You'll get us caught, Cowboy." Then she rolls off me and points toward the fields. "Give me a five-minute head start. I'll tell everyone I was out for a run."

My eyes close so I don't have to watch her walk away. It's a sight I'm pretty used to by now. But that doesn't mean I'm not getting awfully tired of it.

—

It's lunchtime before I get even a glimpse of Tally again. She's carrying a tray of food and setting it on the picnic tables right as I'm finishing up staining the last of the bed frames. The Liberty Ladies showed up this morning with quilts and new bedding. Rayna insists she bought too many sheets—claims she's got an obsession with testing out every one she finds and forgot she ordered an extra fifteen pairs. I can see right through her lies, but I appreciate it nonetheless. We can use all the donations we can get at this point so I can avoid taking any more money from Frank's loan.

Gail follows behind Tally with two jugs of homemade iced tea. There are fresh tangerines floating in the tea, which Tally told me is her secret ingredient to make it the perfect sweetness. Babs, Rayna, and Penny set out plates, and the guys from the fire department appear instantly, as if they can smell the food, despite the fact that it's only sandwiches and cookies.

I'm just heading over to grab a sandwich myself and hope-fully get a minute sitting beside Tally when Babs pats the spot beside her. "Have you given any more thought to the bakery?" Babs asks Tally.

Penny rolls her eyes with a smile on her face. "Please, she's probably got a countdown on her phone for how many days she has left in Hope Harbor, right Tal?"

Tally almost stumbles and drops the second plate of sand-wiches. "Um, what?"

My eyes narrow and I reach for the plate, setting it down for her.

"Yeah, Tally has big plans this summer," Gail says. "Like her daddy always said—"

The entire group of them finish her sentence: "You can't keep a wildflower in one place."

The words are said with a smile, but I see the hurt flash in Tally's eyes. The rest of the town doesn't see how much she's been trying to open up since arriving home. She's been work-ing day in and day out for this farm, and still they don't see her. I'm angry for her, but when I go to open my mouth and defend her, she scowls at me.

"Don't," she mouths with a shake of her head.

It's a reminder that we're not even dating, and it stings. So I grab my sandwich and head toward the cottages to eat alone.

Chapter 36
TALLY

Breathe, just breathe." My father's voice calls to me right as I start to spiral at the anger vibrating from Walker's every pore.

I inhale a deep breath as he storms away from the group. I should stop him. I should reach for his hand to reassure him. And yet somehow I can't give in to him when everyone is around.

It's only been a week since we said fuck it and started playing. I've never had more sex in my life and yet I'm constantly hungry for him. Constantly finding ways to taunt him into being just short of reckless. There is this thrill of almost being caught that I can't help but chase.

But right now it doesn't feel hot. It feels damn complicated, and I don't know how to handle this. It doesn't matter how much people love my cupcakes or my scones; I don't have the experience to make a name for myself yet, and eventually everyone will realize that. Hell, my mother and Penny already know it.

And Walker will tire of me at some point, too. Nobody has ever wanted me long-term.

Before I can open my mouth, Eli walks out of one of the cottages, practically barreling right into Walker, holding an old worn-out and faded LEGO box. "Found this in one of the closets. Garbage?"

My heart pounds as I stare at Eli like he's holding a bomb. Since the Daffodil Festival, I've only focused on Walker. He's been a perfect distraction from my grief and guilt over missing last year's festival with my father, but seeing that old LEGO set blows every sense of peace I've stitched together to smithereens.

Everyone's looking at me for a response, but words fail me. I'm sure my sister and mother feel the same way, but I can't look at them right now or I'll break down and lose it.

"I'll take it," Walker says, his voice softer now, his anger diminishing. I want to rush toward him and throw my arms around him. Want to thank him for dealing with my daddy's LEGO because apparently my mother, my sister, nor I can do it.

"I've got to grab something," my mother says, her voice filled with emotion.

I glance toward her right as Penny nods to me. "I've got her."

The two of them disappear, and I feel my heart teetering on the edge of shattering. I want to go to them. Want to help. But I never know what to say. And I can't get my feet to move.

Walker grabs the box from Eli, turning on his heel to get back to work.

"Oh, before you go," Rayna calls, somewhat breaking the tension. "Are you going to be at the town meeting this week?"

Walker turns around and frowns. "Why would I?"

"Because of the grand marshal campaign," Babs explains.

"I'm not running," Walker grounds out.

The entire group gasps in surprised shock.

"You're not?" Rosie asks.

"He doesn't have a choice in the matter." Rayna cuts him with a hard look. "One doesn't say no to being nominated."

"Why?" Walker deadpans.

"Because you don't," Rayna retorts before turning to me. "Tell him, Tallulah. Tell him how much it meant to your daddy."

"I—um, yes he—" As I struggle for words through the sadness, I feel Walker's hulking presence behind me.

Breaking my rules, he places his hand on my hip and squeezes. "What time is the meeting?"

Rayna's lips curve in satisfaction, and suddenly I don't want to be around any of them anymore.

"Seven p.m. on Thursday," she replies. "We'll see you then. Tallulah, are you going to sit down and take a break?"

"No," Walker replies for me. It takes exercising every muscle in my body not to relax into his chest in relief. Because with him, I'm safe. With him, I'm seen. "*Tally* is coming with me. We've got flowers to deal with."

"Is 'flowers' a euphemism for 'sex'?" I ask as Walker drags me into the house.

Walker doesn't reply. Instead, he paces ahead of me toward the kitchen until something stops him and he spins on his heels, stalking back to me. I back up against the door, not sure what to make of his hard jaw and wild eyes.

"Why do you do that?" he hisses.

"Do what? Make jokes about sex?" It's a weak attempt at our usual banter, and Walker's palm landing with a thump against the door, right beside my shoulder, makes it clear he thinks the same.

He heaves in a long breath. "Why do you let people treat you that way?"

I frown. "Huh?"

"Your sister, your mother, Rayna Fucking McGovern.

Why do you let people treat you like you don't care? You have absolutely no problem putting me in my place. Why didn't you put Rayna in hers?"

My eyes roam over his face and then, when I can't stand to see the desperation there, the way he's trying so hard to understand me, I look away. My gaze lands on the dining room table, with all of my father's papers strewn on top. His chair sits just behind, and my heart sinks at the sight.

Gently, Walker cups my chin and pulls my focus back to him. "It's okay to miss him, Tally. It's okay to say you want me to do this grand marshal thing because your dad did. Or fuck, I don't know, it's okay to feel something for me."

His brown eyes dare me to disagree with his words.

"Walker," I start. "We promised we weren't going to do this. We said no getting attached, remember? My inability to stand up for myself isn't your problem. I'm not your responsibility; I'm just someone you fuck."

"No." He spits out the word.

"You're not going to bully me into telling you I'm falling for you."

He doesn't react, so I push on.

"You're not going to bully me into admitting that seeing you doing all the things my dad used to do makes it impossible to separate the two of you. That I find comfort in sitting in the kitchen with you at night and talking to you about absolutely nothing because that's what we used to do." Once I start talking, spewing my every thought over the last few weeks, I can't stop. "Or how seeing that damn chair—*his chair*—pushed back from the table makes me think maybe he's just in the other room, but then my chest hurts so much it becomes hard to *breathe* when I remember that he'll never sit there again. Or how I'm so damn guilty that I missed last year's festival. And the parade, and every other little tradition this town has that my parents love so much. How I missed out on all of the days leading up to his last one and I don't know how to move past that. How he hired you since I wouldn't come back. *You're here because I wouldn't come back.* You're here because *he's not.*"

I push against Walker's chest, but he doesn't flinch. He takes the hits as I pound against him until I'm pulling on his shirt and forcing him to hold me. I rest my head against his chest, somehow managing to speak through heavy sobs.

"And then I feel even *more* guilty because I'm glad you're here. Because I like you and I feel like I'm betraying him."

Walker's arms squeeze me tight, and he presses a gentle kiss to my forehead. "Get it out, Wildflower. I'm right here."

Now, I'm crying broken, ugly tears. And still, Walker doesn't rush me. Doesn't try to give me false condolences. Doesn't remind me that I'm not selfish, or tell me that I'll do better with time. He just lets me cry until the tears run dry and my throat is sore.

My head falls back against the door, and I let out a long sigh. "I'm sorry."

Walker's head shakes as he cups both of my cheeks and smooths away the remnants of my tears with his thumbs. "We're not going to do that. You're not going to apologize for feeling." His lips pause and he presses a kiss to one cheek. "We're not going to pretend we don't feel something just because you're leaving." He brushes his lips across my face and kisses the other cheek to swallow my tears. "This is real, Tally. I'm here. For sex, yes, but I'd also like to be your friend. The sneaking around is fun, but what I crave is these moments. Just the two of us, when you're real with me. I want you to be real with me always. Dressed or undressed. Out in the fields or in the bedroom. While we're sitting together or while you're riding me. Can you do that?"

"Where did you come from?" I whisper. My sister would have dreamt up someone like him. But me? I never imagined someone could be so caring, so comforting, and so incredibly dirty at the same time. Walker is perfect, and I don't deserve him.

He lets out a deep sigh. "Your dad found me, sought me out. Would you like to hear that story?"

I nod and he takes my hand, leading me toward the kitchen. I don't know if he knows that's where my dad and I always had these conversations or if he does it because it's where we've had so many of them since I got here.

I settle on the stool closest to the wall and watch as he walks to the fridge. He pulls out a glass bottle of diet coke, pops the top, and adds a straw before pushing it toward me. My heart squeezes even tighter at the gesture; it's exactly what my dad would do to calm me down.

Walker pulls out the stool next to mine and begins to speak as he sits. "I grew up a few towns over, but for as long as I remember, I've wanted a farm like this." His gaze dims as though he's gone somewhere else.

"I spent every spare minute I wasn't in school working on farms in middle school. And then, in high school, I entered the agricultural program and spent even more time doing the things I loved. It was an escape for me." He sucks in a breath and then lets out a long one. "My life wasn't like yours, Tally. My mother wasn't around, and my father didn't like me. He died when I was eighteen, and honestly, it was the best thing to happen to me and Billie." I wince but Walker pushes on. "He was a mean drunk, and with him gone, Billie could have a shot at life. With the little money I saved working through high school, I was able to afford an apartment and keep food on the table for her, plus go to school full-time. My sole focus was looking after the only family I had left. I wanted to be needed. To mean something to someone." His shoulder lifts. "And I did that."

"How?" I ask softly.

"By working hard?" He runs a hand through his hair and shrugs again. "I don't know. I got this nickname: the soil whisperer. I guess your father heard about me. And I assume you know how he was when he got something in his head."

I smile. "He didn't stop until he made it happen."

It was one of his best and worst traits. There were countless LEGO sets throughout our house because my father never saw one he didn't think he could put together. Though they never quite looked like the image on the package.

Walker nods. "About a year ago, your dad showed up at the farm I was working at and offered to buy me lunch. I don't trust many people so I told him I was all set, but he showed up again the next day and brought a sandwich for every guy on the farm. I couldn't very well turn him down then, and he knew it. So we talked and he told me about this place. The problems he was having. His vision for the future. He asked me to give him an hour, to come over and see it. He said that whatever I thought, he'd take me to the brewery afterward for lunch. If it was a waste of my time, then at least I got a meal out of it, right?"

I smile, because this is exactly something my father would do.

"Now, I want you to listen to this next part, Tally, because it's the most important."

My slumped shoulders straighten and I nod.

"Your father never expected you to come back to this farm."

The words aren't a surprise, yet I'm unprepared for the ache that burrows into my chest. Walker reaches for my hand, which is braced around the bottle, and strokes it with his thumb. "He wanted to extend the season, and we agreed to do it together. We'd share in the profits. *That's* why I'm here. He knew you had other dreams, Tally, and he didn't need you to share his. You shouldn't feel guilty, wildflower. Your dad would be unbelievably proud of you. He *was* unbelievably proud of you."

Tears pool in my eyes. "Really?"

Walker nods. "It's not selfish to chase your dreams. Your dad did it. Penny did it. Hell, I'm doing it. Why shouldn't you?"

I shake my head. "Because wanting those things kept me from being here."

"You know what your dad always said?"

I offer a sad smile. "You can't keep a wildflower in one place."

He nods. "But I don't think he meant it the way you thought he did. He didn't mean you couldn't stay here, Tally. I think what he meant was that you're a force to be reckoned with. Someone who goes after what she wants and doesn't stop until she gets it. He understood you, Tally. So do I. And he was proud of you. Just like I am."

I laugh despite the tears streaming down my face. "God, I'm such a mess."

Walker smiles at me. "You're the most stunning mess I've ever seen."

"Flattery will get you laid." I swipe at my nose, and I'm pretty sure drool comes off on my arm.

He hands me a napkin. "As tempting as that sounds, I actually have other plans."

I blink, embarrassed that I've kept him here for so long when he clearly has a job to do. "I'm sorry."

Walker runs a thumb beneath my eyes and cups my cheek. "None of that, remember." He glances at the clock. "I think we both deserve a break today. What do you say we bring Quinn an ICEE before his game and then grab dinner with him and Billie?"

A soft smile plays at my lips. "That's sweet, though I'm surprised you're actually going to take a break."

"Well, someone told me there's more to life than work." He hums. "I'll go tell everyone that we're done for the day. You gonna shower and come along with me?"

I bite my lip. "Okay."

His face lights up. "Really?"

"Really, Cowboy."

And for the first time, I let myself think that staying in Hope Harbor *could* be the dream after all.

Chapter 37
WALKER

HOPE HARBOR TOWN CHAT

FLETCHER: Hi Walker! We're so excited that you signed up to judge the derby race! See you Thursday at the town meeting!

RAYNA: Hi Walker. The PTA thought it would be fun to have you come in to talk to the first grade about being a farmer. Does Wednesday at 10 work?

STEW: Hi Walker! Was wondering if you wanted to join us guys for a beer at the bowling alley Friday? We could use another player in our league.

"Oh, for fuck's sake," I grumble when my phone buzzes in my hand again. This is what I get for having my own people.

ELI: Want to grab dinner at the diner this week? We can go over campaign ideas?

I glare at the text, confused.

ME: Aren't we running against each other?

I groan, realizing what I just texted. Did I really just ask him if I'm running *against* him for grand marshal? Goddammit, this town drives me nuts.

ELI: Sure are but it'll be more fun if we do it together.

With another roll of my eyes. I drop the phone on the windowsill of the cottage I'm just finishing painting.

"I saw that."

I practically jump at the sound of Eli's voice. "Why the hell are you texting me if you're *right* there?" I drop my head down and groan. We're back to working nonstop hours, but Gail, Penny, and my family are joining us at the big house for dinner tonight. I say "us," even though Tally and I are still sneaking around. We made it through our first two weddings over the weekend without any major problems. Billie assisted Gail and Tally stuck by my side, but now the pressure is on when it comes to getting everything ready for the Hall event.

"Figured I'd test out the waters, suss your mood before I asked you this next thing." Eli's grinning when I turn around.

I motion to my face. "Is this scary enough to avoid any more questions?"

He chuckles. "Nah, I'm like Teflon. Nothing bothers me."

I roll my eyes, but my lip twitches in betrayal. It's hard not to smile when the guy is trying so damn hard.

He must see that momentary weakness because he pounces. "Do you have a date to the Spring Fling?"

I groan. "What?"

"The Spring Fling. Do you have a date?"

My teeth grind together. "Are you asking if you can take Tally?"

"Do you think I have a death wish?" Eli laughs. "I was just thinking we should go shopping for suits together."

I shake my head. "We're not doing that."

"Come on. I'm wearing blue, we should coordinate." I kill his enthusiasm with my silence. "True, blue is so not your color. Maybe green then?"

"Fuck's sake, I don't know why I try," I grumble.

"Because you're going to like the information I just heard about Tally."

I immediately stand to attention. "What did you hear?"

He turns toward me like he doesn't want anyone to over-hear, despite the fact no one is with us. It's ridiculous, but for some reason I lean in as well. "Word on the street is, the old bakery she used to work at has been put into the town resto-ration project."

"Huh?"

"It's this fund that restores old buildings and offers re-duced rent so the downtown remains vibrant. It's the only building empty on the whole street."

My tongue goes to my cheek. "You don't say."

—

A few hours later, I'm trying to forget about what Eli told me and instead focus on helping Tally make dinner. She's wear-ing another one of her pretty dresses; this one is red and floats down to her bare feet. I wonder how she will act in front of everyone this evening. Because here, in this kitchen, she looks a hell of a lot like mine.

"Oh, what smells so good?" Gail asks as she appears with Penny and Billie in tow. Quinn must have booked it back outside, typical. Mid-April has brought with it warmer weather and bluer skies—much better than the gray New England experiences so often in winter—which means it's nearly impossible for my sister to get Quinn inside at night.

"Tally's making brisket," I say before greeting each of them with a quick kiss to the cheek and a hug. Billie and Penny are focused on how I move around Tally, though Gail seems more tuned in to her daughter.

"Haven't had that in a long time," her mother murmurs as she steps up close, leaning over Tally's shoulder and taking in the impressive spread.

"Daddy's favorite," Tally says softly.

Gail rests a hand on Tally's shoulder and squeezes. "It sure was."

Tally relaxes her head against her mother's hand, and something between them settles, an acknowledgment that although they might be grieving in different ways, they still have each other.

"I'll go get Quinn, and we'll set the table," I say quietly.

"Penny and I can do it," Gail offers. "There are six of us so we'll need all the settings," she tells her daughter. Tally's shoulders seem to tense, and I remember how she reacted last time someone sat in her father's chair.

"Why don't we eat outside?" I suggest.

Gail lights up. "That's a great idea, Walker. It's a beautiful evening."

She's not wrong. The moment I step outside, the warm breeze greets me. I take a deep breath of the fresh New England spring, which is almost as sweet as a Tally dessert, grateful that I get to live on this land where acres of color greet me. Lively green grass rustles in the wind, and daffodils dance for me.

Each day I discover another spot on this farm that I love, and tonight it's a long wooden table big enough to fit both Tally and my family. It sits beneath a string of twinkle lights that hangs from the tall sycamore trees surrounding it, and it's the perfect place to watch the sunset.

Quinn makes himself known immediately as he zips by me, pretending he's a superhero. I carry the plates to the table and holler at him to help. For the next fifteen minutes, he fills me in on the superhero he's made up, the stats for every single play on his baseball team, how much he hates his English class, and how his science teacher has the coolest fake eye. He's barely taken a breath when the girls appear out the back door.

"That boy can talk," I mumble to my sister as she settles in beside me.

Billie laughs and pats the spot beside her. "Come on, Quinn, I think your Uncle Jesse needs a few minutes of silence."

"Well then, he's living in the wrong place," Penny teases as she sits on the other side of Tally.

"What are you trying to say?" Tally says, feigning offense.

Gail rolls her eyes as she takes the seat at the opposite head of the table. "How's the campaign going, Walker?"

"Campaign?" Billie queries.

Tally wears a devious expression. "Oh, he didn't tell you?"

Beneath the table I reach for her knee and squeeze. She bites her bottom lip but doesn't look at me.

Billie looks toward me, then back to Tally. "Nope."

"Walker is running for Daffodil King," Penny says in explanation.

My face contorts. "I am not."

Tally giggles. "He is."

"I am not."

Gail's grin matches her daughter's. "He is. And he's going to win."

"Only if he starts actually campaigning," Penny declares.

"I am campaigning."

Tally snorts beside me.

"What is a daffodil king, Uncle Jesse?" Quinn tilts his head, trying to follow the conversation.

A grumble works its way up my throat. "It's the grand marshal of the parade."

"Which is lovingly referred to as the Daffodil King," Penny says.

I glare at Tally. "You never told me that."

She shrugs but doesn't try to hide the grin spreading across her face.

"Do you have a daffodil queen?" Quinn asks.

"Yeah, Jesse, do you?" Billie teases.

I ignore the question and take a bite of food.

"So what does he have to do to campaign?" Billie asks the rest of the table.

"Well, let's see. He has to attend the town meetings. First one is tomorrow," Penny reminds me.

"And there's Derby Day next week," Gail adds. "They do a cool old-fashioned car show before it, too. You should come, Quinn."

My nephew lights up, and my sister nods. "Sounds fun!"

"And don't forget the Spring Fling. That's May fifteenth," Tally adds. "You guys should come next weekend to the farmers market, though. With Quinn by your side, it'll make you seem more friendly."

"I am friendly," I grouse, and Tally arches a brow.

Billie laughs, and the sound sends a jolt of warmth through my chest. "We wouldn't want you to miss out on a shot at being Daffodil King, Jess. We'll definitely be there."

"Do you get to wear a crown?" Quinn asks.

I'm about to say no when Tally nods dramatically. "Yes! I have a picture of my dad in his crown!"

She pulls out her phone, and after a few seconds of searching, passes it around the table. When it finally makes it to me, I find myself staring at a beaming Peter with his arms wrapped around all of his girls.

"He loved the crown you made." Gail laughs as I notice the daffodil crown on top of his head. Oh, for fuck's sake.

Tally grins at me, and I know with every fiber of my being that I'll do anything she asks, even it if involves wearing a damn flower crown.

—

"Is everyone gone?" I search the kitchen for any spare family member or friend who could hop out and interrupt our night.

I relax when I'm greeted by no one but Tally. "Just me."

"What are you doing?" I'm moving toward her before she answers. She stands in front of the counter, still in that damn red dress that makes my mouth water, a slew of ingredients in front of her. I swear this girl is never not baking something. I smile at the memory of what Eli told me earlier.

"Making your favorite cupcakes," she says before turning back to the counter. I settle right behind her, and she reaches for both of my hands, placing them on either side of her.

Stepping up closer so I can feel every breath she takes, I glance over her shoulder and watch as she measures her ingredients.

"This is all it takes?" I stare at the few things she has beside a bowl.

"Well, this is just for the frosting. Honey—three tablespoons plus more for drizzling; three cups of confectioners' sugar, two tablespoons of heavy cream, one teaspoon vanilla—" I dip my head into her hair and inhale. She laughs and pushes me back with her butt. "Pay attention, Walker. I'm only teaching you once, and there will be tests."

"Oh, you're teaching me, huh?" I grin even though she can't see it. "Will I get a prize if I get the answers right?"

She tips her head back and stares up at me. "Yes."

That one word is filled with so much promise I force my attention back to what she's doing. "And we use sea salt because you like the salted honey buttercream," she continues.

"Oh, I do?"

She leans back again and licks her lips. My hand goes to her cheek, and I tug her to an angle where I can taste her. One quick peck is all I get.

"Yup. Pretty sure you said you would like to lick it from the bowl."

"I could think of other places to lick it from," I mumble, settling my head over her shoulder again and watching as she takes me through each step.

As soon as the ingredients are mixed together, she dips a finger in the bowl of frosting and holds it up to my lips.

My brows arches. "You have a kink you haven't been telling me about?"

Her resounding laugh is loud. "No, I don't want to watch

you eat. Though I guess that is a sort of kink for me. I love watching you enjoy something I've made."

I suck her finger into my mouth and swirl my tongue around it, moaning loudly at the burst of flavor. "I enjoy everything you make." I lick the remnants off my lips as she pulls her hand free. "So if you don't want to watch me licking it from the bowl, is there somewhere else you'd like me to lick it from?"

Her eyes dance. "Now he gets it."

I grab her hips and lift her onto the counter, then push her bare knees apart. I pull the red fabric up to her waist and stare down at the pretty matching lace panties she's wearing. Dragging a finger across the edge of them, I watch the goose bumps pebble across her flesh. She sucks in a hiss of air when I tap my fingers against the damp spot between her legs. "Is this where you want me to put the frosting?"

She taps her collarbone. "How 'bout we start here?"

I scoop an absurd amount of frosting and spread it right across her chest, making sure to avoid her dress.

"I think I should take this off," she says, starting to undo the buttons of her dress.

I don't argue. And when she tugs at it, I pull down her bra, too, exposing those gorgeous tits of hers, right before rubbing the frosting all over them. Tally's moans mingle with my own as I roll my fingers over her nipples. "Like that, Wildflower?"

She nods, her amber eyes hooded. "Yes."

"Need something more?"

My gaze trails up her heaving chest; over her long, pretty neck; and all the way to her lips.

"Your mouth," she begs. "I need your mouth on me. Please, Walker."

She doesn't need to ask twice. My mouth sucks the sweet cream frosting from the side of her breast and then I glide across to her nipple and flick my tongue repeatedly over the tight bud. She curses and digs her fingers into my hair as she holds me in place. I'm practically humping the air with need but continue to lick and suck until she's a puddle of want, begging me to spread the frosting in other places.

I rip her panties from her thighs and then, using two fingers, I scoop another dollop of frosting and swipe it right down her slit. She falls back, her elbows landing on the counter, and she watches me as I shove her legs wider before setting my mouth exactly where she wants me. I lap up the taste of the frosting mixed with her arousal. Tally is easily my favorite thing to eat in this kitchen.

"Love you spread out on the counter, my favorite frosting all over this beautiful pussy." I slide two fingers back and forth between her lips, leaving her bucking her hips in search of more.

I suction my lips around her clit and suck. I don't come up for a breath until she's feeding me with her orgasm.

Needing to be inside her, I grab a washcloth and clean the leftover sugar that I missed off her.

"What are you doing?" she asks.

"Taking care of what's mine," I tell her as I get in every crevice.

She giggles in response. "That tickles."

"Well, I'm about tickle you with my dick, so hold tight, Tally girl."

She rolls her eyes as she laughs. "Men and their dick jokes. Should we go upstairs, maybe?" She glances around the kitchen, and I realize how reckless we've been. It's late but not that late. And though her mom's cottage isn't nearby, she could walk in here at any moment.

"Just give me a few more moments with you like this," I say as I slide off my jeans.

Tally bites her lip. "Fuck, you know I can't say no when you take that out."

I give myself a tug just to ease some of the pressure that's been building. I know for a fact that if I had hours with my head between Tally's thighs, I'd come multiple times from the taste alone. But I need to be inside her now, to feel that wet cunt squeezing me tight. So I pull her right to the edge of the counter, line myself up, and push inside her.

Tally wraps her legs around my waist to pull me closer, and her inner walls flex around my cock.

"You keep squeezing me like that and I'm going to have to pull out," I growl.

She smirks as if she's got me by the balls. I wrap my free hand around her throat.

"Maybe I should, though," I taunt, pulling back just a little, my shaft glistening as I tease her with just tiny thrusts in and out. Tally whimpers at the loss of contact.

"Maybe I should make you watch me jerk off instead." I pull out a bit more. Now it's just the tip that stays inside her, and I stare down at where we join, her tits out, her lips puffy, her eyes and hair a wild mess, my cock so hard it's pulsing. I pinch her nipple, and she whines some more.

"Please, Walker, make me come."

I shake my head. "Not yet. I want you to hold that feeling for me. I need you to squirt all over my cock again, and we won't get there with a quick fuck."

Her eyes roll back as she grips the counter and tries to

push herself forward, sheathing herself on my cock. I press a hand down against her pelvis and hold her in place. My thumb is right on her clit, but I don't move it. "Be my good girl, Tally, and lift your leg up for me."

She relaxes her legs, and I slide her ankle onto my shoulder. I stare into her eyes and thrust deeply inside her.

Tally screams out in pleasure and I grunt because goddamn does she feel incredible. My hands slide down her bare leg, and a cascade of goose bumps follow in my wake until I make it to her hip. While my other hand starts to tease her clit, I slide my thumb toward her other hole and tap gently against it before doing anything. "Anyone ever had you here?"

Tally's eyes widen, and she shakes her head.

"May I?"

"I—oh God, are you sure?" She's breathless, and I can tell she wants me to continue even though she's nervous.

"Yes, Tally. There isn't an inch of you I don't want to devour. I want to lick this ass and make you scream while you come around my cock. I want to own every piece of you. Promise I'll make it feel good."

"Holy shit."

Even as she says it her legs widen a little, and when she nods, I press my thumb against the tight hole. I slide my thumb up and cover it in her wetness and then bring it back down before pushing in more. She sucks in a shocked breath that turns into a moan the more I continue to work her with both my thumb and my cock.

"Play with your clit, baby. I need my other hand."

Tally doesn't hesitate to take over for me as she rolls circles around her swollen clit. Her body arches and her head falls back. "That feels so good. Fuck, I need more."

Her asshole swallows my thumb, and I keep up my steady cadence, thrusting my cock as deep as she can take me. "One day soon I'm going to fuck this ass and you're going to come so hard you won't know what to do."

Her pussy flutters around my cock, and I know I'm going to come the second she does. "Come on, beautiful. Make a mess of my cock." I lean down and press my mouth to hers. She releases on a scream, and it feels as though my orgasm goes on and on.

Long after we've both finished, I'm still lying on top of her, our hearts beating rapidly at the same pace. Damn, I don't ever want spring to end.

Chapter 38
TALLY

"You ready?" Walker is leaning against the door as I come down the stairs, his keys in hand, his Wranglers on, along with a black T-shirt that molds to his broad chest. He's not wearing a hat, and his jaw is freshly shaved.

The man had me spread out in the kitchen last night and has taken me in almost every inch of this house and the farm. Yet my stomach still swoops in excitement the moment I lay eyes on him.

I feign indifference. "For what?"

He sighs as he pushes off the door. "The town meeting."

"You're going?"

He levels me with another one of his no-nonsense stares. "Are you ready?" he asks again.

I smile. "Are you asking me on a date?"

I'm wearing a new navy dress that I bought in town last week when Rosie and I forced my sister to take a break and go shopping with us. I've got my pink cowboy boots on, and my hair is down and styled.

"It's a goddamn town meeting, Tally. You think for our first date I'd take you to hang out with a bunch of busybodies who fight over what color Mr. Simmons paints his mailbox and how many different ways we can celebrate spring before it's summer?"

I shrug. "Is that what happens at town meetings?"

"How the fuck would I know?" he practically yells.

I fold my lips into my mouth to stop myself from laughing. Of course that's what happens at town meetings. "Fine, Cowboy. I'll not go on a date with you to the town hall meeting tonight."

He runs his hands through his hair, which looks freshly styled, exposing some of his beautiful muscular forearms.

"I really like seeing you flustered." I push on. "You get this little flare in your eye, and eventually you take it out on my body."

He stalks toward me, his swagger slightly exaggerated. "Christ, woman, you're goddamn perfect. Better get out of here before I change my mind and do exactly that."

—

"Oh, I didn't know you were going to be here!" My sister cheers the second she sees me before looping her arm in mine and leading me to the front of the room. While I've had plenty of time for heart-to-hearts with Walker, I haven't had any real conversations with my sister or my mother since arriving home. Maybe it's because I'm afraid to admit how much I wish I could stay here. Afraid they'll be disappointed in me for staying away so long when my dad was alive and for giving up a plan I was hell-bent on for so long.

I glance behind me to make sure Walker is following, but he's already been waylaid by Mr. Simmons and I'm pretty sure he's giving Walker an earful about the photos his wife sent Walker last month. My cowboy is holding up his hand

and shaking his head, and I swear I can almost hear him say he didn't want to see them, though the crowd is louder with their clacking of hellos and gossip.

"Incoming," Penny mumbles as I'm tugged to a stop and return my focus to the front of the room. Nothing I can do to help Walker right now.

"Oh, I'm so excited you both could make it," Babs says as she and Ruby block our way to the chairs.

I thumb toward the back of the room. "Looks like your husband is having a word with Walker, Mrs. Simmons. You might want to go handle that."

She waves her hand. "A little jealousy keeps the men young and virile."

"Not sure that's how it works," Penny mutters.

"You know my son is a doctor," Babs cuts in, a twinkle in her eye.

"Isn't he married?" I ponder aloud.

Ruby shakes her head. "We don't like the wife."

"She doesn't eat meat," Babs explains. "Or vegetables or fish. No pasta, no chocolate, no gluten, no sesame. I'm sure if you show me a food, she'll tell you a reason why she doesn't eat it."

My jaw drops as I try to figure out what she *can* eat.

"Exactly." Babs points to my face. "Which means we're on operation divorce. You want to be a mistress?"

My eyes pop. "Me?"

Babs grins. "My oldest always thought you were cute." Penny snorts, and that draws Babs's attention back to her. "What about you? Ever consider being the other woman?"

"Oh my God," I mutter.

"Think about it." Babs grins as she and Ruby head over to their next unsuspecting victim.

"Why are we sitting at the front?" I ask Penny as she guides me to the first chair opposite the lectern. I place my purse on it and move to sit on the second one, but Penny pushes me down farther so I'm seated beside Fletcher, who's staring at a note-covered paper on his lap. "Hi, Fletcher."

He grins a hello before I turn my attention back to my sister who merely shrugs. "I don't want to miss anything."

"You don't want to miss our neighbors arguing over complete nonsense? Or trying to set you up with their married sons?"

"I know the small-town thing isn't for you, Tally. But I love it. Minus the matchmakers. And as a business owner, it's important to get involved."

"Whoever said small-town living wasn't for me?" I mutter.

"Up." Walker appears out of nowhere and stands in front of me, arms crossed, glaring.

I raise an unimpressed brow. "We leaving already?"

"I'm only staying if you sit next to me, so like I said, up." He motions for me to stand, and I giggle as I wait for my sister to move down a seat so I can sit next to Walker. He takes the seat on the end, where he'll garner the most attention, and his knee bounces as he sits and waits for me to settle beside him.

My sister leans over. "Is this a date?"

I plop into the seat between them. "Nope. Walker was very clear. This is *not* a date."

Walker lets out an aggressive sigh, but when I cross my legs and rub the bottom of my pink boot against his calf, his bouncing leg comes to rest. Marginally.

Penny twists so she can look at Walker. "Why won't you ask my sister on a date? You just stringing her along like all the other men your age?"

My lips fold in on themselves again as I stifle a laugh. Walker sinks deeper into his frown before his eyes narrow. "Why's your mother up on the stage?"

I glance up, and sure enough, my mother is up there, along with the rest of the town council. I shrug, but Penny leans across me with an answer. "Every owner of the big businesses in town has a shared seat on the town council. They alternate monthly."

"What?" The waver in Walker's voice makes me turn and study him.

Penny nods. "Yeah. Rosie, Eli, Babs. I'm sure there's others. Not me, though. The bookstore isn't big enough."

"Yet," I say with conviction. "The bookstore isn't big enough *yet*."

My sister gives me a soft smile. "Thanks, Tal."

"You say it like you want the position." Walker scowls.

"Everyone wants that position," she explains, and the pride in her tone takes me aback. My sister really does love this town. I always knew she loved the store and her books, but this passion for the community? It's shocking. A bolt of something akin to jealousy hits me because I want to feel that way about my career.

"Not me," Walker gruffs.

I smile and pat his thigh. "Then it's a good thing you don't own anything."

He swallows heavily, and I ignore the niggle of a worry that bubbles in my stomach. "Remember, Walker, you love this town and the farm. You are so excited to be the next grand marshal. Now sit up straight. Everyone's watching you."

It's a torturous two hours. Fletcher can barely get through his list of agenda points without someone interrupting him every five seconds. When the meeting finally ends, Walker grabs my hand and drags me from the meeting before another person can stop and say "Hi, Walker." Now that he's running for grand marshal, he has to respond, and I think it's driving him batty.

"You done peopling?" I ask with a smile as he tugs me out onto the sidewalk.

April has brought with it slightly warmer weather and flowers on almost every stoop. There are trailing petunias in wicker baskets hanging in a cascade of colors and wreaths bursting with greens and yellows welcoming the new season. I can't help but feel slightly nostalgic seeing our town all dolled up and ready for the spring parade. I'd forgotten that this time of year is by far my favorite.

Walker lets out a grunt as he stops under a street lamp and turns to face me. As he runs his hand through his mop of hair, my fingers twitch to do the same. "You want to maybe grab dinner downtown? Or go for a walk? Check out some of the stores?"

I try to hide the way his simple question, asked with a lilt of vulnerability, makes my heart swoon and my lips curve. "That sounds oddly like a date."

He shakes his head. "Not a date, I promise."

"So we're just two people who like to kiss—"

"I like to more than kiss you," he mumbles as his hands flex by his sides.

"And we're just going to grab dinner and walk around town?"

"I'll probably ask you questions, and you'll drive me nuts and do that girly giggle thing a lot."

"That tracks," I say, nodding along as my stomach swoops again.

"We'll probably split an appetizer or two, and if you get something I like, I'll probably eat from your plate."

My heart picks up as this crazy pull has me taking a step closer to him. "What about dessert?"

"I'd let you order whatever you want." One brow lifts as he waits for my next challenge.

"And then when the check comes?"

He lets out a ragged breath and grumbles, "If you touch the damn check, I'll turn your ass red as soon as we get home."

I smile. Absolutely giddy. "Right, so you'll pay for my dinner—"

"And your dessert."

"And I'll be ending the night in your bed?"

His chin dips quickly in acknowledgment.

"So what keeps it from being a date, Cowboy?"

He shakes his head slowly as he stares at my lips like this one thing will kill him. I lick them, waiting for a response.

His eyes fall shut on a curse. "Because I won't walk you to your door and kiss you good night."

"Oh." It comes out as a whimper as I imagine him doing just that—walking me down the gravel of my long driveway, holding my hand, stroking his thumb back and forth. It'll tickle but leave me hungry for more. I'd walk up the steps and pause by the door. He'd brush a stray hair from my cheek, and his lips would lift at something I said. And then there'd be that moment, right before our lips pressed together, when the possibilities of what happens next feel endless. When hope and excitement bubble together to create that swirly feeling in my chest.

"I think I'd like you to, though," I admit.

Surprise flares in Walker's eyes, and he takes one small step closer. His fingers flex again, and his lips curve up, just like I imagined they would.

He reaches out his hand to me. "Okay, Tally. Would you like to go on a date with me?"

I grin right back at him and accept the gesture. "I thought you'd never ask."

Chapter 39
WALKER

The crackle of the fire dancing in the restaurant's large hearth is the only sound aside from our spoons hitting the bowl. When we'd first arrived, the dinner crowd was already long gone so I promised the waitress she'd get a nice tip if she asked the kitchen to stay open for just a bit longer—and if she gave us a seat by the fire. The temperature had dropped considerably from when we first arrived at the town hall. The sun in the springtime is like that; it brings a warmth during the day but the night chills considerably after it sets.

I've always loved a fireplace. Though I never had one until I moved to the farm. The first thing I did when I moved onto the farm and Peter told me the fireplace wasn't working was clean it out so we could light it. We spent that night with a bourbon in hand, the fire crackling in front of us, and he'd told me all of his dreams for the farm. The smell alone now is like a beautiful memory come to life.

"Favorite color?" Tally asks me to a roll of my eyes. She's been asking weird questions since we sat down. I think she's nervous and I kind of like it, the idea that she may want this as much as I do.

"Favorite color?"

"Actually, let me guess. Blue like the sky."

I shake my head.

"Brown like the dirt."

"Black like my soul," I tease.

Tally rolls her eyes. "Black isn't a color."

"It's also not my favorite." I lean forward, my focus on her eyes. "It's yellow. Well, actually, not exactly yellow. Maybe more of a marigold. An amber of sorts."

"Like sunflowers?"

"No, Tally." My voice is a rough whisper as I reach across the table for her hand. "It's the exact shade of your eyes when I sink inside you."

Tally's mouth opens but no words come out. I drop her hand and, using my thumb, push her chin up to close her mouth. Then I slide my thumb across her bottom lip. "Second favorite color would definitely be peach. Like these lips. I have an unhealthy obsession with your mouth." I take a bite of my ice cream and play her game. "What's your favorite color?"

"Well, any answer I give now is going to seem juvenile since you had to go and be all . . ." She waves a hand in my direction.

My brows lift in question, and my smirk grows.

She shrugs and I have to wonder if she's ever been out on a real date before.

"Favorite flower?" she grinds out.

"Wildflowers."

Another eye roll. "Cute."

"I'm being serious. They've always been my favorite. Wild, unconfined, bursting with color. You never know quite what you'll find in a wildflower field. They're sturdy, they come back year after year, and they don't need too much, just sunlight and open land. Plus, they can take over an entire field. It's why I picked the cottages facing the wildflower meadows to work on first."

Tally licks her lips until finally, after another breath, she asks, "Aren't you going to ask me mine?"

I shake my head. "A man who's interested in you shouldn't have to ask you these things, Tally. Your favorite color is whatever makes you feel pretty that day. Some days you love yellow, but it also hurts because the color reminds you of your father. Most days you prefer bright pink. Even if it's just the strap of your bra, you've got pink somewhere on you."

"You have an unfair advantage. You saw my underwear today."

I don't smile. I don't want to flirt. I want Tally to know that this is about more than sex.

"You wear bright colors because you think that without them, you'll go unnoticed. It's a way to be loud without making a sound. But Tally, in every room, no matter what you're wearing or what you're saying, you have my attention. So, yes, I saw your underwear today and I'll see them again on my bedroom floor within the hour, but I know the color of everything you have worn since the day you arrived because you have owned my attention since the first moment I saw you."

She glances down at her unfinished dessert. "Can we get the check?"

We barely make it to my truck before she's trying to push me up against it, though I throw her hands away.

"You told me what you wanted, and I'm going to give it to you," I explain.

She blinks up at me with lust-filled eyes. "Right. Well,

what I want is your dick inside me within the next three minutes or I'm going to explode."

"No." I reach around and unlock the door. Then I lean in close and press a gentle kiss to the spot right below her ear. "What you want is to be taken on a date, wooed, driven home, and then kissed on the porch." I nip at her neck again. "I know you, Tally. Even if tonight is our first date, *I know you.*"

I say the last words slowly, making sure to enunciate each one, and the little puffs of air from my lips being so close to her ear has her breaking out in shivers. My fingers toy with the pink bra strap right beneath the stitching on her pretty dress. "And yet I can't get enough of you. I want to know every thought that goes through your pretty head. Want to hear your every desire." I press my lips to her cheek and then nod to the open door of the car. "But I can't do that until you get in."

Tally's quiet for the ride home. I'm in my head, too. And as much as I tell her I'm trying to give her what she wants, I'm also doing this for me. I'm doing this for the boy who never felt he could go after something just for him. Who put everyone else first.

Tally is it for me. And I know she feels the same. I want this to be the best first date ever so it's also her last first date. I'm not sure when it happened, or what I'll do with myself if she leaves, but I've fallen for this woman. So hard that it sometimes feels impossible to walk out the door in the morning and start my day without her next to me.

"You going to get out of the car?" The soft lilt of her voice coaxes me back to the present. I'd hardly even registered that I'd parked.

She reaches for the handle and I growl. "Don't you fucking dare."

I make my way over to her side. She's smiling when I open the door and hold out my hand to her.

"I had a really nice time tonight," she tells me.

I swallow my nerves and lead her toward the porch. "Me, too."

When she takes the first step, she grips the banister and then laughs as it wobbles beneath her hand. Glancing up at the sky, she shakes her head. "I know, you'll get around to it."

I frown. "Hmm?"

"My father." She sighs. "He always had projects."

She shakes the wooden structure again, showing me it's loose, and then points to the rocking chair in the corner of the porch.

"I wouldn't sit in that chair, either. Pretty sure the back leg wobbles under too much weight."

It feels as though she's only talking to fill the silence, and I smile as we step up to the front door, happy that we are both feeling whatever this is building between us.

My hand goes to her cheek, and I stroke her smooth skin with my thumb. Fuck, she's beautiful.

"Hi," she whispers nervously.

I swipe my thumb across her lips and lick my own. "Hi, Wildflower."

I take a step closer, and the moment I lean in, her lips lift into a smile. Our mouths touch and it's gentle at first, like a first kiss despite the fact that we've done this countless times now. She moans as my tongue slips into her mouth before gripping me tighter until the kiss turns ravenous.

"Need you," she mutters.

"Not nearly as much as I need you." I lean down and scoop her up, carrying her back down the steps.

"Where are we going?" she asks on a laugh.

"The cottage. I don't want to risk anyone interrupting us. Tonight is all about you."

"It's about us," she says, and then she's kissing my jaw, my neck. By the time I kick open the door to the cottage, we're both impatient. I stalk toward the bedroom but slow the moment we get to the bed. Gently, I place her feet on the ground. Then I kneel in front of her, easing her pink boots off her feet. I press my lips to the inside of her ankle before staring up at her.

"In case you didn't know, I'm crazy about you, Tally."

Tally's eyes are warm as she reaches down to stroke my face. "Oh, Cowboy. I'm a bit obsessed with you, too."

I suck in a surprised breath. "Thought we weren't supposed to share our feelings."

She rolls her thumb across my lip. "Nah, we weren't supposed to catch feelings. Though I thought you'd noticed I don't always play by the rules." She pauses before pushing on. "I don't know what this is, or what we're doing, but I don't want to stop."

I nip at the side of her thumb. "Good, because I don't plan on letting you go."

I undress quickly, but I take my time with her. I start with the bottom buttons on her dress. I swear she buys dresses with buttons just to fuck with me. Though I can't deny I love taking my time with her. Love the way her breath hitches as my hands get close to her pussy. And the way she trembles as I make my way to her breasts until her dress finally falls open and I'm the one with my heart in my throat.

"You're so fucking beautiful, Tal. I could stare at you for the rest of my life and still not get enough."

"Walker." Her voice is a soft rasp.

I start at her thighs, taking my time to pepper every part of her body with kisses until I'm straddling her, my cock heavy and aching to be inside her.

I hold myself above her, not sure if there are words to express the way I feel as I hover right between this moment and the next. Knowing that I'll be chasing this feeling for the rest of my life.

I almost tell her. Almost whisper the words that don't even begin to describe what I'm feeling. *Love.* The word is trivial in comparison to this, to the way this woman has healed me, the way my heart settles when she's near. How all the darkness makes sense to me now that she's shown me the light.

"Walker." My siren calls to me, and since I don't have the words, I dip my mouth to hers and slide inside her. We rock back and forth slowly as I make love to this woman, pushing her hands up above her head, linking our fingers, and staring into the eyes that have become my home. I kiss down her neck as I roll my hips, never once pulling out fully, keeping our bodies as connected as our souls.

She shatters around me without warning, and as she comes apart in my arms, crying out my name, I revel in the feel of her and hold myself back. I make love to her for hours, keeping myself right at the edge. I fuck her from every angle, softly, gently, then roughly as I tug on her hair from behind and bite down on her neck. Devouring every ounce of her pleasure, I don't stop until she's crying out and begging for me to empty inside her. Only then do I give her the last of me.

Chapter 40
TALLY

I wake up deliciously sore, wishing I could relive last night a hundred times over. From the moment Walker kissed me on my daddy's porch, I knew things had changed. Then he had to go and carry me to this cottage—a place I've come to lovingly think of as ours—and settled me on the bed, slowly undressing me until I knew in my soul that this man is it for me.

The banter during the last few weeks has been addictive, but last night was real, and so much more than a first date. I've only been here a little more than a month, and in that time Walker and I have been slowly getting to know each other, but now we've peeled back another layer. We've taken off the proverbial armor, and we're letting each other in.

So when he crawled on top of me, I didn't tease him about needing his cock in my mouth, or ask how many times he thought he could make me come. And when he finally sunk into me, he took my mouth in the sweetest of kisses, and I swear something inside me flipped.

Waking without him here now has my mind racing. I rush to get dressed and run through the fields in search of him. And when I find my mother instead, and she tells me she saw him fixing the banister up at the house, I run until I can stand and watch as he tightens each of the porch railings under the early morning sun.

What have you done to me, Jesse Walker?

—

The next two weeks continue in much the same way. There's so much work to be done, but Walker makes sure I know how important I am to him every chance he gets. We missed Tally Tuesday this week because the mattresses were delivered and we spent the day finalizing the last details on the cottages. The Hall ceremony is this weekend, and guests are arriving tomorrow for the welcome dinner, which will be held at the brewery.

It's also officially May, which means I leave in three weeks. I couldn't be less ready.

I promised him another day like we had last week, when we hid out here in the cottage and he read me the book club pick. I never knew how I felt about a woman being taken by two men, but after hearing Walker read it aloud, fuck, I was sweating. Walker assured me we would never be acting out any of those scenes with anyone else, but I didn't mind. Walker's dirty mouth and smiles are enough for me.

Outside the moments he's with me, I've caught him far more stressed than I'd like. Part of his anxiety is about the big event, I'm sure, though I have a feeling it's more than just that. We're both aware of my time in Hope Harbor coming to an end, and every time my phone beeps with another message from my boss in Nantucket, Walker disappears and I feel an insane pressure mounting. I don't even want the job anymore. I just wish I had a valid reason to stay. And being Walker's personal sex toy isn't it, no matter how much I enjoy it.

I sink into the sheets and suck in a long breath, frowning as I smell something familiar. *Is that my—It couldn't be—Is he?*

No, I shake my head. There's no way.

I throw the covers off the bed and tiptoe to the bathroom door, which is slightly ajar, and inhale again. My smile grows. Stepping inside, I reach for the shower curtain and pull it back. "Caught red-handed."

Walker's hand, which is already strangling my shampoo bottle, squeezes tighter as he hisses, "Jesus, Tal."

I'm laughing as I shake my head. "I thought I was going crazy. I couldn't figure out how I was going through so much shampoo."

Walker's head falls forward and he sighs. "You're never going to let me live this down."

Confused, I ponder, "Do you like the way your hair smells when you use it?"

Walker squeezes his eyes shut and drops the shampoo bottle on the side ledge. Then he rubs the shampoo between his palms and brings his hands up to his nose.

"No. I was the one going crazy, sniffing your damn shampoo so I wouldn't go after you."

I smile when he finally looks at me. Water drips down his hard body, and the smolder he hits me with has my thighs clenching.

"You aren't trying to not go after me anymore, though," I remind him. "You have me. So what were you doing with the shampoo?"

His eyes bore into mine, but he doesn't answer.

"Wait, were you more than sniffing, Cowboy? Were you—" My eyes narrow. "Did you?" My gaze drops. His dick, heavy between his legs, practically bounces at my interest. "Did you rub yourself with it?"

Walker grunts as he squeezes his eyes shut, like he's embarrassed to admit what he's been doing.

"Show me."

His lashes flutter open, and he hits me with a surprised moan. "Take off your clothes and get in here," he growls.

Within seconds I'm naked and in the shower with him. He steps back so I'm under the stream of water and then his fist goes to his cock and he begins to tug slowly.

"What would you think about?" I ask as I watch him, entranced.

"Your tits." His fist tightens.

My fingers go to my nipples and I squeeze. "What else?"

"Your mouth. Your perfect cunt and how good you'd feel. How, when I sank inside you, this smell would be everywhere." His hand falls against the tile to the right of me and he pushes me against the wall, still fucking himself while his forehead lands on my shoulder. He sucks at the skin of my neck, and I watch his fist work. He's desperate for release, and I can't decide whether I want him to take it now because I'm dying to see exactly what he looked like all those times he did it by himself, or if I'd rather prolong it for both of us.

"Don't come yet." I breathe out the words, and he strangles his cock with a groan.

I tilt my head and he claims my lips with his. His hand circles my neck and he squeezes gently, stealing just a bit more of my air. Holding me steady by the throat, he takes his other hand and slides it between my thighs, pinching my clit. He swallows the scream that follows with a kiss. "No whining," he mumbles against my lips before kissing me again.

The lack of oxygen makes me slightly dizzy, which somehow leaves the rest of my body hanging like a live wire, ready to combust. By the time he slides a finger inside me, I feel like I'm floating away. His thumb massages my clit while he continues to fuck me with his fingers.

When he releases the pressure on my throat and gives me a second to breathe, he pulls back and watches his fingers fuck me. "You going to come on my fingers, or you want to make a mess of my cock?"

"Make a mess," I answer belligerently. Because who can think when a man this sexy is looking at them like this?

He flashes me a wicked smile as he presses another kiss to my lips and returns the pressure to my throat. "Good answer." He nips at my lips and pulls his fingers back, much to my disappointment. "Hands on the wall, bend over, ass up."

I don't even remember turning, but suddenly I'm facing the draining water, my hands cool against the tile as his palm lands on my ass in a loud smack.

I shoot him a look from the side. "What was that for?"

"Another thing I thought about while fucking my fist with your shampoo," he grumbles right as he slides his cock inside me in one thrust. Clenching around him in surprise, I cry out as we devolve into nothing but bodies slapping and rolling, both chasing the orgasms we've worked hard for. Walker leans over and cups my breast, squeezing. "Fuck, I love being inside you, Tal."

He kisses down my spine and then the hand on my breast moves lower and, while making shallow thrusts, he rolls his fingers over my clit, massaging the tight bud into oblivion.

His fingers squeeze my hips as he unloads. I can't turn myself around quick enough to wrap my arms around his neck and kiss him while he slides right back in me and continues to fuck me even as he goes soft. What is this? What is this feeling? And how the hell am I ever going to get over it when it ends?

—

After an actual shower, during which Walker washed my hair and rubbed my favorite body wash over every inch of me, I'm feeling like a new woman.

"Why are you putting on clothes?" Walker hooks out an arm and wraps it around my waist, pulling me back into bed. I giggle as I fight against his tight hold, but the scuff on his face burns deliciously against my bare shoulder as he nuzzles my neck and tries to hold me down. "You promised we'd stay in bed all day."

I glance up at him over my shoulder. "No, I was promised a Tally day. And you're still getting one."

"I'd prefer a naked Tally day," he mumbles, but he releases me so I can grab my sundress that's fallen to the floor.

"I was thinking," I start as I pull my dress over my head.

"Oh no, I can already feel that I'm going to regret your thoughts."

I chuckle and push against his chest. "Stop being so grumpy."

He juts out his lips in a mock pout. "I'm exactly who I was when you met me."

As I start to work the buttons on my dress, I assess him. Walker couldn't be more wrong. He's nothing like the person I met; he's more open, and he smiles more than he frowns. And God, does he make me smile, too.

I turn to tell him my thoughts, to kiss the frown right off his face, when I hear a loud banging on the door.

"Walker!" My mother's voice has me pulling back and frowning.

"Mom?" I leave the bed and head toward the front of the cottage as the door swings open.

My mother's face is crazed, her hair a wild mess. "Where's Walker?"

I motion behind me. "He's in the bedroom. What's wrong?"

She stalks past me and into the bedroom without hesitation. I follow behind her and almost snort when I see Walker pulling the sheets over his body. My eyes fall to his erection, which makes an obvious tent as he grabs a pillow and holds it over himself.

"What is with you Darling women?" he grits out. "You're supposed to knock and then *wait* to be let in."

My mother shakes her head, not phased in the slightest by what's in front of her. "It's the cake."

"The what?" I ask, trying to get her to look my way.

Finally, she turns to me. "For the ceremony. It was delivered last night. When I went to check on it this morning, the refrigerator was dark. It's broken. The cake's ruined."

Walker bounds out of bed at her words, wrapping the sheets around his waist and rushing out of the cottage. My mother and I chase after him, but when we finally make it up the path and to the shed that houses the makeshift kitchen caterers use for weddings, we find him standing in front of the warm, dark fridge, his shoulders slumped.

"Is it ruined?" I ask, even though I know the answer. The frosting has melted down the cake, and the floral decor has wilted. "It's a cream-based filling," I murmur to myself. Even if we could salvage the outside of the cake, we can't serve this. There's too much of a risk that people would get sick.

"What are we going to do?" my mother asks, sounding drained as she stares at the melted masterpiece. My heart aches for her, for everything she's lost this year. I reach out to wrap an arm around her. This ceremony was supposed to be the thing that saved the farm, but if we've destroyed the cake, I can't imagine we'll be saving anything.

Walker turns around, and his gaze settles on me. "Well, Gail, I guess it's a lucky thing that we have a baker on staff, huh?"

I shake my head and hold up my hands, pulling away from my mother. "Oh no, I can't—"

With one hand tightly gripping the sheet around his waist, Walker smiles at me and nods. "Yes, you can."

I blow out a breath. "I don't have anywhere to bake. I'd need a commercial kitchen. One stove isn't going to cut it."

Walker stares at me while he works out something in his head. "What if I could get you a commercial kitchen? Then would you do it?"

I roll my eyes. "Where would you find that?"

Walker smirks. "That's not the question, Tally girl. If I get you a kitchen, will you do it?"

My stomach swoops, and this time, it's not nerves. It's excitement.

My mother reaches for both of my hands and squeezes, her brown eyes wide and hopeful. "Please? Everything you've made since you arrived has been heavenly. I'm sure you'll make a better cake than this one."

My heart pounds. I've never made a cake for such a high-profile couple, not to mention a couple whose original cake was destroyed, but before I can get ahead of myself, I close my eyes and listen for my father. *"Breathe Tally. You got this."*

I take a deep breath, then turn to them both and nod. "Okay. If you can get me a kitchen, I'm in."

My mother beams and throws her arms around me, pulling me in for a hug. When she pulls back, she glances at Walker and her brows knit together. "Really, Walker, why don't you put on some clothes?"

Chapter 41
TALLY

D o you trust me?" Walker asks as we park on Maple Street, right across from my sister's store. My heart races when I realize we're in front of Mabel's Bakery.

"Of course I do," I mumble, even as I try not to get my hopes up.

Walker rounds the truck, and when he opens my door, holding out a hand to help me down, he flashes one of his dimple-popping grins.

"Good." He nods toward the bakery. "Welcome to your kitchen."

Walker wraps his arms around me and settles his chin on my shoulder, forcing me to stare at the bakery I've loved since I was a child. "Just breathe with me for a minute, Wildflower. Take a look at the storefront, and breathe."

My eyes flutter closed and I smile. "What did you do?"

"I just got the keys from Rayna so we can use the kitchen. Thought maybe you could test out making some cupcakes and see if everything is up to snuff. If it all works, then tomorrow it's yours to make the wedding cake."

"Can we really go in?"

He nods against my cheek, and I squeal when he drops the keys to the bakery over my shoulder and into my hands. I don't wait even a second before I rush forward, dragging Walker with me.

The moment the key notches in the lock and the door

opens, something clicks into place. I forgot how bright it was in here. How, even in the evenings, the sun cuts in off the harbor, creating this golden hue that makes the whole space seem magical. Something blooms within my chest as a million memories race through my mind. Mabel's was the spot where I fell in love with baking.

"What do you think?" Walker's smooth voice breaks through my thoughts and I turn to look at him, at this man who's captured my heart in such a way that sometimes it's hard to breathe.

"It's just as I remember." I sigh as I walk toward him. "But can we really use the kitchen for this?"

Walker nods. "Got it approved by the owner."

"You actually *talked* to Rayna?" My jaw drops in mock surprise.

"I'd do anything for you, Wildflower." Walker chuckles and thumbs toward the door.

"Get comfortable. I'm going to grab the ingredients from your sister. She picked them up for us earlier."

I shake my head at Walker in wonder before allowing myself to focus on the bakery. Refamiliarizing myself with the space, I'm amazed at how everything is exactly as I remember. Mabel died more than two years ago, but it's clear that Rayna has spent money to keep it in decent shape in hopes of renting it out, I suppose. It's clean but dated. I look to the worn wooden counter where I used to take orders and ring up customers on the old-fashioned black register. I tap on it and it dings, the noise echoing through the tiny store. As I move to the back kitchen, I find six ovens and an eight-burner gas stove. I turn the dial to test if it still works and suck in an excited breath when a flame roars to life.

"So will it work?" Walker asks when he reappears, now holding two shopping bags. He sets them down, and I peer inside. Of course he's got exactly what I need to make his favorite cupcakes.

"It'll work." I bite my lip as I lean against the counter. "Are you sure you want me to do this, though? What if I screw up the cake and ruin something else for the farm?"

The words are whispered. No one in my family has ever relied on me. At least not since I was in high school and my dad was asking me to help him out in the fields. Even then, there wasn't much I could screw up. He was always by my side, guiding me if I needed it. But now it's just me.

Walker brushes a hand against my cheek, reminding me that I'm not alone.

"But what if you don't? What if you take this risk and save the event ? What if you stop worrying about whether you're good enough and just try? Remember, it was your cupcakes that started this whole thing. You had a line of people raving about them—including the Liberty Ladies, and you know they complain about everything. You have family who moan in delight every time they eat your food."

I try to hide my smile. "I think you're hearing your own reaction."

Walker wraps an arm around me and pulls me against his chest. "Damn right I am. Every meal you make is incredible, just like you."

Resting my head against his chest, I glance up at him. "You really think I can do it?"

"Tally, you can do whatever you set your mind to."

I will myself to believe him. Part of me feels like I'm not

ready for any of this, that I need to go to Nantucket and then to school. I need to become this whole person before I'm ready for him and this life he's laying out in front of me. But another part of me is tired of waiting to start living.

Determination wins out, and I nod. "Okay, let's make some cupcakes."

"That's my girl." Walkers drops a kiss to my lips and then empties both grocery bags.

I locate some bowls and an old mixer, relieved that everything is clean and will do the job.

Walker settles next to me, and I can feel his eyes watching me as I set up. "You're making me nervous. Don't just stand there, say something."

Walker folds his arms across his chest and leans against the counter. "Okay, do you like weddings?"

I snort as I crack one egg after the next.

He shrugs. "What? Don't all girls love weddings?"

I shake my head. "I wasn't one of those girls who pictured every minute of my wedding. That would be Penny. *She's* the romantic." She may say she's done dating, done with *men*. But she's full of it. I know this weekend Penny will be staring wistfully at the way the groom watches his bride like he's in a damn fairy tale. I smile. "She used to come down to the kitchen at the house, wearing one of her dresses and pretending she was a bride. My father would put on music and spin her around." My voice catches as I realize how he probably thought that one day he'd do that with both of us for real. Maybe even on our farm. A vision flashes in my mind of my daddy walking a bride down the aisle. The sun is setting in a brilliant burst of magenta behind the dance floor, and he's spinning her around to "What a Wonderful World." I drop the eggshell on the counter and bring my fist to my mouth to choke back a sob.

Walker grabs my shoulders and pulls me flush against him, pressing kiss after kiss against my head. "I'm sorry. I wasn't thinking."

"I didn't realize I even cared about some imaginary wedding that now I'll never have."

Walker squeezes me tighter. "You will. It might look different than what you imagined, but you'll get every everything, Wildflower. I'm sure of it."

I let out a loud breath to get my emotions under control. "What about you?"

"What about me?"

I glance at him. "Did you ever picture your wedding?"

Walker is silent for a second too long, and my stomach swoops in realization. "Wow, you did, huh?"

Walker groans.

"Oh, there's a story there."

His jaw hardens. "No."

"No, you never pictured your wedding, or no, you don't want to tell me about your dream event?" I bite my lip and settle back against the counter. "Let me guess, you planned on wearing a cowboy hat and some spurs?"

He snorts and shakes his head. "Sounds like a better wedding than what I'd have planned."

I raise my brows in question as jealousy singes my stomach. It's such a surprising feeling that I find myself cracking the next egg I pick up in the palm of my hand. I stare down at it in shock before going to the sink to clean it off.

"What happened?" I ask over my shoulder as I dry my

hands. I grab another egg from the carton and attempt to focus on the job at hand.

"Not much to tell. Gina and I were together through high school, then college and quite a while after that. I asked her to marry me, and she told me she was seeing someone else. I haven't talked to her since."

The eggs drops on the floor with a loud *splat*.

"*Tally*," Walker growls.

Breath short, I glare at him as the egg continues to spread. "She did what?"

Walker shakes his head and then grabs a towel to clean up the mess.

"It was years ago, and I'm over it. I told you before, my life wasn't like yours. We were extremely poor, and my father was—" He blows out a breath. "Not like your father. My sister needed me. Every penny, every ounce of extra attention I had went to Billie. She's my only real family. Gina needed more than I could give her, which"—he flexes his fists—"was fair."

"No, it's not." This isn't the Walker I know. The man who's sure of himself, who's surly because he can be, because he's right most of the time. "There's never an excuse for cheating."

Maybe it's because I watched Penny go from one bad relationship to the next in the hopes of falling in love, desperate in her chase of a beautiful love story. Or maybe I'm naive because I've never been in a relationship, but to me, choosing to be with someone doesn't mean they need to be perfect. It just means that you need to show up for each other in the best way you can. I grab Walker's hand and squeeze. "I'm sorry that happened to you."

Walker's face softens. "It's okay, Tally. She did me a favor. Truly."

I scoff. "Well, obviously. Because now you're with me."

Walker's smile spreads all the way to his eyes. "Yes."

I press a kiss to his jaw and then turn back to the ingredients, telling myself I won't break any more eggs. "When I first showed up, you mentioned your sister wanting the job to help my mom. Is she still interested?"

Walker tilts his head. "The weddings will be done by the first weekend in June. It's already May, so I'm not sure how needed she is."

"If we had more flowers, though . . ." I sigh as the words die on my lips. The reason we don't have enough flowers to get us through the season is because of me.

"No indication we'd have more weddings, Tal. Don't beat yourself up."

"But you were fixing the cottage for her and Quinn, right?" It's the topic we've avoided since my mother mentioned it weeks ago. And because I've come to think of it as our cottage. Stupid really, considering I'll be gone before she moves in.

"Billie's stubborn," he says with a smile. "Kind of like someone else I know."

I flash him a grin. "I like her."

"I was just trying to give her another option to consider. Quinn's father has never really been in the picture, and it's hard being a single parent."

"You're a good brother. I'm sorry I got in the way of you being able to do that."

"I'm not. She needs to want to make the change and she's not there yet, but you being her friend, and including her in stuff with Penny and Rosie, means a lot to her. It means a lot to me."

"Of course," I say quickly. "We're a team. Just like you're helping me right now, I want to help with the farm. I want to help your sister. I want to help *you*."

Walker frowns as I drop the whisk and turn toward him, placing my hands on his chest.

"What are you doing, Wildflower?"

"I'm making you smile."

His lip twitches, but he's not strong enough to fight it. "Oh yeah, and how do you plan on doing that?"

"I have my ways," I whisper against his cheek before pressing a kiss to his rough skin.

His lips hook into a smile, his dimple popping out with the movement.

"I think maybe you didn't always have the time to be happy because you were too busy being strong for everyone else," I whisper against his neck, peppering light kisses up to his jaw.

His voice comes out scratchy. "Oh yeah?"

"Yeah, Cowboy. But I'm here now. You don't have to be strong anymore."

Chapter 42
WALKER

May

"*You don't have to be strong anymore.*" Tally's words echo in my head from two nights ago, when it took everything in me not to blurt out the three little words that would change everything.

It became even harder yesterday—after surprising her at the bakery—when I watched her single-handedly bake the most beautiful cake I've ever seen.

"Don't move," I had whispered in her ear as I wrapped the gift I'd bought her around her waist.

She had been holding a whisk in one hand, covered in some type of frosting, but she dropped it the moment I finished tying her new apron in a bow.

"Jesse Walker! Did you buy me a present?" she'd squealed.

From the smile she gave me, you'd think I gave her diamonds rather than a canvas apron with the word WILDFLOWER scrawled among different flowers.

I've never felt this way about anyone. I've wanted Tally from the moment I laid eyes on her. But after our first date a few weeks ago, when I'd walked her to the door of the house, stared into those beautiful golden eyes of hers, and took my time kissing her good night, I've been a total goner.

Now, as I stand with my sister, staring at Tally's cake, I know without a doubt that I'm in love with her.

"That cake is . . ." Billie shakes her head as she stares at the seven-tier butter cream–frosted cake that boasts a cascade of wildflowers waterfalling down the side into a pool of daffodils at the base.

"Gorgeous, right?" I can't hide the pride in my voice.

My sister's eyes are wide when she turns to me. "Walker, everything, every single little thing that you've all done is incredible. The cottages, the venue, this cake . . ."

"Our girl did good, right?" Rosie says, appearing next to us. The ceremony is about to start, but the bride, Hannah, wanted to get a few pictures of the cake before sunset. She was thrilled when she found out one of the owners of the farm made it and that local flowers were used for decoration. She said it made it even more special, and the surprised smile on Tally's face made all the stress of the last few weeks worth it.

Now Hannah asks Tally to get in a picture with her and her groom in front of the cake. After they've got the shot, Hannah turns to hug Tally before heading down to the wildflower field for the ceremony.

"Need help with anything else over here?" I ask Tally, who is fixing the last flower decorations.

She shakes her head. "Just going to get this back in the fridge until after the ceremony. You guys go ahead and make sure the ceremony goes off without a hitch."

"I'll help her," Rosie promises.

"Me, too," Penny agrees.

Tally meets my worried eyes. "It's fine, Cowboy. I promise

we won't get out our coffee cups yet." She blows me a kiss and I chuckle as I guide Billie away from the trio of trouble.

"Oh my God," my sister mumbles, pausing to stare at me.

"What?" I glance behind me, panicked at the thought that the girls already knocked down the cake. But they're all just standing there, and the cake is intact. I shake my head and smile. They'll probably still be talking when the ceremony is over.

"You just laughed."

I glance back at my sister, my brow furrowed. "I did not."

She nods her blond head exaggeratedly. "You did. Tally blew you a kiss, and you freaking laughed. And now you're smiling!" She points at my face like I'm an exhibit in a criminal proceeding. "See! Right now!"

I groan as I slide my palm down my face. "So? Is that a crime?"

She shakes her head and her mouth opens and shuts like she doesn't know what to say. "No. It's just . . . you're happy. Like truly happy." Her gaze flits back to the girls. "Because of her."

I swallow, nervous to admit it. Because if I tell her yes, I'm happy, that I want Tally to stay, she'll think she has no reason to come work here.

I don't know how to be a good brother to her, a good uncle to Quinn, *and* go after what I want.

"You don't have to be strong anymore."

Everything I've ever done up until these last few weeks has been for Billie and Quinn. But somehow I lost sight of that the minute Tally's lips touched mine.

"Walker, do you have any idea how rare this is?" my sister says, stepping closer to me.

"What is?"

"This kind of *love*." The word doesn't even scare me. My sister says it like she expects me to deny it, but there's no denying how I feel. I love Tally. I know that.

Billie's eyes fill with tears. "Walker, you need to tell her."

"She's leaving, Billie." My eyes fall shut and my shoulders sag because she has to go, and I'm not naive enough to believe she'll stay.

"Who says she can't be happy here?" My sister motions to the land around us. To the fields, which are now in full bloom, bursting with pink and purple tulips, white dahlias, yellow daffodils. And the goddamn wildflowers that make my chest ache every time I see them.

"She doesn't even know the truth about the farm. She'll hate me when she finds out."

No matter what I want to do, eventually I'll have to tell her why I'm really here. And when I do, she may never forgive me.

My sister's eyes dance toward the cottages, and she offers me a half smile.

"Not if she sees what you've been trying to do. You should tell her Peter's plan. It's your plan now, Jesse."

I blow out a breath. I can't tell Billie that's what I want to do because then she'll never agree to move here. It's a lose-lose situation. In the end, I need to do what's best for her and for the Darling girls.

Billie and Quinn stay here and they're happy. Tally goes to Nantucket, and then to school, where she's happy. *This* is what's best for everyone.

"You don't have to be strong anymore."

Tally said I have her, but she's supposed to leave in three

weeks. It's officially May, and while normally I'd be thrilled about the warmer weather and the longer, sun-filled days, it all feels like a countdown that I don't want to hit.

"I'm not an idiot, you know," she says.

I balk at her words. "I don't think you're an idiot."

"You know the girls do this thing . . ." She shakes her head, and her lips hook up again. "I don't have champagneso I can't cheers you and force you to tell me the truth. But if I agree to tell you the truth, will you do the same?"

I roll my eyes and let out a huff of air. "You can talk to me, Billie. We don't need to play some truth-or-dare game."

She gives me this look that is so Billie, one I've seen a thousand times during my life. One that signals she's about to call me out on my bullshit.

"I'll go first," she says before licking her lips and pausing. "I gave my notice at the hotel last week."

My eyes widen, and she shakes her head to let me know she isn't done.

"I should have done it a long time ago. I should have listened to you when you told me I was working too much and missing all of these moments when Quinn needed me. I wanted to prove to you that I could do something on my own. Wanted to prove it to myself, too. I didn't want you to have to fix something else for me. I'm stubborn, I admit," she says with a half smile.

I laugh. "You think?"

"Where do you think I get it from, grumpy old man?"

"I'm not that old," I mumble.

"My whole life you've protected me. Given up things for me."

I open my mouth to object, and she holds up a hand to

stop me. "Don't even try to say you haven't, because you have. Our grandfather lost this land, and all we ever heard about was how the Darlings stole from us, how they owed us. It made Dad a miserable person, just like his dad. You could have been the same way. But you are good. You protected me. You worked hard. And Peter saw that. You didn't con him into giving you this land. He came to you because he needed help, and he knew how much this land meant to our family. To you. You deserve good things, Jesse Walker. Peter saw it, I see it, and Tally will see it. You need to be honest and admit that you don't *need* me to come help with the farm. You *want* me here, with you. I know what's best for Quinn and me and, as long as I'm welcome here, I promise I'm moving in. Whether I work on the farm or not. Now tell me why you're letting Tally leave rather than fighting to keep her. Because Walker, I've never seen you smile this much. And I can't tell you the last time I heard you truly laugh."

Well, shit. I tug my sister beneath my arm and squeeze her tight right as the music starts up to signal the ceremony is about to begin.

"When did you get so smart?" I whisper, emotion keeping my voice quiet.

Billie grins up at me. "Well, I had this really wise older brother."

I smile at her before we turn our attention to the ceremony. From our spot on the hill, we have a perfect view of the part of the meadow we'd cleared for the ceremony. Like Tally's cake, flowers from all over the farm trickle down to the clearing to where the white chairs—decorated with wildflowers—are set up, a cascade of daffodils and tulips lining the walkway to make the entire space seem as though it is part of the flowering farm. A genius idea my sister had and that Gail and Penny helped her make happen this morning while Tally worked on the cake.

Golden fairy lights twinkle from the green foliage as a little boy runs down the aisle screaming for his mama, much to the amusement of all the guests. The groom rushes after him, lifting him up in the air and flying him past the line of groomsmen, who are clearly all hockey players. They stand, each of them oversized with a black eye or two and big smiles. Each of the guys fist-bumps the toddler and then the groom hands him off to an older man sitting in the front row.

Apparently the couple were married right after they had their son, but the groom wanted a bigger celebration so Hannah agreed to this ceremony. It's sweet that he's the more excited one. I think in a different life, if I'd been raised differently, if Billie didn't need me the way she had, I could have been like that. And when I spot Tally standing in the meadow, a pretty smile on her face as she catches me staring, it's easy to imagine that maybe I still can be.

Chapter 43
TALLY

If you get cake in my hair, I will murder you, Daniel Hall!" the bride shrieks as her husband plays airplane with a piece of cake.

"Is it weird seeing someone destroy what you worked so hard to make?" Walker asks.

"No. Nothing makes me happier than seeing someone enjoy something I've fed them." I lick my lips and my eyes widen. "You going to try my cake, Cowboy?"

He smiles knowingly. "You know I love your cake."

I lean into him and we laugh, and God, does it feel good to just relax with this man. Between getting the farm ready for the Daffodil Festival and preparing for this vow renewal, these last few weeks have been extremely stressful. Especially for Walker, who I know takes everything personally. But standing here now, I feel like we've accomplished something amazing. My father would be so proud.

The party gets rowdier as the night wears on. Because boy, these hockey players can drink. I'm surprised, seeing as they're still in season, but apparently they're all enjoying their night off. My favorite moment, however, is when the bride and groom head to the dance floor with their son between them, rocking back and forth as their friends surround them and sing the lyrics to "Adore You" by Harry Styles.

They're just about to start the family dances when Walker grabs my hand and tugs.

"What's up?"

"Come with me. Our sisters have this part covered," he tells me.

My heart races when I realize Walker's taking me away right as the father-daughter dance is about to start. This man. He leads me toward the wildflower field, and I shake my head, pulling his arm backward. "What are we doing out here? We can't get naked while a wedding is going on! People will see us!"

He chuckles. "I was thinking maybe you'd like to dance with me."

I hide my face in his chest as he pulls me toward him and we sway in time to the music.

"Did you have a good time today?"

Chin on his chest, I smile up at him dreamily. "The best."

He presses a kiss to my nose, and my cheeks pink.

"You know someone might see us," I warn him.

He shrugs. "Couldn't care less."

"Because you like me?" I don't know why I'm so nervous to ask him. Of course he likes me. But my question is loaded, and we both know it.

Walker pushes a golden lock of hair behind my ear and cups my cheek.

"Fuck, Tal, I more than like you." He traces a finger across my jaw, and the feel of it sends an electric current through my body and straight to my heart. "I'm crazy about you, and the thought of you leaving and meeting someone else . . ."

I turn into him and rest my palm on his jawline, tweaking

his chin to force him to look at me. "I've never dated anyone but you. And I think I make you happy." My fingers smooth over his rough skin, my thumb coaxing him to relax. "That you smile more when you're around me." His eyes soften. "Maybe most people wouldn't call this dating, but it's the most real relationship I've ever experienced."

Something sparks in his eyes. "Yeah?"

"Yeah. I've never been happier than I have these last few weeks with you."

"Will you be my girlfriend?" Walker's words take me by surprise. The boyish innocence of them.

"Really?"

A laugh looses from his chest. "Yeah, Wildflower, really. Will you date me? *In public.*"

I bite my lip, but before I get a chance to respond, Walker presses on.

"I know you're still leaving. I'm not trying to keep you. I just—"

I press my finger to his lips to silence him. "How about we don't talk about the future? How about we just live in the now, together?"

He nods with a goofy grin. "I'd like that."

A huge smile blooms on my lips. His mouth twitches into one, too, before we both lean in to savor a long, languid kiss.

"Are you two ever coming back?" Penny calls.

Walker and I turn to see Rosie and Penny standing at the top of the hill, both beaming as they watch us.

"Yeah, what are you guys doing out here? The party's back there!" Rosie shouts.

The corners of my mouth twitch up as I settle against Walker's chest and holler back. "We're dating!"

Chapter 44
TALLY

ROCHELLE: Tally, I wanted to go over the recipes you've been testing. Do you have time tonight?

ROCHELLE: Hi Tally, could you give me a call?

ROCHELLE: Are you still interested in joining me this summer?

My boot-covered foot taps wildly against the ground as I wait for Walker, trying like hell to avoid looking at my phone and the many messages that call for a response. My future boss in Nantucket, Rochelle, has texted me three times since last week, but due to the wedding cake debacle, I've been distracted. And now, well, now I actually don't know if I can answer her question because last night Walker asked me to be his girlfriend as we danced in the wildflower field. Can we really have a future if I leave? But can I really stay because of a boy? Or, in Walker's case, a beautiful, wonderful, excellent-in-bed, swoony, makes-my-toes-curl man?

I chew on the inside of my cheek as I stare out at the farm. The Halls and their guests are still here, staying in the cottages until tomorrow. It's clear as day that this is the future of the farm. A mini-resort on the prettiest piece of land, with weddings in the spring, and I'm sure Walker already has a slew of ideas for the other seasons. Everything will continue to grow, bigger, better, and more beautiful, and I can't imagine missing it all.

But how do I stay? Walker wants Billie to move here. The cottage is supposed to be her and Quinn's new home. It's the right thing for them and for Walker. And for my mother. Having them around all the time lights her up. I've come to realize that they aren't replacements for us. But they do bring her joy in their own way, and all I want is to see my mother happy.

And I have to admit that as much as I love this farm, it's not what makes my heart tick like it does for her and Walker, or like it did for my dad. So I should go to Nantucket. I should save up the money I make there for school and maybe one day I can come back here. Maybe take up Rayna on that offer for Mabel's. But that day is not today.

I'm still having these thoughts half an hour later as I set up my table at the farmers market when Quinn comes bolting down the brewery steps. His head whips back and forth like he's searching for something. I round my table and head his way.

"Hey, Quinn."

The moment he spots me, his lips tip up into a grin, exposing a missing front tooth. "Hi, Tally! Have you seen my Uncle Jesse?"

"Did you lose something this morning?" I ask him with a laugh.

His face falls and he looks around confused. "I don't think so? Why? Did you find something at your house that I left?"

I snort. "No. Your tooth." I point at my own front tooth.

"Oh yeah!" He reaches into his pocket and produces a five-dollar bill. "And look what the tooth fairy gave me!"

"Wow, five whole dollars. What are you going to do with that?"

He leans in close. "Can you keep a secret?"

I nod earnestly.

"I wanted to see if Uncle Jesse could make me a bouquet for my crush."

Urgh, my heart. "Oh yeah?"

He nods and I hold out my hand. "Well, let's go find him and see."

He sets his tiny, warm hand in mine, and we head toward the line of tables where all the gorgeous men are lined up. It really is genius marketing keeping all of them together.

Walker is helping one of the guys fix the leg on his table, and from his bent-over position, I get quite the eyeful of my favorite denim-covered ass. He huffs and runs his hands through his hair as he stands, his face lighting up when he spots Quinn. Or maybe it's the two of us. Because there's a look in his eye that makes me think he's picturing a life years from now. One where I'm holding another little boy's hand.

Shit. The man calls me his girlfriend and my brain starts conjuring up babies. I shake my head and force a big smile. "Look who I found!"

"You here to help?" Walker asks and nods toward the farm table where my mom is fixing the bouquets that are lined up in glass jars that say ROSIE'S BREWERY on them.

"I'll leave you two to it," I say as I release Quinn's hand. "Make sure he gives you the prettiest one," I tell him. Walker looks at Quinn, intrigued, and I spot his cowboy hat on the table. "And make sure he's wearing that while he prepares it for you."

Walker's resounding chuckle has me smiling as I head

back to my table, where I see a line forming. "What's happening?" I mumble to Rosie.

"Oh my God, are you the girl?" a teenager says as I settle behind the table.

I glance at Rosie. "I don't know, am I?"

Rosie snorts. "What can we get for you?"

"Would you make my cake for my sweet sixteen? Can you do it like this?" She pushes the screen of her phone toward me, and I see a photo of the wedding cake from last night. Wow, word around town spreads fast.

"Did someone put a picture of it in the town chat?" I ask Rosie.

"Oh my God!" I hear Penny scream from my mother's table. Her chair tips backward and she lands in the dirt, though she barely reacts as she crawls toward us. When she reaches us, Penny jumps up and pushes the phone at me. "Your cake is viral!"

"My cake is viral?" I parrot, not understanding what she's saying.

"Yes! Hannah Hall tagged the farm in a post of her and Daniel kissing behind your cake! She tagged the farm and it's gone viral! The photo already has fifty thousand likes!"

"Holy shit."

The girl in front of me nods. "Yeah, so do you think you could do it? My mom said I have a budget of two hundred dollars."

My eyes widen. "You want to pay me two hundred dollars to bake you a cake?"

Someone from behind her yells "Can I have one, too? It's for my mother's eightieth birthday."

"What is happening?" I murmur to Rosie.

She smiles at me. "Looks like you, Tally girl, are famous."

The next few hours are a dream. The line at my table hasn't stopped, so Billie comes over to help handle money while Penny and Rosie take orders and I answer questions about my recipes. Are things gluten free? No, but I can work on that next. Does something contain peanuts or sesame or coconut extract? By lunch, I have an entire menu in my head that I can make for next week so I can sell even more items for all those with food allergies and other dietary restrictions.

"I have to go to the bathroom," I mumble as I look at the line that hasn't let up. Thank God I made so many treats. We're making a killing on Walker's favorite honey cupcakes with the salted honey buttercream frosting.

"Grab another bottle of prosecco on your way back!" Rosie calls.

I've just made it inside the brewery when I'm pulled back and shoved against the wall. I don't have time to scream because Walker's hand goes to my mouth and his brown eyes glow with mischief. "Shhh, Wildflower, it's just me."

A thrill runs through me when I realize he's got me pressed against the wall right out of view of the window to the market. Where all our friends and family are.

Walker is wearing the cowboy hat I love, but it's going to get in the way of what I really want, which is his mouth on mine. So I reach up and toss it to the floor. Walker licks his lips. "Hi."

"Hi, yourself," I whisper.

He dips his head and suddenly he's kissing the life out of me. My stomach swoops in excitement at the idea of getting caught, and I wrap my arms around his neck to deepen the kiss. Walker's hands go to my hair and he tugs as he licks into my mouth.

"Fuck, Tal," he mumbles against me as his hand trails down my back and he cups my ass. "You're like a damn celebrity out there. It's turning me on."

"They really like my cupcakes," I purr.

"I like your cupcakes," he says before sucking on my lip again.

I chuckle and push against him. "I have to get back. Someone's going to come looking for me soon."

"Good, let 'em look." His fingers dip beneath the back of my shirt and I suck in a breath at the feel of him against my bare skin.

"Later," I say, pulling away. If I don't, I'm liable to start stripping.

I slip out of his arms and toss him his hat. "See you out there, Cowboy." Then I rush into the bathroom to douse my face with water.

As soon as I get outside, I notice my table has a temporary lull.

"Everyone wants to talk to you, so they're coming back later," Penny says in explanation.

Rosie waves a finger in my direction. "You've got sex hair."

My mouth falls open as I stare at her and then glance in Billie's direction, willing my best friend to shut her mouth.

Rosie grabs her mug and tips it my way, but before she can say anything, I just laugh. "I'm not hiding anything. You can't threaten me with your bad sex because I'll happily admit that I'm Walker's girlfriend and having all the good sex."

Billie coughs out a laugh, and I hold up my hands. "Sorry!"

She giggles. "Oh, I totally knew you were sleeping with my brother."

As if she's summoned him, we turn to see Walker coming down the steps of the brewery and heading toward us. He's got this mischievous look on his face and a glint in his eye that tells me he's up to no good. As he passes us, he drops his cowboy hat on top of my head.

"Oh!" Penny squeals. "You know what they say about men and their cowboy hats!"

I smile because I know it means Walker is marking me.

Walker opens his mouth to say something right as Quinn comes running up with a bouquet in his hand. "Can I give them to her now?"

Walker nods, and Quinn steps up and pushes the bursting bushel of tulips, daffodils, and wildflowers in my direction.

"What are these?" I ask.

"These are for you," Quinn says with a big smile.

"*She's* your crush?" Walker grumbles, and the girls all break out in a fit of giggles behind me.

"Aw, Quinn, thank you," I say before pressing a kiss to his cheek and putting Walker's cowboy hat on his head. "Now you can be my cowboy."

Chapter 45
WALKER

"What are you doing?"

Tally's voice startles me and I blow out a breath as I let go of the rocking chair I just set on the porch and turn toward her. The cicadas hum around us as the sun drops behind the rolling New England hills. The water in the harbor laps against the shore, gently swaying the pretty sailboats and glistening orange and pink hues. Tally blends in perfectly in the peach-colored spandex she threw on when we got back from the farmers market. Her wavy golden hair, which is tied up in a loose ponytail, jostles back and forth in the warm breeze, and the sweet scent of spring, fresh air, and sugar, which I've come to associate with her, dances around us. "I—ugh—" I motion toward the two rocking chairs and the lavender plants I've set out in large yellow ceramic planters to keep the bees and mosquitos away.

Tally had been busy at the brewery with Penny and Rosie for hours after the market, going through the hundreds of messages that were pouring in on the farm's Instagram account. Everyone wants to know how to order one of Tally's cakes. I know she's overwhelmed, and I wanted to set up a little surprise for her so she could relax tonight and celebrate what a huge accomplishment this weekend has been.

She walks toward me, those big golden eyes of hers widening as she takes in the scene.

"You mentioned your father wanting to finish the porch for your mom." I shrug.

Tally blows out a breath and blinks a few times.

"Hell, please don't cry." I take the steps two at a time, pulling her to me as soon as she's within reach.

Tally squeezes me tight, and I memorize the feel of her like this. How much longer do I have her? Fuck, I can't think about it or I'll be the one crying.

Tally wipes at her eyes before turning her gaze to me. "I'm sorry, this day has just—" She blows out a breath. "Thank you."

I smile at her. "Baby, you never have to thank me. This weekend was all you. How many more messages did you get after I left?"

She laughs and rolls her body into my side, guiding me up the steps with my arm still wrapped around her. Then she smiles at one chair before settling into it. Her eyes close as she rocks. "So many. Everyone is asking me if I can make their wedding cake." She blinks her eyes open. "Crazy, right?"

It takes effort to sit in the rocker beside her rather than pull her into my lap. "Why do you think it's crazy?"

"Because I'm not a baker. I don't have a degree. I'm just me." She says it like it's true. Like she doesn't see herself the way everyone else does. The way I do.

"Tally, nobody ever has everything. Maybe some people have degrees, but they don't have experience. Maybe some people have both but not the personality. There's a reason your boss in Nantucket sought you out to help this summer. You're talented. Don't wish away all of these experiences because you don't think you're enough. It's okay to take your dreams by inches and not by miles."

Her rocking chair creaks as she jolts forward. "You really think I could do it?"

I reach for her hand, stopping her chair for a moment. "Tally, I think you could do whatever you set your mind to. So, tell me what you want. Tell me, if you could have anything, what would your perfect life look like? Because I want to help you make it happen."

She bites her lip before letting a smile free. "Well, right now, I want to dance with my boyfriend on the porch of my daddy's house."

"Alexa, play country music," I say to the device I set on the porch. Then I stand up and hold out a hand to her. "Eli asked me if I had a date to the Spring Fling."

Tally takes my hand and lets me guide her away from the chairs. "Oh yeah?"

"Told him I'm going with you."

She snorts. "Oh, you just assumed, huh?"

I glance at her. "You are my girlfriend."

Her entire face lights up. "Well, then, I guess we'll have to go shopping for a new dress."

"*Tally.*"

"Come on, Cowboy. I need to look pretty when you get crowned Daffodil King."

My head falls back and I laugh as I come to terms with all the things I'm going to do just so I can be crowned king and Tally can be on my arm, smiling like the damn queen of this town she deserves to be. "You're lucky I really like you."

"That's good, because I forgot to tell you there's a dance-a-thon at the Spring Fling."

I cough out a laugh. "Hell, Wildflower. A what?"

She rolls her eyes. "I'm sure it sounds like the worst thing ever, but each couple picks a cause and whoever remains dancing the longest wins the pot of money for their charity."

I tug her closer. "So I have to dance with you all night?"

She nods. "Your worst nightmare."

I smile as I lean down and press my lips against hers. "I don't know Tally. I can think of nothing better than having you in my arms all night."

We twirl in a circle and I dip her right as Morgan Wallen's "Spin You Around" starts up.

"What are you doing, Cowboy?" she asks from her new position.

I tug her back to my chest, swaying us to the music. "Dancing with my girl."

"Is this practice for the Spring Fling?"

No, I think, *it's practice for the rest of our life*. But I can't tell her that. Can't tell her that every moment with her feels like a test. Like I'm trying to prove to her that she should stay here, in Hope Harbor, with me.

So I don't answer her question, but when one song changes to the next, and we continue dancing until the sky turns an inky blue and the stars start to twinkle, I think it's obvious that I have no interest in letting her go.

—

Later that night I'm still out on the porch, staring at the land I've come to consider my home. In the house behind me is the woman I know is my home. She's showering off the excitement of the day, and I'm looking forward to sinking inside her tonight to remind her, once again, how precious she is to me. But first, there's something I need to take care of.

It's clear that Tally is nervous to take the leap. But I want her to have the choice. So I take out my phone and start a new group chat with Fletcher, Eli, and Rayna McGovern.

ME: Hi, I think I might need another favor.

I'm smiling as I wait for the messages to roll in. I can only imagine how shocked they'll all be.

My phone buzzes and I glance down, but my smile falls the second I see the message.

FRANK SEYMOUR: You screwed up. Looks like the farm will be mine after all.

Fuck.

Chapter 46
TALLY

HOPE HARBOR TOWN CHAT

RAYNA: Did you all see this? Our Tally Darling is FAMOUS!
<link to Instagram post>

BABS: I remember when she was just a little girl, working in Mabel's Bakery. Rest in peace, Mabel.

RAYNA: Sweet Mabel.

MINDY: How did she die again?

RUBY: I think in her sleep?

BABS: In bed for sure.

ROSIE: Why does that sound dirty?

BABS: It's a talent of mine.

STEW: Please make it stop.

FLETCHER: LADIES!

* * *

I'm not sure I've ever been as out of sorts as I feel sitting in Babs and Mindy's salon, and for once it's not because of the inappropriate comments Babs likes to make. It's because the eyes of everyone in the salon are on me, and I don't like to be the center of attention.

"You need to reply to these, too." Penny points to the comments on her phone beneath the second post Hannah Hall made, which features all the vendors and designers for her ceremony. She tagged me personally for the cake. I swallow hard as I think about how lucky we were that Hannah was so agreeable to switching out cakes after we told her what happened. Another bride might have lost her mind. And it seemed it worked out for the best; a ton of people who attended the vow renewal ceremony have commented that it was the best cake they'd ever tasted. Aiden Langfield—the freaking star center of the Boston Bolts—shared it on his story, too, and now I've been tagged in hundreds of comments asking how to order from me.

I nibble on my lip, trying to not fall victim to the overwhelming sense of imposter syndrome that threatens to take over. Yes, the cake was gorgeous and tasted delicious. But it was one freaking cake. Eventually people will find out that I was just a fill-in. Like I am in so much of my life, helping during the seasons but never actually a part of the kitchen. Pitching in at the farm until Billie arrives and takes my place.

I think of how I felt last week, though, with Walker in Mabel's old bakery. I didn't feel like a fill-in there. No, I felt alive and like I was right where I belong. Shit. I don't want to leave.

I sigh. "I don't even know what to say to these people. I'm leaving in two weeks." Or at least, I'm supposed to leave in two weeks. I still haven't replied to Rochelle, and I'm absolutely dreading that ferry ride to Nantucket.

Rosie holds up her mug. "Is there any prosecco left in that bottle?" Babs is folding foil into Rosie's hair so she's stuck in her chair for the time being.

When I'd shown up this morning for our appointment, I didn't see the day going this way, but we're four glasses—or mugs, I suppose—deep and this is the second bottle we've polished off if it's finished. Which I suspect it is.

My sister lifts it up. "Feels empty to me."

I hop up from my spot on the couch and grab it from her. Sure enough, there's not a drop of booze left in it. "Definitely done."

"There's more in the cooler," Rosie reminds me.

"You girls could just sit still and not drink prosecco," Babs suggests.

"What would be the fun in that?" Rosie dangles her mug between her fingers as I stand to grab it and head for the cooler.

The Spring Fling is in ten days, right before I'm set to leave, and I've been beyond busy between the weddings at the farm, the grand marshal activities, Tally Tuesdays with Walker, and replying to all these messages on Instagram every night.

The truth is that every day I'm in this town, every moment I spend with Walker, I wish I wasn't leaving. The last eight weeks went by way too quickly, and the excitement I once felt about working on the menu with Rochelle isn't there anymore. I've come to love this place that I used to avoid, come to see the beauty in the townsfolks' meddlesome ways. The way in which they would do anything for one another.

More than all of that though, I've fallen for Walker. Hook, line, and sinker.

I promised myself I'd be open to new possibilities, to new dreams, but I think my dreams have changed more than I realized.

"Okay, don't kill me, but look at the link I just sent you," Penny says from her seat.

I've been avoiding my phone because there's always more messages that I don't want to deal with, but I huff and do what she asks. As soon as I open the text messages, there's a stream of links.

I laugh as I shake my head in disbelief. She made me a freaking website. And a TikTok. And an Instagram. All for a business I don't have. Tallulah's Tasty Cakes. It's catchy, I'll give her that.

My fingers dig into my forehead. "You are insane."

"It's a good idea," Penny says, shifting forward.

Mindy sighs. "If you keep moving, you're going to end up with bangs again."

Rosie snorts. "Uh-oh."

"Penny, there's likes fifty messages on this Instagram." I groan. I can't possibly keep up with this.

Rosie leans forward. "Let me see!"

Penny holds up her phone, waving it in her hand dramatically. "I'll message it to you. Don't go messing up your hair."

I laugh, but I can't ignore the excitement swirling in my chest.

For a moment everyone is silent while Rosie stares at the links Penny just sent her. "I don't know, Tal, this looks pretty good to me." She glances up from her phone. "And every day people are coming into the bar, asking if we have your cakes. You're famous. You should strike while the iron's hot."

I shake my head. Could I really do this? Open a bakery and start my own business? It seems . . . a smile pulls at my lips. Damn, it seems pretty exciting.

My sister spots my smile. "See, I knew you'd like it."

I try to straighten my lips, but they keep tugging up. "Okay, well, if I was to do this, would you be able to help me set up a rate sheet? And help me research what I can even charge? God, there's so much I'd have to do."

My sister smiles as she picks up her phone. "I thought you'd never ask."

I glance down at the text to find a link to an article on costs of wedding cakes.

"We can start with that. Since you're just starting out we should keep prices on the low end, but I'll make something on Canva tonight."

I tap my foot, staring at the website again. "Am I really doing this?"

The women all look at me expectantly. "I can call Rayna about Mabel's?" Babs offers.

I shimmy my shoulders in excitement and let out a nervous squeal. "Okay, but can we talk about something else right now? I'm kind of freaking out."

Penny grins with pride, and I revel in the feeling for a moment. For so long I felt like I didn't belong. Like my sister didn't truly see me. Like none of my friends or family did. It's clear, though, that those beliefs were grounded more in my insecurities than in reality, because she's been fully supportive since the moment I showed a true interest in the bakery. Just like everyone else.

"Did you see that Jake Montgomery released a new book?" Babs muses, changing the subject. I imagine the only person she could be talking to is my sister, so I glance back at Penny to gauge her reaction. Sure enough, she's sucking on her bottom lip, and though she nods at Babs in response, she doesn't say anything else.

Mindy runs her fingers through Penny's hair. "That boy ever get married?"

Penny's shoulders lift. "No idea."

"We should read it for book club this month, right?" Babs continues.

"It's not a romance," Penny grumbles.

"Oh, so you *do* know what it's about," Mindy teases.

"Leave her be," Rosie growls. "You ladies are so nosy."

I tune them all out while I pop the cork on the next bottle. They are nosy, but they're also harmless and their interest comes from a good place. Besides, I'm celebrating.

"Have you given any more thought to my son?" Babs is saying to Penny when I deliver Rosie's glass.

"Your married son," I remind her.

She sighs. "You keep harping on that, but Penny's already a woman of a certain age."

"I'm not even thirty," Penny grumbles. "Why do I come here again?"

"Because it's what neighbors do," Babs tells her. "Just like we all go to Rosie's brewery even though not one of us likes beer, and we'll all read Jake Montgomery's bad book because he used to be a Daffodilian—"

"That's not a word," I interrupt.

Babs shushes me. "And it's why we all buy enough flowers from your farm to cover that loan your daddy never should have taken."

I'm just about to toss back another snarky comment when her words register and my head whips back in her direction. "What did you say?"

With eyes the size of saucers, Babs snaps her lips shut. I look at Penny. "Did you know about this?"

Penny eyes are wide and she shakes her head. "No. Mom never said anything."

It's like a punch to the gut. Ever since being back on the farm, I've known something seemed off.

"I'm sure it's not a lot of money," Penny offers hopefully.

"Well, I wouldn't really say a hundred thousand dollars isn't a lot of money," Babs mumbles. "But I guess that's really Walker's problem now since he owns it."

"*He what?*" Rosie growls, jerking her head around and glaring at the woman.

"You're going to have streaks," Babs hisses as she holds a piece of foil in her hand that was just coated in hair dye and wrapped around Rosie's hair.

"I can pull it off," my best friend says before standing and turning to me. "What do you want me to do?"

Ignoring Rosie, I focus on Babs. "What do you mean, Walker owns it?"

She nibbles on her lip. "I don't think you were supposed to know that."

"We deserve to know," Penny proclaims. "It's *our* farm."

My stomach sinks as I remember all the times I'd said those exact words to Walker when I first arrived. And then I recall the looks he'd give me. At the time, I thought it was because he didn't like the fact that it was mine and Penny's. But now I realize it was because he knew it wasn't. All along, the farm has been his.

Chapter 47
WALKER

No matter how many times I look at this piece of paper, the numbers don't change. The farm is in the red. Seriously in the red. And Frank is calling in the loan. Motherfucker. After everything we've worked so hard to achieve, we missed one fucking clause that made it all worthless.

"You weren't supposed to transfer the land," I mumble to Gail as I read over the letter from Frank for a second time. I'd been at the brewery when she called, panic stricken, and I'd told her to bring the letter here. I've known for a week that we had a problem, but this is the nail in the coffin. Frank's threats weren't empty.

She blinks at me from across the table, tears in her eyes, and shakes her head. "I don't know what to do."

Years ago, Peter took out a line of credit from Frank Seymour and mortgaged the property. For years, Peter made the minimum monthly payments, but it ballooned in June and now the payments will be nearly quadruple what he was previously paying. That was bad enough. Everything we'd done over the last few months was supposed to mean we'd be able to make that first balloon payment in June and buy some time until I was able to prove to a bank that we had what was needed to refinance the loan. But we missed one tiny detail: When Gail and Peter gave me half interest in this property, it was a violation of the loan agreement they signed with

Frank, and now he's calling the loan. We either pay off the entire thing or he forecloses in July and we lose it. *Fuck*. Fuck, fuck, fuck.

I have nothing to sell other than my old truck, and we'll need that if we have any chance of coming out on the other side of this spring. No, the only thing that would fix this is an influx of cash.

"We're going to need to sell some land." I don't say it easily. I'd been avoiding this last resort since January, when Frank first showed up and told us about the balloon payment. I'd gone around and around on what could be done, but it can't be avoided now. There is no quick fix other than that.

From across the table, Gail nods at me. "The wildflower meadows make the most sense. Developers have been after those plots forever because they look out toward the harbor. Peter could never bear to part with them."

My swallow is heavy as I imagine Tally's reaction to losing her favorite place in the world. To saying goodbye to a future house on that spot.

"We need to tell the girls."

"Absolutely not." My head snaps up at Gail's pronouncement. Her lips don't quiver, and her face is a mask of seriousness.

"Gail—"

She shakes her head. "Tally will stay if she knows the trouble we are in. I promised her father I wouldn't let her do that."

A rush of defeat runs through me, and I hang my head. I know Peter never wanted the girls to feel obligated to the land. I know Gail forced me to keep quiet since Tally came home because she promised her husband just that. Hell, she held an NDA over my head and I agreed. But now? Now all of that seems so fucking pointless. Tally's heart will be broken, and I have no one to blame but myself. I should have told her, should have fought Gail harder to tell her.

"She doesn't want to stay in Hope Harbor. She likes to travel . . . that's her thing," Gail continues.

I shake my head because she doesn't know her daughter at all if that's truly what she believes. Though I don't think she's completely to blame for that. Everyone's been hiding pieces of themselves under the guise of protection: Tally, Penny, Gail, Billie, even me. But that all needs to end. Tally and her sister deserve to know the truth. About everything. They'll be upset, yes, but in the end they'll understand.

"She deserves to live her own life," she says. "If we can't figure out a way to keep the farm, that's on me. *Us*. I don't want to put that on her."

My jaw hardens because I don't want to put that on Tally, either. But lying to her, hiding the truth, is only going to end badly. "Eventually she needs to know about the land, Gail."

She shakes her head. "Why does she? She'll never understand. She'll only try to fix it."

My teeth grind together because Gail's not wrong. Already, Tally has been trying to find a fix to the unfixable. And that's just the problem, isn't it? The way the business is currently running is dead in the water. Changes need to be made. And we don't have the money to make them unless we sell the land.

It makes perfect sense to me. We have too much of it. But still, I know Tally won't agree. I'll need to figure out a way to slowly give her all this information, to make her understand that this isn't a bad thing.

And if Gail is right, if Tally's leaving just like she's planned to all along, then what does it matter? Telling her will only have her digging in her toes and fighting for something she doesn't want.

I don't want to lie to her any longer. But I know if I tell her the truth, she'll stay. And as much as I want that, I know she doesn't. Tally needs to choose her own destiny, to chase her own dreams.

"Promise me you won't tell her," Gail pleads.

I gnash my teeth together but give a simple nod.

"Thank you, Walker. I'll talk to the Realtor and see if any developers would be interested in a quick deal."

My head bobs again and lead settles in my stomach as she gets up and disappears out the door. The sale won't happen quick enough. We'll still miss the payment due on the first, but we'll be able to pay off the loan relatively quickly when the cash lands so it will be worth it. And Tally won't be here to see it, which will make everything easier.

I'm still trying to work out how I'm going to solve this when the sound of a chair being pulled back startles me. I look up to find Eli and Fletcher sitting down at my table. "Thanks for inviting us for lunch."

Confused, I stare at them both. I definitely did not invite either of them for lunch.

Fletcher chuckles. "He said you wouldn't agree on matching suits so we're here to find out what color you're wearing so we can coordinate. Also, Stew told me you're joining our bowling league and I wanted to go over the rules with you."

Oh, for fuck's sake. "When did I tell Stew I was bowling?"

Fletcher's face crunches in confusion, but Eli laughs good-naturedly. This guy.

Fortunately, the server appears at that moment, cutting the conversation short. "What can I get you?"

For some unknown reason, I order lunch and then proceed to sit there and listen to the rules of bowling. I even agree to bringing the beer. Apparently, the bowling alley is bring your own.

I also learn that they wear matching shirts, which is where I draw the line. Eli told me I looked to be a large, which means I'm sure I'll have a damn shirt on Friday.

I have this whole conversation on autopilot as I think about how I just agreed to break the heart of the woman I love.

"So when's the big reveal?" Eli asks, pulling me from my thoughts.

I blink in confusion.

"The bakery," Fletcher prods, reminding me of how we've been spending our spare time lately.

I sigh. Pretty sure that will all be for nothing, too.

"Rayna's so excited. As is the rest of the town," Fletcher continues. "I'm just so happy the revitalization fund is being used."

My head snaps up, and it's like all the pieces fall into place at once. "What else is the fund being used for?"

Fletcher scratches his cheek. "Just that project and then we've kept an eye on all the parcels around the harbor. There are funds set aside to keep the harbor from being overbuilt."

For the first time since Gail showed me her letter, I smile. "What if I told you I had the perfect spot for the town to invest in?"

Fletcher grins. "Tell me more."

Chapter 48
TALLY

"You sure it's okay if I stay here?" I ask Penny as she makes up the pull-out couch for me. I couldn't bear to return to the farm after everything we learned today. I don't know how to face Walker, how to come to terms with the fact that everything he ever told me was a lie.

And I hate myself even more because he warned me he was hiding things. He told me in no uncertain terms that I wouldn't like what my mother had done and that he couldn't tell me what that was. And still, I went and fell for the man, anyway.

He basically told me the farm was in trouble, and I chose to fall in love rather than dig deeper.

"The better question is, are you sure you want to stay?" My sister slips a pillow into a pillowcase and then fluffs it once, twice, before tossing it at me.

It lands with a thunk against my chest, and I let out a disgruntled laugh. "Yes. Why wouldn't I want to stay?"

"Because before Walker you hated it here, Tally. You've been avoiding Hope Harbor for the last eight years in any way you can. And only eight weeks ago, you came here kicking and screaming, complaining that you weren't staying a minute past May twentieth."

I sigh. I can't fight her right now. Instead, I move the conversation on. "I have some money set aside; maybe I can use it to help with the loan."

Penny looks around her apartment. "I've got nothing. Everything I had I sunk into the store."

"I'm not asking you to fix this. Walker did this to us, and I should have listened to you when you said he was up to no good."

"Maybe." Penny's voice is soft, like she doesn't believe it.

"Maybe what? Maybe the fairy tale is dead? Maybe I'm just like every other cliché; the girl who falls in love with the villain, despite him telling her he was hiding something—"

"You love him?" Penny's cuts me off.

"What the hell does it matter?"

"Tally, of course it matters."

I don't say anything for a beat. Walker isn't some white knight in shining armor. But he's not an evil villain, either. The truth is, he's just a man trying to do what's best for his family. He told me why he took the job, told me how he wanted to help Billie and Quinn. It makes sense why he did what he did, but it still hurts.

"I never hated it here," I blurt out, dropping to the edge of the pull-out couch.

Penny plops down beside me and chuckles. "That's all?"

I roll my eyes and then focus on the bookshelves that line her walls. She's got a tiny apartment above her store. It's got one bedroom, an open living space with a small kitchen, a table that can fit no more than two chairs, this sofa bed, and rows and rows of bookshelves.

There's an entire store downstairs, filled to the brim with a rainbow of colorful spines, but that's not enough for my bookworm of a sister. Up here are her trophies; the books that she's read and loved over the years. Some have barely been opened, displayed only as beautiful treasures. Others are tattered and worn, like she searched every page for a word of comfort. I don't miss how Jake Montgomery's books are the most worn of the bunch. Though there's not a drop of romance in Jake's thrillers, I get the feeling Penny's still searching for the love story.

That's how my sister has always looked at the world, with rose-colored glasses, searching for beauty in all the black and white. Whereas I've simply been turning from page to page, living my life like it was an instruction manual.

Ironically, never once have I followed a recipe to the letter. Baking was the one place I allowed myself to go with the flow, and I thrived because of it. The same thing happened when I met Walker.

A smile tugs at my mouth. "I never hated this town. And I wasn't avoiding coming home. I just never thought I had done enough to come back."

Penny furrows her brow. "So you planned to come back?"

Turning to face my sister, the words spill out unfiltered. "I always wanted to open a bakery here. In Mabel's old spot maybe." I shrug at my sister's shocked expression. "I'd spend the early hours baking, and after a morning rush, I could walk across the street and sit in your bookstore and we'd swap stories over a coffee. One day we'd meet men, and after work they'd take us to dinner on a double date. Or—" My eyes light up. "We'd go to trivia night at the brewery and annoy Rosie with requests for every odd drink we could think up to have her make."

Penny laughs lightly.

"Eventually we'd both have kids, and we'd bring them to

the farm to see Mom and Daddy—" The words catch in my throat, and I blink, trying to stop the tears that I'm never quite ready to let flow.

Penny squeezes my hand. "That's a good dream."

My chin wobbles as I nod. "But now Daddy's not here and I have no idea if there'll even be a farm to come home to."

"Tally." Penny shakes her head. Like me, she's just as lost when it comes to that dream. I know she shared it once. But now we're both working with an entirely new plot.

"I just wish I knew what he was thinking when he took out that loan. What he used the money for. I wish we had a portal to summon him and ask these things, or that he left us a letter or a journal. I feel like that's what happens in all good books . . ." I glance at my sister, and she nods for me to continue my ramblings. "I want answers, and the thing that sucks about death is that I don't think we'll ever get them."

"Well, there is one way to get answers," Penny says softly.

I shake my head. I can't face Walker or my mom right now. Penny sighs and the bed dips as she turns to face me completely, her knee coming between us.

"Tally, things can't always be perfect. If you're waiting for your life to be packaged in a pretty bow, you'll be waiting forever."

"You sound like Walker."

She shrugs. "You should talk to him. Keeping secrets is what got us into this."

"No." I shake my head, my eyes brightening as an idea comes to me. "What we need to do is to talk to the guy who wrote Walker that letter, offering to buy the farm. I bet he's the one who holds the loan. If we can find a way to pay it, we can try to get the land back from Walker. Dammit, what was his name again?"

My sister—who has a photographic memory—blows out a breath and closes her eyes as she says, "Frank Seymour."

"Yes!" I lift my phone, and ignoring all the texts I've received from Walker asking what time I'll be home from my day at the salon, I google Frank's name. "Look. He has a farm down in Connecticut! Sounds like it's time for a girl's trip!"

Chapter 49
WALKER

HOPE HARBOR TOWN CHAT

RAYNA: Does anyone know where the Darling girls disappeared to? I just got an email that book club is canceled?

BABS: Book club is canceled?

BABS: I just stopped by the store. The bookstore is closed. It's never closed!

I shake my head and scroll past the town group chat and down to the one that's been silent for hours.

TALLY: Last minute girls' trip with Penny. We'll be back in a few days.

ME: where are you going?

ME: Did you get there okay?

ME: Tally, please just let me know you're okay. I'm going out of my mind here.

Her last text was sent this afternoon, and now it's almost dusk. I'd been busy meeting with Fletcher, the town's lawyer, and Gail, trying to make this impossible situation more tenable for everyone. But if Tally doesn't answer her phone soon, I'm going to storm out of this meeting and go search for her. Something's very wrong. I can feel it.

"Are you sure this is what you want to do?" Fletcher taps his pen against his finger, one, two, three times.

I glance over at Gail and she nods.

I practically swallow my tongue trying to answer. I have no idea if this will make things better or worse. I just know that we need to pay Frank his money and get him out of our lives forever.

I hope Tally forgives me, that one day she understands I did this all for her. I pick up my phone again and then drop it; a message hasn't miraculously popped up. Taking a deep breath, I take the proffered pen and sign page after page, forever changing the ownership of Darling Daffodils Farm.

Hours later, I'm pacing the porch, at my wit's end. No one knows where the girls are, and if anyone has a clue why they disappeared, they're not talking. Rosie merely looked at me and said "You screwed up, Cowboy" when I tried to talk to her.

I'm trying not to worry Gail. Fortunately, we were so busy sorting out everything today, I don't think she's noticed the girls haven't been home. Plus, she isn't big on using the phone so I doubt she's seen the messages in the town chat.

I type out another desperate message.

ME: Tally, please baby, whatever I did, I'm sorry. Just tell me you're okay.

Chapter 50
TALLY

My head hurts, and I'm starving. Those are the first two thoughts that enter my brain when I wake up. Though I barely slept in the first place. Between the spring from this pull-out bed that kept jabbing me all night and the endless loop of worst-case scenarios I continued to run through in my mind, I hardly slept a wink.

We are supposed to start out for Connecticut this morning. Leaving last night seemed like a bad idea, especially once we pulled out the wine and some old LEGO sets my sister had stored here for Dad. We spent hours laughing and crying together as we reminisced on old family memories and discussed our hopes and dreams for the future.

Penny told me things I never knew about her relationship with Dick, and as much as I thought I'd be able to commiserate and talk bad about Walker, I just couldn't bring myself to do it. It was too hard trying to come up with anything bad about that man other than the fact that he broke my heart.

I let out a long breath and my stomach rumbles again. Okay, I really need to feed myself.

The bed creaks, and I remember the text I sent last night. Not the one in response to Walker's many texts but the one to Rochelle.

Despite everything, I know sending that message was the right decision and already it feels as though a weight has been lifted from my shoulders. I throw off the sheet and pad softly over to the kitchen, trying not to wake my sister, who is sleeping soundly in her bedroom.

Her pantry is pathetically barren, and I know it's because she lives on coffee and treats downstairs in the shop. Dammit. A glance at the clock tells me it's only 5:53 a.m., which means that nothing is open in town, either. Just as I'm giving up, my stomach offering another hungry growl, I spot the plate of cupcakes covered in plastic wrap on her counter.

Yay for small wins!

She stole those the other night after helping me make several dozen for the farmers market tomorrow. I grab the one with the most frosting and take an enormous bite.

As the sugar and cinnamon hit my tongue, it unlocks a treasure trove of memories. This is so much more than a cupcake. It's the late nights in the kitchen, getting to know each other. It's words of *I can't* and then moans of how good everything feels. It's frosting spread across my body and a hot tongue licking it up. It's Sunday mornings at the farmers market and whispered dreams while slow dancing. It's falling in love with a grumpy man who smiles so wide his dimple pops. It's an entire spring's worth of memories: messy and beautiful, a little rain with a lot of sun.

Oh my God, what am I doing? Walker believed in me when no one else did. And I didn't even give him the opportunity to explain. I didn't believe in *him*.

Without thinking, I grab my sneakers and rush down the back steps of my sister's apartment. Fortunately, I slept in my normal spandex, so after tying my shoes, I head out onto the quiet street.

The glow from the street lamps guides me through my

sleepy town and past the dark storefronts. The waterfront is still and the world is silent as a I rush past, the calm broken only by the gentle lapping of a few boats in the harbor and the squawks of one lone gull.

My chest burns by the time I hit the crushed gravel that leads to the farm. A farm I thought I loved more than anything, though recently I've come to realize that it's the people in this town who mean more to me. And most importantly, the ones who live here: my mom and Walker, my soulmate.

When I finally make it halfway down the driveway, the sun is casting a gentle glow across the meadow in a greeting that feels like a beckoning, a reminder that this is where I belong. I gulp down the New England air as the shape of the man who's taken hold of my heart comes into view.

I don't slow. I rush to him, begging that he'll have answers to the questions turning in my mind. But mostly I hope that somehow, someway, after we speak, this will still feel like home.

Chapter 51
WALKER

Bleary-eyed and exhausted, I blink a few times, sure that I'm seeing things. But when I open them again, I know that what's in front of me is real: Tally, a blur of peach in one of her spandex outfits, her golden hair bouncing behind her.

I'd been walking the meadows for hours, trying to figure out how to fix things. How to find her. And here she is, right among the wildflowers. I almost laugh at the irony of it all.

Without thinking, I reach for her as soon as she gets close, but she pulls back and holds up a finger, catching her breath as her head falls down.

"I've been going out of my mind, Wildflower. Where have you been?"

She winces and shakes her head, then lets out a heavy sigh. "I was trying to forgive you for breaking my heart." Her voice cracks on the last word, as does my damn heart.

"Tally—" I step forward, but she shakes her head again.

"My father gifted you half the farm. *You* own this farm. Not me."

Fuck. I don't make her wait for an answer. The time for secrets is over. "Yes."

She blows out a breath and nods like she thought there was a chance I'd deny it. But I'd never have lied to her if she'd asked me point-blank. And I certainly won't do it now.

"Can I explain?"

She shakes her head and a tear drops down her cheek.

"I know—" I blow out a frustrated breath. "I know I fucked up by not telling you the truth. But I did tell you, before anything happened between us, that I was keeping secrets."

"I didn't know it was this," she cries.

I squeeze my fists to keep from reaching for her. "The farm is still your family's."

Her head tilts, and I hold up a hand. "And mine. And if you give me a chance, I can explain. Please Tally, if I ever meant anything to you, just give me five minutes."

She blows out a breath and nods.

"I didn't know how to tell you everything. Didn't want to show you all my ugly. Because my family's history with this land *is* ugly. My grandfather lost it to your grandfather in a poker game. Fucking New England and its storied history."

Tally's eyes widen. "What?"

"Growing up, I hated this land with a passion. This farm made my grandfather and my father angry. It made them bitter. I was raised to think that your family was evil, despite knowing that true evil was the back side of my father's fist."

Tally's face softens, but I shake my head. I don't want her feeling bad for me.

"When your dad showed up at that farm and offered me this job, I'd wondered if he knew what he was asking of me. But as I got to know him, I realized he knew precisely what he was doing. He needed help, Tally. He was underwater, and he knew that the only person who could save this farm was someone who was just as invested, who could love the land just as much he did, and who would do anything to keep it from becoming a development of new houses or an apartment complex."

Tally steps closer.

"And then we lost him. Your mother lost the love of her life, you lost your dad, and I lost the first person to truly believe in me." My chin dips as I try to contain my emotion. "Your father was incredible, Tally. Even more than I'd realized, now that I've seen a whole other side of him from being with you, from seeing the way you love him, the way this town loves him."

She nods, and I take it as a signal to push on.

"Even after he died, he's continued to teach me things. Through you, through our friends. He taught me to ask for help, and that's what I did when I realized we were really going to lose the farm. I asked our friends to help with the cottages, and fuck, Tal, everyone showed up. You were right all along. We *need* people. So when the loan came due and I knew we had no other options, I turned to Fletcher and we made an agreement. The town purchased the wildflower meadows."

Her eyes widen, and I hold up a hand to ease her worry. "With a stipulation that nothing can ever be built on that land."

She shakes her head, and her eyes fall shut. "You sold the wildflower meadow to the town?"

"Tally, I—"

Her eyes fill with tears. "They're safe now. No one will ever build on them?"

The dread in my chest lifts as I realize she's not angry. "I couldn't bear to have you lose them, too, after everything you've already lost. But I can't take all the credit. Fletcher swept in and saved the day. If that didn't work, I was going to sell the land in the east."

Her face scrunches in confusion. "That's where the tulips are."

I shrug.

"Walker," she hisses and then pushes against my chest. I barely move. "You could have gotten so much more money from a developer. Why'd you do it?"

There's not just one answer to her question, there's a myriadof them, but they all revolve around the same thing. So in the field of wildflowers that she loves so much, I give her my truth.

"Because I love you." Her eyes widen in shock. But I'm not done, and now that I've said it, I just want to say it again. "I love you, Tally Darling, and I want you to come back. Fuck, I want you to stay but know you need to live out all those big dreams of yours. But when you're done, I want you to come back and live this dream with me. Because *I love you*." I choke on a laugh because it feels so good to say those words. "Tally, I love you, this farm, this life of mine. But none of it is my dream if you aren't here with me. So, no, this farm doesn't only belong to me. Yesterday I signed papers to transfer ownership to you, your sister, your mother, my sister, and me. It was my only stipulation to your mom. I'll continue to run the farm as long as all of you own it with me."

Tally's swipes wildly at the tears that cascade down her cheeks. "What?"

I nod. "So go to Nantucket. Go become the person you need to be. The farm is safe. I promise I'll never take a thing from you."

She bites her lip and shakes her pretty head. "But I don't want to go to Nantucket." She looks so goddamn adorable with a pout on her face and her hair blowing in the early morning breeze.

"Dammit, woman, you are confusing the hell out of me."

She laughs. "You asked me last week what I wanted. Ask me again."

"What?"

"Ask me again," she says slowly as she steps up and sets her palms flat against my chest.

I swallow nervously. "What do you want, Tally?"

She smiles. "I want this." Her arms swing out, and she motions to the land around us.

"What?"

She settles her hands back on my chest and slowly enunciates, "I. Want. This. This farm. This land. Every day waking up with you. Tally Tuesdays. Our cottage." Her smile grows. "Sundays with the girls, drinking out of my coffee mug and making fun of you while you wear that stupid cowboy hat at the farmers market. I want to go to the brewery on Friday nights and slow dance with you and laugh with my friends. I want to walk into town and visit my sister's bookstore and spend hours with her doing absolutely nothing. I want to have family dinners with my mom and sister, and your sister and Quinn. I want this farm to be my home. I want *you* to be my home. And I want to make whatever dream you and my dad thought up come true."

Damn. The way she's looking at me makes me believe that just maybe she really could be happy here.

"But why?"

She snorts. "Stupid, stubborn Cowboy." She shakes her head. "Because I love *you*."

"You do?" My heart pounds.

She rolls her eyes, but she's smiling. "Yes. And you can't do everything on your own."

"I know. But what about Nantucket? And school? Tally, I

didn't fix everything. The loan on the farm may be paid off now, but it's still going to take a lot of work to get this place profitable."

She licks her lips. "I gave Rochelle notice yesterday that I wasn't coming to Nantucket."

"Tally—"

She holds up her hand. "It wasn't what I wanted." She shrugs. "It would have made me happy once. But not anymore. And about school." Her eyes drift to the horizon and then come back to mine. "I'm going to take the money I've saved and talk to Rayna about leasing the bakery. I figure it's about time I start chasing my dreams on my own time. Take the dream by inches and all that." She bites her lip, her eyes going a bit shy at that admission. "I just need a place to live. So what do say, Cowboy? You ready for a permanent roommate?"

I pull her into my arms and finally, fucking finally, I kiss my girl. When I dip her dramatically, she giggles against my lips, but quickly those giggles fade as our kiss deepens. She tastes like cinnamon and sugar, like cupcakes and all my dreams coming true.

We pull back and smile stupidly at one another. "I love you, Tally Darling."

"I love you, Jesse Walker."

"You know, I had this whole speech planned."

"Oh yeah? How were you going to do that if I was in Nantucket?"

"I was never letting you get on that ferry."

"Were you going to chase me down, show up at the boat, and, what? Hold up your phone and blare Taylor Swift's 'Cowboy Like Me'?"

My smile falls. "That's not our song."

She snorts. "Says you."

"That's not our song. And no, though that sounds wonderfully dramatic, my gesture is a little bigger."

Her eyes dance, and in the early morning light they glow brighter than the sun. "Well, what are you waiting for? Grovel away."

My hand goes to her cheek and I stare into those gorgeous amber eyes. They're the color of the sun right as it comes up over the meadow, a hue of pink and orange tinging the corners like it's reflected off the wildflower field. "Give me an hour, woman. I've got to round up the brigade."

Her eyes dance. "Oh, your people are involved, too?"

"No, Tally, *our* people are involved."

And I laugh because who the fuck ever thought I'd find one person in this town as amazing as Tally. But somehow I've found a whole community of them: people to help whenever someone needs it, who show up for farmers markets and festivals, who rebuild a farm that's on its last breath, who made my girl's dream come true. Now *that* is a dream worth chasing. A life worth living.

I smile at the woman I've fallen so head over heels for. My wildflower. Wherever the wind blows us, I know she'll be happy because we'll be together.

I scoop her up and carry her toward our cottage. "Oh, I guess I can tell you one of your surprises."

She squeals in excitement when I land on the steps of our cottage and then kick open the door. "This is our home now."

Tally smiles at me. "I was hoping you'd say that. But what about your sister?"

"She's moving into the house. So is your mother. Quinn will take Penny's old room, and Billie will take my old room."

"You mean *my* old room." Tally sticks out her tongue. Brat.

I grab it with my lips and suck on it. "Yes. Your old room. That okay?"

Tally's grin is radiant. "Yes. Yes, to all of it. We're really going to live out here?"

I nod. "Yeah, Wildflower. I can't think of anywhere better."

"I can think of one thing that would make it better." Tally's tone is pure sex.

"Oh yeah?"

"Yeah, Cowboy. Drop those pants."

Chapter 52
TALLY

My stomach flutters in anticipation the moment Walker swings open the door to the cottage. *Home.*

"Where do you want to christen first?" he asks with a roguish grin as he holds me in the entryway.

I roll my teeth over my bottom lip, completely famished, and yet still I can't help but tease him. "Doubt there's an inch of this place we haven't already touched."

Walker smirks. "That a challenge? Because I promise, Tally, there are ways I haven't had you in this house." A kaleidoscope of positions flip through my mind, and he chuckles like he can see the Rolodex of ideas. "Dirty girl, you were fucking made for me."

I won't argue that. "We've got a lifetime to test out all those positions, but right now I just need you, inside me. No games, no teasing. Make love to me, Walker."

His eyes light up like that's the best thing he's ever heard, and without hesitating, he carries me toward the bedroom. There's a pale yellow comforter on the bed and more pillows than I can count. It looks beyond cozy and not at all the same as yesterday. "Where'd you—" I shake my head. I don't know why I'm continually surprised by this man's thoughtfulness.

Walker ignores my question as he tosses me onto the bed. And then, with one hand, he reaches behind him and pulls his shirt over his head, exposing an expanse of skin and muscles for my eyes to feast on. Walker's own eyes smolder, holding mine as he slips off his shoes and unbuttons his jeans before pushing them down with his boxers. His cock springs up, and my mouth waters. God, I love this man.

And because we're no longer afraid to tell each other that, I say those three words out loud.

His fiery gaze softens, and those brown eyes caramelize. My chest grows hot under his loving stare. "I love you, Tally girl." Then that wolfish grin returns as he grips his cock and gives it a firm stroke. "Now strip."

Hungry for a taste, I sit up and reach for him but he pulls back. "Tits, Tally, I need to see your tits. Then you can swallow me down or do whatever you fucking want. But please, baby, let me see you first."

I smile and tug the spandex over my head, and he hisses the second my breasts spill into view.

Reaching out, he tweaks one and my head falls back. There's nothing like the feeling of his skin against mine. Not a thing compares to his hands on me. "These are my fucking favorite," he rasps. "Want to lick them and bite them and fuck them and come all over them."

"You telling me your list of things again? Getting forgetful in your old age. I already told you that we have forever to try it all out."

He chuckles and pinches my nipple, making me whimper. "Brat. Think I'm going to drag out that orgasm now. Make you really work for it."

My eyes light up. Sounds like a reward to me.

As if he can read my mind, Walker shakes his head and laughs. "Get over here, Wildflower. I want to eat that pussy while I fuck your mouth."

I shake my head and curl my finger, ordering him closer.

Walker drops a knee on the bed and wraps his fist around his cock again. "What? You can't wait that long?"

I shake my head. "Not today. Right now I need you inside me. Need to feel you pulsing as I come all over your cock."

"Fuck, Wildflower, you're—" He shakes his head, wonder in his gaze. "I fucking love you."

"Show me," I beg.

Walker settles between my open thighs and drags a finger through my sex. "You're more than ready for me."

I nod, aware that I'm soaked, before I reach up and wrap a hand around his neck, tugging him down until his lips are pressed against mine. Then, with a shared breath, we hold each other's gazes as he presses inside me.

Between one heartbeat and the next, I'm complete. As Walker's hips hit mine, and he sinks fully inside me, my mouth opens and his tongue tangles with mine. What starts as a slow, sensual kiss becomes more desperate as the seconds bleed together. I wrap a leg around Walker's waist and hold him to me while he fucks me with a raw intensity I haven't experienced before.

"More," I whimper desperately, not sure what I'm even asking for anymore.

Walker kisses down my jaw and then sucks on my neck, and I arch into him. When he bites my nipple, I feel the slow build low in my belly.

Five fingers wrap around my throat and squeeze gently. "Don't ever leave me again," he warns as he holds me in place and fucks me slowly. It's decadent, being devoured by this man. I'm molten as liquid rushes through my limbs, forcing my toes to curl.

"Never," I promise him.

Walker's mouth returns to my own, and he kisses me as I go over the edge, ecstasy blinding me the moment he pulses inside me, coming with my name on his lips.

—

"You ready yet?" Walker calls into the bathroom, where I'm just straightening out my dress. After our mind-blowing sex, we both fell asleep and I woke up with Walker still inside me. A shower was necessary after that.

I smile at my reflection as my heart pounds in my chest, wondering what the hell else this man has up his sleeve for today.

"Breathe, Tally," my dad reminds me.

That's a lot easier to do now that I've admitted what I really want in life. I can't wait to meet with Rayna this week to discuss the lease on the bakery. I've got dozens of emails with requests for cakes, too. At this rate, I'll be booked through the year.

When I leave the bathroom, Walker is there, wearing a pair of Wranglers, a white T-shirt, and his cowboy hat.

"Aw, you didn't have to play dress-up for me."

He chuckles and smacks my ass as I pass him. "Brat."

I stick out my tongue and take off at a jog toward his truck.

I'm standing at the driver's-side door when Walker finally catches up to me. "Not a chance," he says with a grunt.

I put out my hand.

"Tally, I love you, but no."

"Please." I pout.

"No, woman. And stop distracting me. We have somewhere to be." I stomp a stubborn foot in the ground, and dirt blooms up around us.

"You done before you make more of a mess?" Walker chuckles as he follows me to the passenger side, making sure to open the door and help me up. "I promise it's better this way."

The moment Walker gets in, he settles his palm on my bare thigh and squeezes. "Remember when you first got here and kept questioning why I had the tulips covered?"

I nod. "How could anyone forget the great deflowering?"

He snorts. "Anyway, like I was saying," he points to the fields as we pass them. As far as the eye can see is a mass of color: magentas and purples, yellows and baby pinks. "One of the reasons I had them covered is because science tells us that the dark, cold winter will bring the most beautiful flowers. And I think it's kind of beautiful in a way that the flowers are Mother Nature's promise that even when things get dark, on the other side of that there's beauty waiting for us." He glances over at me and his eyes soften. "That's what you are to me, Tally. My life was so dark before I met you. But I think I needed to weather all of that so I could come out on the other side to this beautiful life you've helped me create."

My heart pinches, and I lean across to kiss Walker's cheek.

"But want to know a secret?"

My brows raise.

"Wildflowers don't need that. They don't need darkness or sun; they don't need extra rain or more seeds to bloom; they don't need anything but the stalks themselves, and they somehow figure out a way to multiply across fields, season after season."

I bite my lip. "You got a point here?"

"You, Tally Darling, don't need another day of training in

a kitchen, or schooling unless you want it. You've got this, all on your own."

I shake my head as tears prick my eyes. Sucking in a steadying breath, I stare out at the crystalline harbor that winks at me as the sun hits the water's surface. As we turn onto Maple Street, it's clear that the whole town is out and ready to enjoy the beautiful day.

I laugh as I spot the group of men sitting on the corner, drinking their coffees and gossiping. About what, one only knows. Probably something Rayna said. As we continue down the street, I smile as we pass every store, each decked out with more flowers than ever before. Hope Harbor is certainly ready for the Spring Fling and the start of summer.

Right as we pass my sister's store, Rayna steps out into the street.

"Stop, you're going to hit Rayna!" I shout.

Walker chuckles as he pulls into the spot right in front of her. "Don't you know? Cars stop in this town."

I glare at him. "You're acting weird. And what are all those people doing over there?" I ask, pointing to the human wall tightly packed in front of the bakery. I don't take my eyes off the group of people, who I can now make out one by one. Rosie, Eli, Fletcher, the Liberty Ladies, Penny, my mother.

"Wait, what are my mom and Penny doing here? What's going on, Walker?"

Somehow between the time we stopped and all my questions, I didn't even realize Walker had gotten out of the truck, but now he's at my side, door open and staring at me. "Do you really want to stay in Hope Harbor?"

I press my hand to his forehead. "Did you hit your head or something?"

"Just answer the question, Tally."

I sigh. "Yes."

"Well, we really wanted you to stay, too. We wanted you to feel like you had a place in this town, and turns out, so did your dad."

"What?"

"The loan, Tally. Your mother finally told us what it was for."

"I'm so confused."

Walker motions for my mother and Penny to join us, and the four of us stand in a circle.

"I'm so sorry I didn't tell you girls the truth," my mother says, reaching for Penny's and my hands. Her eyes fall shut and I can see how exhausted the last few days have made her. When she opens her eyes, they're filled with tears. "I just didn't know what to do when we lost your father." She blows out a breath, and I squeeze her hand. "I thought that if I pretended to be okay, if I pretended everything was okay, maybe it would be. And I didn't want to pull the two of you down with me."

"Mommy, no," Penny murmurs, leaning her head against our mother's shoulder. "We should have known. We should have tried harder."

"I was determined to follow your father's wishes," Mom says, and a smile creeps over her face. "All your daddy and I ever wanted was for you two to be happy. For you to chase your dreams." She sucks in a breath and straightens, looking at my sister. "Which is why he set aside money to help you open your store."

Penny nods and then my mother turns to me. "And why he set aside money for you to chase your dreams, too."

"I don't need any money, Mom. I just want you to have the farm. I can take care of myself."

My mother smiles knowingly. "He knew you'd say that, which is why I wasn't supposed to tell you our plans."

I hold my breath, waiting for the next words to come out of her mouth.

"His plan all along was to sell off some land, keep just the house and some of the small fields so I would always have my flowers, and then you and your sister would each be able to chase what you wanted."

"I'm still lost. Are you saying there's some money for me to fix up Mabel's?" I ask, turning to the building in front of us.

Walker squeezes my hip. "Better than that. The town and I—"

"The town is not its own being, Cowboy," I say with a grin in his direction.

"You sure about that? Because we had a whole meeting on this."

"You attended a town meeting without me?"

"I'd do anything for you, Tally. Anything at all." Then, like they've choreographed it, the crowd next to us opens up and Walker waves a hand toward the bakery. "Welcome to Whisk and Wildflowers Bakery."

My hand goes to my mouth and I bite back a sob when I see the most beautiful pink sign, complete with a yellow whisk and a host of wildflowers in all different shades.

"It's perfect," I rasp.

"The town voted on the name, but if you want something else . . . ," Walker mumbles.

"Personally, I liked 'Whipped and Wildflower' better," Babs says.

"'Whisk It Good' was my favorite," Ruby chimes in.

Walker groans as I laugh loudly. God, I love this town.

"The name is perfect," I tell him, already itching to get inside. But before I do, I look back to my mother to make sure she's all right.

She flashes me a grin. "He would be so proud of you. He *was* so proud of you. Now go on and enjoy your surprise. The cowboy did good."

With her approval, I rush toward the bakery, pausing just for a second at the door, where the hours are listed. I snort when I see the words "Tally Tuesdays, store's closed" scrawled on the second line.

I push inside and gasp at what awaits. "Walker, what did you do?"

"It wasn't just me." He clears his throat. "Everyone helped."

Pink and yellow tables with matching chairs dot the fresh space. The counter—which just last week had been a weathered wood—is now sanded and sealed, and the old-fashioned cash register has been shined so thoroughly, it looks brand new.

I continue my tour to the kitchen, now decorated with teal cabinets that contrast beautifully with a yellow mixer that stands proudly in front of the picture window framed by pink curtains.

I rush over to see the view, and my breath catches at the sight. "I can see the wildflowers from here!"

Walker steps up behind me and rests his head against mine. "It's like it was meant to be." He presses a kiss to the spot below my ear. "Are you happy?"

I spin around and throw my arms around him. "Happy?! Walker, this is the best surprise ever."

"I can't take all the credit. Your dad had this vision. With the limited hotel options for tourists, he wanted to clean up the cottages on the farm for an extended wedding season.

And now that we've fixed up the cottages, we've finally got a fighting chance of making it all work. It was his dream, and it became mine. But he knew it wasn't yours."

I open my mouth to object, but he stops me.

"I think he might have been wrong. I think you could be happy here. So now you have this kitchen, and I hope maybe you'll want to do all of this with me. Run the business, feed more people, *bake*."

"It's incredible," I say through more tears, though I'm smiling. "It's everything I could have ever dreamed of and more. Thank you. For everything."

"So what do you say to a little baking? All the ingredients you need to make my favorite cupcakes are in the kitchen, and you've got a line of customers outside waiting to try your desserts."

I wrap my arms around Walker's neck and press the first kiss of many to his lips.

"They can wait," I say with a smile. "I've got cowboy things to do first."

Epilogue
TALLY

HOPE HARBOR TOWN CHAT

RAYNA: Don't forget to get your tickets to the Spring Fling! Last chance!

BABS: You can also get them at the door right? My son wants to come but his wife isn't. Wink wink, Penny Darling!

ROSIE: This is a public chat, Babs! Reign. It. In.

ROSIE: Also can you confirm my hair appointment for 11?

BABS: You're all set.

STEW: Mayor, I thought this was for announcements and emergencies only!

FLETCHER: Ladies, please start your own group chat.

RUBY: Has anyone confirmed that Walker is coming? He's not on the list.

BABS: Walker?

RAYNA: It's not optional.

TALLY: We'll be there!

BABS: Did you hear that ladies? She said WE!

* * *

"You know we don't have to go," I hear Walker say as I touch up my lipstick.

"You're going," Billie replies.

Their voices get closer, and when I spin around, Billie is walking into the kitchen, rolling her eyes. Walker follows just behind, and I clamp my teeth down on my bottom lip to keep from laughing at his yellow tuxedo. Walker was stupid enough to tell Eli that yellow was his favorite color, and this is the result.

Walker cursed seven different ways when he saw it, but he has no choice but to wear it, seeing as there are no spare tuxes lying around the farm. And we can't buy a new one because, hell, I'm not even sure we've got a hundred bucks to rub together right now. But we'll be okay. Walker's plan to turn the rest of the cottages into rentable Airbnbs means we're only a season away from turning some sort of profit. Even if it's just breaking a dollar above even for a bit.

"You could come," Walker suggests.

Billie smiles. "Next year. Tonight Quinny and I have a date with the sunset and some ice cream."

"Mom!" Quinn calls from outside, embarrassed.

Quinn's taken over Penny's room, and Billie is in my old

one. Walker and I moved out to the cottage last week, and my mother is getting ready to move back into her room. She's just waiting on Walker to finish her shower, which he plans to do next week.

Things are changing, but for the better. The farm has more life now. I like to think that would have made my dad smile.

"But you better promise me that the moment he's crowned Daffodil King, you'll get videos and pictures," Billie continues, bumping my hip conspiratorially. "I need every second of it documented."

Walker lets out another curse. "It's Grand Marshal, not Daffodil King." Both Billie and I glare at him, and he holds up his hands in surrender. "Fine. Whatever. I'll wear the damn crown."

"If you're lucky enough to get selected," my mother reminds him as she appears in the kitchen.

I smile at her. She's finally starting to look like herself again. She's dressed up for the event in a pale blue chiffon dress that drops to the floor, and her hair is in a pretty updo since we all visited A Breath of FresHair earlier in preparation for tonight.

The moment I saw how Babs was doing my mother's makeup, though, I said I'd do my own. The eighties style is strong with that woman.

The back door swings open, and Quinn appears with a gust of wind. The moment he sets his sights on me, his eyes go wide.

Walker chuckles as he settles beside me, squeezing my hip. "Think you've got him dumbstruck, Wildflower."

Quinn's eyes narrow. "I'll let you borrow her for tonight, but remember, she's *my* girlfriend."

It takes everything in me not to giggle. But somehow I manage to maintain a straight face as both Walker and Billie begin to object. Billie's been trying to let Quinn down easy, and clearly Walker doesn't know what to do. I, on the other hand, find his crush adorable.

"You tell him, Quinn." I hold out my arms, and he rushes into them. From my crouched position, I spin us both and look up at Walker. "Doesn't your uncle look handsome?"

Quinn shrugs. "The yellow is a bit weird."

—

"You've got to be fucking kidding me," Walker growls as he spots Fletcher and Eli walking toward us.

"What?" Eli's wearing a wolfish grin along with a dark navy tuxedo with black accents. Against his golden hair, chiseled jaw, and blue eyes, he looks nothing short of dashing. Fletcher's in a classic black tuxedo, the curls on his head giving him a boyish charm that I still can't quite figure out how Rosie resists.

"You said we were wearing matching tuxes." Walker points at Eli's classic navy tux and then back at his bright yellow one. "This is not matching."

"And you said we needed to wear different colors. It's the same brand, same style." Eli stretches his arms, showing off how good he looks. "I just happen to wear it better."

"Bright side?" Fletcher cuts in with a reassuring smile.

Walker glares at him. "My suit. Yeah. Ha. You're hysterical."

Fletcher shakes his head. "Nope. The bright side is that

no one will be looking at a single one of us with Tally around. You look gorgeous."

My lips tip up in a surprised smile. "Aw! Fletcher!" I throw my arms around him in a hug. "I have no idea why my best friend hates you so much. You're the best of the bunch."

"Jeez, thanks," Eli mumbles as Walker growls, pulling me back to tuck me beneath his arm and into his chest. "Stay close."

"Because you want me to distract everyone with my beauty?" I bat my lashes up at him.

Walker doesn't take the bait, though. His eyes are warm as he stares down at me. This is how he looks at me all the time now. As if, since the weight of all the secrets has been lifted, since we all just agreed to start being honest—even when it hurts—he's lighter. "Because I love you and I don't like peopling unless I'm with you."

My chest grows tight, as it does every time he says those words. "That's 'cause I handle the talking."

He arches an unimpressed brow as I press a kiss to his chin. "I love you, too."

When I pull back, I take a moment to look around the brewery. The whole building is covered in flowers from the farm, and as my eyes focus on the end of the bar, I spot my sister talking to a man. "Is that Jake Montgomery?"

Rosie appears out of nowhere and leans across the bar, whispering, "Yeah, he came in here all depressed because his book flopped. He didn't realize we were closed for a private event, and I didn't have the heart to tell him. Don't let Rayna know he got in here without a ticket."

"Wait, he told you his book was a flop?"

Rosie snorts. "I'm a bartender. I *overhear* everything."

"I actually liked his book," Eli offers.

"You read it?" Rosie asks.

"It was our bowling team's read last week." He turns to Walker. "If you ever showed up, you'd have read it, too."

Walker rolls his eyes and bends down to murmur in my ear. "Want to go over and say hi?"

I glance in Penny's direction again. Her cheeks are flushed, and she's beaming. I haven't seen her smile that big since—I bite my lip—actually, I haven't seen her smile that big since prom, when she spent the entire night sitting in the corner with Jake Montgomery.

"Nah."

Walker shrugs just as we're interrupted by a hollering Rayna. "Mr. Mayor, Mr. Mayor!" Behind her, the Liberty Ladies stand with my mother in tow, each of them in a different color to celebrate the many flowers of spring. My mother chose pale blue to represent the blue irises that were always my daddy's favorite.

My dress has splashes of all different pastels as a symbol for the wildflowers.

"What can I do for you, Mrs. McGovern?" Fletcher replies, all business.

"It's time to announce the grand marshal." She winks in Walker's direction, and I feel my heart leap.

There's no way this crazy town didn't vote this man in. If only for the fact that they love to make him talk when they know it's his least favorite thing to do. But truly, I think it's because they saw a man who needed people. Who needed community. And that's what the residents of Hope Harbor do when they see people in need. They act. They provide.

Fletcher makes his way to the stage as I turn toward Walker and fiddle with his suit, making sure his tie is properly done. Then I kiss him, because from the way he's looking around, like a deer in headlights, I can tell he's considering bolting. Fletcher calls all the nominees up and talks about what an honor it is to stand next to the men and women who represent the best of this town.

"Enough dillydallying," Babs hollers. "I want to see them take it off!"

Fletcher flounders for his words while Rayna gives Babs a swift smack to the back of the head. "No spicy jokes here. This is a sacred ceremony."

Babs rolls her eyes. "Buncha prudes."

Penny sneaks in between my mother and me. "What did I miss?"

"They're about to announce the winner," I whisper.

"But Babs told them to take it off," my mom explains.

"And then Rayna hit her," I finish.

Penny nods. "Cool, cool. Business as usual." Then in a louder voice she yells, "Let's give the people what they want, Fletch! Announce our Daffodil King!"

Fletcher blinks down at the piece of paper in his hand and shakes his head before opening it. "It is my great honor," he says, a huge smile spreading across his face, "to be the first to congratulate Jesse Walker as our grand marshal."

My sister, my mother, and I all let out loud whoops of excitement as Fletcher motions for Walker to come up to the mic to address the room. Walker steps up and Fletcher holds out the daffodil flower crown that my mother made this afternoon. He stares at it before shaking his head, dumbstruck.

"Come on, Walker. Say something," I mutter aloud.

"Hi, Walker!" Rosie screams from behind the bar.

Walker's chin falls down as he chuckles.

Eli follows with it up with another "Hi, Walker," and then suddenly the entire room is greeting the man who always claimed he doesn't like peopling. Too bad for him.

His gaze searches the room, and when it settles on me, his face brightens.

"Hi, everyone. Thank you for—ugh—making my girlfriend's dreams come true." He motions toward the daffodil crown in his hand and finally places it on his head as everyone laughs. "As most of you probably know, I didn't grow up here. I didn't know my neighbors. People didn't say hello to me; they didn't really say hello to one another, either. And I thought that was good thing. And I suppose it was until I came to Hope Harbor and you all refused to let me by without acknowledging me."

Penny nudges me in the arm. "Look at Walker with all the words."

"Right? Who knew! By the way, Jake Montgomery!"

Penny's cheeks pink right up as my mother shushes us. "Girls, pay attention."

We look back to Walker, whose attention is still on the three of us. "Meeting Peter Darling was the greatest thing to ever happen to me." My hand goes to my chest. "Because he introduced me to this town; he gave me community, a purpose. And now I'm lucky enough to live on a farm doing the things I love, with the woman I love by my side."

Walker closes his eyes for a second, and when he opens them again, it's as if something settles within him. "So thank you all for making me your grand marshal. It's an honor."

The entire room erupts in applause when he steps back and then it takes him a good twenty minutes to make it through the crowd as everyone congratulates him.

"Want to get some air before you speak to anyone else?" I ask him when he finally reaches me.

He presses a kiss to my forehead. "You know me so well."

"Hey," my best friend calls. "Before the two of you disappear, we've got to do a toast."

Walker and I look at each other nervously. If the expression on Rosie's face is any indication, she's about to hit us with a doozy of a cheers. I shrug. "Make it Fireball."

Walker's hand settles on my back, and he pushes me toward the bar, where my sister, Fletcher, and Eli sit.

Rosie lines up the shots and then waits until we each grab one. "To going after our dreams, each and every one of us."

"I'll cheers to that," Walker says as he holds up his shot glass. He tips his against mine and winks.

Smiling, I watch as every one of my friends hesitates to do the same. Guess I'm not the only one who struggled with figuring out what my dreams were before I started chasing them. I nudge my sister in the shoulder. Her eyes have already circled the room one too many times searching for her long-lost friend. "Remember, the only thing worse than no sex is bad sex."

She coughs out a laugh, taps her glass against Rosie's, and says, "Okay. To chasing our dreams."

And because I'm not about to risk being called a liar, as soon as I finish my shot, I grab my dream by the hand and tug him out into the warm spring night.

We don't return for the dance marathon, but I do spend

the night in Walker's arms with only the moonlight as our witness. Amidst the pink and yellow tulips, the lavender lilacs and bourgeoning white hydrangea, we sway in the fields I'm lucky enough to call my home as I make a whole list of dreams I still want to achieve.

And I tell Walker every single one of them.

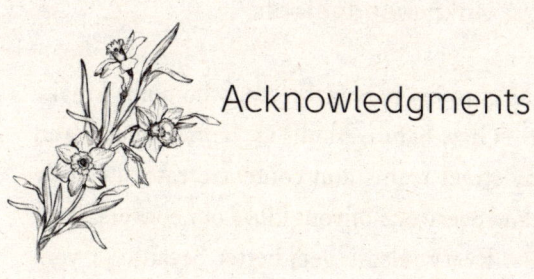

Acknowledgments

Thank you so much for traveling to Hope Harbor with me. As I write these acknowledgments, I can admit that a year ago, I never thought that one of my books would appear in bookstores around the world. Dreamed maybe, but never actually truly believed that would happen. So when I say that you, my dear reader, have made my dreams come true, I mean that in the most literal sense. This series is a dream come true.

It also wouldn't be possible if not for some really amazing people. First and foremost, Jessica Muscio, thank you for trusting me with your fabulous idea. For giving me this brilliant canvas and all the tools to create what I know we are both so proud of. And to Tara Carlson, for believing in this idea with only a few words written and helping us create this world I know we all want to live in. I appreciate the entire team at Evermore, Putnam, and the whole Penguin Random House family, for believing in me and this world and giving me the opportunity to meet so many new readers.

If you know me, you know without my PA Sara none of what I do would be possible. But that's especially true when it comes to this series because she told me there was an email from a publishing house that I absolutely could not ignore and then we spent approximately ten minutes screaming to each other on the phone. When it comes to my career, I have no greater support, no better fan, and the best friend a girl could ask for. Thank you Sara.

A special thanks to my personal team, who helped make this story better—Glav, Sarah, Madison, Jamie, Janelle, and Andi, and to my street teams and content creators, I truly appreciate each and every one of you. I love our conversations and our tangents. Every release gets better because of you! And to my wonderful author friends, especially Jenni and Daphne, who I would be lost without. I adore you all.

And to my family. Mackenzie and Jack, being your mom is my favorite dream come to life. John, you are the reason I believe in love stories and why the grump who loves only her is my favorite trope!

If you want to follow along on my writing journey and have sneak peeks into all the characters in my world, follow me on Instagram, join my awesome Facebook group Britt's Boozy Book Babes, sign-up for my newsletter and follow me on TikTok.

Return to Hope Harbor with
Bonfire and Bliss Books
Coming next Fall

On a station platform, with nothing to read,
and a four-hour train journey stretching ahead of him...

That's where the story began for Penguin founder Allen Lane.
With only 'shabby reprints of shoddy novels' on offer,
he resolved to make better books for readers everywhere.

By the time his train pulled into London, the idea was formed.
He would bring the best writing, in stylish and affordable
formats, to everyone. His books would be sold in bookstores,
stationers and tobacconists, for no more than the price
of a ten-pack of cigarettes.

And on every book would be a Penguin, a bird with a certain
'dignified flippancy', and a friendly invitation to anyone who
wished to spend their time reading.

In 1935, the first ten Penguin paperbacks were published.
Just a year later, three million Penguins had made their
way onto our shelves.

Reading was changed forever.

—

A lot has changed since 1935, including Penguin, but in the
most important ways we're still the same. We still believe that
books and reading are for everyone. And we still believe that
whether you're seeking an afternoon's escape, a vigorous debate
or a soothing bedtime story, all possibilities open with a book.

Whoever you are, whatever you're looking for,
you can find it with Penguin.

evermore

Love, spice and sleepless nights.

The hottest new romance publisher at Penguin Random House UK.

Prepare for excessive swooning, devouring love stories and dangerously high standards for your own happily-ever-afters.

Proceed with caution... and an open heart.